RESTLESS
ARE THE SAILS

RESTLESS
ARE THE SAILS

BY
EVELYN EATON

INTRODUCTION BY
A.J.B. JOHNSTON

Formac Publishing Company Limited
Halifax

Formac Publishing Company Limited acknowledges the support of the Cultural Affairs Section, Nova Scotia Department of Tourism and Culture. We acknowledge the financial support of the Government of Canada through the Book Publishing Industry Development Program (BPIDP) for our publishing activities.

We acknowledge the support of the Canada Council for the Arts for our publishing program.

Cover illustration: *Burning of the Prudent* (1771) from a drawing by R. Paton, Maritime Museum of the Atlantic M73.95.1.

National Library of Canada Cataloguing in Publication

Eaton, Evelyn, 1902-1983
      Restless are the sails / by Evelyn Eaton ; introduction by A.J.B. Johnston.

(Formac fiction treasures)
First published: New York : Harper, 1941.
ISBN 0-88780-603-1

      1. Louisbourg (N.S.)—History—Siege, 1745—Fiction. I. Title. II. Series.

PS8509.A96R4 2003   C813'.52   C2003-905185-4

Series editor: Gwendolyn Davies

Formac Publishing Company Limited
5502 Atlantic Street
Halifax, Nova Scotia B3H 1G4
www.formac.ca

Printed and bound in Canada

Evelyn Eaton (c. 1923) (Boston University)

Presenting Formac Fiction Treasures
Series Editor: Gwendolyn Davies

A taste for reading popular fiction expanded in the nineteenth century with the mass marketing of books and magazines. People read rousing adventure stories aloud at night around the fireside; they bought entertaining romances to read while travelling on trains and curled up with the latest serial novel in their leisure moments. Novelists were important cultural figures, with devotees who eagerly awaited their next work.

Among the many successful popular English language novelists of the late 19th and early 20th centuries were a group of Maritimers who found in their own education, travel and sense of history, events and characters capable of entertaining readers on both sides of the Atlantic. They emerged from well-established communities which valued education and culture, for women as well as men. Faced with limited publishing opportunities in the Maritimes, successful writers sought magazine and book publishers in the major cultural centres: New York, Boston, Philadelphia, London, and sometimes Montreal and Toronto. They often enjoyed much success with readers at home' but the best of these writers found large audiences across Canada and in the United States and Great Britain.

The Formac Fiction Treasures series is aimed at offering contemporary readers access to books that were successful, often huge bestsellers in their time, but which are now little known and often hard to find. The authors and titles selected are chosen first of all as enjoyable to read, and secondly for the light they shine on historical events and on attitudes and views of the culture from which they emerged. These complete original texts reflect values which are sometimes in conflict with those of today: for example, racism is often evident, and bluntly expressed. This collection of novels is offered as a step towards rediscovering a surprisingly diverse and not nearly well enough known popular cultural heritage of the Maritime provinces and of Canada.

INTRODUCTION

R EADERS of historical novels generally want to know if the story before them is true — well, more or less. No one expects a work of fiction to be accurate in every detail; after all, it needs invented characters and imagined dialogue. Yet the conscientious "history" reader is naturally curious about the basic shape and tenor of the story. He or she wants to know if the key events are accurate to the time and place presented by the author.

In *Restless are the Sails*, Evelyn Eaton puts her characters through a great many settings as she tells the story of Paul de Morpain and a cast of others. In a plot-driven narrative that never quits and barely rests, the novelist sweeps the reader on a journey — on land and sea — from mid-18th-century New England through to Louisbourg and eventually on to France. It is above all a romance with a leading man and a couple of leading ladies. The heart of the story takes place at the one-time French stronghold of Louisbourg, as it first anticipates and then undergoes the siege of 1745.

Since the history of Louisbourg was at the centre of my professional career for nearly a quarter-century, I am probably qualified to comment on where *Restless are the Sails* ranks on a historical scorecard. One-word assessments, however, are not what historians like to provide. Our preference is to say something about the "context" of the work before issuing any kind of judgement. In the particular case of Evelyn Eaton and her historical novels, familiarity with both her personal life and the period in which she wrote is essential for an understanding of the works she created.

Evelyn Sybil Mary Eaton (1902–1983) was born in Switzerland to Canadian parents of some prestige. Though the wealth was not always there to match the aspirations, the family strove to place itself in the upper-class circles of both Edwardian England and Canada. The mother's side of the family, the Fitz Randolphs, had an entrée into certain levels of high society, though apparently not as high as they would have liked. As an adult, Evelyn would look back on her youth and comment that the people that mattered to her mother were, in order of importance, the British Royal Family, God and the Fitz Randolphs.

The Eaton children received the best education their mother could provide, and they enjoyed opportunities to travel in Europe. Yet Evelyn came to feel like she did not fit comfortably in the privileged world into which she had been born. A rivalry with an older sister who possessed all the right attributes, including blonde hair and blue eyes, was perhaps part of the alienation. So too was an independent personality. Later in life, looking back on her childhood, Evelyn commented that she always felt like "an alien from another place."

Evelyn gave vent to her independent spirit by seeking to live life on her own terms, regardless of whether her family or peer group approved. From an early romantic liaison she gave birth to a daughter and became a single parent. This was a source of considerable scandal for well-born ladies in the first half of the twentieth century. When a subsequent marriage ended in divorce, Evelyn encountered new complications and additional stigma.

Evelyn Eaton's desire to chart her own course was a trait that made her life more difficult than it might have been had she accepted the status of her birth. At the same time, it was a quality that led her on a journey of self-discovery and to become an author and a creative writing teacher.

The first writing Eaton tackled was poetry. Later she turned her hand to novels. *Restless are the Sails* was the second of three historical novels she authored that were set in eighteenth-century Nova Scotia. At a later turning point in her life, Eaton moved to the southwest United States where she developed a profound interest in, and sympathy for, aboriginal peoples and their cultures, specifically the Paiute and Arapho. The initial spark for this attraction was a belief that she was descended in part from the Mi'kmaq or Maliseet. Which group, and on which side of the family, is unknown. If her belief was well-founded, it may explain why she felt out of place in some of the circles that her mother wanted her to move as a child. In any case, in the latter half of her life, in the United States, Eaton became a regular attendee at sweat lodges, endured fasts, and came to feel that she had finally found a way of life meant for her. Eaton continued to write, only now her publications related to her quest for understanding of Aboriginal spirituality.

As a young woman, in the late 1930s, Evelyn Eaton came to live in Nova Scotia where she had family connections. When she moved there, she had no intention of researching and writing stories set in the eighteenth century. That idea came from her literary agent in New York, who suggested she try to write a historical novel. Evelyn replied: "How can I? I never even read them." Nonetheless, she needed the money at the time and, fortuitously, an inspiration came to her. She remembered a rainy afternoon spent at Fort Anne in Annapolis Royal, where her uncle had been the curator of the local museum. Colonel E. K. Eaton had showed her a collection of letters written by different French governors about a sometimes tempestuous and always intriguing woman named Louise de Freneuse. Recalling those letters, Eaton found the spark she needed to write her first historical novel. Years later, she stated that she banged out that first novel on her typewriter a chapter a day.

As a strong and individualistic person, Evelyn Eaton inevitably placed unconventional women in her novels. She probably could not have done otherwise and been true to herself. The first novel, *Quietly My Captain Waits* (1940), featured the independent Louise de Freneuse, a real-life historical figure from the late the late 1690s and early 1700s at Port-Royal. The novel became so popular in the United States that a Hollywood producer paid Eaton $40,000 to purchase movie rights. That was a huge sum of money at the time, yet no film version of the book was ever made.

It is Eaton's second novel, *Restless are the Sails* (1942), that is the focus of this introduction. In it Eaton invented, or embellished, two female figures, one Mi'kmaq (San) and one French (Anne du Chambon). Neither woman is the leading character, however, for the military storyline revolving around the 1745 siege dictated there had to be a man at the centre of the story. Nonetheless, a good part of the plot revolves around one or the other female figure.

Eaton's third and final historical novel set in Nova Scotia was *The Sea is So Wide* (1943). The central event in that tale is the 1755 Deportation of the Acadians. Once again the author has a woman at the heart of the story, Barbe Comeau.

A glance at the publication years of the three novels set in Nova Scotia reveals they were all written during the Second World War. One would perhaps expect that since the novels were written in the 1940s they would demonstrate pro-British sympathies. After all, Eaton's family background on her mother's side was staunchly pro-British, Great Britain was under constant threat throughout the war and Eaton's main marketplaces were in Canada, the United States and Britain. Once again, Eaton went her own way. The leading characters and the narrative focus in all three novels are French. This led to some disappointment or controversy, especially in connection with her novel on the Deportation, where her sympathies are clearly with the Acadians, not the British. Yet the author was never one to be influenced by the opinions or criticism of others.

Though Evelyn Eaton's venture in historical novels was not something she had initially wanted to do, she took to the genre after her initial success. She explained the attraction and the importance of writing fiction set in past time periods in this way:

> ... the men and women of the past are responsible for the present and we might as well be interested. The mistakes they made involved us, the triumphs they score advanced us, the ideas they held influenced us, and the struggles they endured liberated us.

Eaton's motivation in choosing the New Englanders' 1745 siege of Louisbourg as the subject of her second historical novel is not known. Perhaps her New York agent suggested it, since a tie-in with one of the formative achievements of the Anglo-American colonists had the potential to sell well in the United States. If that was the thinking, however, Eaton did not deliver a book exactly tailored to the American market. While the opening sections are indeed set in New England, what follows is not a novel that celebrates the New Englanders' conquest of the French stronghold on Cape Breton Island. Instead, Eaton develops a story that mostly unfolds from the perspective of her French characters, especially the leading man, Paul de Morpain. Eaton had little or no interest in trumpeting the accomplishments of the New Englanders. Instead, she explores the missed opportunities and the sufferings of the French civilians at Louisbourg.

None of the characters in the novel has great depth or complexity, for Evelyn Eaton was not Henry James or Fyodor Dostoyevsky. Her stories are driven by action and romance, not psychological insight. That being said, the reader still learns about the lives, hopes and fears of the French characters, and to a much lesser extent about the Anglo-American actors in the drama.

So, at last, what does a historian of eighteenth-century Louisbourg think of the accuracy of the story presented in Evelyn Eaton's *Restless are the Sails*? Starting at the most elementary level, most names mentioned on the French and British sides of the Louisbourg campaign were real-life figures: William Vaughn, Parson Moody, acting governor du Chambon, and many more. The leading characters, however, are strictly Eaton's creation. Paul de Morpain is an ingenious invention because there was a renowned mariner and sometime privateer sailing out of Louisbourg by the name of Pierre Morpain. Eaton presents the well-known real person as Paul's uncle. She adds the "de" to make him sound grand or more French, but that is not justified.

To make the story move, Eaton gives personal quirks, attitudes and foibles to all the characters, including the historical figures. This is sometimes disconcerting for a historian, especially when the personal traits Eaton pins on a few characters are based more on her plot requirements than on evidence. The Anglo-Americans are the least well-developed; some are little more than caricatures. This is the case with Parson Moody, whose evangelical zeal is presented as almost that of a madman.

On the French side, Eaton selects du Chambon, the commandant of the French fortress during the fateful siege of 1745, as one of her targets. Although the author does not make him a villain, she does paint him as an incompetent. (He is also the father of a love interest for Paul de Morpain). The underpinning to the entire story is that if only the previous commandant, Duquesnel, were still governor, or if only du Chambon had listened to Paul de Morpain's early warning about the coming of the New Englanders, then the military outcome would have been different — the French might not have lost Louisbourg in 1745. That makes for an appealing interpretation if you are a romance novelist, but no historian would accept that theory.

It is, of course, possible that if Duquesnel had lived he would have conducted his defence differently than du Chambon did, perhaps more aggressively. Yet that would not likely have been enough to stave off a French defeat, given the effective blockade the attackers were able to impose and the vast superiority in soldiers they enjoyed. Similarly, advance warning that the besiegers were on their way would not have enabled the French to have implemented any preventative measures that would have made a significant difference. Another artificial contrivance Eaton injects into the plot is to have Anne du Chambon at the Royal Battery just as it is about to be abandoned to the advancing New Englanders. It is next to impossible to imagine such an occurrence.

Nonetheless, the 1745 siege of Louisbourg that Eaton describes is more or less authentic. And yes, there was a mutiny in the French garrison the previous December, which meant that morale was low. The author clearly did her research, a fact that is underlined to readers by the occasional insertion of asterisks in the text. They indicate that an exact period quote has been used. Eaton probably read most of what was available at the time — the first full-length history of Louisbourg, by J. S. McLennan, was published in 1918 — and she mentions meeting with individuals who helped her to envision Louisbourg and the siege events. Two names — Dr. J. C. Webster and Katharine McLennan — stand out in the acknowledgement to the original book. The first permanent museum devoted to the history of the French stronghold opened at Louisbourg in 1936. It contained a large number of maps, plans, artifacts and objects associated with the sieges and other events in the history of the place. Evelyn Eaton surely visited the museum, spoke at length with Miss McLennan, and took careful notes on the layout of the fortified town and the principal locations where the events of 1745 occurred. People today are used to thinking in terms of the one-fifth reconstruction of Louisbourg that stands as a major tourist attraction. Eaton was not so fortunate. The immense research and reconstruction program that resulted in the Fortress of Louisbourg National Historic Site did not begin until the 1960s, twenty years after the publication of *Restless are the Sails*. Thus, Eaton's accomplishment in bringing the town and its fortifications to life is considerable, in light of what was available to her.

There are various small and mid-sized errors concerning the 1745 siege of Louisbourg that crop up in the novel. The broad sequence of events that marked the progress of the New Englanders, however, are in the right order. Nitpicking over details seems unimportant in comparison with the major issue that arises when twenty-first-century readers pick up the novel, which is Eaton's depiction of the Mi'kmaq and Maliseet. Like Thomas H. Raddall and many other writers of historical novels prior to the 1970s, Eaton regularly describes the aboriginal people as "savages." Equally bad as that offensive term, she depicts the Mi'kmaq and others as either child-like or as virtual servants of the Europeans.

Eaton's interpretation was not unusual in the era in which she, Raddall and others wrote. Right from the discovery of the Americas in the late 1400s, Europeans developed twin traditions of seeing the new peoples they encountered as either fearful "savages" or as heroic (usually tragically) "noble savages." We know it today as racism, but it was around for centuries before it was regarded as what it really is. Racist attitudes surfaced not only in books but in innumerable paintings and sculptures in which Amerindians were depicted in kneeling or other subordinate positions in comparison to Europeans. With the introduction of mass-market cinema early in the twentieth century, racist stereotypes became even more entrenched. Hundreds of Hollywood movies were made in which African, Asian or Aboriginal people were portrayed as dependent individuals capable of uttering only monosyllables. The malice was probably unintentional on the part of the movie-makers; it was simply the way the dominant culture looked at non-white people. Yet seen today, the old films come across as either insulting or laughable, depending on one's point of view.

The overt racism of bygone periods has passed, pushed into oblivion by a sea change in people's attitudes — and, of course, by legislation. To meet racist stereotypes in the novels produced in earlier eras, such as those of Evelyn Eaton, T.H. Raddall and others, is a startling experience for today's readers. The big question is how do we handle these books — and similarly some works by Mark Twain, Joseph Conrad, William Shakespeare and other writers — when they offer what have become unacceptable comments?

In the particular case of Evelyn Eaton's *Restless are the Sails*, the question is particularly intriguing. We know that later in life she believed she had Mi'kmaw or Maliseet ancestors, and that she came to embrace what she understood to be aboriginal spiritualism. Her books on those topics are still in print and in demand. This makes the lack of sensitivity she showed to such issues during the 1940s when she wrote her novel of the 1745 siege of Louisbourg a sad irony. Did she know then that she had an aboriginal ancestor and simply ignore or suppress this detail? Was she simply going along with the stereotypes of the period, which required that the Native characters show deference to white men and women? There are no answers to these questions, just speculation. The character of San that Eaton introduces into the story must have ultimately posed a major challenge to the author. Eaton presents the Mi'kmaw woman as strong, dynamic, and unconventional, yet nonetheless subordinate to Paul de Morpain and to the other woman in his life, Anne du Chambon. That Eaton found it difficult to deal with the Mi'kmaw character she had created, is revealed — to this reader at least — by the abrupt and unsatisfying way in which the author removes San (and her child by Paul de Morpain) from the story toward the end of the novel.

One imagines that when Evelyn Eaton looked back as an older woman on the three novels she had written in the 1940s about eighteenth-century Nova Scotia that she wished she had shown more understanding of the aboriginal characters she presented in the stories. For questions of racism aside, the literal truth, now recognized by all historians of the period, is that the Mi'kmaq and Maliseet were important players in the way events unfolded in the Maritimes. By the mid-eighteenth century their numbers were reduced from what they had once been; nonetheless, the French continued to value the aboriginal inhabitants of the region as important allies. On the other side, the British and New Englanders feared them as warriors and as sometime privateers. This dimension does surface toward the end of *Restless are the Sails*, but in an exaggerated way and still with the Mi'kmaq in subservient roles. The military aspect aside, Eaton erred seriously by not representing the aboriginal characters as fully developed and autonomous individuals.

Should the racism inherent in Evelyn Eaton's historical novels keep anyone from reading them? For some, it will be a deterrent. Others, however, may wish to challenge themselves. By that I mean they may want to embark on a fast-paced historical romance written more than a half-century ago and enjoy it for what it is. Yet at the same time, the challenge will be to read beyond and to correct for the stereotypical depictions. There is not much doubt that Evelyn Eaton herself would want something like that. Her own life story demonstrates how a person can learn and change.

Evelyn Eaton's *Restless are the Sails* is a romance novel in which the author's imagined characters get caught up in the dramatic events of the 1745 New England siege of Louisbourg and the 1746 d'Anville expedition. The broad sequence of events, and some details, are based on historical evidence. The characterizations and interpretations, however, come from Eaton's imagination and the requirements of her plot line. Those details, and the personalities of the actual historical figures, are sometimes based on evidence, and sometimes not. *Restless are the Sails* offers its readers a swirling glimpse into a period that was one of the most colourful in the history of Atlantic Canada.

A.J.B. Johnston
Halifax 2003

A.J.B. (JOHN) JOHNSTON is the author of many studies of eighteenth-century Louisbourg. They include *The Summer of 1744* (Parks Canada), *Life and Religion at Louisbourg* (McGill-Queen's University Press), *Control and Order at French Colonial Louisbourg* (Michigan State University Press) and *The Phoenix Fortress* (Nimbus Publishing).

DEDICATION

To the EATON FAMILY of Nova Scotia, in particular
the late VERNON EATON, R.C.H.A.
MYRA EATON, his widow,
TERRY, their grandchild.

"Omnia vincit veritas"

"The wind blows, and restless are the sails."
— *The Prophet*: Kahlil Gibran

CONTENTS

AUTHOR'S NOTE

THE figures in the foreground of this picture of some parts of the New World during the years 1744-1746 are fictitious. Paul, San, Hortense, Anne, Marie, the Merciers and others have left no trace of themselves in history. The figures in the tapestry behind them have been taken from the record. Governor Shirley is the same Governor Shirley responsible in large measure for the expulsion of the Acadians a few years after the close of this story. Parson Moody was the Senior Chaplain of the expedition against Louisbourg, noted for the length of his prayers and the strength of his venom. A contemporary records watching him hack down the altar in the church of Louisbourg with an ax he had brought with him from New England for that purpose. Abbé le Loutre's strange figure and his great influence over the Acadians and the Micmacs are well known to any student of the period. François Bigot was the last Intendant of Canada, and has been immortalised in *Le chien d'or*. He was dishonest, rapacious and an important contributor to the downfall of the French in Canada, but records show that he was an honest and amiable administrator in Louisbourg and that his career took its downward turn when he came back to Canada after the close of this story. William Vaughan, William Tufts, officers Forant, Perelle, Thierry, Boularderie, and Bonaventure, a descendant of the Captain de Bonaventure in *Quietly My Captain Waits*, are authentic. Pierre de Morpain, Paul's uncle, was a well-known privateer, whose crew, like that of other pirates and privateers of the period, was composed of Micmacs and other savages. There are also recorded instances of savage crews mutineering, and working the ships they seized, to the terror of the coastal towns. Governor du Chambon is remembered, among other things, for having fathered Vergor, the traitor of Beauséjour, which after the fall of Louisbourg was the most important French stronghold in Acadia; its ruins have been reconstructed, and can be visited as can those of Louisbourg. The incidents of the French manning British prizes, the abortive attempt to sail against Annapolis in Acadia, the virulent plague that devastated the fleet, the suicides of the commanders and the terrible voyage back to France are all history.

Some actions by unnamed persons have been pinned upon the characters. For example, it is known that the secret of the impending attack on Louisbourg was given away to Boston by the too loud and earnest prayers for guidance of a member of the assembly, who informed the Lord in detail of the proposed expedition and was overheard. Whether this gentleman and Parson Moody were one, I do not know.

When actual words, written or spoken by the characters, are quoted, this is indicated by asterisks. The songs in the text are my translations of French songs of the period and earlier, still sung by the descendants of the Acadians.

Louisbourg is in Cape Breton Island, then called Ile Royale. Annapolis Royal, once the great French fort of Port Royal captured by the British in 1710, and Chebucto, the modern Halifax, are in Acadia, which comprised, roughly, all Nova Scotia, all New Brunswick, some parts of Maine, some parts of Ontario and Quebec. Damariscotta and Kittery, today in Maine, were then in New Hampshire, as Maine did not exist. A map giving wherever possible both the French and English place names of the period will be found in the end papers.

The main sources for the material used in the book are: *A Half Century of Conflict*, Francis Parkman; *The Rise and Fall of New France*, Vol. II, George M. Wrong; *The Jesuit Relations*, Vol. LXVII; *William Shirley, Governor of Massachusetts*, G. A. Wood; *Lettre d'un habitant de Louisbourg; Transactions of the Royal Society of Canada*, Fort Anne Library, Annapolis; *America Sails the Seas*, Frank C. Bowen; *Ships and the Sea*, Lt. Commander E. C. Talbot-Booth, R.N.R.; *All About Ships and Shipping*, Edwin

P. Harnack; *Competition for Empire, 1740-1763*, Walter L. Dorn; *Louisbourg*, two volumes of correspondence from Fort Anne Library.

My thanks are also due to Dr. J. C. Webster for material on Abbé le Loutre, to Miss Katherine McLennan, Curator of the Louisbourg Museum, for material on the siege, to the Mariners Museum, Newport News, Virginia, for prints and material on sea fighting and ships, and to Ethel Comstock Bridgman for research and proofreading.

Fundy Tide, 1941.

PART ONE
NEW ENGLAND 1744-1745

CHAPTER 1

IT WAS a stormy day. Sea and sky lowered at one another. The sea raised great fists of spume in the sky's face, and shook them furiously. It thundered, it threatened, it crashed upon the rocks. Through the turmoil of sound and spray a northeast wind blew shoreward, shining, blustering, dying away to rise again among the spruce trees on the cliff. Its murmur became a moan, the moan a roar that shook the forest.

Sea gulls added their screaming to the din, an old crow barked its way overhead, three more crows squawked in answer. From the distance an irregular sound that was neither the bark of an animal nor the cry of a bird drifted along the beach. Two figures were making uneven progress over the rocks, the sound of their words coming in bursts above the storm.

Presently there was a lull. The wind dropped. The tide had turned and was going out, sucking at the seaweed, dragging at the rocks. It left a beach of gray pebbles heaped in careless ridges, smooth and shining in the sun. The more picturesque of the two figures left the rocks and stepped forward.

It was a young man, fair-haired, with high-colored cheeks and blue eyes, so blue that one looked twice before believing in their color. He was dressed in motley, as though he had scrambled on what hodgepodge lay to hand, but the carelessness in his dress was studied. Doublet, breeches, lacy shirt, long knee-stockings and buckled shoes carefully chosen to set off the figure were no more than he owed himself, being like his father before him at nineteen, a graduate of Harvard, and now lieutenant in the newly raised militia.

He climbed the first mound of pebbles and flung himself down upon the next, regardless of the wet spattering upon his clothes. His companion followed more slowly. He was younger, slighter, smaller, with dark hair, dark melancholy eyes, and pallid skin. He was dressed in a suit of close-fitting black, darned and patched about the elbows. His shoes were plain, without buckles. He did not fling himself down, but sat gingerly, as though he must take care of what he wore. His hands, long and flexible, with restless curved fingers, scrabbled among the stones.

Presently he found something. A gleam of laughter flashed in his black eyes.

"Master Vaughan!"

"To hell with Master Vaughan when we're alone."

"Well, Will, then, look at this. Does it remind you of something?"

He held out a rock with a strand of seaweed hanging from it. William Vaughan took it from him and turned it over.

"Captain Waterbury's whiskers?"

"No. This is less luxuriant. There's a bald patch there." He pointed with his sensitive fingers. "See it?"

"Bald patch? The cat at Damariscotta."

"No."

"I give it up."

"Mistress Moody's head without a wig."

"How could I be expected to guess that? I've never seen it."

"Neither have I without a nightcap. I wager that's what it looks like, the old bezum!"

"Paul!" Will's lips curled in distaste. "No gentleman . . ."

"Oh, I know, but I'm not a gentleman. I'm a prisoner of war, a Frenchie, a Catholic, a fish out of the sea!"

"A fish out of water, do you mean?" Will inquired coldly.

"I mean Mistress Moody's maid-of-all-work!"

He flung the rock he was holding down at his feet. Then he went to the water's edge, and stood looking out to sea. Will watched him for a moment, then he rose and went to stand beside him, awkwardly. He put his hand on Paul's shoulder.

·[4]·

"I know it's hard for you," he said. "I've told you what you could do to come with me."

Paul laughed. Will took his hand away.

"You're a damned determined Frog," he said, "and you're a fool, but for six years we've known each other, we've been friends. I thought you would like the chance to serve with me . . ."

"Thanks, Will. Six years is a long time."

He looked out to sea as he spoke, and his expression changed. He was thinking of his home in Louisbourg, in Ile Royale, hundreds of miles to the north of where he stood, wondering what changes six such years had made. There was his father's death; killed by the English who had taken his ketch, his seamen and his son. How long did his mother wait before she gave up hope? How did she make her living with three girls and two boys all under eight years old? Eight and six—fourteen—Marie was fourteen now. He saw her, saw them all, gathered about the table in the dusk, candlelight on gleaming plates, firelight on faces, Maman with her rosary. His hand went up to cross himself and stopped midway. Six years ago! Six years since he had heard a Mass or seen a rosary.

The ketch became the property of Will's father, who owned most of the land on either side of the Damariscotta River, and presided over the settlement he had established there, sixty miles north of Boston, with a garrison house and a trading station for timber and for fish. He had a fishing station on the island of Matinicus; that was where the ketch was sent, to join his fishing fleet. Paul had seen her since, graceful against the sky line. She brought a lump to his throat.

The two seamen captured with him were exchanged for prisoners in France. They did not go back to Louisbourg direct. Perhaps they were there now, perhaps they returned from France, perhaps they had given news of him and of his father to the people at home. Perhaps. His gaze grew clouded, misty, he wiped his eyes.

"The spray gets into them," he said.

Will looked at him.

"I hate to be going."

·[5]·

Paul nodded.

"To be secretary to a man like William Shirley . . ."

Paul nodded again.

"Shirley and your father plan the expedition against Louisbourg."

Will looked troubled.

"You know how it is," he said. "Father has lost a good deal lately. The fisheries are threatened by your—by the French. Louisbourg is the headquarters for all that sort of thing."

"What sort of thing?"

"Now, Paul. . . ."

"What sort of thing?"

"Well, since you must have it, piracy."

"Ha!"

"Why do you talk of it? You know the French privateers are a terror to all the trade routes of the Atlantic. They collect in Louisbourg, in the harbor there."

"I never saw anything but the fishing fleet, boats like my father's. I suppose he was a privateer!"

"He was fishing in our waters."

"Your waters!"

"We'll only disagree. Let's not talk of it."

"Yes, yes. I want to know."

Will shrugged. "They have decided something must be done. The French have built a fortress there bigger than Versailles."

"Nonsense!" Paul began, then stopped. Perhaps if the English were to believe Louisbourg so big, so important, they might let it alone. He knew it to be a struggling little place, where the fishing fleet came in, a rugged settlement, perched upon a rock, fortified indeed, but as for these wild tales—Versailles!—it was nothing more than a desolate outpost, guarding the doorway to Canada, by the great river leading to Quebec.

"So you see we cannot, we of the colonies, allow France to continue and to dominate. . . ."

Will paused for breath.

"I see," Paul said with a strange smile, "there is to be an expedition to attack."

"Yes." Will drew himself up. "It is a secret. I tell you because

·[6]·

I am your friend and I should like to see your condition bettered. But you must swear to secrecy."

"I swear," Paul said. "Tell me some more. It is a change. I spend my days so tamely, carrying wood for the Moodys, doing chores."

"That's it. You are a fool, when you could be set free. You could be in the militia."

"I?"

"You could be. You could be of help. You know Louisbourg, you could tell us of weaknesses in the fortress. You could act as guide. They would engage you, if you took the oath of allegiance. My father said . . ."

"No—no!"

The words came out in a sudden croak. "No!"

Will looked at him sharply.

"I could not do it. And if I would, I do not remember weaknesses. But it is kind of you to have thought of me."

"I would like to have you with me. I must have a body-man."

"I see."

"Shirley will organize the expedition. Probably he will go with it. Perhaps he will lead it. I shall be with him. If he does not go, the militia will, and I shall go with that."

"I see."

"This is the last time we shall take a walk together."

Both were silent. Paul put his hand into his breeches pocket. He brought out a miniature silver tuning fork, the only thing he had brought with him from Louisbourg, and struck it on the stones. Then he lifted up his voice, clear and true, with a rare quality.

"What are the words?" Will asked. He concealed his passion for music from his father and his Harvard friends—it was an unmanly weakness; but with Paul, who had a voice and could sing, who played the flute and the harpsichord with no self-consciousness, he could let himself go.

"The words!" he insisted, humming the air.

Paul translated haltingly.

> "I leave tomorrow for the isles,
> Sweetheart will you come with me?
> No, and I will not go,

·[7]·

Each handsome lad to go
To those isles is lost to me."

They sang it together. Then it was time to go. They walked along the rocks to where they had left their horses, fastened to a spruce. Will loosened his, and swung himself up with the easy mastery of a born rider, seldom out of the saddle. Paul mounted more awkwardly. He got little chance to ride. He was a fisherman, a sailor by nature, ill at ease out of a boat. He followed Will at a canter, with the stinging wind in his face.

"This promenade has been good," he panted when he caught up with him. "I wish it might not end."

"Think over what I said to you and come with me," Will shouted back. Paul shook his head.

"No, and I will not go!" he bellowed.

Will shrugged, settled himself more firmly into the saddle and cantered on.

CHAPTER II

THE two riders separated when they reached the outskirts of the settlement. Will took the horses toward his father's imposing stables, nestling behind the well-built house that dominated the settlement; Paul turned on foot toward the modest two-story frame building that sheltered the Moody spinsters from the elements, Mistress Moody, a formidable old harridan of seventy-two, Mistress Susan, a spineless nonentity of seventy, and Sarah Town their maid.

Mr. Vaughan had been tutored by their younger brother, the Reverend Samuel Moody, now Minister of York. He had taken a fancy to the tough old man in spite of his irritable temper. He had seen past the uncompromising, dominating, dictatorial pastor, shouting at sinners in his congregation to reform, dragging them bodily out of taverns, shaking his fist in the street, to the warm-hearted, bewildered man, giving his all in charity, so that his family had to resort to stratagem to prevent his beggaring them and himself. "Father Moody" as he was called behind his back—he would have resented the name to his face, since he looked on the Pope as Anti-Christ and all Catholic priests as heathens—had once pulled Mr. Vaughan out of a bad scrape and set him on his feet again.

In memory of this, when the fishing industry prospered, Mr. Vaughan took over the two sisters, who were the only spinsters in a colony where women were scarce and wives in demand, and established them in a house on his estate. When Paul was captured from the French, Mr. Vaughan gave him to the two ladies to make use of.

"He will make you a body servant," he said.

Paul hated the place, hated the women who lived there, and despised himself for serving them. Mistress Moody was at the window as he came in, her wig could be seen bobbing back and forth. Wicked words formed in Paul's throat as he looked, but he took off his cap and presented himself with civility.

"Well, zany, so you've come back at last! I wonder you deign to show us the light of your countenance at all, you beggar on horseback, you! Today of all days, when the dispatch is come! We are to go to my brother, and you stand there, with all the packing and the arrangements and the journey to be made, and you the only servant that we have! Fine doings! I'd as soon have a haddock for a servant, fins and all. Riding cockhorse through the woods!"

She paused out of breath. Paul inquired politely what she would have him do.

"Do? Do? There's a mort of things to do, you dizzard, ninny-hammer, hoddy-doddy."

Paul solemnly inclined himself. "I need not put up with this," he thought, "I could go with Will. I could be a soldier. If it were against any other settlement but Louisbourg!" He hummed, unconsciously, ". . . to the isles . . ."

"What Satan's song is that, looby jobbernowl?"

"An incantation taught me by the Jesuit fathers," he said wickedly, "for use when one is sworn at."

He backed himself out of the room before she could recover.

"What is the matter here?" he asked of Sarah, whom he found bustling aimlessly about the disordered kitchen. "What are the old hags up to now?"

"Master Paul! Such language is unseemly."

"How did you know whom I meant, if the description didn't fit? Come, Sarah, tell me what's to do. I left them knitting their samplers, when I return the whole house is carrying sail."

"You know as well as I do. I heard the Mistress telling you. They're away to the Reverend."

"It isn't I that would stop them," Paul replied, "nor fret if they wanted to stay there. You and I will have some pleasure and some peace, as we did the last time, remember?"

"But this time you're going with them."

"I? Not I!"

"Paul. . . . Paul. . . . Sarah!" the cracked old voice called querulously toward them.

"There!" Sarah muttered. "Get along with you, don't you hear her calling?"

"Tell her I'm in the privy."

"Master Paul!"

"In the woodhouse, then, or better still, I've gone to the woods to get some more logs."

"Paul! Sarah!"

"Coming, Mistress, coming!" Sarah wiped her hands on her apron, gave a tweak to her cap and wig and waddled toward the door. Paul slipped out the back. He crossed the yard, and entered the stable.

There were three oxen in the stalls, patiently relaxing from their work. They lifted drooling mouths, incurious eyes, and blinked at him. Paul pulled a handful of hay from the rack above their heads and gave it to the nearest.

"You and I," he said, patting the heaving flank, "are leading the same life—work, then rest, then work again, for masters that are alien flesh. You have adapted yourself and I cannot."

The ox chewed stolidly. The other two looked round at him, mild reproach in their large eyes. "Why," they asked, "should one of us have hay and the others not? We have worked in the same yoke all day."

"Why indeed?" said Paul, running his hand along their rumps.

"Paul!"

"Master Paul!"

"Paul!"

"Crénom!" he said. "Can't postpone it forever, I suppose."

He emerged reluctantly and walked toward the house. After he had explained that he was seeing to the oxen, that he had come as soon as he could, he dodged a box on the ears, bowed his head to the storm of words that broke over it, and set himself to the work in hand. There were boxes to be fetched, cords to be found, messages to be run, contradictory orders given. While he worked, he thought:

"If I go with them, to York, I shall be nearer to Boston and Governor Shirley. I shall hear news of the expedition. Perhaps I shall find French prisoners and hear some word of home. I can escape from the old hens now and then. They should be better tempered, visiting. I doubt if Mistress Moody will swear so much before her brother, and he a minister! I shall have to attend his long-winded meetings, though."

Through the window came the sound of the wind, howling across the forest, blowing from the sea. Paul raised his head to listen. He pictured the scene of the afternoon, himself and Will standing by the waves. Across them, far to the north, was Louisbourg. There, at this hour, in the old days, his mother would be setting about the supper with the help of her Indian maid. Delicious odors would fill the house. His father, sitting on the "old man's bench" outside the door, would light a last pipe and look up at the sky, judging tomorrow's weather, before he came in smiling, stamping his boots on the sill.

Paul always pictured the rare occasions that his father was ashore when he thought of Louisbourg, because that was the time when he himself was there. Mostly, of course, they were in the ketch *La Belle Louise*, renamed the *Trident* now, and its Captain dead. He brushed aside the present to continue with the past. Now the table would be set and all would come to it, his father, his mother, himself, Marie, Tomas, Andrée, Louise and Pierre. The children's faces were indistinct. He could not remember very well how each one looked, nor what they wore. But he could see the cover lifted in his mother's hand, the steam fly up, the pewter gleam. They had three pewter dishes, more than most families had. He could hear his father's deep agreeable voice, his strong laughter, great as the sea over which it rolled. He could see his mother's face.

"Paul . . ."

"Yes?"

"Yes what? you insolent numskull."

"Yes, Mistress Moody."

·[12]·

"Find me the bale of villymot cloth and my stammel red silk. I'll have them made up in York."

Paul bowed and went to look for them. "Villymot!" he mimicked. He knew by the color of the cloth when he found it that it was "feuille-morte" that indescribable rusty-gold that his mother wore. "Villymot indeed."

He pictured the sharp-faced old maid decked out in her new finery. "Something one wouldn't believe!" He was kept on the run. It was late that night before he could climb to the hole under the eaves allotted to him for his own. Then, not bothering to undress, for it was cold and he was exhausted, he rolled himself in a heap and went to sleep.

CHAPTER III

THE sails of the *Trident* bellied in a stiff breeze. Sunlight played from white canvas to whiter foam on green wave. Paul sitting on the after rail stared moodily at the sea. He had not seen the *Trident* close to since he sailed in her as *La Belle Louise*. You could still see the *Lou* under the white paint chipping off her side. It gave him the strangest sensation. All about him a thousand familiar details leaped to life and called to him: "remember this and this and this!" He was astonished at all he had forgotten. Putting a curtain between him and the day that he had seen his father die, and had been taken prisoner himself, he had put a curtain between him and the things that made up life, between him and even these, the boards, nails, ropes, that he had known. A lump came in his throat. It was too brusque, this tearing down of curtains.

He took it hard that Mr. Vaughan chose this ketch to transport himself, Will, the two ladies and Paul to York. He did not know much about York, except that it was roughly halfway to Boston, from Damariscotta, and had a good harbor. He would have enjoyed the trip, the chance to see a new part of the coast, but for having to wait upon them all. He was there for that. He could not even help to sail *La Belle Louise*. There was an English crew—the *Trident's* crew—while he was a landlubber body servant—on his father's boat!

He took it hard, but to be on the seas at all was some relief. The sea spelled comfort, liberation, life! The strong salty breezes filled his nostrils in the old remembered way. Sailing thus before

·[14]·

the wind was exhilarating. They were keeping to the coast. They had fair weather, though the sea was moderately rough. York Harbor lay before them, to starboard. Paul looked at it and looked away. He had no mind to land, to carry things, to be ordered about. It was some satisfaction that his old cats were sick and lay abed. Their sense of propriety forbade his waiting on them there at least. They held the basin for each other—it gave them something to do, and him a chance for air.

Will walked the length of the deck to him.

"Well," he said, "this is better than watching it from the beach."

Paul nodded. Will would not remember that this was *La Belle Louise*, even Will. He said with an effort:

"She's a good vessel."

"Oh, yes—old-fashioned, though."

Paul laughed. *La Belle Louise!* It was true that she must be old, his father brought her out from France in 1710, the bad year when the English took Port Royal from the French. She helped in the risings of 1711, and was one of the few vessels that got away. She wasn't new then. It was thirty years since she left France. Yes, Will was right, *La Belle Louise* was old, but she was beautiful.

"Father says a ketch like this isn't as good for the fishing as a sloop. He says if he could get any peace or security from the French he'd build a fleet of smacks for offshore fishing, lobsters and scallops, there'd be money in that."

"Yes, but I think the deep-sea fishing more exciting, more of a man's life! Pollack, cod, and tuna fish—sometimes there are sharks. A good fight with a shark, when you harpoon it, haul it in and take it home, and all the people shout on the shore as they see it tied to the bow, that's something!"

Paul's eyes lit with excitement, his whole expression changed. Will looked at him curiously.

"I forgot that you were a fisherman," he said.

"On this very ketch."

There was an awkward silence. A hand bell tinkled in the cabin. Paul got up. He looked at Will for a moment, shrugged his shoulders and went to answer it. Presently he reappeared, carrying a basin which he emptied overside. His expression was grim. Will, suddenly shy, turned his face away and looked toward York Harbor. They were approaching it rapidly.

His father shouted orders. Will glanced at him appreciatively. Mr. Vaughan was in his element upon the sea. Headstrong and rash, he embraced obstacles, and would stop at nothing to sweep aside anything in his way. Stories were told of him along the coast. Once Will had known him order a number of small boats to leave Portsmouth for Matinicus for his fishing trade. It was a wild March day, the sea was mountainous, his men advised him that his boats could not be launched and carry sail. He would not listen, but embarked himself with Will, ordering the men to follow. One boat was lost at the mouth of the river, the others, after a terrific beating, made Martinicus and landed them. He laughed as he set foot on the rocks and shook his fist at the sky.

His restless force made him a power to be reckoned with. It ran through the family, Will mused. His grandfather had been Lieutenant Governor of New Hampshire. His father was more of a buccaneer, in business on his own. He was fast making a good thing of the fishing trade. If the French marauders could be checked, if Louisbourg, their stronghold, were destroyed, the road would be clear to greater things. Therefore he was on his way to confer with Governor Shirley, Will's new master, the English barrister who emigrated to Massachusetts in 1731 and ten years later rose to governorship. Will knew all about him. Governor Shirley had been in office now three years, was able and liked by all; he was just the man to push the grandiose scheme that the Vaughans were maturing. The governor thought himself a military strategist—a fig for that! The point was that he was energetic and influential. If anyone could raise an expedition, he could.

The ketch wore round, slackened sail, making for the landing stage. The usual curious crowd lounged on the beach. Now all was bustle to meet the incoming ship. The stolid crew eased her in, furling the sails with deliberate care.

Paul laden with packages appeared at the cabin door in time to see the mooring. He stepped upon the deck and dumped his load.

"Where you from, sailor?"

·[16]·

Paul didn't answer.

"Stiff necked? I said where are you from?"

"Ask the master." Paul jerked his thumb toward Mr. Vaughan, leaving the ketch with Will beside him. His questioner, a big, red-faced, truculent individual, who might have been anything from harpooner to second mate, drew back a step or two, growling into his beard. Paul returned to the ketch for a second load.

The old ladies appeared, the worse for wear, and followed the Vaughans ashore.

"Hey, you!" Mr. Vaughan called to a boy gaping at the ketch, "run to the minister's house and tell the Reverend Samuel Moody that his sisters are here, there's a penny for you." Then to his son: "We'll see the ladies disposed of, then you and I will to the tavern and upon our way. If we accept to dine with the worthy minister we'll miss the tide." He raised his voice: "We sail in an hour, men, for Boston. Get yourselves a meal at the Sailor's Den and then stand by. Here," he delved into his cloak pocket, bringing out a handful of silver. He counted out five shillings and gave them to the bosun for the men. "I'll settle for the supplies you take on board when I return," he added, giving his arm to the two yellow-faced old ladies, still hiccuping into their handkerchiefs in a genteel way. They moved off toward the town. Paul followed with his bundles, cursing the cobblestones that hurt his feet. His shoes were wearing thin, his temper thinner. He followed the strolling group with bitter words behind his tongue.

They reached the brow of the beach to perceive a black-frocked old gentleman scurrying to meet them with his hands outstretched.

"Well, well, well! The Lord be praised! We must offer up thanksgiving. Charlotte, Susan," he kissed the Mistresses Moody heartily. "And you, sir, and you, William," he paused uncertainly before including Paul with a "you, my lad. This is a joyous occasion. You will dine at the manse?"

Mr. Vaughan declined.

"We must be under way."

He saluted the Moodys good-by. Will took his leave. He looked at Paul, who looked at him.

"Sure you won't change your mind?"

·[17]·

Paul shook his head. Will smiled.

"Good luck," he said.

"Good luck," Paul answered, smiling back.

Mr. Vaughan frowned. He did not like this familiarity. He liked it still less when Will, as a parting reminder, lifted up his voice and sang, not a good rousing English drinking song, bad enough, unsuitable indeed before the minister, but a finickity French song with heaven knew what licentious words!

"That's enough, William," he said crossly, "you're disgracing me."

Will stopped singing. Paul shrugged expressive shoulders. The bundles upon them jiggled up and down. He moved off after the Moodys without looking behind him at the ketch or the sea.

"Good-by—Master Vaughan!"

CHAPTER IV.

SNOW fell heavily. There was a thaw, the ground froze, it snowed again. The houses of York village nestled in drifts as high as the people who went in and out of them. Pathways must be cut, stamped, cleared. It was Paul's duty to keep the approaches to the Moody property clear, and since the manse stood by itself a hundred yards from the road, he had a good deal of work on his one pair of hands. He dug whenever he was not requisitioned for anything else. Once or twice he went out into the cold of the night and shoveled beneath the stars. It was pleasant work, outdoors, healthy. It gave him the illusion of freedom, and time to think his own long thoughts.

He was shoveling thus, one morning, after a flurry. The sun shone out of an ardent sky, over the sea, over the white counterpane dotted with houses, over everything, making the shadow of the forest trees show long and purple against the snow. It brought a million glittering diamond points upon the shovelful Paul scooped and carried. The whiteness of everything was dazzling. Paul blinked his eyes. Raising his head he looked upon the village.

A team of oxen dragging a rough sledge was plodding patiently knee-high in snow. Their frosty breath and the heat of their bodies steamed in the air about them. The driver, standing on the wooden block that they were dragging, flourished a stick in his hand and shouted "Gee!" to them. Occasionally he rapped them on the rumps. He was a young driver. Paul smiled to see them patiently, unhurriedly go on. So fast, no faster. We can be set in motion, we cannot be made to go.

Behind the cart two famished-looking dogs, like wolves, struggled for a bone. Mistress Turf had set out her washing above them. Frozen stiff, a creaking shirt flapped and struck the dogs. They growled and kept on tugging. Round the end of the village street, on the road that led to the world, two riders appeared, trotting smartly, one behind the other.

Paul looked at them eagerly. For a moment he thought that Will—but no, the second figure though it had Will's height and general shape had not his bearing. This was no horseman, Paul thought sympathetically, rubbing his own behind, as the space between saddle and seat appeared. Crénom, how it hurt for a sailor to ride! Perhaps this man was a sailor too?

He watched the figures approaching, leaning on his shovel. They went briskly through the village. They were coming to the manse. Presently he could see distinctly who and what they were. The first man was tall and strong with something pompous in his bearing that proclaimed him Somebody. He bent a sober, bourgeois face on Paul, as he stood aside to let them pass. It would have been smug, but for the eyes. Strange eyes, Paul thought, in such a face, with their look of candid surprise, as though a little boy looked out on a baffling world. He beckoned to Paul to follow him. The second figure passed. Paul drew in his breath. Spit and image of Will—absurdly like, and yet he could never be taken for Will, whoever he was. The uneasy way he sat his horse, the diffidence with which he pressed after the first man, proclaimed him a servant, no less than his clothes, which were like Paul's, too thin for the time of year, and shabby. All this flashed through Paul's mind as he ran after the horses and took the foremost by the head, in time for its rider to dismount and throw him the reins. He did not wait for Paul to announce him but strode into the house, leaving the two servants together.

"Who is that?" Paul asked, smiling at this portrait of Will.

"Mr. William Pepperell, of Kittery."

"Where's that?"

"Don't you know Kittery? Kittery Point? It's within easy riding distance from here, to the north, on the coast. Mr. Pepperell rides here frequently."

"How long will he be staying? Are the horses to be unsaddled?"

"I don't know. Yes, I suppose so."

"They will have to be put in the stable, anyhow. They cannot stand in the cold. You will have to dismount," Paul said, taking charge of this diffident stranger. "The stable door's too low for you to ride your horse into its stall. Follow me, I'll take you there."

The fellow slid off his horse, awkwardly, all of a heap. He coughed as he reached the ground, with a painful, racking spasm. It passed. A smile of relief lit up his handsome, troubled face.

"Lead ahead," he said.

Paul pitched his shovel into a drift and led Mr. Pepperell's horse away. He opened the stable door. Horses and men gratefully entered the dark warmth of the place, crowded with oxen, chickens, cows and horses, all lending the heat of their bodies to the atmosphere.

"It's good in here," the stranger said, when he had thrown a blanket over his horse.

"Did you ride from Kittery?"

"Yes, a long, cold, bitter ride, and I hate riding."

"I too," Paul agreed. "Horses hate me as much as I hate them. What's your name?"

"Randolph. They called me Randy here. I'm—I was trapanned."

"Trapanned?"

"Yes. Surely you've heard of trapanning? It happens all the time."

"I'm sorry, I have not heard."

Randy looked at him curiously.

"Your a foreigner by your speech."

"French, a prisoner of war."

"Ah, I see. And that is why you do not know trapanning, although if you have been in these colonies any time you must have met with us."

"Tell me," said Paul, settling himself upon the edge of an empty manger. He added: "if you want to," seeing the other's face darken as he thought.

Randy joined him on the manger.

"Trapanning is kidnaping," he said. "It does not go on in France or the French colonies."

"But kidnaping does go on in France . . . lettres de cachets

·[21]·

. . . disappearances . . . many people are taken for ransom, spirited away."

"This is a different kind of kidnaping altogether. You've heard of indentured servants?"

"Emigrants bonded to the merchant company or owner of the vessel transporting them? Yes, I have heard of them. They work to repay their passage."

"Ha! They bond themselves. Trapanning's different. Get a boy, a girl, a child, a man, a woman, on board a boat, blackjack, gag, bind, throw them in the hold, set sail, and there you are. You can sell them into slavery when they land, it's all profit—so many years for their passage money, enough to cross seven times in a comfortable cabin, so many years for their start in life, which may never come. None of them see home again. Trapanned!"

Paul was silent with horror and sympathy. He stretched out his hand.

"I feel for you. I was captured. I saw my father killed. I have never recovered. I am a prisoner of war, it's hard enough, but your story's worse."

"If you could have seen the horror of that hellship! I was a child of ten. I don't know why I tell you this, but I was nobly born, richly reared. The suit I landed in was satin and lace, and it was not even my best suit. My first master's son wore it afterwards, and the gold chain about my neck was taken too."

"Paul! Paul!"

The housekeeper's voice could be heard calling across the courtyard.

"There!" Paul said, "they want the horses."

"I don't think so," Randy answered, but he rose and stretched himself.

"Paul, you are to bring Mr. Pepperell's servant into the kitchen. They are to stay the night. He will sleep with you."

"I'm glad," Paul said, "for now we shall have a chance to talk and know each other better. One can dispense with formalities when one has been trapanned. The miserable of the earth must unite. It is a new word to me but an old story." He smiled. "Shall we see if we can trapan a bowl of coffee for ourselves?"

They walked toward the kitchen, each of them content. A mysterious fusion had taken place between them.

·[22]·

CHAPTER V

THE REVEREND SAMUEL MOODY was proud of his dining-room table, made from beams washed ashore from the wreck of a French privateer. He had stumbled upon them one night on his way to rebuke three parishioners whom he suspected of drinking and gambling together in a disused hut by the beach. Black in the moonlight lay the trove.

Seasoned wood was badly needed in the settlement for many purposes, the trees in the surrounding forest were young pine and stripling birch. Anything larger had been cut as far as safety from the savages allowed of woodcutting parties. This was oak. The discovery compensated him for the disheartening expedition, he claimed the beams, and such was his authority with the rest of his flock that nobody disputed his claim, and willing hands were found to set up his table for him.

With a vague picture of the Last Supper in his mind, although he did not trace the source of his idea, putting it down to the length and the strength of the beams, and the pity it would be to change their shape, he had a long refectory table made of them, supported upon stumps of cedarwood, still smelling of its origin. Every time that Paul stooped over to serve a dish or remove a plate, the fragrance of the forest rose into his face, nostalgia of freedom, of hot sunny days, cool nights, and solitude.

Seated at either end the Mistresses Moody frowned or simpered, they were simpering now at Mr. Pepperell. He sat opposite his host, with Randy behind his chair. Paul stood behind whichever Moody claimed his services, contriving to signal to Randy unobserved. During the intolerably long grace or invocation which dealt at length with the past, present and future of the Pepperell family, the state of the weather and the deplorable condition of the minister's flock with special reference to games of chance, Paul and Randy caught each other's eyes and exchanged sly glances of mingled weariness and contempt. Paul had never before found a face reflect his own emotions. If Will had caught his eye, he would have looked a little shocked, and certainly embarrassed. Will could not forget that he was his father's son, but expected Paul to forget that he was his! There had been friendship between them, of six years' growth, but it had not the foundation of sudden comprehension, of shared emotion and common feeling that his few hours with Randy had developed.

It made the tedious routine of the meal exciting. Each time that he obeyed the contemptuous summons of Mistress Moody's arbitrary finger, or the timorous beck of Mistress Susan's uncertain one, accompanied by vague nods, he caught Randy's eye and knew that he understood the years of impotent hatred Paul had felt for these two fools. When he stood behind the Reverend Moody's chair and that gentleman raising his elbow suddenly spilled the dish Paul served to him and slapped his face for carelessness, he felt run through his veins the generous warmth of Randy's sympathy.

The meal dragged on.

"Are you going to the Assembly, Sir?"

"If my duties here permit me, Sir. The care of a flock as unruly and stiff-necked as mine allows of little time for the conduct of the national affairs."

"There is an important issue to come before us, I have been informed. It cannot, of course, be discussed—ahem—here."

Mr. Pepperell bent his oxlike face on the gathering, his wide eyes coming to rest on Paul's expressionless face, one cheek crimson, one a yellow-white.

"I purposed asking you to share my trip to Boston. I am going in the sloop. Mistress Pepperell is accompanying me to indulge in a little society. I believe that some silken goods have arrived in Boston. It is early in the year for them, and perhaps the report has been misunderstood, but it was enough to whet Mistress Pepperell's appetite."

He smiled at Mistress Susan whose tongue was protruding from her mouth with eagerness. Mistress Moody frowned at this ungenteel display but fidgeted with her villymot and looked toward her brother. He did not observe these manifestations of excitement and put an end to the ladies' hopes by saying decidedly:

"I will accompany you with pleasure, Sir. There will be room for my servant, I suppose?"

"Oh, yes. I am taking mine."

Randy and Paul looked at one another. Paul was not the minister's servant, he belonged to the old hags, but in moments of social importance he was borrowed.

"It should be a stirring occasion, an unusual assembly," Pepperell said, "every vote will be required. I don't know how you feel about the enemy. . . ."

"Feel? I pray, preach, and order my daily life against those infidels! Popish idolators! But the cause of the Lord will triumph. Look at these!" He swept his hand over his table. "These beams were on their way to Louisbourg, or some other stronghold and citadel of Satan. Now they serve for us to eat upon. There is a moral in that. The Lord will place our enemies beneath our feet."

Paul's face darkened. He bent over to replenish the minister's bowl with the mixture of tea and rum that he preferred and oddly enough did not consider drink. Randy poured wine for his master at the same moment.

"It must be gay in Boston now," Mistress Susan said wistfully. Mistress Moody frowned at her again. The two men ignored the remark.

"Well," said the minister rising, "if you will pass into my study, we shall not disturb the ladies further."

The ladies thus rudely given their cue rose hastily to their feet. Mr. Pepperell saluted them with formal gallantry. They passed from the room, and the two men lingered only long enough to take their bowls with them. Randy and Paul were left to clear away. Randy raised his eyebrows.

"So it goes," said Paul.

"I wonder how we stand it."

"What else can we do? We are servants."

"Cattle."

"Slaves."

"It is worse at Kittery. I get thrashed there once a week."

"Oh, I get thrashed here too, by all of them."

"It was worse still before Pepperell bought me from my first master. I hadn't got used to the idea of being a servant then. It took time. That family thought that I was proud and they should break my pride. They broke everything else, but not that. I'm still proud, I'll be proud till I die, and what I'm most proud about is that I'm not one of them!"

"Hush, Randy, not so loud. The old hags will hear us and come back. Wasn't it funny to see them ogling and hankering after an invitation to go to Boston in the sloop? We shall be going, though, and if we can get together there it will be gay."

Randy's face cleared, as Paul intended it should. He was seized with a fit of coughing, then he spoke.

"What's to prevent our meeting? Boston's a town. We will be sent on errands, we can slip out of nights. I wonder how long we will stay? Some little time, to judge by the importance of the Assembly."

"The Assembly!" Paul burst out. "Did you hear what old Pious-Patter said about Louisbourg and the French? My town, my people! Something's afoot and I don't like to think what it is."

"An expedition against Louisbourg," Randy said promptly.

"Then you know, too."

"Of course I know. Pepperell talks of nothing else. But it isn't voted yet, and perhaps the Assembly will turn it down. It means getting help from England, and the authorities at home may not want to help at this time. The Duke of Newcastle has other things in his mind, I wouldn't worry if I were you. There will be a lot of talk, of strong words, a curse or two, but nothing more will come of it."

"You seem to be well-informed."

"Even a slave has ears."

"And sympathy for the French?"

"I'm English, and loyal to England, but not to these colonies or the dogs who enslaved me."

"It was an Englishman who trapanned you, though."

"No, it was a colonist. At least I like to think that it was. I well believe the Englishmen who trapan and kidnap do it without knowing what lies at the journey's end for those they sell. I must believe it so. It sustains a core of faith in me to believe that these are different from those. I have vastly more sympathy for Louisbourg and the French than I have for Boston and the colonists. Inevitable—the French have not enslaved me and these have."

"It is the complacency with which they degrade us I resent," said Paul. "You come from a great family, and I of good Norman stock. My father was poor, and a younger son in a large family. He left his inheritance to carve a better place for himself in New France. He was every bit as wellborn as Pepperell and as for the Moodys!" He made an expressive gesture. "But because I was not old enough to wear a uniform when I was caught, they do not treat me with the respect they would give a private in the French army. He would be exchanged, I am made a slave."

It was Randy's turn to console.

"Tell me about Louisbourg," he asked, "and New France."

Paul was silent for a moment recovering himself. Then he muttered:

"It's a good place. The people are gay and devout and happy-go-lucky there. They have not the puritan element. They are not heretics. Forgive me, you are Protestant."

"No, at least I do not think so. I have nothing in common with these people's faith, and I remember a chapel at home in my father's house and a priest in vestments. I suppose I was, I may have been, a Catholic."

Paul gave a cry of delight.

"We are neither of us better than pagans now," he said, "but I like to think we told our rosaries once, and attended Mass."

"I don't remember a rosary and I don't remember Mass. I can't remember much of anything of those times, except that I was happy. It is all very long ago now, and I was just a child."

He passed his hand over his forehead, and coughed again, painfully.

"Paul!"

The housekeeper was calling.

"Hurry! We should have finished. Help me, quickly."

They speeded up their efforts and left the dining room.

·[27]·

CHAPTER VI

THE homeward-moving sun gave up its daylong struggle against gray skies. A light snow began to fall. The woodland trail grew darker, indistinct. Spruce and undergrowth looked black, their outlines blurred as the snow increased. Paul shivered. He released his right hand from the reins, cautiously reaching for his collar. Any sudden movement might antagonize the brute he straddled. Frogsmarch derived the name from his unwilling and erratic gait. "Father" Moody riding ahead, astride the gentler mare, turned in his saddle, motioning Paul to come up to him. Paul motioned in return, silently because of the danger of attracting attention from Indians or wolves, or hostile coureurs de bois. He urged Frogsmarch forward.

"We must go faster," Father Moody murmured. "In an hour's time the twilight will be here."

Paul nodded. There was no need to stress the danger of being caught by night in the winter woods. Father Moody spurred the mare and cantered forward. Paul followed wearily, cup-and-balling on his sore behind, cursing, silently of course, the stiff jerky canter Frogsmarch lolloped into, also the coming night, also the minister, also the snow that stung his eyes and went into the places unprotected by his clothing, wetting neck and wrists, running down his chest. Paul hated riding at any time, riding in the winter—he set his teeth and lowered his head, the better to escape the worst of it. They must press on.

The trail, roughly discernible, wound in and out of trees. Now the undergrowth slowed them to a walk, now a clear space allowed of cantering, now they could break into a lumbering trot.

After what seemed eternity, when Paul was wet through and the luggage tied behind him, bumping into his back, was a sodden mass, a clearing through which they cantered opened upon a wider trail than any they had traveled, which gave in turn upon a good-sized road.

"In good time!" the minister turned to shout. Paul spurred up to him. He knew that the long silence had been torture to his loquacious master. Now he would roar admonitions and crack hearty jokes until they arrived at the very gates of Kittery. Paul was anxious to arrive there speedily. Apart from being wet, he wanted to see Randy. It was New Year's Day. At home this would be kept in great festivity. He had plans for keeping it, too. He had stolen a bottle of rum from the mate of a whaling ship, drunk enough to invite him on board and fool enough to let him see where the rum was kept. He and Randy would drink together at least. It would be a surprise for Randy and something for Paul to do, something to take his mind off the minister's eternal nagging.

"My man," the minister called him. Man he was, but not the minister's. It was a far cry from *La Belle Louise* to lackeying. He dismissed it with a shrug of his powerful shoulders. His mind was still his own. He was coming into his strength rapidly, in spite of hardship. He stood five feet nine in his slippers, now. He was thin but wiry and very strong. It was good, this strength, it was his own, something nobody could rob him of, although they could exploit it. Vague visions of torture, of death, rose up before his mind. These too he dismissed with a shrug and a twist of the lips. They were morbid and fanciful, also the old fool who thought he owned him had been speaking for some time.

"Oh, indeed," he answered earnestly, it was a formula which had served him before for yes or no.

"There she is." They rounded a corner and Mr. Pepperell's spacious house spread before them in the dark, its candlelighted windows shining. "There she is."

Paul spurred Frogsmarch. The ugly beast pricked his great hairy ears and put his feet down with more resolution. Lights

·[29]·

twinkling across the snow meant stables. There would be corn, warmth and rest. Frogsmarch broke into a trot.

A sound that had been with them distantly and faintly now grew loud and clear, the swirling waters of the sea sucking at islets and island rocks, the breaking of the surf against the shore, again, again, again! Paul drew a deep breath. Below him a wide river added water to the sea. He pointed.

"What is that—sir?"

"The Piscataqua and the Isle of Shoals."

He repeated the names. They sounded like the sea about them. His mind as usual flew across these breaking waves to the surf-beaten rocks of Louisbourg Harbor. With every roar and crash he imagined that the waves were breaking on the reefs beneath his home. It was New Year's Day—the Jour de l'An when everyone in France or in her colonies brought gifts to celebrate. His eyes grew sad, his face lengthened, even as he rose between the gate-posts of the Pepperell estate and came to a halt beneath the portico. He dismounted mechanically and went to hold the minister's horse. The door opened. Randy in livery said:

"This way if you please, sir, you are expected."

He winked at Paul behind the old man's back, and jerked his shoulder as much as to say: "Let me just get the fellow settled, I'll come back to you." Paul interpreted the gesture correctly. In a few minutes Randy had returned.

"Take the horses round to the stable," he said. "Give them over to William. He'll look after them. Tell him to bring the luggage to the house. Come in quickly after that and get dry. Those clothes are not heavy enough for a snowstorm."

Paul nodded. He walked off with the horses, dispirited. But it was at least a break in the monotony of his servitude to spend the night at Kittery Point, to set sail in the morning for Boston. That would be good. He snuffed the air. It was the good, strong, salty breeze that a man should draw into his nostrils every day and all day long and all the night. Unconsciously he lifted his head. Color came into his sallow cheeks. He was a handsome, animated man with promise of passion in his smoldering dark eyes and in the set of his shoulder blades. He strode across the stable yard, but there was nobody to see him so, and by the time he had

·[30]·

reached the door his customary mask of blank stolidity returned to him.

Randy was waiting.

"I'm glad to see you again," he said, and then: "I will give you some clothes. They are not very good, but you will prefer them to livery."

"Why not livery," said Paul, "if it's warm?"

Randy looked at him. The bravado of Paul's tone did not deceive him.

"Very well," he said. "There are two suits of livery besides the one I wear."

Paul followed him to the kitchen, and through the kitchen to a woodshed. Here Randy slept on a bale of straw and kept his meager belongings in a chest. The liveries were hanging on a peg. Paul drew off his soaking things and shivered into dry ones. He followed Randy to the house and was pressed into service by a flunkey with a sour-looking face under a wig too large for him.

"As a member of the Governor's Council," Pepperell was saying, "and President of the Board, I cannot feel . . ."

There was a flutter of white and foamy pink as the ladies of the household disclosed themselves. Paul looked at them critically. It was a long time since he had waited on anything younger than the Mistresses Moody. These were not very pretty, he decided, nevertheless their presence woke an aching nameless longing within him, a dissatisfaction with his life and with the future as it now appeared, a nostalgia for Louisbourg and the French women that stifled him. He made his way with the decanter and tried in vain to forget the sound of the liberating sea and the sight of these disturbing girls. Randy opposite him was having the same trouble. Paul read it in his face. From time to time Randy was shaken with a spasm of soundless coughing. Once as he fought for breath, he coughed aloud.

"Take your spluttering out of here!" roared Pepperell. "Oaf!"

Randy slid out of the room. The flunkey boxed his ears as he passed. Paul felt himself go red with rage. The conversation went on, the men guzzled, the ladies simpered, Paul, hungry and tired, looked at them all with contempt. Suddenly he was startled to find his gaze being caught and held and returned with interest.

·[31]·

One of the girls, the youngest, was eyeing him shrewdly, pene-tratingly. Paul dropped his eyes upon the plate he held. But he was startled out of his rage. The eyes that had looked into his were like, so very like, those of somebody he knew.

He went about the rest of his work mechanically, clearing the table, helping in the kitchen, carrying wood to the hall fire. Randy and he, at length, found themselves free of immediate duty. They stood at the kitchen windows looking over the sea. Each was gnawing a bone he had picked up.

"The sea!" sighed Paul, listening with the drumstick in his hand. He spoke as a lover might.

"I hate the sea!" Randy said. "It brought me here. What do you think of this house?"

"It's big," Paul answered indifferently, "and I suppose it's beautiful."

"But not so big nor so beautiful, nor so well furnished as my father's house in England."

Randy's voice rose.

"He does not expect me to believe him," Paul thought, laying his hand upon Randy's shoulder for a moment to quiet him. The hysterical note in his voice diminished.

"It is a consolation, Monsieur," he said to Paul, rolling out the French courtesy title, "it is a pleasure, sir, to have made your acquaintance."

Paul bowed ceremoniously. A sudden hoarse cackle of laughter behind them recalled them to themselves. The cook and the flunkey were laughing at them, laughing and laughing.

"Mongseer," the cook mimicked, "sir, your servant," then his tone changed. "You, Randy, get along there, and empty the swill to the pigs, and mind you don't eat any of it, you and your French nobility!"

CHAPTER VII

BOSTON HARBOR was full of vessels. Paul saw them first as the weathered headsail of the Pepperell sloop came over on a tack he made toward the wharf. At the last moment Mistress Pepperell was indisposed and could not come, entrusting each of them three times over with patterns and instructions should the new silks have arrived. Even without her, the *Olim* was hardly big enough for the load she carried. Mr. Pepperell, the minister and Randy stayed below, in the stuffy little cabin, while Paul and the crew, consisting of two sailors, one of whom styled himself the "sailing master," ran the sloop before a winter wind, through an angry sea.

Now they reached the harbor. Paul was impressed. He had a southeastern view of the town, grander than anything he had seen. Marseilles and Paris were bigger. It was hard to conceive of such a thing. He counted nine steeples strung out through the city, a large dome, smaller domes, and how many houses! They all seemed to be stories high, some two, some three. It was incredible.

"A big place," he ventured to the sailing master, who grunted and said without removing the corncob pipe he sucked:

"Twenty years ago I mind my father telling me—he came from Boston, worked at Wentworth's wharf—there were nigh three thousand houses, a thousand of 'em brick, the rest timber, near twelve thousand people. Look at her now! She's grown since then. Oh yes, she keeps on growing, and there's always something new, each time we dock."

Paul blinked.

"Look at there!" the sailing master continued, sweeping his hand to the right. Ships of all sorts lay between them and the town, some letting go, some weighing anchor, some like the *Olim* tacking in for a berth. There were barques and barquentines, brigs and snows, ketches, sloops and fishing smacks, and small lug-sailed craft. Behind these, at the wharfs, ships were loading and unloading, some were out of the water being calked and scraped. It was a gay scene, there were so many sails, so many pennants, so much movement in the harbor, men in the longboats shouting and waving to each other or to the shore, others pulling silently with officers aboard. Paul drew a deep breath.

"There's the *Shirley*," said the sailing master, pointing to a schooner on the port side, "carries twenty guns. Captain Rous commands her. There's the *Caesar*, twenty guns. That there to leeward that's a snow, carries sixteen guns. Ah, and see, there's a privateer, taken from the French."

Paul craned to peer at her.

"And the Government sloop the *Tartar*, from Rhode Island colony. Carries fourteen carriage guns and four swivels. I've sailed in her. Taken French ships with her, too. There's the *Boston Packet*. Sixteen guns. Quite an armament."

"Are there always so many fighting vessels in the harbor?"

"Depends on what is up. I've seen more, I've seen less. Look lively there, with the tiller. Ready about! Hard alee!"

Paul ducked mechanically as the boom swung over, his eyes still fixed on the French privateer. Perhaps if she were captured recently there would be prisoners still in town. He turned to ask the sailing master, but he and the "crew" were both busy bringing the sloop into the wind. It was not the time to bother them with questions.

"Stand by to lower sail," the sailing master shouted. Paul stood ready. Mr. Pepperell was coming up from the cabin, squaring his shoulders with an air of sturdy indifference to the elements. Paul who had heard him grunt and retch below was not impressed. He moved aside, the sailing master touched his cap, and the *Olim* glided forward to the wharf. Only when she was made fast and stationary did the minister appear, green to the gills.

"Your servant's sick with more than seasickness," he said to Pepperell.

"Oh, nonsense," Pepperell shrugged. "He's strong enough if he didn't give in to himself. You, Randy! Stir your stumps. We're in port. There's more for you to do than to lie wallowing there! Up with you!"

He sprang ashore, brushing the salt from his sleeves, and smoothing out his wig. The minister followed. Paul followed him, and Randy, pale as a ghost, staggered after them. He held a handkerchief to his mouth. When he took it away, Paul thought that it was spotted with red, but Randy smiled at him. They stooped to take up the baggage, following their masters to the town.

Pepperell was going to the Governor's house, the minister to lodgings in King Street. They parted in Union Street, going in opposite directions. Paul watching Randy stoop beneath his load and move away after the portly figure of his master, checked in his stride. He wanted to make an assignment with Randy for the night. He whistled softly and held up his right hand as the minister trotted forward and Mr. Pepperell stopped to greet an acquaintance on the opposite side of the street. Randy turned his head.

"Let's meet in an hour," Paul mouthed. "I'll wait for you at the inn."

Randy nodded, to show that he understood, mouthed: "If I can get away," shifted his bundle and plodded on. It was Paul's turn, presently, to run into an acquaintance. At the window of the tavern to which the minister was headed, a young man lounged, waiting. It was an elegant young man, dressed in a velours coat of the newest cut. He sprang up as the minister came in sight, and hastened out to him.

"My father wants to see you at once, sir, as soon as you are rested," he said. "He is with the Governor now. They are expecting Mr. Pepperell. Is he not with you?"

"He is on his way to the Governor now. We parted in Union Street. Paul, get the packs undone and give me my best coat. I'll wait on them immediately."

·[35]·

Paul moved toward the house to obey, but first he hung back for a moment to be greeted in his turn.

"Oh, hello, Paul." There was a trace of patronage in Will's voice, and his smile seemed a little forced. "Did you have a good trip?"

"Good enough," Paul answered. "You look well."

"Oh," Will laughed a little awkwardly. He glanced at the three young officers at a table near them. Paul saw the glance.

"Good-by, Master Vaughan," he said quietly, moving off toward the inn.

"Good-by," Will answered. He turned to the minister with a shade too much eagerness in his manner. "Will you have a glass with me, while we wait for your things to be unpacked, sir? Shall we sit at this table?"

Paul looked back at him for a moment sorrowfully, as he waited at the door of the inn to be shown the minister's lodgings. "Poor Will," he thought. "Whatever I had of him is lost to me forever. He has come to his father's way of thinking about our intercourse. He was afraid those friends of his would hear me addressing him without due respect." He followed a servant up the narrow stairs, thinking as he went, "If I had not found Randy I would feel this desperately. The loss of a friend, of Will, would come very hard to me. I would be desolate. As it is . . ." he shrugged.

Then a sudden rage came to him. "Damned popinjay! How dare he stand there patronizing me! How dare he think that because I am a prisoner I am no better than the servant they have made of me! How dare he take complacently the change in our positions when we meet. At home, in his father's house he was glad enough to make a friend of me. Here in Boston he is ashamed, Jésus, Marie, Joseph! Tous les saints du Paradis!" he crossed himself. "Give me patience. Grant that I may not spit in his face for a turncoat coward. Grant that I may not hate him. Grant me this!"

He spread the minister's best cloak upon the bed and went to summon him.

CHAPTER VIII

THE General Court of Massachusetts was sitting. Paul, standing with Randy by the door, watched the members stomaching in, pompous merchants, solemn rustics, grave lawyers, Puritan clerics, all alike in their self-importance. "Father" Moody was in his element, with the Reverend Thomas Prince on one side of him, and the Reverend George Whitefield on the other. The Reverend George Whitefield was leader of a religious ferment known as "The Great Awakening" which was sweeping the countryside. He puffed at the chest like a pigeon, and Paul could hardly keep his gravity as he listened to the minister's final instructions.

"See that there is a hot meal at the tavern after the assembly."

"Yes, sir."

Mr. Pepperell followed with Mr. Vaughan, leaning on his arm. They were talking in low tones together. They paused in the doorway as people pause at a funeral before they enter. Paul and Randy touched their hats. Mr. Pepperell threw his cloak to Randy, who caught it with an effort. He was tempted to put it on, for the weather was bitter and they had been standing there for three-quarters of an hour.

There was a murmur among the men at the entrance, gathered to watch the court assemble. A burly man with a leather case under his arm appeared, walking beside Will Vaughan. This was Governor Shirley and his secretary. Paul looked away. He did not want to be ignored for the second time. They passed quickly through the doorway. There was a buzz of conversation, a scraping of feet, an outburst of coughing and a shuffle, from the inside. A voice could be heard droning:

"On this day of January seventh in the year of our Lord one thousand seven hundred and forty five . . ."

"Come on," said Paul impatiently. "Will you stand there all day, holding out his cloak? They've gone in. We have time to ourselves."

Randy started.

"I forgot," he said. "You're right, it is cold here."

They started to explore the streets. They wandered along Cornhill, down Water Street to the docks, where they stood a long time, watching the shipping, talking to dock hands lounging on the wharfs. Although it was bitter weather, these men stood for hours, looking at nothing, waiting, spitting, chewing, all they desired was to be near the sea. Paul found a sailor among them with a wooden leg newly fitted. He had news of Louisbourg. He had seen the French fleet draw off and sail for France, leaving the place unprotected for the winter, except for its own privateers. He repeated gossip taken from the militia returning from the defense of Canceau—that the fort at Louisbourg was weakened by a mutiny, and provisions were fallen short.

Paul pondered this, and asked as many questions as the old man would answer, until he lost patience and told him to be off. Randy meanwhile was hopping from one cold foot to the other, bored and tired. He did not like the sea, nor sailors, nor anything to do with docks. He brightened as they returned up the crowded lanes that led from the water front, past peddlers, tinkers, fishmongers, a watch and clock maker, a blacksmith and a merchant of silk. Paul remembered Mistress Pepperell's recommendation. He made a long nose at the bales displayed. The merchant saw him and shouted angrily. Randy took his arm and drew him away.

"They are Puritans here," he said, "remember that."

He draped his master's cloak about him and struck a pompous attitude. Paul laughed. For once his immediate surroundings were pleasant, he had leisure to forget his servitude. It was agreeable to explore the city with Randy, in search of an adventure. Round the next corner they thought they found it.

Two girls were coming down the narrow walk in earnest conversation, with baskets on their arms. They were plump, rosy-cheeked, and plainly dressed, fishermen's daughters or servants at an inn perhaps. Randy stepped forward. Sweeping the cloak about him, he bowed.

"May I have the pleasure of carrying your basket, Mistress Madison?" he asked of the prettiest of the two, laying hold on it.

The girls stopped, wide-eyed and stared at him. One of them began to giggle.

"Sir, you are mistaken," said the other, with an attempt at haughtiness. "My name is not Madison." She twitched the basket out of his hands.

"It's Lawless," giggled her companion.

"Lawless?" protested Randy. "Oh, no, not as bad as that."

The plump girl made an effort to follow her companion, already moving forward, smoothing her stomacher and trying to frown. The humor of the situation overcame her, she turned to explain.

"Lawless, her name is not Madison, but Lawless."

"Ah," said Randy, "now I understand. I am more lawless than she, we must be related. Cousins have privileges." He swooped down on them, gathered the girl into his arms and kissed her lustily. Screams, shouts, the sound of running feet, windows thrown open . . .

"Hurry!" said Paul, "Randy, let her go."

Randy took another kiss, flung the cloak about himself and fled, running after Paul up the first side street toward the town.

"You must remember they are Puritans here," Paul quoted when they slowed to a walk. "If anyone had been about we would have been jailed or put in the stocks. Tell me, was it good?"

Randy shook his head regretfully.

"She tasted of stale cheese," he said, "or Puritan pie."

"She probably thinks she is damned and done for then," Paul said, "like the first girl I kissed. I kissed her on the mouth, and she cried so bitterly I asked what was wrong. I got it out of her at length. She thought she would have a baby. Imagine that, a baby everytime one kissed a girl!"

"You and I could populate the New World easily at that rate," Randy said. "Have you any children yet?"

"No. What would I breed children for?"

Randy laughed. "For the fun of it," he murmured.

Paul laughed too. "That was a silly way to put it. I mean I've taken care in my chance encounters. After all, there's enough trouble in my world without that."

They were getting near the courthouse now. Signs of bustle about its steps made them mend their pace. Randy had taken off the cloak and was shivering again in his rags. They joined the muttering crowd pushing themselves to the front.

"Secret vote!" said a man over his shoulder to Paul. "What do you make of that?"

"What can it be?" asked another behind him.

"The Governor asked for a secret vote."

"Secret vote!"

They heard it on all sides. The Governor had announced that he had a communication to make of the gravest urgency, so critical that he wished the assembly to swear to secrecy before he disclosed it to them. That was all the onlookers knew or would know. One by one the members reappeared, pompous, portentous, their expressions grave. Here and there signs of amazement and agitation showed the Governor's proposal to be an extraordinary one. "Father" Moody's face was red. He had the expression he wore in his pulpit when denouncing some more flagrant backsliding than usual on the part of his flock, or when he talked about hell. Mr. Pepperell was white. His mouth was set in a resolute line, but his eyes betrayed a dull wonder. There was uneasiness in his bovine face. Randy arranged the cloak about his shoulders. Paul attended on the minister. In silence they set out for the Governor's house. The Governor and Will remained behind. They would follow presently.

"I wonder what it is?" Paul and Randy signaled to each other. Paul thought that he knew. It was something to do with Louisbourg. The proposal to send an expedition perhaps, but why a secret vote? Everybody must know by now that an attack on Louisbourg was in the wind. There was always talk and muttering against the French, but this time with the fleet withdrawn to France, it might be wise to attack before the ships returned with fresh supplies for the colony and troops for the garrison. His face darkened, a nerve in his throat tightened as he thought of home. The expression of cheerfulness and excitement that his afternoon of freedom in the streets of the town had summoned, left him. Things looked grave.

"O mon pays, mon doux pays!" he said beneath his breath. Randy looked at him inquiringly. The minister and Mr. Pepperell parted on the Governor's doorstep.

"Your servant, sir."

"Servant."

Mr. Pepperell and Randy disappeared.

"Well, well, well," said Father Moody. He sucked in his breath in anxious contemplation of the Governor's news, "tut, tut, tut!"

CHAPTER IX

". . . and, O Lord, guide me in this my momentous decision. If it be Thy will that we should smite the idolaters, even as Thou didst smite them of old, hip and thigh, if it be Thy will that we should smite them alone without help of the mother country—(England, as Thou knowest, Lord)—if it be Thy will that we should smite them relying on our own resources, and those of the colonies—(although the Governor does not expect co-operation, Lord, save from Connecticut, New Hampshire and Rhode Island, besides the four New England colonies, in which, as Thou knowest, Lord, and above all in Massachusetts, burns a pious zeal)— O Lord, if it be Thy will that we strike without the help of the mother country, while the French fleet is withdrawn, Thy will be done. For if we wait for help from England, Louisbourg will be reinforced and the golden moment gone. Lord, enlighten me, Lord strengthen me, Lord show me how to vote aright. And if I am to vote for the immediate reduction of Louisbourg, relying upon our own right arms and Thy defense of the right, then let the other deputies vote likewise, Lord. Be with us when we sally forth against the Popish infidel, uphold us till we overthrow the idols. With my own hand will I hew down and overthrow the images. O Lord, amen."

Father Moody, wrestling with his soul in prayer for guidance over the Governor's secret proposition, far into the night, forgot, in his anguished perplexity, that tavern walls were thin, that his voice when it was raised in prayer would awaken the dead, let alone the sleeping tavern servants, and that a curious chambermaid with her ear to the cracks could gather what the hullabaloo was about—an expedition against Louisbourg, without the help of England. Such a thing had never been dreamed of before. England's help had always been taken for granted as the major part of any attack.

The news spread through the town. By morning it was spreading through the province. From there it went abroad, carried on the wind. Governor Wentworth heard it in New Hampshire, stroked his chin and told himself: "I am the man to lead that expedition." Benjamin Franklin heard it in Philadelphia, and wrote to his brother in Boston: "Fortified towns are hard nuts to crack, and your teeth are not accustomed to it; but some seem to think that forts are as easy taken as snuff."* Roger Wolcott heard it in Connecticut and set about gathering five hundred men. Henry Sherburn, of the New Hampshire Regiment, threw himself on his horse and rode to Boston.

The town hummed with agitated groups. Seamen and old soldiers cheered. Calking parties and building hands attacked their work with extra vigor. Youths and idlers lounged near the courthouse, discussing militia prospects, spitting as they talked, each peering with a hopeful eye for the recruiting officer. The Assembly met and voted the measure down. Conservative heads wagged sagely, while the adventurous were depressed. Shirley, walking disconsolately down King Street, ran into James Gibson, a merchant in favor of the expedition. They entered his counting-house and drew up a petition together. Gibson obtained the signatures of other merchants from Salem, Marblehead and towns along the coast. The measure was reconsidered. This time it passed, by a single vote. (One of the members of the opposition broke his leg as he hurried to oppose it.)

Governor Shirley rubbed his hands. The expedition was authorized by the Assembly. It only remained to launch it. Recruiting began at once. Volunteers were offered sixpence a day, furnishing their own clothing and bringing their own guns. Shirley chose Captain Tyng to command the navy, consisting of those ships already in the harbor and any packets or privateers that he could muster. Captain Tyng had taken a French privateer the year be-

* Asterisks indicate actual words written or spoken.

·[43]·

fore, with his own much smaller vessel. He was the right man. Nevertheless Shirley also wrote to Commodore Peter Warren, who was in Antigua with a small force. He sent an express to find him with his three ships the *Superbe*, the *Mermaid*, and the *Launceston*. For transports they would use the fishing boats thrown out of work by the war. Salem and Marblehead were full of them.

Command of the army presented pitfalls. Shirley appointed Pepperell. He was popular, he was sensible, and though no soldier, he would be competent. Knowing that Governor Wentworth wanted the command himself, Shirley made Will pen a letter to him saying that he would gladly have given it to him, were it not for his gouty legs. Wentworth was furious. He declared himself willing and able to assume the full responsibility. Shirley dictated the answer to Will:

"On communicating your offer to two or three gentlemen in whose judgment I most confide, I found them clearly of opinion that any alteration of the present command would be attended with great risk, both with respect to our Assembly and the soldiers being entirely disgusted."*

"That will keep him quiet for awhile," he said, "and Will, pen a letter to the Reverend Samuel Moody. I shall make him senior chaplain of the expedition. If our guns and our men do not take the place and raze the fortifications, his blistering invective will! He could pray the place to ashes, judging from the sermons I have heard him deliver."

When Father Moody heard the news he retired to his room. This time he let himself go. The admiring chambermaid ticked off adjectives of thankfulness upon her fingers. Her ears burned when he got to work on the French. He consumed, blasted, and blistered the enemy to the Lord for three-quarters of an hour. Paul, coming upon her with her ear to the crack, took hold of her by the arm. She shook him off.

"Let me alone, Frog!" she said, tossing her head. "You're no better than a heathen idol, as the master says. Ought to be in the stocks. You will be, too, when the soldiers get ahold of you."

Paul opened, then shut his mouth. The events of the last few days, confirming his worst fears for Louisbourg had also opened his eyes to his own unenviable position. He was a French prisoner of war, he would be left in Boston with other prisoners of war, as a hostage. This meant the crowded jail, the filthy stench of neglected humanity behind four stifling walls. Summer would come and find him there, penned helpless like a beast. Or else he would be killed in some street brawl as a hated French Frog. The Mistresses Moody would not take him back, even if he could make his way to York. They would be afraid. Their brother, busily haranguing against the French would not be interested in his servant's fate, he was not interested now. He hardly spoke to Paul. Once he snapped:

"Get out my ax and polish it. I'll take it to Louisbourg and hew down the idols myself!"

They were all mad with fanaticism. About this time a wild idea formed in the background of Paul's mind. Three nights running he awoke to find himself screaming: "They are gathering, they are coming!" to his blanket instead of to the Governor of Louisbourg. It was an omen to dream three times. He began to turn the impossible project this way and that. Then Randy made his discovery. They had formed a habit of walking together along the coast, as Paul used to walk with Will at Damariscotta. They poked among the rocks for crabs and looked for gold dust in the stones. Gold had been found that way. But it was something more useful than gold that Randy found one evening, in the falling light. It was a lugger, beached in a cove, a lugger small enough for two to handle. Paul came up to look at it. They stared at each other. Without a word the desperate project took shape in both their minds. They turned together, running to the town. Before they reached the first lantern Paul stopped and put his hand on Randy's arm.

"If you will come," he said, "if you will help me to reach Louisbourg and warn the town, I'll see that you get to England, I swear it on the Mass."

Randy nodded.

"There will be dangers first," Paul went on desperately. Randy nodded again and cut him short.

"I would have gone with you anyway," he said. "Whether we get there or not, we will draw a few free breaths."

"Randy, you hate the sea."

"Not if she carries me home."

·[45]·

CHAPTER X

IT WAS midnight, winter moon and frosty stars. Paul, stooping
beneath his heavy sack, could see the stones in the frozen dirt
of the Boston road. He walked quickly. He had run into
better luck at the inn than he expected, now if there were no
pursuit he would be safe. Almost in answer to his thoughts, a
shout arose behind him. Angry voices called into the night. Paul
held the sack tighter and began to run. The noise behind him
lessened. It was not for him, they had not perceived him in the
darkness. The load felt heavier, he slackened to a walk.

There were six loaves of bread he had taken from the ovens
half-cooked, to cool in his sack; there were two flasks of spirits,
and a water bottle filled with well-water; it was glass, that in itself
was valuable; there were two coils of rope, a hatchet and a mal-
let; there were a cloak, a coat and a pair of leather boots; there
were two cold fowl and the half of a ham. Best of all, there was a
leather pouch full of gold pieces. It would be hanging if he were
caught with the sack and he might as well hang for the gold as
for the other things. He hurried on.

Suddenly a door opened. A stream of light from a lantern fell
across the road.

"God give you good night," said the man who was coming out
of the house. He tripped, lurched, and saved himself. Paul walked
on, trying to set a pace that would get him away from there, and
yet look unconcerned. The sack grew mortal heavy to him, he
bent beneath it, panting with fatigue and with his fear.

"It's a bitter night," the man announced. Paul grunted. He did not want anyone to hear his French turn of speech. The man was in uniform—one of the new militia recruiting officers, Paul guessed, the very last person whom he wanted to meet.

"That's a heavy load you've got there," said the officer, running a practiced eye over Paul's muscles as he stepped into the light. "It's a bad night to be alone on the road with a burdened back. You should join the army instead, and fight the accursed French. Good pay, light duties, plenty of loot at Louisbourg. How does it sound?"

Paul looked at him. He was a brawny six-foot two. He had a stick in his hand and a pistol at his belt. There was enough light to see his calculating expression. "Here's a man for my company," it said, "I'll force him if he isn't willing, I'll take the head money for him, anyway. He looks strong enough for war."

He took a step nearer. Paul lowered the sack as if he were considering the question. He scratched his head with his left hand, loosening the fastening of the sack with his right. The man came nearer still. Paul thrust his right hand into the sack with a careless movement, as though unaware of what he was doing. His fingers closed about the ax. The man was barring his way. There was an air of bullying authority about him now. He eyed the sack inquisitively, and it was plain that he would not allow Paul to escape. There would be investigations, followed by the noose. Paul whipped the ax from the sack and struck. The officer dodged, the ax missed his head and sank into his shoulder, with a spurt of red on either side. Quick as thought, Paul pulled it out, flashed it about and struck again, with the blunt end. This time the blow went home and the man rendered stupid by surprise, went down like an ox.

Paul stood over him, listening intently. There was no sound from the house, there was no sound from the road, there was no sound but the beating of his heart, unnaturally loud and fast. No one had heard. He bent over the officer to take the pistol from his belt. He dragged the belt from beneath the body. It was full of cartridges. He searched the coat, fingering the lace enviously as he went over it. There was a silken purse half full of gold pieces in the breast pocket. Paul took it up. Then he straight-

·[47]·

ened himself, pushed at the body with his foot, shouldered the sack and turned away.

This was not the first man that he had killed, but there was a difference. The others had been in fair fight, beside his father, on *La Belle Louise*. Fighting was different on the sea, somehow. Perhaps the clean immensity of water changed the atmosphere. Death was not so ugly when the waves took the corpse from sight, washing it clean of blood and lust. *This* would lie in the road, for the dogs to sniff at, until it was found. That might be at any moment. Paul pressed on.

He reached the cove where the lugger was beached and looked about him for Randy. There was no sign of life. He dumped the sack into the boat, and began to go over its equipment by the light of the setting moon. She seemed a well-built craft. The owners—here he raised his head to peer into the darkness—evidently believed in things shipshape. The lugger as she lay was ready to be launched at once. There was even fresh water in a keg under her bow deck, and a spare anchor aft. Paul wrinkled his forehead. More likely than not the owners lived in one of the houses near, that one, or that. It might be difficult to steal the lugger without their hearing it. Certainly it would be noticed soon. They were not the sort to leave their boat for long.

Where was Randy? Perhaps he had decided not to come. Perhaps he had been caught stealing his provisions, and they had got the project out of him. Perhaps there were men of the watch on their way to catch Paul now. He looked at the tide. It had turned and was going out. Just as they planned, perfect for launching the lugger, the tide would sweep them well to sea before dawn, they would not have to wait for an offshore wind.

He stirred restlessly as he peered and listened, eager to be off. Suddenly he stiffened, all alert. Somebody was running down the beach. "Hush there, hush!" he muttered angrily. The sound of running feet in the night brought people to their doors. Running feet meant Indians, French privateers, fire, alarm, or simply urgent news. Running feet were never ignored. The owners of the lugger would hear, think of their boat and come to see. Randy was a fool to run so noisily, if it were Randy coming.

Panting could be heard above the stumbling feet. Paul could

make out a figure now, carrying a sack, sobbing and coughing as he fled. Randy had altogether lost his nerve, his senses. Paul looked behind him to see the pursuit. The need for Randy's desperate rush was suddenly obvious, as seven or eight lanterns appeared behind him on the road, bobbing up and down.

"Here," said Paul, "lift and run the boat out, now, with me. Quick, Randy, quick!"

They tugged and tore at the lugger. It hardly stirred beneath their efforts.

"Harder! Harder! It's hanging if we don't get away!"

Randy threw himself at the stern, dug his feet into the beach and shoved with all his body's strength in a frenzy till the lugger began to move. The lanterns were coming nearer.

"Harder!" grunted Paul as he seemed to lift the bow upon his shoulders, "harder, Randy, now!"

The boat began to slide across the stones, crunching and scraping. Now it was in the water, now it was near afloat.

"I figured it would take us an hour to launch this thing," Paul whispered, "Randy, push!"

Randy flung himself upon the stern again, and pushed so frantically that he fell in, wetting himself to the shoulders. Paul clambered in and pulled him aboard.

"Well," he said, "we're afloat. The tide will drift us out, but we must stand them off if they try to rush us now."

They stood ready but the lanterns went bobbing by on the road above the shore. Apparently the pursuers did not think of the beach. They passed in a string of small, excited will-o'-the-wisps on the Boston road.

"Ah," said Randy exultantly as they watched them disappear, "I thought I might have shaken them off. I did, see that!"

"How did you come to be chased?" Paul asked, feeling the tiller answer to his hand.

"Mr. Pepperell caught me stealing his compass and the sextant from its case. They're in the sack. Brrr, it's bitter cold." He began to shake.

CHAPTER XI

THE lugger was heeling over to a following wind that sprang up providentially. The sea ran high around the boat, occasionally breaking against the stern and sending its bitter chill into the two boys' bones.

Paul, watching the stars fade before a gray winter dawn, hearing Randy cough desolately where he was crouching in the bow, began to measure the difficulty of the desperate quest they were embarked upon.

Louisbourg was about five hundred miles from Boston. They must hug the shore, then cross toward Cape Sable, skirt the Acadian coast for three hundred miles or so, coming at length to Ile Royale and Louisbourg.

He had made the journey from Louisbourg to Cape Sable and back again many times in *La Belle Louise*. Even then, with a big seaworthy ketch and a full crew, they had dreaded the treacherous waters around the cape. Plenty of ships had been wrecked there, broken upon the reefs. It was no place to tackle alone on a stormy day. Paul was singlehanded, virtually alone. Randy would be no help, eager though he might be. Paul looked at him in the light of the dawn. He was a landlubber, seasick already, while Paul felt at home on the sea. The motion of the boat beneath him gave him confidence.

With a fair, following wind like this, with luck and no mishaps, no English privateers, no pirate ships, they would make the journey in a week. Of course the wind would veer before then, it could not hold so long, they would not be in Louisbourg as soon as that, but still, within a week's distance of them lay the fort, Paul's home, that he had not seen these bitter years.

Why had he not ventured to steal a boat before? He would not have ventured now, but for the urgency of the mustering troops, the armaments, the earnest gathering of an expedition. He had been sunk in apathy over his personal fate, waiting from day to day for whatever might betide. It was the menace to Louisbourg that roused him from this servitude.

He grinned. "Father Moody will be surprised when he lifts his ax against the walls, to see me there opposing him. And that's a time that I'll remember old scores and settle them—when the militia come, if they get so far."

Suddenly he remembered Will. The thought sobered him. He would not care to fight against Will, to see him killed, wounded or taken prisoner. No, he would not care for that, for past friendship's sake.

Randy stirred and shivered, lifting his head to stare at the gray waves.

"Where are we now?" he asked.

"Hard to say," Paul answered. "Under God's good sky, in a good boat with a following wind. Some fifteen miles, perhaps, toward our goal."

"It's cold," Randy muttered. His cheeks were feverishly bright, his cough more evident. The wetting of the night before had done him little good. Paul tossed him a loaf of bread from his sack and told him to open a bottle of wine.

"That will warm us both," he said cheerily.

"How long will it take us?" Randy asked, when he had uncorked a bottle and taken a swig at it.

"About a week," Paul told him absently.

His arm ached from the unaccustomed pull of the tiller. His years ashore had changed the set of his muscles, he would have to learn seamanship afresh.

The boat rode lightly, too lightly. The sail of reddened canvas was too full for her. If they ran into wind, any kind of a blow, he must look out. Meanwhile she was lolloping on her journey, shipping little water.

The sun rose higher. They would be warmer soon . . . brrr

. . . this bitter February weather! No one but a madman or a fisherman would set out on a day like this to travel so many leagues.

Louisbourg. He would see his country's flag, his home. He did not believe it yet. Much might happen to prevent his landing there. If he should founder in this lugger, who would warn the fort? Get ready, get ready, the New Englanders are there, arming their militia, gathering their men, casting their cannon, provisioning their ships. Fanatical ministers are preaching a crusade, get ready, Louisbourg, they mean to take your batteries and turn your own guns against your citadel. Get ready or they will raze you to the ground. They are coming, this is no time to sleep, waiting for the return of spring and the French fleet.

Randy startled him.

"What's that over there?" he said. "Is it a sail?"

Paul cupped his eyes, stood up and raked the seas. He could see nothing where Randy pointed.

"Where? What did it look like?" he asked anxiously.

"Something that wasn't water, gray, brown, black . . ." Randy shrugged.

"A porpoise, probably."

Paul hoped it might have been. He had no wish to meet a sail here. No French ship would be so near to Boston at this time, a sail could only mean an English ship, and hanging for both of them, or a pirate ship, and serving as unpaid crew, beaten and bullied by all aboard, walking the plank in the end. No, let them see no sails until they were further out. A French sail then might be a help, but the French fleet had returned to France, and the Louisbourg privateers chose this time for repairs; that is if all went on now as it had when he was there. He raised his face to the wind. It was veering. Diable! They would have to tack instead of running along so swiftly over the waves . . . tacking, coming about, working slowly up to Cape Sable.

"There it is," said Randy suddenly. "Look at the beautiful sails and the people on the deck. What a noble-looking ship! See, they are greeting us."

Paul looked about him wildly. There was nothing to be seen, nothing but gray-green sea and stormy sky.

"Where, Randy?" he asked, looking intently at him.

"Why, there, of course!" Randy lifted his right hand and pointed down to leeward, "There! It's gone about, it's sailing parallel. Look at the people laughing and beckoning to us!"

Paul said nothing. A horrible misgiving came into his mind. His father had told him stories of the phantom ship of Death. It appeared out of the atmosphere, and sailed close to its prey. Its crew was composed of seamen who had died in the sea, its captain was Death himself, in a long white cloak and an admiral's hat.

Randy was watching something with a strange look on his face.

"I can see the captain now," he cried.

Paul groaned.

"He's beckoning," Randy said. "Do you think they want us to go aboard? We'd get to Louisbourg quicker, it would be better, let's go aboard."

Paul shook his head. He looked at the empty sea and the lowering sky.

"Randy," he said, "Randy, look at me."

Randy turned. His face was flushed, his eyes bright.

"Have some more wine." Paul handed the flask forward. Randy unstoppered it and drank. Then he looked back for his ship.

"Why it's gone!" he said disappointedly. "It's sailed away from us. What a pity! It would have been so comfortable."

His voice sank to a murmur, his head dropped on his breast, he began to sleep and to snore. Paul heard the snores with relief. He was left awake, alone. Perhaps the accursed vessel had sheered away this time, perhaps it was waiting there, waiting for them. He shivered. From time to time he looked to leeward at the mist fast rising from the sea, obscuring everything.

CHAPTER XII

FOR three chilling days and three freezing nights, the lugger beat slowly upon its way. It plunged and slithered over a dark, unfriendly sea, beneath heavy clouds.

Randy slept most of the time, groaning and shivering in his sleep. Paul slept, too, in short uneasy snatches, wakened by the pull of the tiller in the crook of his right arm, numbed by cold cramping fatigue.

They ate their cold provisions, and drank the warming wine. Its glow soon died out, leaving them colder than ever and more susceptible to cold. There was nothing to look at but the black sea, breaking with little hisses, green against the boat. No land, no sail, no life, long weary hours waiting for the dark, longer wearier hours waiting for the dawn. Paul steered by compass while he could see, and by the stars at night. Randy could not give him much companionship. He had a feverish chill, and lay most of the time in the bottom of the boat, moaning now and then, now and then standing up to wave at imaginary friends, or at the ship which he was sure was following them.

Paul kept an eye upon him, plying him with wine. If they could only endure. Five hundred miles! It was a stupendous trip in wintertime. Paul brushed the salt from his eyes and shrank within his clothing to keep warm. Feeling had left his arms altogether. He knew that he was holding the tiller, and that from time to time he came about and trimmed the sails, performing all the motions necessary to sail the boat, but he had ceased to connect himself with any of the things that he was doing.

The sun came out, a pale, wintry sun, cheering even so. The wind dropped, the sea grew calmer. The boat rocked gently. There was an hour or so of this altered motion, then a new wind sprang up behind, the sails filled and the lugger forged ahead with a following wind again. Paul lashed the tiller and crept forward to rouse Randy.

"Let us eat," he said, shaking him awake, "the wind has changed and we shall be traveling now."

Randy started up and smiled at him. He looked better, refreshed. He spoke like his old self, and fell upon the cold ham and stale bread. He even looked about him with eager interest instead of cowering away from the sea because he hated it. Paul brightened. If Randy were going to recover and be a companion to him, the journey would be easier. He could even imagine them coming through it, when Randy was like this.

The wind freshened from astern, blowing harder. Paul had to shorten sail. The lugger plunged and kicked, without enough ballast to stiffen her. Randy crouched down again, his back to the bow. The noise was too great for them to hear each other unless they shouted. Even then, the wind tore the words away, killing half of them. Paul's cheeks were whipped to scarlet, his breath came hard, spray whitened his lips. The little boat began to pitch, shipping water over her bow. Paul shouted and pointed, making the motion of bailing, to Randy, who picked up the wooden dipper and began to collect the water in it, wearily.

The lugger plunged on. Presently the wind increased to a shriek. Paul took in more sail. They were in for a blow. He looked behind him at the darkening skies. A storm was coming up. It looked a real tempest. What an undertaking! Fool that he had been! To warn Louisbourg, to return home, to see his mother, to be free, these were things worth straining nerve and sinew for, worth enduring cold and hunger and fatigue, but life itself—that was another matter. Better to be alive and a prisoner, than free, swinging to and fro beneath these angry waves, torn at by sharks and swordfish, eaten by the eels. He shivered. The wind snatched at the bit of sail still showing. The lugger lifted her stern skyward, then shot nose first into the seas. A drenching spray clouded the air about them. The wind screamed and roared, and rose to a

·[55]·

gale. Paul lashed the tiller and staggered forward to lower the sail. There was nothing else to be done. They must ride out the gale if they could. It was blowing in the right direction, that was one good thing, taking them upon their course. Perhaps it would blow itself out. He curled himself up in the stern, and covered himself with a cloak. Relieved of her sail the lugger was not shipping very much water now. He must get out of the wind or be chilled beyond recovery. He could not feel his hands or his feet but his body kept its temperature. He was not frozen yet.

The stout mast quivered and shook, this way and that, as the wind tore at it. Beneath him the lugger pitched and heaved, surging forward. Randy crouched in front of him, sheltering his chest. The noise was horrible. All hell had broken loose. The light began to fail. Storm clouds hid the setting sun, night came upon them suddenly, without moon or stars.

There was nothing between them and the angry swollen sea, the savage shrieking wind, the growing hurricane, nothing between them and the hostile elements, but this small boat of hollowed logs and rough planking, held in place by clumsy wooden pegs, this fragile shelter constructed by human fingers, floating in defiance of the night.

CHAPTER XIII

LIGHTNING split the sky like the strands of a frayed rope. Thunder that roared and crashed above it was drowned in the louder roar and crashing of the sea.

Paul clinging to the tiller, strained his eyes through the darkness. He welcomed the sizzling flash that blinded him for a long moment, afterwards making the blackness blacker. It revealed the reefs that he was striving to avoid, leaving the image of them printed on his aching eyelids, so that he threw his weight upon the tiller and by a succession of miracles missed striking this rock, that rock, this that scraped the side.

The lugger driven by the storm reached Cape Sable long before Paul thought she would. It was good to be thus far upon their way. It was bad to navigate the treacherous shoals about them in a storm at night. It was impossible, and yet the boat remained afloat, though each new flash showed breakers awaiting them. He looked helplessly at Randy when the flashes came. Randy was huddled shaking beneath the bow. He had huddled there for hours, for days, for nights. Paul could not think how long. Poor Randy. Presently he would be thrown into this icy sea, in the black night. It was Paul's fault, this desperate quest. As for the storm, he should have counted on one storm at least, February was a bad month on the sea. But that the storm should overtake them here, should drive them here, in fact, helpless, with lowered sail, to the most dangerous point in all their dangerous course, that was a bit of extra devilment he had not counted on. God was on the side of the New Englanders after all, as Pastor Moody often affirmed. Poor Randy, he would perish here. Poor Louisbourg, attacked unwarned. Poor Paul.

"Madone," he prayed between clenched teeth, "thou who art the Star of the Sea, help us poor seamen now."

A brighter streak than the rest flashed out above him. Directly in the lugger's path, he saw a reef. Its wicked outline, jagged, black, spread out on either side of them. He tried desperately, straining against the tiller, to make the boat come about. A mountainous wave behind him lifted her up . . . up . . . they hung for an eternity upon this crest of water, then they crashed. The bottom was ripped out of the lugger and they were thrown into the sea.

Paul gasped. Icy, numbing cold enveloped him. He fought for breath, he grasped the sides of the lugger, floating by the reef, and holding by one arm, plunged the other into the breakers, feeling for Randy. He shouted. Randy's voice replied, near him on the other side.

"Help," it said, "I'm sinking. Help."

Paul let go the side and struck out to find Randy. He was flung against him by a breaking wave, and seized his wrist. The iciness of the water was fast making Paul lose control of his muscles. He gathered himself together for a supreme effort, caught the gunwale, held on to it with his arms, taking Randy's collar in his teeth. Randy was silent. Paul wondered if he were still alive, or if the shock and cold had finished him. Kicking out with his legs, numbed to the knees, he found that he could stand upon the reef. It was about three feet beneath the water. He braced his feet against it and slackened his hold on the lugger, shifting his right hand beneath Randy's armpit. The force of the storm made him lose his footing, for a moment he floundered wildly, then he found the rock again and stiffened himself against the sweeping waves. Another flash lit up the scene. Paul saw that land was nearer than he supposed. Perhaps if he could walk along this reef, if it shelved so far, he could get within swimming distance of the shore. The cold might numb him so that he could not swim, but if he stood here longer, waist-deep in water, he would be numbed anyway, frozen and swept from the reef. He must try to make the shore. He must try. He must drag Randy with him, too. He shook Randy's shoulder and slapped him. It was no use. Randy was frozen or had fainted. Randy would die unless he could get him to shore. This responsibility more than his own danger, spurred him to collect his forces. He began to wade, striking his numbed feet against the rocks, cutting them to ribbons without knowing it, falling, recovering himself, always keeping his hold upon Randy, dragging him beneath the water and on top of it, advancing unsteadily in the darkness, hoping for more lightning to show him where he was. Once he fell off the reef and was swept away. It took him a long time to regain the rock, an agony of straining in the darkness, eyes, nose and mouth filled with the bitter sea.

He began to fall more often, to stagger as he got up and to fall again, but all the time he kept his hold on Randy, and all the time he crept forward slowly, a painful foot at a time. The wind snatched and clawed at him, whistling through his wet clothing, freezing it against his breast. Each breath he drew hurt, cutting him. He could no longer feel his legs, even when he struck them against the rocks. Suddenly, when all thought had ceased in him, except the force that kept him in forward motion, he came to the end of the reef. The water shallowed about him, hissing against his feet. He fell forward, letting go of Randy, who was dragged away, face downward, washing to and fro like a drifting log. Paul lay gasping, drawing agonized breath till he recovered enough to go after him. He hauled, pushed, pulled Randy to safety, rolled him upon his face and straddled him, working his arms to pump the water out. The bitter wind swooped round them, chilling Paul to the heart that beat so slowly now. Unless he could get warmth, some warmth, some heat, some warmth, he was going to die. Randy was dead already and he was going to die. The thought traveled through him slowly rousing only dim wonder, dull resentment. He ceased to work over Randy, painfully straightening his back. Then he saw the fire, flickering ahead of him, the fire in the woods upon the shore. It was a big fire, a good blaze. There was warmth there, ahead of him, a fire in the storm. It was foolish to build fires when the wind was as high as this, foolish and dangerous but it was warm. If the fire that was leaping there started the forest burning that would be warmer still. But he could not feel the heat of it down here. He must make an effort and go to the fire, since the fire was not coming nearer him. He dropped upon his hands and knees and crawled forward, cutting his bleeding legs afresh upon the rocks, feeling them not at all, intent upon the blaze.

PART TWO
FLIGHT THROUGH ACADIA 1745

CHAPTER XIV

T HE fire, when Paul reached it, was banked about by rocks, like the open-air oven the Acadians used. It burned fiercely, shooting flames above the stones. Sparks whirled away by the wind came down in showers to be quenched in snow.

Paul fell down. Everything went dim. He found himself being helped. A girl was helping him. She was a squaw, that much was visible in the firelight. A sharp fear went through him as he looked at her. Then he remembered. He was not in New England, where the tribes were sullenly hostile, and the women not to be trusted, crueller than braves. This was Cape Sable in Acadia. Indians here would be Micmacs or Malisites, or wandering Passamaquoddy, all branches of the peaceful Algonquian race, friendly to the French.

He raised himself on his elbow, stammering a greeting in Micmac. The girl—she was very young—answered him in French. It was the beautiful, cultivated French of the noblesse. Coming from a savage in the forest it was inexplicable, grotesque. It made Paul feel that he must be delirious, and as if to confirm this, she ran brown probing hands over his chest and forehead.

"If you will come this way," she said with the tones of Madame la comtesse showing guests into the salon, "if you will lie down here."

She indicated a bed of spruce boughs covered with bearskin. Paul dragged himself toward it, then he remembered Randy, stopped and managed to gasp:

"There is another man with me, a sick man. He is unconscious.

You must send some of the men to bring him here, to warm him. He is so cold that he will die."

He sank into the warm relief of the litter of spruce and waves of comfort began to rise about him from the bed and from the fire. He was reassured that he had done his best for Randy. He had told this girl to get her people to send some braves. Perhaps he should have sent for the chief, but he was tired. She would deliver the message, they would take Randy on a litter and look after him. Meanwhile it was safe where he was, and warm. The pounding of the seas receded to an indiscriminate roar, fading, fading . . . he slept heavily.

When he awoke the sun was in the sky, shining full upon his face. It was a winter sun, but it was warm. The wind had dropped, the storm was over, the day was calm and clear. Below him on the reefs he could hear the sea breaking, still rough and angry, not subsiding with the wind, the black defiant sea! He smiled to think that he had defeated her somehow. . . . How? It all came back to him. He propped himself on his elbow to look for the Indians, for Randy. He saw nobody and there was no encampment, only this stone fireplace, the litter on which he lay and the kneeling girl. She was kneeling on the other side of the fire, attending to something Paul could not see. He watched her for a moment before speaking. It was so good to lie in the sun, warm and cared for, safe, alive.

Alive! He remembered Randy.

"Bosool," he said to the girl. "Greetings and gratitude. What have the men of your encampment done with the other man?"

"There are no men of my encampment," she answered in her polished French. She had the melodious voice of her people, with its murmuring liquid lilt. It fitted the French tongue perfectly.

"I am alone," she said. "The other man is here. He lives, but he will go to the Great Spirit."

She squatted back on her heels, looking down at Randy before she looked at Paul. He saw now that she was very young, and for a savage handsome, almost beautiful. Her face had the quality of her voice, there was strength and harmony there, mystery, too.

She looked at him with searching, honest eyes, and there was something warm in her gaze. It was as though the warmth and light of her fire had drawn his body. After a moment she looked down.

"He speaks in English. He is not French. I have tried to save him. Is he your friend or your prisoner? Your friend?"

Paul nodded.

"Although he is English he is my friend and we must save him," he said. "What have you done for him so far?"

"You can see for yourself."

Paul hoisted himself to his feet, and she moved aside. He reflected on her strange dignity, it puzzled him. She did not say, as most squaws would have said: "The white man can see for himself." She said "you," and she spoke perfect French. It was the first time he had heard French spoken in a woman's voice for many years. It stirred him with a strange excitement, as he bent to look at Randy. He was lying with his mouth open, his eyes shut and shrunk in his head. His cheeks were scarlet and his breathing hurt him, he groaned after each short breath. From time to time he muttered thickly, turning his head from side to side. "It's the white peacocks I like the best," Paul heard him say, "the white peacocks, Mother, on the west terrace. They're so pretty at feeding time." Then he shook his head and shouted: "No! No! You can't strap me. You can't! I won't sail on this dirty ship, I want my father, you can't! You can't!"

Paul smoothed his forehead.

"It's Paul, Randy, it's Paul. It's Paul. You're going back to England, you're going to your home. But you must get well first. We have to go to Louisbourg, first."

He had forgotten the squaw altogether as she stood beside him with a handful of melting snow for Randy's thirst. When she heard "Louisbourg" she turned her head and looked at him, startled, puzzled, mistrustfully. But he was kneeling beside Randy, trying to gather him into his arms.

Randy sighed, stirred and flung up his arm. "The rose-garden," he said, "not in the rose-garden, Patricia, we will be punished if you dig up the bed."

"We must put him nearer the fire," Paul said, tugging at the litter as he tried to move him. "Poor Randy, he is dreaming of his home."

·[65]·

CHAPTER XV

THEY banked the fire high. Paul and the squaw lay down with Randy between them and the heated stones. Paul fell asleep. From time to time the girl rose, silently stepping from bed to bed, then reassured that the sleepers were not frostbitten, she would pile wood upon the fire and lie down again.

Her thoughts were strange, strong, exciting. They flowed within her as the river floods in spring. It was impossible not to take the white men's coming as a sign. She knew herself to be taking it for more than that.

Pictures of the last few months, and of before, and of her childhood, gathered in her mind. They were clear and sharply colored like the picture writing of her people on a ceremonial skin. That was it, she was seeing the picture. She bent over Randy, listening to his difficult breathing, attending to him with the one half of her mind, while in the other half the pictures grew.

She saw the woods where she was born, woods like these. She remembered a spring of childhood, when the green of the hills sloping to the blue of the sea was greener, fresher than it had ever been, everything was new and wonderful. She ran in the forest, happy from her forehead to her feet. And then . . . and then . . . Koospem told her she was nothing but a squaw. He told her cruelly, out of childish vanity. They were playing by the water— was it that she swam too well that day? He laughed, and flung the contemptuous words at her like arrows, Koospem, her brother. Then he stretched himself arrogantly above her.

"I'm a brave. You're a squaw but I'm a brave."

Even now the words could wound, then they were like lightning, tearing through the sky, lighting up the darkness on either side of it, showing the road ahead.

She had always seen her mother treated like a beast of burden, and the other women too, doing all the dirty work, standing humbly in the prescribed manner when the braves were there. She had seen them taking beatings from her father and the rest. She had eaten with her mother after the hunger of her father and her brother had been fed, but she had never thought these things through to the end. She understood then, for the first time, as she looked at her brother's bronzed sleek body with its undeveloped muscles rippling while he laughed, that she was a squaw, and misery lay ahead.

Other women liked the labor in the fields and in the wigwams, the toting of bundles and burdens, the building of a fire beneath the cooking pots. Other women liked the stench and laughter in the lodges, the blubber pots, the skins, the sewing and the beads. Other women liked the clutter round their feet, babies and children, dogs and other squaws. But she liked the things her brother liked, the clean streams, the deep recesses of the forest, trapping, hunting, shooting. She shot better than Koospem, ran faster, swam farther, and yet she was a squaw.

At this time in her life things might have gone ill. She might have given herself up to the dwindling sickness that carried away so many dumb with miseries they could not cure. But the French missionary, Abbé le Loutre, came to the encampment. He made a talk. He said that he needed girls. Young squaws were decked and sent to him. He made another talk and said that it was not he but the church that needed girls, and they were not to be old, but children.

She laughed as she remembered the pursed lips and furrowed brows of the braves and the medicine man. It was not the custom, they told him, for children to be taken for any man's bed so young.

Abbé le Loutre shook his head and stretched out his arms.

"It is not for what you think. Give the children to me and not a hair of them shall be harmed!" he cried. "We will bring them up as good wives and mothers and return them to you when the time is ripe."

He made a long speech. In the end the children were sent, and she was one of them.

What a place the convent at Port Royal was! Clean beds, clean clothes, good treatment, and the dignity of living there! One was not a squaw to nuns, but a soul, something precious to be saved, and life went smoothly, sweetly, in the convent to an aroma of incense and candle-wax. It was here she had her first small triumph over fate. The nuns asked her name. "Wosowechkul-seguwaat, blossoms of the sunrise." "Have you no shorter name?" they asked, dismayed. She thought quickly. "Yes," she said, "I am called San. I am not called anything but San." San was a boy's name, equivalent to John. The nuns did not know Micmac well enough to challenge her. The other children did not care enough to report her. She was San. A wicked glee came over her each time she heard it said. If she could not be a brave, she would have a brave's name, some of its virtue would flow into her. She was different, set apart.

The nuns taught her to sew, to say her catechism, to cook and to play in the convent garden. She learned to speak French, to read it and to write it. The nuns were all great ladies, who came from the province of Tours. The Mère Supérieure came from Paris. She played the harpsichord, and taught the children to sing their hymns and say their prayers to her.

Sometimes the walls closed in upon the Indian children. Sometimes the ordered procession of the days stifled and oppressed them. Sometimes they broke away to breathe the free air of the forest, but they always returned. San ran away twice, the first time for a week, the second for three days. She had been glad to return, crouching at the door for seventeen hours, until they would let her in. The Mère Supérieure christened these runaways "petites courseuses de bois" and shut the gates against them rigorously. But patience and determination won. San wore down their resistance in the end, and entered the convent again, this time to stay until the day the Indian children dreaded came upon her, the day when her father sent for her to be married to a brave.

San wanted to stay in the convent. She said she had a vocation and would be a nun. When she pleaded with the Mère Supérieure to be allowed to take her vows, la Mère was firm with her.

"You have no vocation," she said, "only a fear of your own people, and a distaste for the rough hardships of the squaw. But your mission, daughter, is to marry among your people and bring more of them to the true faith. By the way in which you fulfill your duties as an Indian wife and mother you will bear witness to your training here. The prejudice of your people toward us will disappear, more and more children will be sent to us for education, and the tribes will be Christianized. Of course you must be prepared for hardship, for rough treatment, for ordeals. You will be lonely, you will miss us here, and you will find hostility toward you. It is your duty, your duty as a Christian soul, to bend yourself to the dictates of your father, and when you are married, of your husband."

Here San had fallen to her knees and pleaded:

"I hate men! Let me live here always, let me, if I cannot be a nun, be a lay sister, anything! Let me live here and work here, I will work, I will do all you say. Don't send me to the tribe, don't make me marry and be a squaw, don't, don't! Let me stay here, I know I have a vocation!"

But la Mère was firm. She had been through such scenes before. And San was firm. She ran away. She ran away convinced that an injustice had been done her, that she had a vocation and a true vocation to become a nun. She would live as a hermit instead, and the fame of her holy life and her good deeds would spread to the convent. Then they would take her back. And she would be glad to go. It was the only safe place she knew.

The day before her people came for her she disappeared. She spent the first part of the winter preparing her camp and trying to pray, and the last part being lonely. Her prayers changed. She realized that la Mère was right. She had no vocation. But she would not be a squaw. There must be some other way, something she was fitted for. And when this Frenchman came to her out of the stormy night, she was sure. Her prayers were answered. She was called to be a wife, a wife, not a squaw! She crouched upon her heels, bending to look at the sleeping men. One of them would die, but the other would be hers.

CHAPTER XVI

WHEN Paul had satisfied his lust for sleep and found his aching muscles rested as he stretched them in the sun, he asked the squaw in the halting Micmac that came to his lips at the sight of her, where the men of her tribe were and how they could be reached.

She looked up at him from the pemmican that she was stirring into wooden bowls and shook her head.

"There are no men of my people near," she said. "The nearest camp is moons away, a great many leagues."

He stared at her doubtfully, remembering the tale coureurs de bois were forever telling about the Indian woman who dropped behind in the snow to make her camp, catching up with the march two days later, a papoose strapped to her back.

The story was usually told to illustrate the decadence of the modern woman, and received by feminine hearers with incredulity and polite distaste. Paul believed it, though his contact with Indians was limited to a few ceremonial meetings between his father and a Micmac tribe. He had heard the coureurs de bois talking among themselves. His uncle, Pierre de Morpain, privateer or private as you chose to look at it, was a close friend of the Baron de St. Castin, a half-breed and coureur de bois whose exploits were famous in Acadia. Paul remembered things he had heard these men discuss, when he was an unregarded child playing beside them.

But this was no accouchement, not even if the child had died. It was not that the girl looked too young to have a child, that, he knew, meant nothing. It was a host of other things. He looked about him at the piles of wood, sawed and neatly stacked, at the stone fireplace, carefully built, and the bed of spruce and wooden pegs, careful preparations for a more permanent camp. As though the Micmac knew what he was thinking, she raised her head and spoke.

"I have spent the winter here. Not a man of my tribe has passed."

She brought him a bowl of pemmican which he began to eat. It was clean and better prepared than most Indian food. He swallowed it hungrily, rose and went to Randy's side. Randy was asleep in heavy stupor. Paul looked down at him.

"We must find men somewhere," he said. "I have to get to Louisbourg, quicker than the wind flies, and there is the sick man."

The girl moved closer. There was a light in her eyes.

"I know Louisbourg," she said, "and how to get there by quick trails."

"Still we must find men to carry the sick man."

"We will make a toboggan for him," she said impatiently, "and snowshoes for you. Tomorrow we can be ready to start on the shore trail. We will pack the pemmican and other things on the toboggan too."

Paul pondered, twisting his fingers in perplexity. The squaw was very likely lying. There must be Indians at hand. For some reason she had left her tribe or been thrust out of it. She was probably taboo. To be found with her might be unwise. On the other hand he could not deal with Randy by himself, or leave him to get help, and there was always the chance that she might be telling him the truth.

"Where have the braves gone?" he asked in another effort to get things straight.

She shrugged.

"Some whaling," she pointed north, "some to the lakes, some—" her expression brightened—"are dead of the plague. You will not find any men, I can assure you."

"Where did you learn to speak my tongue?" he asked, intrigued.

"In the convent. I am a civilized savage."

·[71]·

He threw back his head and laughed. She laughed with him, uncertain of the joke.

"Very well," he said, scraping up the last of the pemmican, "I must take the risk and do as you say, since I have to get to Louisbourg. If you will take me there by quick trails, you shall have all the beads, or a silk dress, if you prefer it, being civilized, or stuffs, or feathers, anything that you desire."

She squatted back upon her heels, considering his suggestion, weighing it this way and that with slow movements of her head. The sun glinted on the bead pattern of her leggings and the gold ornaments of her dress. Her eyes raised to his were wistful, her smile eager, her whole attitude an offering.

He felt his blood stir as he looked at her. Memories of the women whom he had known already in his short career flashed through his mind. Brief furtive affairs with servants and with tavern sluts, bringing momentary release, dissatisfaction, discontent; ladies he had stripped in his mind's eye, while he waited upon them deferentially at table, secret humiliation, unsatisfied desire. Between these two extremes, there were others. One in particular had seemed to love him with abiding love, Margaret, the sailmaker's daughter at Pemaquid. He remembered the first time he saw her. Will was with him. Will tried to win her favor, but she preferred the servant to the master from the first. Paul laughed aloud, remembering the chase she had led poor Will, all the time that she was Paul's. He saw her suddenly look up at him over the bayberry candles she was pouring into molds. Kind Margaret, she had helped to keep him sane.

But this was something else. This was a savage, young, mysterious, waiting to be taken, he read it in her eyes. He felt his blood awaken, leap to life, race through him. He clenched his fingers, rocking a little on his feet. They stood looking at each other in the cold winter day.

Suddenly she took his hand between her hands, dragging at it like a child. He freed himself gently. At the contact of those craving fingers his own passion ebbed away, dwindling through the forest until it lost itself in the long banks of snow beneath the firs. It would come back later, both knew that. The knowledge

·[72]·

was a stimulant, it changed the world. To be desired made one taller, bolder, gayer, undefeatable.

He bent over Randy, with some idea of imparting the vigorous life running through him to the sick boy.

"How is it?" he asked, as Randy looked up at him.

San crouched where she had been when she took his hand. There was a queer expression on her face, bewilderment, awe, trust, joy.

CHAPTER XVII

THE forest stood silent, every bare tree alert. The crunching of snowshoes, the whir and scrape of a toboggan being dragged through snow sounded unnaturally loud. Paul stopped in his tracks. He was hot in spite of the cold. The wind had dropped and there was a feeling of thaw in the air. Thaw, warm weather, spring to come. . . . Paul mopped his brow. He knew the cold dismal weeks ahead, the bleak journey, the bitter winds, but for the moment the sun was warm and he was tired. He lowered the strap from his shoulder, the toboggan came to rest. Randy stirred, opening his eyes.

"Are we there?" he asked.

"Not yet, soon." Paul stooped, adjusting the furs about the gasping figure on the toboggan, something more, something less than a friend, Randy, but also the reason for the dull monotonous ache in back and arms, Randy, for whom he felt protection, pity, fellowship, but also the reason San moved in weariness beside him, her dark face drawn into a frown. All the day and for many days, they had been dragging Randy, making, breaking camp; all the night and for many nights they had lain down with Randy between them, warming him with the warmth of their flesh.

Through those long nights, cramped by the sick man's weight, Paul, looking up at the frosty far-off stars, would think:

"They are gathering now behind me against Louisbourg, all along the coast."

He could see the navy assembling in the harbors, furbishing, refitting, straining to be off. He could see the satisfied New England sailor strutting with the prospect of a fight. On shore recruiting officers beat their drums, proclamations echoed in village squares: "Twenty-five shillings a month. All the ginger you want. Each man bring his own blanket, his own gun." Recruits were flocking, eager, self-conscious, cynical, aflame for adventure. Here and there he could see the groups breaking up, clustering about a minister who exhorted them, stirring up trouble: "Remember Canceau! The French are coming back to destroy us. They are planning to take Boston in the spring."

Then he would begin to reckon how many miles it was to Louisbourg, how many hours of march it would take at this slow rate, burdened with a sick man. He saw the place, rising before his eyes out of the gray sea. Sailing in with *La Belle Louise*, he watched his father scan the changing skies, past Pointe Blanche, around Cap Noir, with Pointe à Rochefort on the left, they skimmed in dangerously to anchor near the Epron du Bastion Dauphin—home.

With the coming to rest of *La Belle Louise* the impressions blurred. When he stepped out of the well-known ketch he became confused. He must seek out the Governor, that much was clear, and stayed with him through all the wanderings of his mind. He must seek out the Governor, not Monsieur du Quesnel, but a new man, it was to be hoped not so violent in his cups, so querulous, so undependable. He would convince this new governor of the truth of his story, of the greatness of the danger. Louisbourg would arm to repel the attack. Paul would see the New England men thrown back, downed, disarmed. He would deserve the Governor's thanks for his services, for the warning, and the part he would play in the siege. The Governor would give him a post, a naval post. He would live in Louisbourg with his family, he would forget the bitter years behind him.

Randy moaned. He would send Randy home, to his family, in the old and beautiful house, with the peacocks and the terraces, the flunkeys and the lawns. Randy's people would make up to him for all that he had undergone. Later Paul would cross the seas to England. He would see Randy established on his estate and laugh with him over the hardships of the past.

Randy moved again, and Paul shifted his aching legs. The

·[75]·

present rushed in, obliterating the future. In the midst of his discomfort Paul became aware of a subtle current flowing through him, bringing with it comfort, warmth and something more.

"This savage girl is exciting to touch, even by my fingertips, with Randy in between us. She wants me. Why does she not lead us to a settlement? We could send speedy messengers to Louisbourg, young men who could run with the warning. We could have Randy cared for, we could be alone."

His thoughts went round and round confusedly. He stood still, taking slow, deep breaths, delighting in the freshness of the air, the warm rays of the sun, the vastness of the winter scene. He watched San bend over the toboggan, saw her straighten herself and heard her call to him. Before he could take a step forward the clearing was full of figures, silent, menacing, wafted from the forest as though by no known agency. One moment there was nothing in front of him as far as he could see but snowdrifts under forest trees. The next moment everywhere he looked there was an Indian. He stared stupidly, unable to believe his senses—it must be part of the confusion of his mind, a daydream, a mirage. Then, as the men drew in upon him, crowding about Randy, thrusting San to the side, his faculties came back to him. He flung up his hands in the only gesture he knew of welcome and appeal to savages. It was a Micmac gesture his father had taught him when he was a child. "If ever you interfere with an Indian and are far from home, do this," his father said, "and perhaps they'll let you go." This gesture and the explanations San embarked on at the same moment seemed to impress the Indians. They paused in a grim circle. There was a movement in the midst of them. Slowly the men nearest Paul made way for a Personage.

CHAPTER XVIII

THE man facing Paul in the clearing was a startling contrast to the Indians about him. He towered above them wearing a rusty black soutane, tucked into buckskin leggings. His head was bare in spite of the cold, and tonsured. He wore a ragged beard which caught the eye among the smooth-skinned, bronze faces turned to his. There was a trace of petulance about the mouth, of bitter arrogance in the thin lips. The forehead, large and generous, was laughed at by two eyebrows growing crookedly. This air of perpetual surprise sat ill with the rest of his features. Just below those clumps of undisciplined hair burned two intensely intelligent black eyes.

The fiery glance rested for an instant on Paul's face, traveled over the toboggan where Randy lay in stupor, flickered from San to Paul and back again and finally came to rest upon Paul's hands. He became conscious that he was twisting them, rubbing them together, carying them up and down in gestures that betrayed his agitation and his fear.

"I am the Abbé le Loutre," said the man in black. "This is a portion of my flock. Who are you?"

Abbé le Loutre! Missionary to the Micmacs, bitter foe of the British, secret agent of the French, more of a coureur de bois than a priest, with a greater influence among the Indians than any other missionary. Who had not heard of him? He lived among the savages, trapped with them, traded and fought beside them.

Paul rallied.

"Paul de Morpain," he answered, "escaped prisoner of war. I am on my way to Louisbourg with important news."

"And that?" The abbé extended a pale hand toward the toboggan where Randy gasped and muttered in his delirium.

"That," said Paul, "is my good friend."

Le Loutre moved swiftly to the toboggan-side. He dropped on one knee in the snow, leaning his head to Randy's chest, his eyes never leaving Paul's face. Paul was fascinated by their inscrutability and the thousand half-formed messages he read in them. He took a step nearer.

"He is very ill," le Loutre said quietly, rising to his feet. He beckoned behind him, saying something over his shoulder in the murmuring liquid Micmac tongue Paul found so hard to understand.

Four savages stepped forward, stooping to the toboggan. They raised it on their shoulders and began to carry it away. San stepped into the sunlight from the shadow of the tree where she was standing. Le Loutre's somber, searching eyes turned from Paul to her. He beckoned. She came forward fearlessly. When she was within three feet of him she genuflected, took his hand, kissed it, and made the sign of the cross upon herself.

"Ah," said le Loutre, blessing her briefly. "A convert, my child."

San nodded, looking up at him.

"Let me see, where?" the abbé murmured to himself.

"The convent at Port Royal," San said.

The abbé looked down at her, smiling. "You must be one of my especial charges," he said. He raised her to her feet. She took a step toward Paul, faltered, and stood looking at him wistfully. Le Loutre looked at him too.

"Your wife?" he inquired.

Paul shook his head.

"Your wife," le Loutre repeated pointedly, "in the eyes of the Church."

Paul started to speak but the abbé had turned his back. Savages closed in upon them and began to sweep him forward. He ran a step or two, caught up with le Loutre and said:

·[78]·

"I am fortunate to have found you, I need speedy messengers. Louisbourg is in danger of an attack."

Le Loutre stopped in his tracks. He eyed Paul shrewdly.

"Your sick companion, your good friend, raves in English," he said. "You are probably an English spy. We pay high prices for English scalps."

Paul drew himself up.

"I am what I have told you, Father," he said heatedly, "a French prisoner of war escaped with important news for Louisbourg. Either speed me on my way or leave me to continue as you found me, there is no time to lose. As for Randy, he is an English boy of a good family, trapanned, who has escaped with me. He is ill."

"He is dying," le Loutre interrupted, "and since he is English, he can die without the help of my medicine men."

In response to a slight gesture, the Micmacs who were carrying Randy's toboggan stopped and set him down none too gently in the snow.

"He is a Catholic, Father," Paul said ironically, "and therefore it is fortunate that we have found a priest."

Le Loutre was silent.

San spoke to the men too quickly for Paul to hear what she said. The abbé nodded. The bearers took up the toboggan again and everyone went forward through the trees.

CHAPTER XIX

EVENING fell. The sun could no longer be seen above the trees, a cold, orange-purple glow filtered through the branches, discoloring the snow. This faded presently, its place was taken by the red and yellow flames of a cooking fire. Three great stakes were planted above it in a triangle, a huge iron pot hung from these. Steam came from this and the rich smell of venison stew and steaks of bear jumbled together.

The Micmacs, a company of fifty warriors, spread through the forest clearing, resting from what was obviously a forced march. A complicated line of sentries sent their signals back and forth, the half bark, half howl sounded so like a wolf that Paul was deceived each time, and caught himself uneasily looking over his shoulder.

He was sitting with the abbé, the medicine man and two other braves, on a bearskin spread for them near the fire. On the other side of the fire two skins had been stretched to make a tent over Randy lying on his toboggan, while a brave crouched beside him, wiping his forehead from time to time, forcing a hot drink into his mouth by blowing it through the stem of a pipe. The medicine man watched gravely. From time to time he grunted, snapped with his fingers, or nodded his head. The evil spirit in the sick man was under control for the moment, and he was able to lend half his attention to the story Paul was telling to le Loutre. The abbé sat with his back to the fire, disdaining altogether what was going on behind him. He fixed his burning eyes upon Paul's face as though he would bore into and through him to the secret truth behind.

Paul answering the questions flashed at him felt how feeble his own powers of observation were. He could not tell the exact number of the vessels in Boston Harbor, the names of the men commanding them, the number of recruits to the militia, who was in charge of the transport, how many firearms, how much ammunition. Le Loutre made little clucking sounds of impatient disapproval. He dismissed Paul with a gesture and turned to the three braves sharing the bearskin with him. A stream of Micmac came from him, he used his soutane in the correct Indian signs, holding a part of it over his head in the state-of-anger gesture, placing a fold of it over his left arm in the attitude-of-waiting. Finally he beat his two closed fists together, which Paul recognized as the Micmac sign for war. During the long, monotonous reply that followed from the braves, speaking in turn, Paul let his attention wander to the colorful scene in front of him.

The Micmacs wore their red and gold war paint, the firelight glinted over the quill work on their leggings and their deerskin coats. Necklaces, rings, bracelets, shells and bear teeth jiggled and danced with every movement. As the hour for feasting approached some of the braves began a ritual dance. It was the dance of triumph-over-enemies, as could be seen by the way they whirled their tomahawks and brought them down upon the snow. It ended as suddenly as it had begun and the dancers grouped themselves about the fire. Le Loutre sat where he was, paying no attention to the pagan caperings of his flock; suddenly one of the men by the fire looked up and said:

"Gdamugwell baasi." Le Loutre rose to his feet. Instantly every brave stood up, Paul rose too, suppressing an inclination to laugh as he watched the abbé intone a Latin grace, the painted savages bow their heads and sketchily cross themselves, after which each man leaped to the pot dragging it off the fire, plunging his hand in, snatching it out again with grunts and laughter, carrying away what he could, gnawing at the bones, flinging them in the air, catching them again, scooping up what was spilt in the snow, dancing and rubbing his stomach. Only le Loutre and Paul and Randy in his tent remained outside the disgusting circle. San caught a piece of bear steak on a pointed stick and brought it to

Paul, who shook his head. She offered it to the abbé, who smiled indulgently.

"We have entered Lent," he said. "When we are on the warpath my flock do not keep it as strictly as they should. Presently we can have some sagamité if you would like that better, as I should. I dare say your wife," he laid his hand on San's head, "will prepare it for us and for the sick man."

"I dare say she can prepare sagamité," Paul said, "but she is not my wife." He added rashly: "I am unmarried."

"There is a lot to be said for these native marriages," the abbé continued cheerfully. "I have always encouraged them. The Indians make good wives, as you will find. The English"—he cast a contemptuous glance over his shoulder in Randy's direction—"do not intermarry with them. If you were English, you might, of course, compromise a Micmac girl, a Christian like yourself, a daughter of the Church, baptized by my own hand; you might take her virginity and shame her. The English are immoral. I hate them!" His eyes flashed. "The motto of my birth place, Morlaix, is: 'If the English bite you, bite them!'* I have lived up to it."

He recalled himself to the matter in hand, but not before Paul had a glimpse of a fanaticism that was frightening, incongruous in a priest.

"You," the abbé looked him straight in the eyes, "are French. You will know what to do about this girl. I shall be happy to marry you myself."

Paul blinked. He did not know how to deal with the situation. He tried evading it. He spoke of Louisbourg, asking questions. The abbé answered them. No, he did not know a Madame de Morpain with five children, the eldest of whom was christened Marie, but then there were many families he did not know in Louisbourg. It was not his parish. Yes, the new governor would be there at this time. His name? Monsieur du Chambon. He was an officer with no experience of war. On the second day after Christmas, for example, mutiny broke out, only two months after he succeeded the old governor. That showed what sort of man he was. The mutiny? Oh, just the usual demands, a question of wood, clothing, butter and bacon; it was mostly the Swiss detachment. The Swiss had begun the whole thing. The Governor would be glad to hear of the threatened attack in time to take precautions not only against the New Englanders but against his own garrison.

"We will press on," said le Loutre.

This was the first intimation Paul had that the abbé intended to go with him. Evidently he was not taking any chances. He could still take Randy's scalp and Paul's too if anything went wrong.

The savages had finished guzzling their greasy stew. San was crouching by the fire now with a small iron pot in which she was stirring sagamité. Paul, watching her stoop and rise again, felt the same strange stirring of excitement that had swept over him before. He felt drawn toward her with a positive aching pull, and hated himself for feeling it. He looked up to find le Loutre's eyes fixed on him. There was a malicious smile at the corner of the abbé's lips, he struck his hands together, the after-supper clamor of the savages ceased.

"Bibouguahan amalkadink," the abbé shouted, calling for music and a group dance, "we shall celebrate a betrothal."

San straightened herself by the fire, startled, and looked at Paul. There was something so appealing, so promising in her eyes that he smiled as he looked back and found himself thinking in a wild moment, as the savages began to take their places.

"Well, why not? The Indian women do make good wives, she attracts me, she will be faithful and easy to rule, I am lonely and poor, with nothing to offer a French woman—why not?"

As he said it his blood began to beat faster, he took a step forward and lowered his eyes, unwilling to meet the abbé's and read what was in them.

All this time he had given no thought to Randy. Out of the tail of his eye he saw that the medicine man had entered the bearskin tent, a fire was burning there now and something aromatic was cooking upon it. He had no time to see more, he found himself pushed into the middle of the circle, San was beside him now, her hand in his. The dancing began about him, rising and falling, leaping and swaying bodies and the insistent beat of the deer-hide drum. Paul found his head reeling, his thoughts became confused but his sensations clearer. He was dancing now with the rest, taking San into his arms.

·[83]·

CHAPTER XX

PAUL'S impressions of his wedding night were very blurred. At the wildest of the dancing, when the Indians each would have taken a woman and run off with her to the shelter of the trees, there came a sudden break. Weddings were not usually celebrated on the warpath with no women present. Two of the savages began to wrestle, others joined in, war cries began. Someone threw more logs upon the fire, the flames leaped up. The red glare showed the intense faces and straining muscles of the wrestlers, now thoroughly aroused. One man reached for his tomahawk. It was then that the abbé intervened. Striding into the midst of the swaying, grunting crowd, he put his hand on the shoulder of the medicine man who was encouraging the others, capering, crying out, grinning foolishly. He choked the excitement out of him by the firm grip of his hands, then he lifted his great voice. The Indians nearest checked for an instant as they heard it, and would have resumed their fighting since the lust in them was aroused, but the voice boomed out again above the clamor and what it said brought every man to a stop. The medicine man standing sulkily silent by le Loutre's elbow now stepped forth. Some of his vigor returned as he took the center of the stage. Rage and bestiality faded out of the faces turned toward him. Slowly a look of exaltation dawned in each man's eyes as he loosed his hold.

Paul, his blood on fire, ran with San to the shelter of a fallen fir tree. He pressed her close, laughing silently, shaken with passion. Just as she reached up her arms to him, turning her face aside provocatively, the abbé's voice boomed out above their heads. Paul lay still, rebelliously, but San struggled to her feet, pulling him after her. The abbé raised his hand and without any further preamble married them.

Paul was torn between a desire to gather San into his arms again and a sense of the grotesque that shook him with laughter as he watched her demurely entering into the service, kneeling, saying the right responses, crossing herself. The abbé paid no attention to Paul but he married him all the same.

There was something sinister about this priest dominating the scene in his shabby soutane. The firelight flickered over his face and he was smiling, something in the back of Paul's mind shouted to him:

"Escape! Escape! Knock him down and get away. Run through the forest. Freedom! Conserve your freedom!"

He heard the voice and recognized the warning but he made no move. One tenth of him might wish to escape, nine-tenths of him wished, craved, to sleep with San immediately.

The abbé's voice died away at length. San's attention returned to Paul. He gathered her into his arms and they disappeared again, this time to a wigwam erected, God knew when, behind them in the the the clearing.

Toward dawn a hand shook Paul out of his drugged, exhausted sleep. He swam back to the world and struggled to sit up.

"Your friend," the voice said in bad French, "your friend he is going to the Great Spirit."

Randy! Paul staggered to his feet and pushed his way out of the tent. The first rays of the sun were traveling through the forest, burnishing the branches, staining the snow a strange copper color, with long purple streaks in the shadow of the trees. The frosty air sprang into Paul's face and awakened him. He gathered his coat about him, tightened his woolen belt, catching his fingers in the fringe of it in his haste and stepped hurriedly forward.

The Indian who had come to call him was on his way back to the wigwam where Randy lay. Paul remembered him confusedly as one of the three men who had shrieked the loudest, danced with the most frenzy, and who would have been at each other's scalps if the abbé had not intervened. He looked sober enough

·[85]·

now, walking silently, sedately across the snow. Paul brushed aside the surprising memories of the night, to be considered later. A sudden smile passed across his lips and was gone. Concern for Randy mounted in him swiftly. He ran across the clearing and stooped at the opening of the wigwam. A strange smell of smoke and pungent herbs rose up and nearly stifled him. He could see Randy's face by the dim light of a bayberry candle stuck to a piece of wood. Randy's eyes were open, they were fixed upon the door.

"I feel much better," he gasped, "much better. I am going home today."

Paul bent over him remorsefully. He had not been near him for seventeen hours. He had left him to the mercy of this ignorant medicine man. There was a wild look in Randy's eyes, his cheeks were flushed, his breathing rattled and tore at him as he spoke. He was very much worse. Paul took his hand. The clammy fingers responded feebly, Randy attempted a smile but his lips were cracked and his tongue swollen.

"You look better," Paul said huskily.

"Better," Randy repeated. "Going home. Any message . . . home . . . ?"

Paul took him in his arms and held him while the medicine man put a heated stone at his back. Randy clung to him with surprising strength.

"It was nice of you to come and see me off," he whispered. "I shall tell them at home that I found a friend out here. My father has a low opinion of the colonists. When he meets you he will 'knowledge mistake . . .'" the voice trailed off into silence. Randy's head jerked forward onto Paul's shoulder. Paul tightened his hold for a moment. The medicine man stood up with a grunt.

"Degayk," he said, and then in bad French: "Gone, put him down."

Paul lowered Randy, thinking as he did so:

"Journey's end. A far cry from his English home. But perhaps he is better off. He might never have got back to England. They might never have recognized him if he did. He might have been taken prisoner again, beaten for having run away, branded for stealing, his nose or ears taken off. There was little ahead for him.

At least he lies here, free. Poor Randy, I am indebted to him. He found the lugger in which we made our escape. He lightened my servitude. There is little ahead for me too, unless I can get to Louisbourg. Now I am alone, but no," he laughed at the absurdity, "I am a married man." His thoughts went rushing back to San and the events of the night. He saw the abbé's enigmatical face. "My fate depends on him," he thought. A chill went down his spine. He disengaged Randy's arms and laid him gently back on the toboggan. The medicine man, shocked at his laughter, was trying to edge him out of the tent. There would be great doings later on. The Micmacs loved a funeral. Randy would go wherever he was going with all the dancing and prancing and shrieking and squeaking and feathers and fire of a dead savage. He would also have the benefit of a French Catholic requiem, no doubt. Paul laughed again, thinking of the family in England, placidly unaware of their son's strange fate. This second laughter was too much for the medicine man, he rose and pushed Paul firmly out of the tent.

CHAPTER XXI

PAUL was wrong about Randy's funeral. A shallow grave was scratched for him beneath the surface of the snow, and he was hastily, unceremoniously covered over. The abbé blessed the grave with one hand, and signed to his men with the other. Camp was struck. The band broke up into groups of five and six who dispersed in different directions. Paul found himself with San beside him, in the abbé's group. Two Micmacs scouted ahead of them and two behind; they swung along in single file, silently, swiftly, by the short trail. It was the quickest traveling that Paul had done. They kept a steady unbroken pace that was almost a dogtrot, lifting their snowshoes expertly just the quarter inch required to clear the snow.

Paul got tired and confused. He halted for a moment to wipe the sweat from his forehead and to take a few long breaths. San, striding behind him, took his arm. She had twisted a blanket round her head, her dark eyes looked out at him from under it with triumphant happiness. The excitement of the night came back to Paul. He smiled at her. She put her arm about his neck, with her right hand she pulled the blanket forward so that it concealed his face as well as hers. This was the traditional Micmac gesture of courtship. Paul thought it convenient. He kissed her. A whistle cut the silence of the woods about them, the short bark and howl of a wolf answered it.

"We must go on," San whispered. "Now we must run until we catch up."

"Let them wait for us."

San put her fingers to his lips. "We can't do that. The abbé is a strange man, a violent man, powerful among my people. We have his protection now, but we must do as he says. He is a true friend to my people and to your people. He has something now in his mind about the French. Moreover it is dangerous here."

The two savages scouting behind them padded up across the snow. They grunted and motioned with the right arm in a fierce gesture forward. Then they dropped back a little. Paul and San started to run. The noise of their snowshoes and their labored breathing was drowned in the roar of heavy surf, breaking to the right of them. The trail led here directly along the coast. It heartened Paul to find the sea so near him, magnificent and surly. The sharp salty tang filled his lungs. San running beside him, shivered, turning away her head; he shivered too, but with delight. The sea! The sea!

A sudden twist in the trail brought them to a cliff. The abbé was lying on the edge of it with two Indians, his hands were cupped to his eyes and he was peering through them. Paul and San dropped to their knees and crept near. Below them they could see a long panorama of surf-beaten coast.

"We should be able to see La Hève from here," le Loutre whispered, "if the day were clear. It is about four leagues away. We should make it tonight, it should be easy to get a boat from there, a sloop, a ketch, a fishing smack or even a lugger. We should be in Louisbourg in three days' time with a fair wind." He grinned, suddenly. "We will put in to Canceau on the way and tell them the great news. The English got their belly full at Canceau."

"I heard about that," Paul said, "when I was a prisoner. If the French had not taken Canceau I doubt whether the New Englanders would be raising an expedition to crush Louisbourg."

"It's a bold enterprise," le Loutre conceded, "and without the help of the English fleet, one must admit that they are brave. We must hammer the danger home to Monsieur du Chambon. I wish that we could hammer it home to the authorities in France. We lost Port Royal to the English because of indifference at court. Indifference and greed." He shook his head. "We must get on."

He crawled away from the skyline, rising to his feet. The others followed. Paul caught a glimpse of him striding ahead of them and thought to himself: "All that I've heard of him is true. He should have been a soldier, not a priest. But perhaps he has more influence with the savages as a medicine man than he would have as a captain, say, in the King's service, subject to orders from his superiors. I suppose he does have to report to the Bishop of Quebec." He smiled, picturing the abbé deferring to another man. "He is strange, fanatical, fascinating and repelling at the same time," Paul thought. A dull wonder took him as he reviewed what had happened since he first saw le Loutre . . . his wedding, Randy's death. . . .

San walking silently beside him, looked up. Suddenly she threw herself in front of Paul and tried to drag him beneath a clump of spruce and fallen logs. Paul, taken by surprise, resisted her. Then it was too late to hide. A flight of arrows hissed among them, falling harmless in the snow. The abbé turned, running back. Iroquois were coming through the forest behind him. They yelled as they saw their quarry, leaping high in the air, dropping to their knees to loose a second flight of arrows. Bullets spat in the snow about Paul and struck the trees, ricocheting round his head. There were three English soldiers among the Iroquois, they could be distinguished even at a distance, even dressed like the savages. Paul looked about him for escape. Le Loutre had reached his side.

"Run," he panted, "down on the rocks along the shore. Try to get through to La Hève by yourself. Don't wait for anyone, get through with the news. We will hold them off here." He raised his voice. "Scatter," he cried to the others, and then: "ai, ai, ai, wetkgonegg."

The Micmacs responded valiantly. Paul hesitated for a moment. San pulled him over the edge of the cliff, they scrambled along the rocks to the shore. The din of the sea drowned the howling of the savages, the cliff cut off all sight of what was happening. Suddenly three ferocious, hairless skulls looked over the edge of it. Paul ducked as the arrows whistled again, falling into the sea. He scrambled faster, perfectly sure that all was lost.

More yells, more arrows, this time one caught San in the thigh. She pulled it out with a vicious jerk, stopping for a moment to squeeze the place with her hands, and squeeze it again. Paul, watching her, remembered that the Iroquois used poisoned arrows. Suddenly there was a silence behind them, the heads disappeared, even the distant yelling died away. A terrible panic descended on Paul. He was convinced that the Iroquois, having seized the others were coming down by another trail to catch him and San. She was running still. He caught up with her, put his arm about her clumsily, they scrambled wildly on, panting and sobbing as they ran. The rocks grew worse. They had to separate and then to crawl. San dashed into the icy water, striking out for a point ahead of her. Paul followed, all that he had seen and heard of fiendish torture at the hands of the Iroquois forming pictures one after another in his mind.

CHAPTER XXII

DARKNESS fell quickly, covering the land. One by one the brilliant stars came out above the sea. A faint glow from the landward side predicted a rising moon over the hills. Paul and San crouching behind a rock, felt the darkness roll up around them with relief. They had swum in the icy, numbing water, they had run with their clothes freezing upon them, over rocks, over stretches of blessed sand, until they could run no more. They had crawled behind this rock, out of the way of the wind, out of sight. The sudden squawk of a sea gull overhead made them start and tremble, then laugh with relief.

They clung together, trying to keep warm. San's breathing became labored, now and then she moved restlessly, once she stifled a moan, Paul knew that she was in pain. Her thigh was swelling, the freezing water and the cold wind did not help the inflammation, it was spreading fast. San pressed close to him for comfort, her eyes, dark and appealing, were lifted to his, infinite trust shone out of them. Paul responded to this appeal. He bent over her magnificent body, attempting to comfort, to soothe, to reassure. They were so lost in each other, so set apart from the rest of the world, in their preoccupation, pain and discomfort, that the darkness came upon them unaware. San's face grew indistinct. Paul stared, he raised his head, both began to shiver; with the darkness came the cold. They would be frozen if they stayed there any longer. It was agony to move. San sank down twice before Paul got her to her feet. The sweat was pouring down her face. He led her from the rock to the sandy beach, they had lost their snowshoes scrambling down the cliff, their moccasined feet sank into the wet sand, the tide had come and gone since they were behind their rock and the beach was wet.

The moon rose from behind the hills, the sea became white foam and phosphorescence against black. San staggered and swayed. Her leg was swollen twice its size, she had no feeling in her foot, but she went on. Paul felt a rush of sympathy toward her. "These savages have courage" he thought. The shadow of a possessive pride hovered about him for a moment, he felt for the first time that perhaps she was his wife, not a flesh and blood fantasy embraced in wigwams and forgotten, but a person like himself, with as much individual existence. He began to wonder why she had married him. Was she coerced by the abbé as he was? Was Paul unreal and vague to her so that the whole thing seemed unimportant, or—he looked at her in the moonlight, startled—could it be that she really loved him?

She put out her hand, reaching for his.

"I cannot walk," she said, like a tired child. She leaned heavily on him and took a few steps more, then she stopped and turned her face to him.

"You go on," she said, "and leave me here."

He shook his head. She was smiling at him. In the soft light all traces of her savage ancestry seemed to disappear. Her hair was tousled out of its sleek, straight braids. Her eyes were flushed with fever, she looked like any tired French child, like Marie his sister, or Margaret who had loved him—this child loved him too, he knew what an exciting body she had beneath that buckskin dress. She was his and he would not leave her. There were just the two of them, he would see her through.

He stooped to take her arms about his neck and hoisted her on his back. She was light. He could feel her swollen leg burning through the damp leggings. Her cheek was burning too. She pressed it against his, murmuring things, intimate little things, into his ear. He carried her step by weary step along the beach in the moonlight. The shore was sandy here, broken up by rocks, but the tide was going out and he could skirt round these. His feet sank deeply into the sand, it was an effort to pull them out. He concentrated doggedly on lifting, counting, setting down his feet toward La Hève.

·[93]·

CHAPTER XXIII

L A HÈVE was asleep. The group of stout little wooden houses huddled together for protection. No light showed in any window. Empty lanterns creaked over the doorways, swinging in the moonlight. The harbor was spacious, sheltered from ocean storms by a promonotory, a group of islands, and its own narrow mouth. A river ran into the far end. A number of vessels were anchored together, ranging from barques to sloops. Here and there a gleam of light showed where an officer kept his watch.

Paul, staggering toward the house nearest him, had no eyes for the beauty of the scene. He did not watch the waning moon give place to the first days of dawn, or the sun rise slowly from the sea. He was exhausted, his feet were bleeding, San hung from his back a dead weight. He had put her down and picked her up a hundred times that night, with stealthy noises behind him filling his ears. His numbed mind obeyed one order, held one preoccupation—to go on until he could reach La Hève.

Now he had reached it, he stood in a daze. Then, sliding San from his shoulders and susporting her in his arms, he scratched on the door of the house. No answer. There was a knocker of twisted iron. He smote upon that. Shutters above him opened cautiously.

"Who's that?"

"The Iroquois are out. They have attacked us. Let me in."

"The Iroquois!"

Instantly more shutters opened, nightcapped heads of all ages appeared. A bearded man with a very red face leaned out and blew on a hunting horn, a long mournful blast.

"Hasten," said Paul, "let us in."

The door was unbolted. A group of women with candles in their hands appeared. They were shouldered aside by the red-faced man.

"How far away?" he asked.

"Not many leagues; if they trailed us they must be at hand."

The man stepped into the street, raised his musket and fired into the air. He ran along the row of houses banging on the shutters.

"Alarm! Alarm! Iroquois!"

Lights appeared, heads followed, shutters were closed and barred. Men and boys tumbled sleepily up and ran to their stations. Peepholes were uncovered, gun muzzles thrust through them, fires were kindled, oil was set to boil.

Meanwhile the women in the first house were attending to San, clucking over her swollen leg—it was discolored and horrible to look at. She had fever—cursed Iroquois with their poisoned darts —ciel, what a country for a woman, even a savage woman!

They were curious and arch; they waited for him to explain, while they bandaged and fussed. One of them brought him a drink of hot rum. It went to his stomach and warmed him for the first time. It loosened his tongue.

The red-faced man had come back from his rounds with two more men, they brought their guns and axes, crowding about Paul, questioning him. How many Iroquois? Where? When? Were there any English too?

Paul answered the questions gravely, warmed by his drink. When he spoke of le Loutre they all crossed themselves in deepest respect. The abbé was a wonderful man. He had been with them only the other day for the marriage of Pépé le Brun. And now he was taken? Did Paul see him taken? No? Ah, then he would give those devils the slip as he had done over and over again. The abbé was as slippery as an eel, or an Iroquois. He would be all right, never fear. Grandmère began a Rosary for him, all the same. Two little girls huddled at her knees, gravely poked the beads helping to keep count. The men stood to their posts. Let the savages come, they would be ready. Meanwhile Paul had done enough in bringing the warning, he and his woman could rest.

The women tended San who had fallen into a heavy sleep. Paul was led away to get back his strength until he was needed. They would call him then. The main thing about an Iroquois attack was not to be taken unaware. La Hève was awake and ready, thanks to Paul.

"You do not know what it means to be in a French village again," Paul said to the child entrusted with him. He babbled more, about his flight through the woods, his marriage, about Louisbourg, and the need for haste, about San dying of a poisoned arrow, poor child—and she was his wife. Then he fell asleep.

CHAPTER XXIV

THE Iroquois did not attack. Slowly the little village resumed its daily business of getting a living from the sea. The house where Paul had taken refuge belonged to a fisherman, like the others. Pierre le Jeune and his wife Marie. It was the usual two-roomed house with an attic above. The outside door led into a large kitchen which was also the family living room. A great square bed stood out from the wall ornamented with rustic carving and covered with a patchwork quilt. A swarm of children slept in it. There was a long pine table, a bench and two rush chairs. The fireplace took up an entire wall, huge logs burned in it and the house was warm; clay and moss plastered the cracks, and the door to the second room was kept open so that it too caught the heat. The attic, used for a storeroom and in summer for an extra bedroom, was too cold to sleep in now. San lay in the bedroom which was a dormitory for three generations. Paul was given a shakedown in the kitchen with the children.

As soon as he was awake and had seen for himself that San, sunk into a heavy sleep, was well cared for, the men of the village gathered to hear his story. Martin le Jeune, Pierre's brother, one of the men who had come with his gun the night before to defend the le Jeune property, put shrewd questions. They were all excited at the news of the proposed attack on Louisbourg, though some of them thought it must have been abandoned as impossible. Jacques Provot thought it must be a bluff. What did the abbé think of it? He was no fool. When he had dealt with the Iroquois —and nobody seemed to doubt that he would deal with them adequately—he would return to his mission at Shubenacadie. Then they would hear from him and know what to do. Paul pointed out the danger of waiting and said that the abbé had urged him to carry the news as swiftly as possible to the Governor of Louisbourg. He would hire a boat and go on at once. There must be one among all the vessels in the harbor ready to sail for Louisbourg. He pulled on his moccasins, tied them with a leather thong, tightened his scarf about his waist, and went out, followed by five of the children, to look at the craft anchored in the harbor. Most of them were fishing sloops, some were being repaired, two of the larger boats lacked sail, and were being overhauled. But there was a brig that caught Paul's eye at once. He had himself rowed out to her.

The brig *Vendange* was not due to sail for three weeks. She was awaiting a double cargo, of pelts from the Abnaki, and ammunition from Quebec. The owner of the vessel laughed when Paul suggested that he should run him to Louisbourg before the cargoes came.

"And have the cargoes seized by another vessel?" he asked. "My winter's livelihood? To love one's king is one thing, Monsieur, to go hungry, another."

"I agree with you," Paul said. "I will pay for my passage, and trust to the Governor to reimburse me. I will pay a good price, and with a fair wind you should get back in time to handle the cargoes as well. Then what do you lose?"

The Captain stared at him, his shrewd eyes took in Paul's shabby clothing, his unkempt hair, his general air of poverty and persecution. He shrugged. Paul took out the purse he had stolen and set it before him. He said nothing, but he began to take a few of the pieces out and ring them carelessly upon the table. The Captain's eyes bulged, he picked up one of the pieces and examined it.

"English gold," he said.

Paul agreed. There was a silence while the Captain did some obvious thinking. Then he began to bargain. Paul was cheated, and he knew it, but he did not greatly care. His chief preoccupation was to get to Louisbourg. After a show of hesitation he accepted the terms. The Captain grew more and more cheerful as sovereigns and half sovereigns rang on the table before him. He swept them into a leather bag and declared himself and the *Vendange* ready to make the next tide. Paul went back to the le Jeunes in the Captain's long boat. He ran into the kitchen and called to Marie le Jeune:

"You must get the Indian girl—my wife—ready at once. We sail in less than an hour."

"Seigneur Dieu!" said the woman, her kind face distorted in horror," she cannot move, she will die if you attempt it. The poor child," she glared at Paul, "may be nothing but a savage, but she is a woman like myself, and if you could see her leg, three times the size of itself, purple from the poison, and she has fever too!"

"We could carry her to the brig," Paul began, "she could have a cabin . . ."

"No, no, it isn't possible," Marie said decidedly. "I shall never agree to it. She will die if she is moved. Perhaps you want to kill her, you men are all alike."

Paul hesitated.

"I will see what she says."

"You will do nothing of the sort. She will want to go with you. Poor soul, she is in love."

Perhaps she was right, Paul reflected. To travel with a sick woman would complicate matters quite a lot. San might be better off where she was, she could follow him as soon as she was well. Pierre le Jeune came in at that moment and Paul turned to him.

"If I leave you some money, will you look after my wife?"

The le Jeunes answered in chorus that nothing would please them more. He must go on his way unhampered by worry about her, she would be all right, the Indian women were strong— Marie le Jeune snorted and tossed her head: "Just like a man!"

Their faces brightened as Paul counted out a little heap of sovereigns. Over and over again they assured him that they would take good care of his wife. One of the children came running in to say that the "Vendange" was getting ready to weigh anchor. Captain Mercier sent word would the Monsieur who had engaged passage with him be sure not to make him lose the tide? The longboat was waiting. Paul nodded. He went to the door of the

·[99]·

second room which was half open, and peered in. San was still asleep, moaning feverishly, turning from side to side. Marie bustled to the bed. She laid her cool hands on the burning forehead. Paul bent over her. San's eyes opened for a moment, drowsily, she smiled at him and went to sleep again.

"Do not trouble her," Marie whispered, "poor soul."

Paul nodded. He kissed San on the forehead, patted her hands, roving restlessly over the blankets, and went out. Marie came out after him. "You must have some wine," she said, more kindly disposed to him now. She brought out a small wooden keg and poured out a tankard full. They all drank from it, passing it around even among the children. Then Paul set out for the harbor, followed by a collection of le Jeunes shouting good luck and good-by.

CHAPTER XXV

THE *Vendange* went out with the tide and picked up a moderate breeze off the Cape. She tacked between three islands, heading out to sea. Paul stood in the waist near the mainmast watching the spray break over the bow. He was jubilant to be at sea again with such a strong deck under him, heading for home. From time to time he left his place and roamed forward out of the way of the crew at their various duties. Some of them looked surly, annoyed that their time on shore should be curtailed, others, like himself, were grinning with the pure joy of finding themselves in their natural element. Paul watched them set the course northeast by east and sheet home topgallant sails and run up outer jib. The *Vendange* heeled over and plunged forward, all sails set, drawing away at a good five knots. She was shipping enough water to make it uncomfortable on deck. Paul went below.

He found the second mate unrolling a chart. He was a sturdy young fellow with a beard and a pigtail instead of a wig. He smiled as Paul came in and made way for him with respect. Paul looked at the chart and struck up conversation. They talked of the attack on Canceau. The second mate had taken part in this, and had come away with some loot, in particular a very fine flageolet. He offered to show it to Paul, whose eyes lit up with interest. It was a long time since he had got his hands on a musical instrument or discussed music with anyone. He followed the second mate to the cabin which he learned he was to share with him. They sat on a chest together examining the flute. It was of ivory with golden stops and curiously carved. Paul thought it worth a fortune.

"Whom did you loot it from?" he asked enviously.

The mate shrugged.

"It was in the Governor's house," he said, "tucked away in a corner, covered with dust. Nobody had seen it. The rest of the house was beginning to burn, I picked it off the wall and here it is."

Paul turned it over. He set it to his lips and began to play. The tone was mellow and sweet, it delighted him. He began to play the old songs: "A la claire Fontaine" and "Petit Oiseau je t'écoute." The second officer listened greedily.

"Do you know this?" he asked.

He played a plaintive air with a seductive lilt to it. Paul shook his head. Before he could ask what it was, the door opened and a sailor came in. He doffed his woolen cap and said:

"Monsieur, the Captain wants to see you."

Paul rose and followed him out of the cabin. The second mate swung himself into his hammock and went to sleep. He had the night watches ahead of him.

Paul stepped along the passageway to the Captain's quarters. He found a spacious cabin for the size of the brig, with panel work and polished wood. The walls were covered with guns and pistols. The room was an extra armory, a safeguard against attack or mutiny. There was a berth in one corner, a table in another, a wardrobe with a surprising amount of clothes hanging in it, for all to see, and a row of buckled shoes. Three wigs were nailed to the wall with hats upon them. The Captain, clearly, was a man prepared for any emergency. He poured out a drink in a pewter mug as Paul came in, and handed it to him with a toast:

"Bon voyage."

Paul lifted the mug.

"Santé," he said.

The Captain eyed him calculatingly. Paul did not like the expression in his eyes. He felt the bag of gold tied to his waist grow heavier, the array of vicious-looking weapons on the walls assume a sinister menace. What was to prevent this man from robbing Paul and flinging him overboard? Patriotism? Perhaps. He would rather depend upon his own good nerve. He pushed his chair back from the table, letting his right hand stray toward his pocket as though he had a pistol there. Let the Captain think so anyway, it could do no harm and at the first possible opportunity it would be true. He took his leave as soon as he could, and the Captain let him go rather as a cat might watch the passage of a distant rat.

"Phew!" said Paul. He went on deck to clear his head. A strong wind had sprung up. The sails were straining, a confused noise of whistling, whining, creaking and splashing blew about his ears. He looked up, the sky was stormy, streaked with mare's-tails. The *Vendange* was designed for bad weather, she was seaworthy, she could take care of herself, and so could Paul. He had grown up in a hard school. He grinned, looking back at the Captain's cabin. Let the heavy weather come! They would make harbor together, the "Vendange" and he.

PART THREE
LOUISBOURG 1745

CHAPTER XXVI

ON THE last day of February, 1745, the town of Louisbourg presented a forbidding appearance. A bleak wind
swept the harbor, rocking the boats at anchorage there,
beating against the shuttered doors and windows of the houses
along the embankment. Across the town on the other side the
Atlantic crashed and roared. It was no day to be out. The fishermen having seen to their boats returned to their homes, thankful
to have a good fireside, a hot stew and an excuse for doing nothing. Even at this early hour the tavern was full of roistering
sailors and soldiers. A few women clutching shawls around their
heads ventured forth to do the marketing. They had the streets to
themselves as they hurried, heads down against the wind, except
for the scavenger pigs rooting in doorways and alleys. Marie de
Morpain meeting one of these withdrew into a doorway. The pig,
a ferocious-looking sow, sniffed at her feet, hesitated, apparently
unable to decide whether the deerskin moccasins she was wearing
would be worth attacking her for. Marie shooed in a rather trem-
bling voice, the pig snorted and passed on. A boy of twelve running along the street in the opposite direction, called out some
friendly insult. Marie called back, beckoning to him vigorously.
The boy good-naturedly stopped and came across to her.

"Where have you been?" she asked. "I looked everywhere for
you, Tomas, and now you can come with me and help me carry
this."

She placed a large wicker basket over his arm and gave him a
push. He made a cheerful grimace and ran along beside her kick-

ing at the snowdrifts and icicles. The market place came into sight, Marie quickened her step, it was the day the Indians brought frozen meats, fish and other things to town. Marie hoped to find the ingredients for a mess of eels, and perhaps a cut of bear or venison. It is not every day that one prepares one's wedding feast. Weddings did not usually happen in the winter when things were inconvenient. She sighed and her thoughts wandered a little from the matter of food. Tomas startled her with a shout. He had run ahead of her to a point where he could see the entrance of the harbor.

"The *Vendange* is coming in! The *Vendange* is coming in!"

"Nonsense!" Marie said rather sharply, "she is not due for another month."

"She's coming in, she's coming in," Tomas sang.

Marie took her place beside him.

"Why so she is," she said surprised.

Tomas put the basket down in the middle of the road and was off before she could stop him, to see the docking of the brig. Marie with a smile and a sigh picked up the basket and hastened her steps. She was curious too, but the dreadful shadow of the wedding feast loomed over her. She thought of all the other preparations there would have to be, and sighed again. There was no one to advise her or to care. She thought of her father whose fate was a mystery. He had sailed out of Louisbourg and had never come back. He had taken his eldest son with him, leaving Marie to stand by her mother, and when she died to make a home and a living for four younger children. Well, she had managed it somehow, she had kept them all alive at least, and now the worst of the struggle was over, there would be a man to help. Her thoughts came back to the wedding itself. Things must be done decently. Perhaps she had better get both eels and bear, and plenty of brandy. Monsieur Mercier was a heavy drinker. Strange that his brother's brig should be coming in out of her time. The Merciers were as regular as clocks. It must be something very unusual. She would see what it was when she could get to the wharf.

Tomas was there already, and a crowd of other children who had seen the brig's sails. Any vessel that entered the harbor was an event. Doors opened along the quay, women came out wrapped in their shawls, a group of lounging men appeared from nowhere in particular watching the brig round to with critical eyes. The wind tore at the sails even as they were being furled. When the anchor splashed overboard the spray that it sent up was carried into the watchers' faces. The men kept up a strict and silent observation of all that was taking place, slapping their arms across their chests, stamping their feet; they saw the longboat lowered, two cases carried down and stowed away, they saw the first and second officers and the contremaître at their places on the deck, the stage set, in fact, for the Captain to come ashore. The mystery of the brig's arrival before her time and without her cargo, for she was riding high, as any child could see, was partially solved when a stranger appeared and took his seat to be rowed ashore. The Captain arrived at last and climbed over the side. The longboat pulled for shore.

Marie came round the corner of her house and set the basket down inside the doorway. She could see the brig from the kitchen window but she preferred to go out and watch it close at hand. Ever since she was a child the comings and goings of vessels in the harbor of Louisbourg had filled her with strange excitement and wistful longing. She did not know whether it was her father's ketch, *La Belle Louise*, that she was looking for, or whether the general sense of freedom and adventure, of contact with the larger world that occupied her daydreams, found its best expression in the hoisting of a sail. She only knew that there was scarcely an hour of the day when she did not snatch a moment by the kitchen window or run out upon the quays. She would miss this house by the water's edge when she was married to Monsieur Mercier. Her face clouded for a moment, then cleared again at the picture before her. The longboat was landing its occupants, among them a dark young man with a strangely familiar face. Marie could not place him at all. She was certain that she had seen him somewhere, or someone like him. She stared as he passed her, noting everything, the burning eyes, the gaunt face, the shabby clothes—it was a strange passenger for Captain Mercier to abandon cargo for and make a special voyage. They disappeared up the street together toward the Governor's quarters. The stranger stopped now and then and looked about him as though he were in a trance.

"Well" thought Marie as she went back to her eels.

CHAPTER XXVII

PAUL walking up the streets of Louisbourg, glanced about him, eager, bewildered, amused. The town looked familiar in every detail, but the houses seemed to have shrunk, the streets narrowed, the quays flattened out. The dream city of his memory, colored by all his childhood values, wavered as he looked at the real Louisbourg and disappeared. There was left a fortified town of about a hundred buildings with stone walls, a stone fortress and some stone houses.

They landed by the first wharf instead of by the third one nearest the Epron du Bastion Dauphin which would have taken him home. He would hasten there presently, but first he must go to the Governor, pay his respects and deliver the warning. Captain Mercier was rather obviously going with him out of curiosity and pique. Paul smiled, he had not only kept his English gold but had added to it, beating the Captain at trente-et-un. He had not been batted about from pillar to post as an underdog without learning something. He had waited on the Captain's sort before.

He waved to the second officer, with whom he had made friends, left on board to keep watch, staring hungrily at his home, which he could see from the deck, then he brushed his way through a cloud of children gaping about his knees. He made for a short cut, mechanically. Captain Mercier shot an astonished glance at him; they walked on in silence.

Paul was thinking: "Well here I am at last! Poor Randy, I wish he could have been with me. Home!"

Pictures of the bitter years behind him surged into his mind.

His youth had been taken from him, his spirit tamed, but enough of himself had endured to bring him safely through. He had shouldered a burden beyond his years, becoming a man overnight before he had lost his first teeth. And now he was home. There was the Recollet convent where he made his First Communion, there was the bakery which sold such good brioches, there was Jacqueline Benoit's house, her mother gave him his first pair of moccasins. Other forgotten incidents surged to meet him from every stone. He walked on quickly, shaken with excitement and regret.

He crossed the courtyard to the Governor's quarters in a dream, and found himself admitted to an anteroom with Captain Mercier, to await their turn. A young officer came in to apologize and keep them company. The Governor, he said, was busy with dispatches from Quebec, and would see them presently. He flung his three-cornered hat on the table, drew up a bench and sat down with them, eyeing Paul until he became aware of the shabbiness of his clothes and his general air of misery. He did not care, let the two men look at him and sneer, the Governor would listen to what he had to say. He leaned back and crossed his legs comfortably, returning look for look.

The young officer, whose name when he tardily presented himself to Paul, turned out to be Nicolas Chauvert, began to tell the Captain all the local gossip. Paul was intrigued, but he tried not to show it. Some of the names were familiar, some he had never heard before. The Captain's brother, he gathered, was about to be married, and the girl was a good-looking little piece without a dowry. Monsieur Mercier, the young officer intimated, could afford to pay for his fancies, but most men would boggle at a brood of brothers and sisters. The girl did not seem to realize her good fortune, either, she had kept him dangling a year or two, but now the date was set, and Captain Mercier no doubt had come home for the wedding. The Captain started to shake his head, then he thought better of it. It was news to him that his brother's wedding date was set, but there was no sense in giving the family away to strangers. The door opened. A sentry saluted.

"The Governor will see you now," he said.

Paul rose to his feet, without haste and without effort he managed to precede both officers and reach the Governor first. The room into which he was ushered was spacious and comfortable. He had been there before as a small boy, peeping in when it was empty. He remembered the big table at which the Governor sat, his head had not reached to it then. He smiled, doffed his hat and bowed ceremoniously.

"Monsieur du Chambon, Paul de Morpain, at your service, Sir."

The Governor rose and bowed. He turned a vague eye on Paul, his right hand shuffled some papers in front of him, he was obviously preoccupied and at a loss to understand the reason for this shabby young man's audience. Paul came to the point at once.

"I am an escaped prisoner of war from Boston," he said, "a great expedition is being prepared against Louisbourg. . . ."

"Your credentials, Monsieur?" the Governor inquired.

"Credentials?" Paul stared, taken aback. So that was the sort of man the Governor was. How pitiable! He recovered himself.

"My news is of more value to you than my credentials, Sir," he said. "However, the Abbé le Loutre will vouch for me, and I am also known in this town. I came from here."

"Monsieur de Morpain?" The Governor asked. "Are you related to the privateer Pierre de Morpain?"

"He is my uncle," Paul said impatiently. "What does it matter who I am? Louisbourg is in danger, on the eve of an attack. You must muster all your resources for the defense at once."

The Governor said nothing for awhile, then he raised his eyes and looked at Paul.

"We must not believe every wild rumor we hear, Monsieur de Morpain," he said pleasantly. "I am glad you have returned to Louisbourg, it is a pleasure to extend an official welcome to you, later perhaps, if there is confirmation of your story. . . ."

"But you have not heard my story yet!" Paul cried.

It was no use, the Governor had risen, he was looking past Paul toward Captain Mercier, bowing in the doorway. Paul took a step toward him and opened his mouth to speak.

"Tush," said the Governor, "New England will never dare to attack Louisbourg. Any child knows that. Put such notions out of your head. Monsieur Chauvert, show Monsieur de Morpain out."

The young officer saluted. Over his shoulder Paul saw the

Governor wink at Captain Mercier. The Captain winked back, then both men tapped their foreheads and laughed. Paul felt the blood mount in his face, he choked with rage at this stupidity, but there was nothing that he could do. He had blundered the interview. He had said "you must" to the Governor and roused his antagonism. A more experienced man would have gone about things differently. Now, if he persisted, he would be thrown into jail or run out of town. He must submit for the moment and find another way. He must try again. But the Governor was a fool.

"If it weren't that I love the place," he muttered, "I would let you all be taken by the New Englanders and rot without my help."

He pushed past the officer and ran down the steps. He had personal things of his own to attend to now.

"Silly old suet-face!" he growled.

CHAPTER XXVIII

T HE de Morpains' house near the Bastion Dauphin was pulled down, not a trace of it remained. Paul, wandering disconsolately through the rubble, came on part of the kitchen floor. The bricks were familiar, he recognized particular stones, worn in particular places. He shut his eyes, trying to recall the scene he had kept so long in his mind. Here maman sat, here père, here he sat himself while Marie and the other children set the table. He opened his eyes; there, buried beneath melting snow, mud and debris of all sorts was home. He turned away, walking aimlessly toward the harborside. He must find news of the family from somebody, but from whom? Puzzling over this, he began to walk along the quay, passing the first wharf, avoiding the little ditch—it was still there—by jumping over it as he had always done. Nothing was changed here, his eye went over the waters of the harbor looking at the Royal Battery with the old pride. It could rake the harbor, with the Island Battery to answer it. Let the New Englanders come. His mind went back to the Governor impatiently. There was that to be attended to, but first his own concerns. He passed the citadel on his right, looking up at it thoughtfully. The walls were stout enough, but were the men?

Ahead of him Paul could see a group of children clamoring around another man. It was the second officer. Paul made for him.

"Monsieur Godet," he said, "you are the very man I want."

Godet stopped in his tracks good-naturedly.

"I did not tell you before," Paul said, "that Louisbourg is my home."

Godet looked surprised. "I don't remember you," he began.

Paul waved this aside.

"I did not want to tell anyone, or to ask news of my family. It is a moment I have kept in my heart for years, the moment when I should step through the door and see them all sitting there, and say: 'Paul is here!' But something has happened, the house is pulled down, there is nothing left." He caught at his friend's arm. "You must help me to find them. You live here, you must know where they have gone."

Godet stood considering. "De Morpain?" he said. "Pierre de Morpain the privateer comes into this port occasionally. I never heard of another de Morpain here. Oh, yes, he has some nephews and nieces who are orphans."

"Orphans!"

"They live in one of the fishermen's cottages, opposite the wharf where we landed. Oh, and I believe one of them is marrying the Captain's brother." He started to say something else, but stopped himself. Paul could guess the sort of thing it was, with the conversation at the fort still ringing in his ears.

"Do you know where this cottage is?" he asked quietly.

Godet said yes, and turned to go back. They walked past the second wharf, along the quay until they came to a little open place with several houses forming half a square. There was a corner cottage with a steep roof. The end wall had one window looking toward the harbor, the front wall had a door and a window looking toward the harbor too, in the other direction. The house was half clay and half stone. It looked sturdy, independent and poverty-stricken.

"I think it's there," Godet said.

Paul stepped toward the door, his heart beating with a variety of emotions. He scratched on the paneling, scratched louder, then banged. It was opened indignantly by a girl of twelve.

"What do you want?" she asked belligerently, "it is rude to make such a noise at people's houses."

She looked as though she might shut the door in his face.

"Mademoiselle de Morpain?" Paul asked, baring his head. His heart was pounding with loud unnatural thumps. He hardly dared look beyond the girl into the living room filled with people.

"That is my sister," she said, then over her shoulder: "Marie, a gentleman wishes to speak with you."

There was a movement in the room behind her. Paul took an uncertain step forward. A figure emerged to meet him. It was a young woman dressed like a fisher girl in a voluminous skirt, an embroidered blouse and a fichu. A shawl was thrown back from her head. She had just come in. Phil caught his breath, she was startlingly beautiful, with a beauty that did not depend so much upon features, as upon a glowing, vital personality. That was Paul's first impression as he took a step forward and made his best bow. Behind him he heard what sounded like a gasp and a snort. Monsieur Godet was also impressed, it would seem.

"Messieurs?" the girl said, looking from one to the other inquiringly.

"Er—I will leave you now," Godet said, backing away as though from a fire. His cheeks were red enough too.

Paul caught him by the arm.

"Not at all," he said, "you will stay with us. Ma sœur, allow me to present Monsieur Godet."

Sister he had said! Marie started. She half drew back, then she sprang forward and threw herself in Paul's arms.

"Paul!" she cried, "it is Paul," she made a half sweeping movement behind her. "Children, Tomas, Andrée, Louise, Pierre, it is our brother that I have told you about, and that we have prayed for so many times, our brother Paul! I knew it, I knew it," she said turning back to him, "something told me today on the wharf."

He kissed her heartily on both cheeks, laughing a little as he did so. The children came forward, shyly, then freely, crowding about him excitedly. Beyond Marie's shoulder and above the children's clamor, Paul was conscious of a room full of people waiting disapprovingly. Marie, still searching Paul's face as though she would find the story of the years that divided them written there for her to see, became conscious of the atmosphere in the room behind her. The light went out of her eyes, the flush left her cheeks, she said in a colorless voice:

"Monsieur Mercier, may I present my brother to you? Paul, my betrothed."

Paul made an elaborate leg and bowed very low. Monsieur

Mercier stared at him coolly for a moment, then he bowed rather stiffly, equally low. Marie standing silent between them turned to the other two people in the room. They were nuns, they stood side by side, arms folded in their sleeves, bowing together. Their bright little eyes missed nothing, and disapproved of all that they saw. Paul felt stifled suddenly, he longed to take his sister and go out into the cold winter street. The air would be frosty and clean. There would be stars later on, he thought confusedly, shining over the harbor. There would be time for Marie to become acquainted with him. They would catch up on the past, and he would hear all that he wanted to hear. But no, the walls of the room closed in upon them all, he found himself staring at a carica-ture of Captain Mercier, coarsened in every particular, mean black eyes, ungenerous lips, fleshy nose and arrogant attitude.

"Well," Paul put his arm about his sister, drawing her close to him, "it's just as well that I have come home," he said. Godet behind him cleared his throat.

CHAPTER XXIX

AFTER half an hour's stilted conversation, during which Paul came to hate Monsieur Mercier, instead of merely disliking him, the nuns took their leave. Paul went with them to the door and held it open. A blast of wind rushed in, rattling the trenchers on the shelf and setting the heavy iron stew pot over the fire swinging, so that it spilt some of the soup. Paul shut the door, and turned expectantly to Monsieur Mercier. He was lolling nonchalantly back expecting to be asked to supper, but the invitation did not come. Marie contrived not to be alone with him or to look his way. What if she were to be married to him in a few days' time? Tonight she had her brother home and would be alone with him. Monsieur Mercier took the hint and took his leave. Paul accompanied him to the door and bowed him out, but when Godet tried to go, he demurred.

"Your family have done without you all this time, they did not expect you for three more weeks, stay to supper with us, that is if there is any supper." He looked toward Marie.

"Of course there is," she said indignantly, but her glance strayed a little anxiously to the iron pot. She had planned to have a simple supper. Monsieur Mercier would excuse frugality, in view of the wedding feast to come, and the nuns had not expected to stay, they were not allowed to eat outside of the convent. They had only come to make some arrangements with her about the children. She frowned, gathering Andrée to her with a sudden hug.

"Set out an extra platter," she said, "and you must help me with the stew."

Andrée nodded, wiping her hands on her pinafore.

"I will help you," Paul said, making for the heavy pot.

But Marie was not satisfied. After all, it is not every day that a brother comes home from the world of the dead, and what if there were no other market day before the wedding feast? She would make the mess of eels for supper. So Paul and Monsieur Godet sat down together among the children to wait. Paul began to look about him and to take in everything for the first time. His eye went to the huge stone fireplace, with the warming pan at one end of it and a dye pot at the other. Half a cord of wood was stacked methodically in the corner. One big log burned under the iron pot, carefully turned from time to time on two massive andirons. There was a spinning wheel in the opposite corner from the dye pot. The light from the fire flickered over a tall dresser with three pewter mugs—how well Paul remembered them—and a silver jug. There was nothing else in the room but a rough refectory table and a wooden bench. A number of wooden stools were scattered about. Paul was sitting on one of them with Pierre prisoned between his knees. The little boy looked up at him solemnly, his clothes were clean but patched and darned. His face was lean and wistful. The bareness of the room, the child's expression, Marie's preoccupation, a hundred other details told the story. When Louise, who was ten, sat down to the spinning wheel hurriedly as though, Monsieur Mercier gone, there was no time to lose in getting on with the business of life, it put the last touch to the picture of bitter poverty bravely disregarded.

Supper came at last. They each had a wooden bowl and a wooden spoon. How well Paul remembered these! Marie must have saved them from the old house when it was torn down. He wanted to ask about that—what had happened to it? Little Pierre said grace and they all began to eat. Paul watching his sister's face, contrasting its anxiety with the placid expressions of the children, their gaiety, felt a rush of protective love toward Marie. He should have been there to help her all these years. When Maman died—when did she die, and why? He longed to ask, but this was not the time—normally he would have been there to help. Marie had had to manage all alone. He looked at her. She was helping Godet to coffee. He was a fiery red. Godet seemed to be

·[119]·

susceptible. That, Paul thought, was a good thing since he liked Godet and did not like Monsieur Mercier. He did not believe that Marie cared for him either. She would not have been so relieved to see him go. He would find that out later; meanwhile here was a good fire, good food and good company. Paul had come home.

When supper was over the children cleared away the wooden bowls and carried them into a corner to be washed and polished, and restored to their places of honor. Marie sat down with the two men before the fire. Paul put out his hand, she took it, they sat thus staring into the flames. Godet not knowing what to say or do, brought out his flageolet and began to play to himself.

"That's an idea," said Paul, "did you save my violin?"

Marie shook her head. "I sold it," she said, distressed.

Paul looked disappointed.

"But there's Mother's harp."

"Give me that."

Marie went to get it. The children who had finished their work, gathered about the fire. Godet began to play his favorite plaintive melody.

"I know that!" Marie said, returning, and she began to sing:

> "Listen all, small and grown
> If you please to hear it,
> To the Passion of Jesus Christ,
> Which was sad and plaintive."*

"Is that what it is?" said Paul. He seized the harp and began to accompany them, improvising chords. They slid into "At the Clear Fountain." They all sang it, going heartily through the nine verses, singing the refrain each time a little differently in emphasis:

> "I have loved you a long time
> I shall forget you never."*

Godet sang it with his eyes fixed on Marie, once she sang it looking at him, Paul sang smiling, watching them both.

On the ramparts of the fort the sentries passed each other with "All's well." Night had come to Louisbourg.

CHAPTER XXX

ONE by one the children finished their tasks, said good night and went to bed in the room off the kitchen. Monsieur Godet rose to take his leave. Marie curtsied to him, shut the door upon him and came back to Paul. They were alone together for the first time in seven years. Paul saw a girl of fifteen, too old for her years, even in New France where women matured early, marrying at fourteen, thirteen, even twelve. In sharp contrast he remembered a child of eight trotting beside him in a pinafore. The straggling mouse-colored hair had become chestnut curls, flecked with red and gold. The sallow, freckled skin looked like peach-colored silk. Only the hands remained the same, rough, strong little hands, work hardened, ugly. She held them out. He grasped them, patted them and let them go.

"There is so much, so much to hear, to tell."

Suddenly she began to cry a little. He watched her gravely while she searched for a handkerchief. She smiled through her tears.

"It has been hard," she said, "since maman died, and before that too. The old governor ——"

"Monsieur du Quesnel?"

"Yes. He was good to us. He allowed maman a pension. This governor has taken it away."

Paul's fingers tightened upon her hand which he had recaptured.

"What did you do? How have you managed?"

Marie looked at the fire.

"Spinning, weaving, making bayberry candles, hatcheling, card-ing, cooking, God knows! Somehow. Lately the struggle grew beyond bounds. Monsieur Mercier became pressing. I consented to marry for the sake of a home for myself, for the children. The nuns you saw tonight came to arrange for the children to be taken care of for a month. He wanted that much time alone with me before they came to us."

She broke off.

"The wedding is in two days' time."

"Was," Paul said.

She looked up, bewildered.

"Was," he repeated. "The wedding need not be in two days or at all unless you desire it."

He put his hand beneath his scarf and slipped it into his breeches pocket. A bag slid on the table between them.

"There!" he said. "Enough gold for a careful housekeeper to last for—how long would you say? Don't look like that! It's no worse come by than my uncle's piracy. He loots, doesn't he? And kills?"

Marie seized the bag and dropped it out of sight beneath the table. She rose and went to the window. The shutters were open. She pulled them into place, dropping the heavy bars across, securing them. Then she looked about her mistrustfully.

"There is no one here but us and the children," Paul said, "and they're asleep."

Marie sank her voice to a whisper.

"If you have any gold, hide it! They will get it from you, somehow."

"Who will?" Paul demanded.

"The Governor. The officers. The sergeant—anyone. They are all thieves here, since the old governor died. You do not know—" she opened the bag and began to count the pieces—"one, two, three—what are these? Not louis d'or."

"English money."

"But gold. Gold is gold and they will take it from you. Four, five, six—you do not know how things have been here, how they are. Seven—I am afraid for you. Eight, nine, ten. What an amount! This will last us, if we can keep it ——"

"Of course we can keep it. We will hide it in the chimney."

"No, not there. Everyone knows enough to look there."

"No one dares come into this house and search it!"

Marie did not answer at once, she was busy counting. "Fifteen, sixteen, seventeen. They will do anything if they know it is here. Does anybody know you have it?"

"Nobody." Then he remembered: "Captain Mercier."

She looked up, startled, the gold falling from her fingers. A piece rolled on the floor.

"The Merciers!" she said. "The biggest robbers of all."

Paul stooped to retrieve the sovereign.

"I am here to protect you from the Merciers, from everyone," he said quietly.

Marie looked at him tenderly, doubtfully, then with more assurance, which faded suddenly, as she looked at him.

"They have the Governor's ear," she said, despondently.

"I've noticed that, though I've only been in the town a few hours. Yes, it's very apparent, they have the Governor's ear, but why?"

Marie shrugged. "Nobody knows."

"But people, being people, surmise? What are the stories?"

"They say," she took the sovereign, putting it on top of the pile, "that Monsieur du Chambon was engaged with them in the fur trade, and that if the King knew what stuck to his fingers, it would go ill with him. They say that Captain Mercier holds the Governor's bond. The Merciers get their share of loot for sure! They took no part in the attack on Canceau, for instance, yet they got more between them than the men who did. They say—they say a lot of things."

"Hmmm," said Paul, "that explains my reception today at the fort."

"Did you see the Governor?"

"I did. I brought him news, stupendous news, firsthand. Captain Mercier discredited me. But even if he hadn't," he added in a burst of candor, "I think the result might have been the same. I handled the Governor badly. I rushed him, I urged him, I even said 'you must.' I forgot the niceties of leisurely approach. Still, Captain Mercier undoubtedly clinched the thing. He tapped his forehead."

"You came on his boat."

"And landed purse strings closed."

"Ah."

"So, though I could have told the Governor every last detail of the preparations for the invasion ——"

"Invasion!"

"Yes, the New Englanders are preparing an attack on Louisbourg."

"Here!"

"Yes, here. They are not waiting for the spring, for England's help, they are coming with an expedition to take us by surprise. I saw the transports gathering in the harbors. I saw recruits for the militia pouring in. I have details. Abbé le Loutre . . ."

"The abbé," Marie murmured, "and you know him. Tell me . . ."

Paul was brought up short by memories of his encounter with the abbé, San, his marriage, which he would have to explain. It would be difficult.

"The abbé," he said, "thought my news of prime importance, but the Governor will not hear what I have to say."

Marie made appropriate sounds of distress. She had finished counting. The sovereigns were back in their bag. She clutched it tightly while she listened. Her eyes went round the room, looking for a safe hiding place.

"We could take up a stone, I suppose."

"What?"

"Nothing. I'm sorry, I was distracted. Tell me more."

"There is no more. Somehow the Governor must be made to listen to me. The New Englanders are coming. Louisbourg must prepare."

"Yes, yes. But they would never attack us in the winter."

Paul snorted.

"They count on just such an attitude. They want to attack in the winter. They will come. Who is there in town with authority and sense?"

Marie pondered.

"The officers are not much good," she said. "There was a mutiny among the Swiss."

·[124]·

"I know of that."

"Nobody knows who is disaffected, who loyal."

"A priest?"

She shook her head.

"The church here and the hospital and the convent are supported by the Governor, the Merciers, and one or two other rich thieves who pay conscience money out of their loot, and the taxes they can screw from the rest of us. No, I can think of no one to stand up to the Governor. It is unfortunate that you should have displeased the Merciers."

"Is it?" Paul asked.

"They are very powerful," Marie said helplessly.

"Unfortunate perhaps, inevitable certainly," Paul said. "The more I hear and the more I see, the better pleased I am to have arrived in time to prevent the wedding."

Marie looked at him piteously.

"Do not jest with me," she said, putting out a hand toward him.

"No jest," Paul took her hand, "I am in earnest. You cannot marry without my permission, you know that, so does Monsieur Mercier. He shall not have it."

"They will kill you."

"I am not so easy killed." Paul said, with a fine show of confidence. Privately he resolved to find a fencing master who would give him lessons in secret. He could afford them now. "And somehow I shall get the Governor's ear. I must!"

"There is one person who might help you," Marie said slowly, "if you are really not afraid of the Merciers. And oh Paul, I must warn you, they are crafty and relentless. You are only a boy, how can you incur their enmity and escape?"

"I've incurred it anyway," said Paul, "and everything you tell me makes me glad. It is worse to have foxes like those for friends than for open enemies, and as for having them in the family— over my dead body!"

"That's what it would be."

This sobered him for a moment. He looked up at her.

"Well," he said grimly, "I am warned at any rate. Now who is this person you were talking about who could help me with the Governor?"

"Madame de Saintonge."

Paul sat back, baffled.

"What can a woman do?" he asked.

Marie laughed.

"This one, plenty," she told him. "She turns the Governor, and the whole place, come to that, round her ringed fingers. She has the temper of a thousand devils."

"Indeed," Paul said, "how charming! And she is the only person you can recommend in this emergency."

Marie laughed again.

"The best person," she said energetically. "And if the Merciers hate you, that will be a strong recommendation to her, for she hates the Merciers, and they would poison her. In fact, there are stories . . ." she broke off. "But look at you! I don't wonder the Governor threw you out. You look like a beggar, a cutthroat. We must get you some clothes." She stared at him appraisingly. "You must have better sleep tonight than you have had for a long time, my Paul. Safe home!"

She turned her cheek, he kissed it. The firelight, all they had to see by, was flickering low. Paul dragged another log from the woodpile in the corner.

"That will last the night," he said. "Good night, my little sister, better dreams."

She hesitated in the doorway.

"I hardly dare to think that the marriage . . ." she faltered, "that the marriage . . ."

"Will not take place."

"I should not let you do it."

"You cannot stop me."

A shower of sparks flew upward from the log, jerked into place. Paul went to the table, he loosened his coat, kicked off his moccasins, put them beneath his head for a pillow, laid himself down and went to sleep. He dreamed uneasily that he was engaged in a duel with a bearded monster who had seven hands and a sword in each of them. He moaned and muttered and finally awoke. When he had taken in his strange surroundings, he settled himself afresh. This time sleep came dreamlessly and deep.

CHAPTER XXXI

LOUISBOURG woke early. Long before dawn bugles could be heard at the citadel for the changing of the guard. Lanterns flickered through the streets, as here and there a fisherman slipped through the dark to see to the moorings of his boat. Candles burned in the church for the first Mass. As the early light streamed across the harbor, doors opened along the quays, children came out, muffled to the ears, blowing cloudy breath in the frosty air, taking buckets to the well. Smoke began to curl out of chimneys. Famished pigs, the scavengers of Louisbourg, started on their rounds. Dogs barked and cocks crew from attics and barns. Shutters began to fly open, nightcapped heads appeared. Day, the companionable, the reassuring, had begun. Another long winter night was over without alarm or accident. The fleur de lis floated upon the Governor's palace. Sentries saluted each other: "pass friend, all's well."

Paul woke from heavy, dreamless and refreshing sleep. A pleasant smell of breakfast pervaded the room. A draft of cold air made him sit up. It was Tomas going to the well. Paul lay down again when the door was shut, but Marie stirring coffee over the embers of last night's fire, sent the children to pull him off the table. He brushed them away and got up laughing.

"Come and put a log on the fire," Marie called, "it's too heavy now that we have a man to do it for us."

Paul complied, stretching and yawning.

"Who would have thought the table such a soft bed?" he asked.

Breakfast was quickly ready, coffee and bread, with a little of the native sweet sirup to sweeten the cups and to spread on the bread. Breakfast over, Tomas disappeared. He earned a little money looking after cattle belonging to one of the officers at the fort. Most of the soldiers, Paul learned, were allowed to get their living scattered through the town in various civilian pursuits, so long as they would muster now and then. Their pay was always in arrears. The Government of the mother country never kept the fine promises with which they were lured to enlist. Discontent, lawlessness and mutiny faced every Governor at the head of these troops.

Marie settled all the children at their tasks, Louise to spin, Andrée to card the wool, Pierre to keep the fire going and to watch the pot already simmering with the midday stew, then she turned her attention to Paul.

"This was to have been a heavy day for me," she said, "with preparations for the wedding, but I have thought it over in the night, and when Monsieur Mercier comes today I know how to tell him . . ."

"You will not have to tell him anything," Paul said, "leave that to me. Give me your time this morning. I want to go about the town and renew acquaintanceship."

"In those clothes?"

"I know," Paul said, following her glance, "perhaps I can borrow some from Monsieur Godet, till I can get some made."

Marie looked confused.

"He is taller than you," she said.

"Well, what would you advise?" Paul asked a little impatiently. "I will go to the tailor as soon as I can."

"I have a cloak here that you can borrow," Marie said. "Later we will attend to the rest."

"A man's cloak?"

"Certainly. A woman's would not suit you very well!"

"Whose cloak?"

"My uncle Pierre's, inquisitive! He left it here for me to mend. I often make extra money sewing."

"Oh."

He waited while she got her cloak and hood, put on a scarf she

·[128]·

brought him, under the cloak. They opened the door and stepped into the street. It was bitterly cold.

"I want to go everywhere," said Paul, "I want to see what the town's defenses are in the light of what I know of the attack."

Marie shook her head.

"You will get a sad surprise."

They set out together.

First he took in the harbor. It was about seven miles in circumference. Islands and reefs blocked the mouth of it, leaving only about half a mile for the passage of ships. The Royal Battery facing this opening commanded a wide sweep of the harbor and could blast at any vessel sailing in. In support of these guns, Goat Island, at the actual mouth was fortified, and could rake the enemy ships broadside. So much for the eastern defenses. The town itself lay on the west, between the harbor and the sea on a promontory, lashed on one side by the breakers of the Atlantic, washed on the other by the harbor tide. The rocky coast of Gabarus Bay formed another natural protection with its high cliffs and narrow coves. In addition to these natural advantages the French had drawn a strong line of defense across the base of the triangle of land, from the sea on one side to the harbor on the other. The ditch was about twelve hundred yards long, eighty feet wide, and from thirty to thirty-six feet deep. There was a rampart about sixty feet thick of earth faced with masonry. It sloped down to the marsh and this marsh was another of the natural advantages of the place. It stretched from the fort to Gabarus Bay, broken now and then by dry ground.

Paul was elated as he took stock of all these advantages which he surveyed from the rampart under the eyes of an indifferent Swiss sentry. But when he came to inspect the fort itself he was not so pleased. The fortress had embrasures for one hundred and forty-eight cannon, without counting its outworks, but Paul saw only seventy-six and a number of swivels. Some of the stone was already crumbling.

The guard was changed while they wandered round, with a great deal of ceremony and bugle calls. Children and a few idlers came to watch. Paul saw the officers collecting for the first levee, Monsieur Chauvert among them. They walked across the courtyard to the ordinance. A few richly dressed gentlemen in civilian clothes went gravely forward. Marie plucked at Paul's arm.

"Let us turn away," she whispered.

Paul following the direction of her eyes saw Monsieur Mercier and his brother, the Captain, advancing pompously behind the rest.

He turned his back, obligingly.

"I have seen enough, let us go home."

He took her arm and they disappeared together by the south gate.

CHAPTER XXXII

WHEN they got home they found the children all excited. Pierre had been to the south gate and as far as Black Point with three other boys. From there he had seen Captain de Morpain's barque, the *Oiseau de Mer*, making for port.

"He'll be here in an hour," Pierre piped, "with this wind and this tide."

Paul smiled at his eagerness. Marie was delighted.

"That will make things easier," she said. "You'll have two strings to your bow. L'Oncle Pierre can present you to the Governor. He stands high as a corsair and just now he is Capitaine de Port. That's the only reason we managed to survive through the hard years, we had his protection. You remember him Paul."

"Very well. I was jealous of him for father's sake and for *La Belle Louise*."

"He stands high with the lady, too," she murmured in a lower tone, "or did. You will have to navigate those shoals with care."

"It strikes me that you know too much."

"It's because I've been poor," Marie told him gravely. "The poor are not protected from life itself, let alone from hearing about it."

"That's true. Well, it can be an advantage. People looking at our young and innocent faces will think us guileless and easy to cheat, but all the time we conceal ineffable depths of depravity and knowledge of the world." Paul's eyes were twinkling. Marie twinkled back.

"We had better go down to the quay and watch him dock," she said.

"Where's he coming from?"

"Quebec."

"Oh." Paul was disappointed. "I hoped he might have come from Boston and seen something of the preparations there. He could support my story."

"He will support you," Marie said, "if you can convince him."

"Perhaps they've heard something of it in Quebec."

It was stiller than usual for a winter afternoon, the sea had subsided somewhat when the *Oiseau de Mer* came in. She rounded the Island, all sails set. A murmur rose from the watching crowd gathered by magic to see her come in. Anyone but Pierre de Morpain would have shortened sail for that narrow, dangerous passage and worked her in under less canvas. Pierre de Morpain was a showman. His barque was the best kept on the seas, his crew hand-picked. Among them there were several Micmacs. He knew to a hair's breadth what could be done with crew and craft. His spectacular entry into the harbor looked casual enough, a piece of foolhardy daring. Actually it was the result of precise calculation and weeks of steady work. The *Oiseau de Mer* rounded to in the wide waters of the harbor, came into the wind, groped for the best anchorage, the sails were clewed up and furled, the anchor splashed overboard. The gleaming cannon fired a salute which shook the houses on the quay.

"Ah," said the delighted crowd as the *Oiseau de Mer* came to rest, and the longboat was lowered. They could see the Captain climbing into it, gold lace, white wig, silk coat and gleaming silver sword. Captain de Morpain was a dandy, who dressed better than the Governor, and was more popular, having that touch of pirate about him that all Louisbourg loved. The longboat manned by his Indian crew, cheerfully half-naked to the winter cold, pulled expertly and rapidly to the first wharf. The Captain landed gracefully and started to walk away. The crowd surrounded him. He brushed them aside a little impatiently, answering the stream of questions with a smile and shrug.

"Later on," he said, "later on I will give you the news, at Saulnier's tavern."

·[132]·

The crowd fell back. Marie and Paul came forward to meet him. He stopped in front of her.

"Prettier than ever," he said, kissing her hand. "And who is this—wearing what looks like my cloak?"

Paul explained himself. Marie commented, the children nodded and smiled.

"You look like your father," de Morpain said, bringing his hand down upon Paul's shoulder. "He was a fine man. We heard that you were killed with him. And so you escaped the New Englanders?"

"Uncle," said Marie, "we need you at home as soon as you are at liberty. Paul has grave news to discuss with you. He needs your help."

"So! And when is the wedding to be?"

"It is canceled," said Paul.

Marie blushed and smiled.

"So!" said de Morpain again. He turned away. Marie called after him anxiously: "You will come?"

De Morpain waved his three-cornered hat, replacing it jauntily on the white curls. He strode away.

"He is a very elegant figure of a man," Paul thought to himself, "but not a patch on my father."

Marie took his arm. They all went back to the house.

"Now," Marie said, "we must find some means of getting you suitably dressed. Perhaps my uncle has brought something with him from Quebec, that we can buy from him."

"Judging from his crew," Paul said laughing, "they do not seem to go in for clothes very much on the *Oiseau de Mer*. Imagine sailing naked in the winter! Brrrrr!"

"Oh, savages!" Marie said with contempt. "They're not human enough to feel the cold, not even as human as an animal."

A strange discomfort came to Paul. He had a savage wife. The more he thought of that affair, the more incomprehensible it seemed that he should have let himself be duped by a fanatical priest into marrying San because he wanted her. Other white men, yes, and priests among them, took Indian women whenever they chose without marrying them. There was something touching about San. Her honesty and her devotion were appealing. She

·[133]·

was exciting physically. He smiled at memories. But after all, a wife! He wondered how she was, whether her wound had healed as well as it should, and when he would have news of her. Marie was speaking, he had not heard what she said, but he gathered it was something to do with his attire.

"Perhaps a gold piece or two would solve the thing," he said. "After all I must have clothes, though with the coming of my uncle perhaps I do not need to cock-a-doodle quite so much to please the Governor."

Marie laughed.

"Didn't you see what he wore?" she asked. "If you had come to me first instead of to the Governor, you might have had a better hearing."

Paul snorted. "Imagine the safety of a town depending upon a pair of breeches and a man's stupid moods."

"Or a woman's. You are forgetting Madame de Saintonge."

"Pah!"

"And how about the ribbons of the King's mistresses?" Marie inquired. "I have heard stories of how a well-turned compliment to the right woman at the right moment had helped more than one minister in his career; flattery in France and here does everything."

"Hush," said Paul, "high treason."

Marie looked about her uneasily, then she laughed. "Now that you've come home it will be a wonder if we don't both get into trouble."

"Let it be together," Paul said twinkling. "God knows we must stir up the garrison somehow to its defense. I will not be a prisoner again, nor see you taken, either, and Louisbourg"—he waved his hand—"deserves to survive. It's the doorway to Canada, which the Governor must have forgotten, but the New Englanders haven't. Whoever takes it, takes the river, and whoever takes the river can take Quebec. It is bad enough to have lost Port Royal, to lose Louisbourg would be criminal folly."

"Dear, you must go to the tailor," Marie said.

CHAPTER XXXIII

PAUL presented himself at three o'clock outside the Chateau St. Louis. He found his uncle there conversing with a gentleman whom he introduced as Monsieur le Commissaire-Ordonnateur François Bigot. Paul bowed as low as he dared. His new clothes were too tight and would have to be sent back for alteration when the occasion for which he had ordered them was over. Monsieur Bigot, like everybody else, seemed to be on excellent terms with his uncle. What a good thing it was that he had arrived so providentially.

They crossed the drawbridge over the moat, passed the chapel on the left. A service was in progress, the three men crossed themselves absent-mindedly, turning toward the Governor's apartments, beyond and above. A great deal of activity was going on in the barracks and the officers' quarters to their right. Paul wondered for a moment, so loud the noise became, whether another mutiny had broken out. Neither his uncle nor the Commissaire-Ordonnateur paid any attention to the disturbance. They walked on together talking about some repairs to the lighthouse tower which Morpain insisted should be done while Bigot maintained that it would be better to put the light out altogether and force such reckless buccaneers as those who sailed in the *Oiseau de Mer* to come in slowly, reasonably, like the rest of the world. Both men laughed. Paul joined in. They reached the Governor's anteroom. Here they found a sentry and came to a halt while he announced them to the officer within. An interminable wait followed. The sentry returned. All four men stood in silence. There was a bench in the anteroom, but no one used it. They preferred to stand, rocking a little on their feet as though they were at sea.

Paul felt more uncomfortable this time, in spite of his good clothes, than he had when he arrived, impetuously full of his important news. He could not help wondering about the success of his mission. He had written out laboriously, with Marie's help, all that he had seen in Boston and along the coast before his escape, and all that he had heard of the preparations from Will Vaughan. If the Governor read it, it should make him at least conscious of the gravity of the situation. Paul stirred uneasily, looking at his companions. They did not seem the sort of men in whom he could have confidence. His uncle was disappointingly lighthearted and lightheaded, while Bigot was one of those dark horses one could not depend upon in an emergency.

Suddenly the door behind the sentry opened for a moment, there was a sound of laughter and raised voices. The door opened farther, the sentry saluted and stood aside, two women swept out, accompanied by an officer. Monsieur Bigot and Captain de Morpain bowed gallantly. Paul, caught unawares, found himself staring as the lady nearest him sank in a curtsy. Her eyes were fixed upon his. They were curious, mocking, provocative.

Captain de Morpain stepped forward.

"Madame," he said, "permit me to present my nephew. Paul, this is Madame de Saintonge."

"Phew!" Paul thought to himself. "So that is the Saintonge. Heaven help the Governor, my uncle, and, yes, me!"

She rose from her curtsy and he from his bow.

"My dear Pierre," she said, "he is the image of you. Bring him to see me."

She put her hand on the other woman's arm, without troubling to present her.

"A companion," Paul thought. He was embarrassed for her. She should have been presented.

The officer with them fixed Paul with a cold stare, nodded to Captain de Morpain, saluted Monsieur Bigot deferentially and went his way in the wake of the ladies. The three men looked after them thoughtfully, the same smile was on their lips.

"The Governor will see you now," the sentry said.

·[136]·

The first thing that Paul noticed when he entered the Governor's room was that Monsieur du Chambon was in a rage. He made very little effort to disguise it, tapping with his fingers on the table, nodding and jerking his head. He acknowledged the greetings of the three men curtly and left them standing in front of him.

"Back again, Captain de Morpain, I see," he said unsmilingly, "and you have brought the young man who claims to be your nephew with you."

"He is my nephew."

"He has paid his respects to me once," the Governor continued, waving the interruption aside, "with a cock-and-bull story of an attack on Louisbourg. The New Englanders have been preparing to attack us ever since the town was built. They seem to have taken your nephew in with their talk while he was among them. Perhaps a year at sea would do him good—clear his head of fables."

Paul blushed hotly; he began to stammer something. Before he could make himself heard Monsieur Bigot spoke.

"Since the attack on Canceau," he said, "the temper in New England has been different toward us. They learned of the war in Europe later than we did. They have always hated us on account of the fishing trade and such marauders as this." He put his hand on Captain de Morpain's shoulder. "We have harried them lately till they see red. I do not believe that they would be so mad as to attack us before the summer. Our fleet can take care of them then. But there may be something in what the boy says. It should be looked into, monseigneur."

Paul was astonished, he had expected his uncle to say a few words of halfhearted defense on his behalf, but not the Commissaire-Ordonnateur. He smiled at him gratefully, and looked at the Governor, who frowned.

"Indeed, Monsieur Bigot," he said dryly, "you must allow me to be the judge of that."

"I have prepared a paper," Paul ventured, "for your perusal."

He laid the document in front of the Governor and stepped backward, bowing. The Governor took the paper up and put it to one side. Captain de Morpain cleared his throat.

"On that last cargo that I brought," he said. . . .

They went into a long and complicated discussion. Paul shifted his feet and stared at the floor. Then he raised his eyes and looked at Monsieur du Chambon appraisingly. Was it possible that the fate of a town, of a settlement, of a whole colony perhaps, rested in the hands of such a shortsighted, self-satisfied, uncertain fool?

"I'll try the lady," he thought, "she'll put pressure on him. Something must be done."

He fidgeted. His uncle spoke of fur. The Governor listened greedily. There was contempt in Monsieur Bigot's eyes. The audience came to an end.

CHAPTER XXXIV

A S PAUL left the Governor's apartment he turned his mind
to the next errand on his list. It was the pleasurable but
hazardous one of calling upon Monsieur Mercier to explain to him why the wedding, postponed for a week, would not
take place at all. He was crossing the courtyard toward the drawbridge when Monsieur Mercier emerged from the chapel, talking
cheerfully to a priest. They both stopped at the sight of Paul. The
priest blessed him, Monsieur Mercier gave him a stiff bow. Paul
went up to them, his hands turning clammy by his sides.

"I was on my way to your house, Monsieur," he said, "to tell
you that my sister's wedding with you will not take place. After
giving the matter full thought, I have decided to withhold my
permission indefinitely."

Monsieur Mercier flushed a dark red and took a step forward.
"Why you insolent villain," he spluttered. "How dare you?"

"It is nothing personal, Monsieur," Paul began.

Monsieur Mercier looked as though he would burst. The priest
laid a restraining hand upon his arm.

"He is within his rights," he murmured.

Monsieur Mercier tried to control himself.

"Give me your reasons," he said with an effort.

Paul looked him up and down without replying. The silence
and the tension grew. Monsieur Mercier was the first to break it.
He raised his hand and struck Paul in the face. Blinded with rage,
Paul fumbled for his sword, drew it and put himself on guard.

Monsieur Mercier, more skillful, had his out on the instant. The priest threw himself between them with a cry of distress.

"It is forbidden to fight in the precincts of the fort!"

Paul paid no attention, concentrating on what he had learned, but Monsieur Mercier lowered his sword an instant, motioning toward the town. Paul lowered his and followed him to a place on the quays. He was thinking grimly:

"Well, here it is. What a fool I was to get into this. I shouldn't have challenged him. That's what he wanted, of course. He'll make mincemeat of me. If he kills me he'll marry Marie." Then he pulled himself together. "Oh, well, I can do my best. I've had a week to practice in and fourteen lessons, two a day. I'm as good now as I'll ever be, and I'm in practice such as it is. Have at him! I commend myself to God."

They set to. Children hearing the clash of steel ran toward them. A crowd formed. Men and women came out of the nearest houses, fashionable strollers on the promenade by the sea, hurried forward, until they stood in a circle, calling out encouragement to both sides.

From the start Paul knew what sort of fighter his enemy would be. He cursed his years as prisoner of war without a sword. He was clumsy and inept. Monsieur Mercier knew it, for he was smiling disdainfully, fighting with a grace and precision that made Paul look like an awkward lout. He was sweating freely, while Monsieur Mercier never turned a hair. The most he could do was to stave off the coup de grâce for as long as he could. Poor Marie!

Then Monsieur Mercier's foot slipped on a cobblestone. Paul knocked the sword out of his hand.

"Ah!" went up from the crowd. Monsieur Mercier stooped sulkily to retrieve it. But Paul recovering from his astonishment, seized his opportunity.

He turned to the crowd.

"He struck me," he called out. "I have knocked the sword out of his hand. My honor is satisfied." He sheathed his sword and started to walk away without looking back at his enemy. The crowd made way for him.

"I would too," a man called out, "if I were in your boots!"

There were snickers, and a few more comments of the same

nature. Nobody had been fooled by the contest. It was obvious that only a cobblestone had saved Paul from being defeated.

They had fought without seconds, there was therefore nobody to arbitrate, and Paul was in his right to accept the satisfaction of disarming Monsieur Mercier.

"Phew!" he said to himself, trying hard not to run, before Monsieur Mercier could insult him again and bring the thing to a more logical conclusion. He was shaking now from the knees downward, and his face was pea green, or so he imagined. But some of the crowd were following him home, and he endeavored to walk jauntily.

Marie came running out, she drew him into the house and shut the door in the curious faces pressing after him.

"Well?" she asked.

Paul disengaged himself and struggled out of his coat.

"Ah," he said with relief as he got rid of it and stood up in his shirt. "I was too hot. That's better. Well, I canceled the marriage in front of a priest, the priest who was to marry you, I believe. Monsieur Mercier struck me, I fought with him, knocked the sword out of his hand, and here I am."

Marie gasped and turned white.

"Oh, Paul," she said, putting her hands out anxiously, "he didn't . . . you aren't . . . ?"

"He didn't kill me, since I am here. He didn't even hurt me. But he would have killed me if it hadn't been for a loose cobblestone, and that's the truth. I know it, and he knows it."

"He will hate you now," Marie said slowly.

"He hated me before," Paul answered lightly. "It's in the open now. The point is that you don't have to marry him."

"Oh, Paul, he'll try again. He'll get you into a trap. He'll have you murdered!"

"I thought of all that while I was fighting him," Paul said, "and I thought of what might happen to you. Listen to me, Marie, these are my orders. If anything happens to me, you are to take the money in the cache and put yourself under Monsieur Godet's protection."

"Monsieur Godet!"

"Yes, and no false modesty about it. He's a good fellow, he

can swing a sword as well as the next man. I'm confident he will look after you, and I hereby appoint him guardian of you and the children."

"Have you consulted Monsieur Godet about this guardianship?" Marie asked demurely.

"No, but I've an idea he won't refuse!"

He looked at her and laughed. She turned away but not before he had caught her eyes, and they had twinkled back at him.

"What happened with the Governor?" she asked, to change the subject.

Paul shrugged.

"He paid no attention. I left the paper there, but I don't believe he will look at it. And all the time the New Englanders are arming. It's incredible. I saw the Saintonge, though, she was coming out as we went in. Quite a fascinator. Her eyes troubled me so that I saw nothing else."

Marie laughed.

"I told you," she said, "that she was a force to be reckoned with. She's troubled many men, better men than you."

"Who?" Paul demanded.

Marie laughed again.

"It would be a long list. You had better ask her yourself when you know her well enough. And you'd better take care or you'll find yourself involved. Perhaps she will even decide to marry again and settle down with you."

"No fear of that. I'm a ma——" Paul stopped. He had been about to say "a married man." But there was no need to spring that yet. He had a feeling it would not appeal to Marie. "I'm a man who knows his own mind," he finished instead.

"She holds her salon this afternoon. Monsieur Bigot will be there. He could present you. I shouldn't ask my uncle. . . ."

"But he did," Paul said. "I know the lady now. I think I shall call on her."

"You will find a number of people there dancing attendance if you do. The Marquis de Vaudreuil-Cavagnal, for one, Monsieur Vauquelin for another. Get them to back your story to the Governor."

Paul nodded. There was a scratching at the door. Andrée

opened it. Two Indians stood outside, with the crowd pressing about them eager to know what their coming meant. Paul drew them in and shut the door. They stood upright in the low-ceilinged kitchen, reciting their message together.

"The Black Father sent us."

"That's le Loutre," Paul said to Marie.

"To tell you to prepare quickly, the New Englanders are on the march. He has sent the news to Quebec. He says never has such a force set out."

Paul nodded.

"Go to the Governor," he said, "tell him the tale, but first, how did the Black Father escape from the Iroquois? Have you any news of my—" he checked himself, "of San, the girl who was with me?"

They shook their heads.

"The Black Father," said one of them, "slipped through the forest and went to Shubenacadie. Then he sent us here when the message came from our brothers near Boston, who are his ears. What shall we take back to him?"

"Say I raised my voice and it is not heard," Paul said. "Say there is folly here and confusion, but the walls are good and the people will fight. It is the leaders who are asleep."

The Indians grunted.

"Tell him he should be here to arouse them."

The Indians grunted again.

"Tell him what the Governor says when you give him your message."

He made the sign of farewell. The children's eyes, watching him, grew rounder, they let out their breath slowly in admiration. The Micmacs bowed, stepped backward, and slipped into the street. They pushed their way through the crowd, disregarding its clumsy curiosity. They disappeared in the direction of the citadel.

Marie went to the window and threw the shutters wide, letting a freezing air sweep through the room.

"I hate savages," she said.

There was a chorus of assent from the children.

"How did you know how to talk to them?" Louise demanded.
Paul smiled with averted eyes.

"I have had more to do with savages than you have," he said
quietly. "There is much about them that is interesting and fine."

"They are no better than animals," Marie said, "not as good
as some animals, cows for instance."

"They are better than we are," Paul insisted, "in many ways."
Marie shook her head.

"We are gods compared to them," she said. "We are the superior race, and they the inferior. I saw and heard enough about
them when I went to school at the Recollet Convent. And when
you think of the death of the martyrs Jean de Brébeuf and
Gabriel Lalemant . . ."

She crossed herself.

"They were killed by the Iroquois," Paul said.

"Everyone knows," Tomas piped up, "that the Iroquois are
crueler than the rest."

"I do not like talk of superior races and inferior races," Paul
said, "we shall never advance with such ideas as that."

Marie shrugged. Men were so illogical in their talk over perfectly obvious things. Advance where? She began to brush Paul's
wig in its three-cornered hat. As she brushed, she thought: "I wish
I could go to the reception with him. I should like to dance in a
silk dress. But he will do better alone, and I have no clothes. There
is the gold . . ." her eye went to a stone in the wall. It looked no
different from the other stones. She smiled, it was good to know
that it was there, even if she must not buy a dress with it. That
would be wicked. It was the family nest egg, for all of them if
anything should happen to Paul. She looked at him anxiously.
Could he steer his way through all the complications of Louisbourg society with so many enemies? He was so young. She
smiled, suddenly, a strange secret smile as she thought of what he
had said: "Put yourself under Monsieur Godet's protection." If
only . . . if only . . . she paused with the brush in her hand,
then suddenly she put it down as though it burned her, and hung
the wig upon its nail.

CHAPTER XXXV

THE salle de réception in Madame de Saintonge's house was a good-sized room on the ground floor. It was furnished more simply than the rest of the house, and the furniture could be quickly carried away to make room for dancing.

Madame de Saintonge was dissatisfied with it this afternoon. She changed two chairs around, pushed the harpsichord farther into the room, sat down before it, sweeping her skirts becomingly about her, played two chords, pushed the instrument away petulantly and stood up. She was bored. It was becoming a chronic malady lately, this ennui of hers. Almost everything bored her, the strutting pomposity of the fort and all that went on there, the Governor's fussiness, Captain de Morpain's bragging, the priest's narrow piety, and the color of the ribbons on her new dress. She had ordered green but they came pink. It was very provoking and just like life. She was sick of it. If only she could go to France or to Quebec—Quebec had much more scope for a woman who wasn't positively ugly. Here she looked at herself in the Louis XIV mirror, smiled, grimaced and turned away. But that was the way things went. She was penned up here for the time being, nothing ever happened, except such mild scandal as she could provide without going inconveniently far. Men were such fools. It was no longer any fun to play them off, one against the other. She sighed and tapped her foot. Usually she looked forward to the day she held her salon as a distraction and amusement. People came, paid compliments and went away. Today she wished they would not come at all. She sighed again and got up restlessly to move about.

The door opened, a footman, one of the soldiers at the fort, drafted for this service came in.

"Monsieur Bigot is here with a gentleman," he announced.

She tapped her foot. She could never get this oaf to address her properly. It was no use correcting him, he went from insolence to insolence, but she had not paid him for five months. She let it pass. The soldier stood aside and the two men came in. She sank in a curtsy as Monsieur Bigot bowed over her hand, her eyes strayed to Paul.

"I expected your uncle, Monsieur de Morpain," she said, as he saluted her. "Where is he?"

"On the *Oiseau de Mer*, getting her ready for action."

"Action? Is he going to the war?"

"No, Madame, the war is coming here."

"Monsieur de Morpain believes that the New Englanders are on their way to attack us," Bigot said. "Two Indians arrived today with the same story."

"How curious, what makes you think so?"

"When I was a prisoner of war," Paul said, taking advantage of this opening, "I saw the preparations well upon their way. I escaped to warn the colony. Abbé le Loutre . . ."

"Oh, wherever there is fighting one can be sure of finding that follower of the Prince of Peace in the thick of it. I would not credit him with anything but intrigue. So he thinks the New Englanders are coming. In the spring, I suppose?"

"They are on their way now," Paul repeated patiently, "and we are preparing for them by doing nothing. We deserve to lose the place and we probably shall."

Madame de Saintonge looked at him thoughtfully, "I suppose you want to rouse the Governor and have him summon the soldiers from all the useful things they are doing now, to stand to their guns and wait."

Paul shrugged.

"They would not have to wait long," he said.

The door opened again. The flunkey announced:

"Monsieur le Marquis et Madame la Marquise de Vaudreuil-

Cavagnal, Monsieur et Madame Forant, Monsieur et Madame Vauquelin."

The room was filled with curtsying ladies and gentlemen bent double. Paul stood aside, conscious that for all his new clothes, he cut a poor figure among them. The servant entered with another footman, bearing wine and cakes. Paul disliked the ceremony of drinking in public. He was sure to be caught for a toast with his tankard empty, or to have his mouth full of cake and have to drink and choke upon the drink. Cake was sticky, it made crumbs, he detested it.

"Give me," he thought, "a good tavern table with my legs stretched out beneath it, and a bowl of hot wine before me. I hate these fal-lals."

A sense of defeat and a sudden craving for the clean air outside came to Paul as he breathed the musk and patchouli rising about him from the ladies' flounces and wigs. Madame de Saintonge caught his eyes and held them with her own.

"She is beautiful," Paul thought, taking in the curve of her naked shoulders, the hollow between her breasts where they showed, pushed up by her velvet dress. Her arms were beautiful too. So no doubt was the rest; disturbing at any rate. He smiled. She smiled back, inviting him to her side. Then as he did not come, she broke off her discussion with the Marquise, set down her wine untasted and said:

"Let us start the dancing early today. I call for a minuet."

She crossed the room to Paul.

"I accept to dance with you, Monsieur," she said.

Paul opened his mouth, closed it again, and took her hand in his. He felt his cheeks burning fiery red as all the men looked at him.

"This will never do," he said to himself. "You may feel like a fool, but the woman is disturbing and beautiful, and can influence the Governor."

He summoned all his resources to make an impression on her. There began an exchange of glances, a language of eloquent looks and silent pressure of one hand upon another, of little motions toward and little gestures away, of blushes and a fan skillfully used to conceal them, of feet advancing a little too near and feet retreating a little too late, of music hummed toward an ear, of all the age-old, delightful, disturbing moves in the game of love, lightly entered into. It was a game Paul had often watched, and sometimes played. He felt more experienced in this field, and rose to the occasion.

The minuet came to an end. Both dancers breathed too fast. Madame de Saintonge moved away from Paul. Her carriage had the old insolence but there was a change. She was no longer bored.

PART FOUR
THE SIEGE OF LOUISBOURG 1745

CHAPTER XXXVI

THE weather changed in March; a mild winter became severe. Louisbourg shivered in the grip of a sudden frost. Ice formed in the harbor, making landing impossible; houses creaked, whined and snapped at night. Fires lost half their heat. People went about morosely, muffled against the cold. After the false thaw it was harder to bear.

The children in the town took to skating, sliding and to making bonfires on the ice. This was forbidden as every stick of fuel was precious, but the fires started, no one could tell how. The regulars in the garrison grumbled. Quarters were cold, sentries suffered from frozen feet, discontent and mutiny were once more in the air.

Paul was unconscious of much that went on about him. He was living in a world of his own, a little blurred, a little misty, full of strange lights and one large star. Freedom! To be a man among men again, with a place in the community, and a sword to defend that place (even if one tripped over it sometimes, even if one had to take lessons from a fencing master on the sly). He continued to live in his sister's house, transformed from poverty to decent comfort. He took the head of the table at family meals. More often than not Charles Godet contrived to be there, and then Marie was animated and grave by turns, unlike herself. Paul was sympathetic to their love affair. Godet and he understood each other well. Godet would protect Marie and the children if the Merciers or one of their friends succeeded in murdering Paul. He did not care about that. He was enjoying life too thoroughly to believe in death, to believe in anything but Paul de Morpain, walking the streets in his own sweet skin. Nothing else mattered, not even Hortense. She was Hortense to him now, the disturbing Madame de Saintonge. She was Hortense, but still mysterious. She held him at arm's length until he felt that she must be indifferent, then suddenly she was in his arms. She was brilliant and witty so that her brain provoked him until he looked at her and saw that she was smiling and was his.

It was exhilarating to know that several people hated him on account of her. He was playing with fire. He justified it to himself when he bothered to think about it at all, by saying that she was influential with the Governor and was pushing him into preparations for the defense of Louisbourg. She believed in it. There was a chance that she might convince Monsieur du Chambon before it was too late.

Day by day Paul walked with her in the morning watching the words they spoke form and dissolve in the biting air like smoke. He discovered ways of telling her that he loved her without saying it in words. They walked back slowly over the powdered snow together with the wind tearing at their cheeks, tugging at her hood. Paul relinquished her at the door with formal courtesy, retreating through the groups of men and women emerging to walk upon the promenade for the fashionable hour, and so home. These were the mornings. In the afternoons he called more formally as early as he dared, snatching time alone with her before more callers came. Sometimes they played together and she sang. She had a low, deep voice, untrained, husky. He found it curiously moving. They sat before the fire, discussing everything: the books that had come from France in the fall; the manners of Boston as he had observed them when he was there; Paris and the Court as she knew them; Quebec; the coming attack on Louisbourg; Paul's part in it; the command his uncle offered him on the *Oiseau de Mer* when the ice broke and she was free to sail. His uncle did not believe the New Englanders would come, but he was preparing in case. He had no use for the Governor's indecision, his weak obstinacy, nor had Monsieur Bigot.

"If Monsieur de Quesnel were here," he said, "it would be a different story."

·[152]·

Paul believed that, but even the urgency of the attack did not come home to him now. He felt so strong in his new-found freedom that he could defend the place by himself. The five hundred and sixty regular troops, the fourteen hundred militia, seemed walking shadows, not flesh and blood of the same substance as himself. So were the enemy, shadows that he could push out of the way.

This exaltation faded abruptly and he came out of his dream when on March 25 the garrison sighted an enemy fleet hovering off the mouth of the harbor. The Governor became alarmed at last and summoned a meeting of his officers. Monsieur Bigot was there. He reported what happened to Madame de Saintonge who repeated it to Paul. Since the mutiny of Karrer's Swiss Company which carried the six French Companies of Marines with them, the officers dared to command only routine services. The town was really in the hands of the mutineers. Their demands of pay for work on the fortifications, firewood, clothing and food, had been granted, but whether they would fight was another matter. Monsieur du Chambon summoned them on parade and harangued them there.

"Men," he cried, "the enemy fleet is in sight. An attack on the town is planned. If you will return to your posts and do your duty loyally to our King, I promise pardon for all who took part in the mutiny."

The men were dismissed. They stood to their posts. The next day the enemy sails could not be seen. Some of the officers ridiculed the idea of an attack. The town went back to its inertia. For a month the sails stood off and on at the harbor mouth while Louisbourg alternately alarmed and reassured did nothing to prepare itself. Then the blow fell.

CHAPTER XXXVII

CANNONS bóomed across the bay, the bells of Louisbourg rang out, doors flew open, men caught up their muskets and ran to join the militia, struggling to their wartime stations with the mutineers. Women, catching up their shawls, ran out to see what was happening. Children clambered up walls and on roofs, crying shrilly that they saw a fleet, a great fleet of transports, boats were being lowered, the New Englanders had come, they were making for Pointe Platte.

Paul was with his uncle and the Governor. They heard the commotion and sprang to their feet. A breathless young officer rushed in to report. The Governor turned pale.

"Monsieur de Morpain," he said, "take what men you can to beat them off. Monsieur de la Boularderie is on watch with forty men. He will join you."

Pierre de Morpain turned to Paul.

"Go and find the contremaître of the *Oiseau de Mer*. Tell him to assemble and arm the crew and to join me at the southern gate."

Paul ran from the room. In his haste he forgot to gather up his sword. It got in his way, he tripped, blundered down some steps and stumbled at the door of a little salon. It opened. A girl was seated there, writing at an écritoire as though no unaccustomed din were sounding round her. She looked up, startled. Paul picked himself up, annoyed at his clumsiness, and shot her an angry glance. But she was not laughing. She looked at him gravely.

"Mademoiselle," he bowed.

It was the Governor's daughter. He recognized her now although he was not conscious of where he had seen her before. She turned to him.

"Monsieur?"

"I must excuse myself. The attack has come."

"I know."

"I am going to get some men to oppose the landing."

She put out her hand.

"Come back safely, Monsieur de Morpain."

"Thank you, Mademoiselle."

He hesitated. Then he stepped to the door. She rose and stood looking at him. He gathered the sword in his left hand and shifted his cloak. The movement swept a scarf from the table. It fell at his feet. He stooped to retrieve it. A sudden mood came over him. Perhaps it was the seriousness of the girl's attitude or her unsmiling face. He had a desire to shock her out of her calm.

"I'll keep this for luck," he said. "It's yours, isn't it?"

He stuffed it into his breast pocket. She looked startled. She looked furious. He laughed.

"Au revoir, Mademoiselle," he said, dashing out.

The streets were full of hurrying men with all sorts of weapons hastily snatched up. Paul ran to the quays and had the luck to find the longboat from the *Oiseau de Mer* just landing with the contremaître and some of the crew. The rest was a wild rush, till they caught up with Pierre de Morpain. Then they all hurried toward Pointe Platte, drawing swords and priming pistols as they ran.

The surf was breaking high along the shore. A strong current ran. It was only a few days since the ice had melted and the floating blocks that lined the coast had disappeared.

"A pity," Paul thought, taking in the scene. "The ice would have made landing impossible and protected us." It had in fact kept the expedition in Canceau for a month.

The boats came on, loaded with grim staring men clutching their muskets. Some of them tried to take aim, in spite of the heaving, tossing sea, and their distance from the shore. An officer shouted, brandishing his sword. Cheering rolled from boat to boat as the men leaned forward, straining eagerly toward a landing. French and Micmac sailors rallied to meet this onrush which outnumbered them. Suddenly the boats sheered off. The flagship behind them was running up a signal. They began to pull away.

"Ah!" Pierre de Morpain breathed his satisfaction. "We have frightened them off. No landing this time."

But as they watched in grim relief, the boats were joined by others and the united party of about a hundred men pulled for another landing place farther up the bay.

"They are going to the Anse de la Coromandière!"

"En avant!"

The watchers needed no urging, but two miles is a long way to run over rough country; the boats had less distance to travel by sea. They beached before even the swift Micmacs could get there, and the New Englanders had time to land, and load, gather themselves together, and rush upon the French. Monsieur de la Boularderie was wounded twice and taken prisoner. Paul found himself penned between his uncle and a brawny New Englander with a long twisted face and a red beard. He kept him at sword's point—luckily this was no Monsieur Mercier—panting and swearing. Sweat poured down his face, though it was cold. He saw two men go down in front of him, dying horribly, their faces turned toward him in astonishment. He set his teeth, concentrating upon his opponent. More and more men dashed through the surf, not waiting for their boats to beach. More boats came behind them. Pierre de Morpain signaled to a bugler to sound the retreat. They began to back away from the New Englanders, leaving sixteen dead and many prisoners. The enemy did not follow. They were busy with the work of landing the expedition now that the way was clear. Discouraged, tired, dismayed, the little party of French retreated to Louisbourg with their bad news: the enemy had landed.

"We must set fire to these houses," Pierre de Morpain said when they reached the town. "Nothing outside the walls must be left for the enemy's advantage. They could take cover here. You must take charge of it, Paul, with Monsieur de la Boularderie's men. I am going to the Governor."

Paul grunted. Monsieur de la Boularderie's men were a rough-looking lot, and the task a distasteful one.

"Here," he cried out gruffly to a peasant and his wife, taking a table out of the first house, "we cannot wait for you to get that stuff out of here. The New Englanders are coming and the house must be ablaze. All these houses must be ablaze within the hour. You should have built within the town. Now there is nothing for it but to lose your homes. Come now, come, it's better than losing your lives. Hé, grandmother, and the little ones too! You can go to the convent; they will take you in there. Hurry, set it alight, men, and along to the next one—quick!"

The men hesitated, loath to destroy the work of years, at a stranger's order. Each man was thinking of his own home. The peasants seeing them hesitate, began to call out to them not to obey, to leave them alone, to go away. Paul signed to the Micmacs. They performed miracles. Seventeen houses were burning fiercely before he turned with his company of sullen soldiers and excited savages toward the gate, followed by a procession of stricken families, beggared of all they owned, carrying a strange assortment of treasures snatched from the flames. A sentry closed the gate behind the last straggler and set the heavy bars in place.

"Now to the fort," Paul commanded. He wiped his forehead. Suddenly he realized what he was wiping it with—the scarf he had picked up in the Governor's salon. He laughed a little dryly, remembering the angry eyes of the Governor's daughter.

"Well, it brought me luck," he said.

CHAPTER XXXVIII

NIGHT fell over Louisbourg, but the town was uneasy. Men and women returned to their houses, shut and bolted their doors, sat down and looked at each other in the firelight, across the children's heads.

"Remember the marsh," they said; "they cannot get across that. Reinforcements will come."

At the fort all was bustle and movement. The Governor was holding a conference.

"I have here a dispatch from Captain Thierry, commanding the Royal Battery. He advises that the guns shall be spiked and the works blown up. The battery's defenses are in bad condition and the four hundred men posted there cannot stand against three or four thousand of the enemy."

"It will be best not to split our defenses," Monsieur de Forant agreed, "but to concentrate upon the town and let the battery go. I am in favor of adopting Captain Thierry's advice."

Monsieur Bigot raised his voice.

"Should we abandon a battery of thirty cannon which has cost the King immense sums, before it is attacked?"

Monsieur de Morpain protested with him.

"Not a shot has yet been fired at the battery, which the enemy cannot take except by making regular approaches, as if against the town itself, and by besieging it in form."*

"It could have been prepared," Monsieur Bigot pointed out, "and a valiant man would make shift to prepare it now."

The Governor frowned.

"Captain Thierry is not here to defend his advice," he said dryly, "it so happens that I agree with it. If any man takes this as an indication that I am lacking in valor, I am ready to meet him." He raised his hand. "I put the matter to the vote."

Monsieur Forant and Monsieur Bigot having made their objections heard, did not think a duel would improve the situation. They voted with the majority. The decision went through to abandon the battery as quickly as possible, call the garrison home and have the defenses of the town itself strengthened by this addition of four hundred men who were not mutineers. Paul, sitting restlessly beside his uncle at the Council, admitted there as secretary and messenger between his uncle and the *Oiseau de Mer*, was shocked out of his fatigue when he heard the decision and further affronted when the Governor ordered him to take a crew and row to the battery to acquaint Captain Thierry with the answer to his request. There was nothing that he could do against so many men in authority unless he wanted to be punished as a traitor. He saluted and left the room.

He found his uncle's contremaître in the courtyard and called to him:

"Give me a detachment of Micmacs and the longboat. Governor's orders."

"How much ammunition and provisions will you want, sir?"

Paul hesitated.

"We're going to the Royal Battery," he said, "with orders for Captain Thierry. I don't know what we may find when we get there. Perhaps Captain Thierry will need our services. You had better provision for forty-eight hours, and give us plenty of ammunition."

"Right, sir."

The contremaître disappeared. Paul loitered a moment, wondering what he would do for the next few minutes while the boat was being manned and lowered. Should he go to see Hortense? He hesitated. It would take some time to get to the house, some time to return; he was dirty and fatigued. He did not feel up to the effort of impressing Hortense, of playing that intriguing, interminable game. What then? Should he go to the tavern for a drink, or home to Marie? While he stood there uncertainly a form glided by him in the dusk, leaving a faint trail of perfume in the air. It was a woman with a shawl about her head disappearing quickly toward the quay. Some soldier's light-o'-love, Paul thought, eluding the sentries. He crossed the drawbridge, making for the quay, turned into the tavern at the corner and ordered a stoup of hot wine. It came, steaming, and put new heart into him. He drank where he stood, threw down a piece of silver and went out.

The longboat was waiting when he reached it, manned by Micmac sailors, naked to the waist. The sight of them made him conscious of the cold again. He stepped aboard and gave the word to push off. The boat drew away from shore, moving swiftly over the quiet waters of the harbor. Suddenly something shapeless and black in the shadow of the bow stood up and began to make its way toward him. By its dress and general shape it was a woman. He could not see her face in the dim light of the stars. He stooped and fumbled for the lantern beneath his feet in the stern. The figure came nearer.

"What does this mean?" he asked sternly. "You have no right to be here. We must put about and make for shore."

"No," she said. Her voice was low and vibrant. "No. On the contrary, Monsieur de Morpain, you must go on. We have no time to lose. No time."

(So she knows my name!)—Paul was angry. He struck a spark from his flint and tried to light the lantern. He fumbled and spilled the oil. He handed it to the sailor nearest him, who crouched over it, muttering an incantation. The woman came nearer, stepping lightly and skillfully without interfering with the rowers or upsetting the balance of the boat. Just as she reached him the lantern went on. Paul snatched it and flashed it in her face.

It was the Governor's daughter. She faced him defiantly.

"Mademoiselle!" he said, surprised and annoyed. He had expected anything but this. "We must put back at once."

"No," she said, "you must go on, Monsieur de Morpain. My father will be furious if you put back. I will tell a story that will put you in a dungeon before dawn unless you take me with you."

In the light of the lantern flashing on her face she looked

desperately serious. Paul saw that she meant what she said. Now she sat down beside him and took the lantern from his hand.

"I suggest that you put this out before the English see."

The Micmacs continued rowing, silent, impassive, incurious. The precision with which they moved, staring ahead of them, the fact that they were savages, made them seem at this moment less than human, merely parts of the boat. It heightened the unreality of the situation for Paul. He put the lantern out and sat in silence wondering what to do. Now that she was beside him, he was aware of the same faint perfume that had brushed by him in the Governor's courtyard. He saw what had happened. She musc have been waiting there for some reason, she had overheard his orders to the contremaître and had acted on them, stowing herself on board. It was quick of her but stupid. The savages had not dared to interfere, but he would not put up with it.

"You really owe me something for the scarf," she pointed out composedly.

He grunted.

"Unfortunately, Mademoiselle, this is not a pleasure party, a cruise around the harbor for the distraction of ladies, but a dangerous mission." He repeated it: "Dangerous. And I do not suppose that Captain Thierry, to whom I am bound will be any better pleased with your presence than I am."

"Indeed. How do you know that I care what Captain Thierry, to whom I am also bound, thinks, or what you think? And as for danger, if you are frightened, I am not."

Paul could hear her breathing beside him. She was frightened and he knew it, but the knowledge did not disarm him. It was just like a woman to do fool things for fool reasons nobody could fathom. He set his teeth and gave his attention to the course. They sat in silence side by side. Once or twice she put her head back to look up at the stars. Once he put his hand out to steady her when the boat rocked.

"How long will it take us to arrive?" she asked. Paul did not answer. She shrugged.

"If I were Captain Thierry or any man, for that matter, I would not spike my guns, I'd use them. I would stay in the battery and fight."

Paul did not answer. It was his own thought, but he would not give her the satisfaction of knowing it. How did she know that Thierry wanted to desert the battery? What had she to do with Thierry anyway? Wasn't he married? Surely, Paul thought, he had a wife in France. The Governor would be pleased when he heard about this visit to a married man! He stirred restlessly. The boat glided on while they continued out of tune with each other, themselves and the night. It was a magic night, a night for lovers, not for batteries and guns and wars.

The boat landed with a scrunching sound. Paul helped her ashore, leaving the Micmacs to tie up. He walked forward. She scrambled after him up the beach. There was a little shelter at the top of the path, a hut built of driftwood and stones. She paused in the doorway.

"Monsieur de Morpain," she said, "will you ask Captain Thierry to wait upon me here?"

There was a tremble in her voice that upset Paul in spite of his impatience against her. He said:

"It would not be safe for you to stay here alone."

"I can call to the savages if I am frightened. I do not care to see all the other officers and . . . and so many men."

"You should have thought of that before," Paul thought, and he was further annoyed that she did not seem to care how her actions appeared before him. Aloud he said:

"Mademoiselle, take my advice, go back to the boat and wait there without seeing anybody. I will accompany you home as soon as it is possible."

"But," she sounded surprised, "you yourself said this was no pleasure trip. I have not come to cross the harbor at night or to count the stars. I have an urgent reason. I must see Captain Thierry. Tell him I would prefer to see him here."

Paul frowned.

"Mademoiselle, I have a sister of your age." This was guess-work. He had no idea how old or how young Mademoiselle du Chambon might be. "I should be loath to see her visit a married man by night, or to ask him to wait upon her alone in a place like this."

There was a faint sound in the darkness beside him. Paul could not believe his ears. It was laughter.

"I am sure you would," her voice came demurely. "But I can assure you, Monsieur, I have not come to tempt Captain Thierry's virtue."

"Tshah!"

She came close to him.

"You do not know me very well. Even if I were the veriest slut, I would hardly choose a moment like this to press my advances upon a man overwrought with the cares of retreat. Retreat!" Her voice grew scornful. "Retreat is what one might expect from a worm like Captain Thierry."

"But Mademoiselle . . ."

"Oh you cannot be blamed for thinking whatever it is you think. Please ask Captain Thierry to come here at once. Tell him there is a dispatch for him. A private dispatch."

She turned away and made to enter the shelter. He followed, perplexed. Against his better judgment he found himself saying:

"Mademoiselle, if there is anything that I can do to serve you, let me do it. Trust me with the dispatch. I will deliver it."

There was a silence. Then she said:

"I wish I knew! I wish I knew!"

Paul stirred, his impatience returning. She caught at his arm.

"Perhaps if you were to say that my father asked you to accompany me," she began, "it would look less strange to Captain Thierry and his officers. I could deliver my message in person and still retain the prestige of virginity."

Paul snorted.

"I assure you the prestige of a thing is more important than the thing itself sometimes."

"Mademoiselle, I have no time to exchange witty conversation with you. I am here on a military mission. I must act."

"Yes, yes, act!"

She drew herself up in the starlight, striking an attitude intended to make him feel pompous. A new light fell upon her face. He looked at her and then away to where the light was coming from. They could see the two towers of the fortification stretching upward, black against the rising moon. She pressed his fingers, smiling.

"Ask Captain Thierry to come here," she said.

He hesitated, reluctant to connive at that secret meeting in the moonlight. He heard himself say:

"I will escort you, perhaps that would be best. I will say that the Governor sent me with you and risk his displeasure. You are asking a lot of me, Mademoiselle."

"Monsieur," she answered with gravity, accepting his arm as she stumbled on a rock, "I have a brother about your age. I should be loath to see him visiting a married woman alone at night, and in the daytime for that matter, for instance, Madame de Saintonge. I should certainly warn him against Madame de Saintonge."

Paul gasped. He took his arm away. She scrambled lightly up the path ahead of him. They reached the battery. There was a lantern over the doorway. A sentry halted them. They were passed inside.

CHAPTER XXXIX

THE first room they entered was a guard room, with a door opening to the Commandant's quarters, and an archway leading to the armories. Everything was dirty and disordered. A great clutter of equipment lay about, rusty, uncaredfor, trailing over tables and heaped upon the floor. More than a hundred hogsheads of rum were stacked in the far corner, some of them broached. The place stank of stale liquor and debris.

Mademoiselle du Chambon shrank against Paul. She put her hand to her head and unwrapped her shawl, throwing it back upon her shoulders. Her hair was powdered beneath it, in cloudy white curls. Her throat and shoulders were bare, except for a necklace of rubies and pearls. She wore a silly silk brocaded gown, already muddied, he noticed with some satisfaction, and torn from the landing and the ascent. She looked what she evidently was, another young lady of fashion, with nothing in her head but powder and intrigue.

Paul was irritated. He drew away from her. He resented being used in a situation that was not clear to him; he was nettled by her reference to his affair with Hortense, annoyed because she had twisted things to make him seem both pompous and hypocritical. He scowled toward the door of the Commandant's quarters, where the sentry had disappeared to announce them.

She turned to him in a sudden panic-stricken movement.

"Monsieur de Morpain," she pleaded, "stand by me! I assure you it is important. I shall never forget your help."

Then as Paul did not answer her at once, she cried impetuously:

"Is it so much to ask that you second me for half an hour? My father would not wish . . ." she hesitated.

"Your father," Paul said grimly, "will probably have a good deal to say about this escapade, for which I make no doubt he will hold me responsible. It is unfortunate that your father has none too high an opinion of me already. I can see trouble ahead."

She was silent. Then she turned to face him and raised her eyes to his. They were honest, large and dark. Paul looked into them and revised his opinion. He shifted restlessly. There was evidently more in this stupid situation than petty intrigue. Mademoiselle du Chambon looked gray about her mouth and cheeks, there were dark lines beneath her eyes, her chin was strained, thrust out determinedly. He thought of a number of explanations for her agitation, all of them natural, none of them complimentary, but when his glance lifted to meet hers, he was ashamed and relieved. There was nothing, he must admit, of the strumpet here.

"Monsieur, if you will stand by me now in support of whatever I say, I will entrust you with the whole story as soon as I can, I promise you."

He bowed stiffly.

The door before them swung open and a man came into the room. Paul eyed him sharply as he bowed and presented himself. He was plump and droll-looking, with a high forehead and a loose mouth above a small blond beard. His clothes presented a remarkable contrast to his surroundings. They were immaculate. A shining silver sword swung against a silk-encased leg, a little portly perhaps, but shapely. Mademoiselle du Chambon sank in a slow curtsy.

Captain Thierry stared at her. There was an expression on his face that Paul could not quite analyze but it was not the look that he expected. There was uneasiness, masked by false geniality, and a man-of-the-world knowingness but no intimacy of proprietorship.

"Mademoiselle? Monsieur?"

He turned expectantly to Paul who was silent, waiting for Mademoiselle du Chambon to speak. She said nothing. He hesitated, then he presented himself.

"I am Paul de Morpain, at your service, Captain, with dispatches

·[166]·

from the Governor. You are to abandon the battery as quickly as possible. Here are the orders, under the Governor's seal."

Captain Thierry put out his hand and took the paper. He glanced through it after breaking the heavy seal. Then he seemed to think that he was not being very hospitable.

"If you will come this way," he said, "we will be more comfortable."

He motioned them toward the door to the Commandant's room, saying over his shoulder to a soldier servant:

"Bring the wine and some rum."

The soldier saluted, unsteadily. Paul noticed he was drunk. Captain Thierry drew up a chair for Mademoiselle du Chambon.

"You will excuse me," he said, "if I give orders to begin the work of demolition."

He left the room.

"Do you want me to stay here while you talk with him?" Paul said.

She hesitated. "No, I suppose not—yes, stay!"

The door opened. Captain Thierry came back. He drew up a chair.

"Captain Thierry," Mademoiselle du Chambon said, "I have come here tonight because I have bad news for you that will not wait. It concerns my brother, or I should not have come. You were expecting a dispatch from him, I think?"

An extraordinary expression passed over Captain Thierry's face. He looked astounded, disgusted, furious and finally unpleasantly afraid.

"My brother sent me a messenger. He got through the English lines yesterday. He is dying in the hospital of the Frères de Charité. He called for me. He gave me the message by word of mouth. Vergor says: 'The Minister's secretary has discovered everything. For God sake tell Thierry not to let the Indians ship any more skins for awhile till this blows over. Tell him to burn all records at once. Tell him to cover our traces, I'll attend to this end.' That is what Vergor's message is, Captain Thierry. I suppose you know what it means as well as I."

Captain Thierry's face grew mottled, beads of perspiration

·[167]·

began to ooze from his forehead and above his lips. Suddenly he wheeled so abruptly that Mademoiselle du Chambon flinched.

"I have only your word for it," he cried. "How do I know this isn't some scheme of that lying devil of a brother of yours to get all the profits for himself!"

"Monsieur," Paul said, "Mademoiselle has come to deliver this message to you at great risk to herself. Her word is not to be doubted."

"Isn't it? Nor yours, I suppose, nor Vergor du Chambon's either!" He sat down and mopped his forehead. "I expected money from your brother, not mysterious warnings and veiled threats."

"It seems to me," Paul said dryly, "that Mademoiselle's brother has acted wisely in sending you a warning. The penalty for being caught in the illicit fur trade is death, as we all know. Death, Captain Thierry."

Captain Thierry shrugged.

"Tell your brother that he is playing a dangerous game, do you hear? Dangerous! And I am not a man to be played with, Mademoiselle, nor intimidated either. And if this is some Government spy you have brought along, that doesn't frighten me, and you don't frighten me. Tell Vergor to send me the money he owes me and have done. And remember one thing, women who get in my way regret it."

Paul caught the appeal in Mademoiselle du Chambon's eyes. He stepped forward, narrowing his gaze.

"Captain," he said quietly, "Mademoiselle du Chambon is not to be confused with the women you speak of, nor to be threatened."

"Oh," Captain Thierry stepped back, his eyes ranging Paul. "So she is under your protection is she?" He threw back his head and laughed unpleasantly. "Well, there's no accounting for a woman's tastes. But if you think you're going to get another share out of the family business you're mistaken."

"Sir," said Paul reddening, exasperated at the position in which he found himself, "you are insulting. Another word and I challenge you."

Captain Thierry put his hand to his sword. Mademoiselle du Chambon intervened hastily.

"I overlook Captain Thierry's remarks, and beg you to do the same; he is distraught. When he has time to think things over he will know the wise thing to do. It is urgent, Captain, urgent. You must for your sake, as well as Vergor's, do what he has said. You know that. You must get a message to the Micmacs at once."

"If anyone but your brother had sent me that message I should know what to think, but your brother is the slipperiest, slimiest thief in the King's New France or old France for that matter. He has played me too many dirty tricks for me to believe him."

"You will not let yourself be hanged," Mademoiselle du Chambon said.

"If I do, I'll see that others hang with me," he said, grinning evilly.

Mademoiselle du Chambon rose and faced him.

"You've accused a man who isn't here of a number of dishonorable things," she said, "but you know in your heart who is the thief."

Captain Thierry choked and glared at her. The door behind them opened. Two soldiers entered, with stoups of wine. Mademoiselle du Chambon turned her back and walked to the door.

"I've given you the message," she said, "do what you like with it."

She walked out of the room. There was nothing for Paul to do but follow. They hastened through the darkness together down the hill.

CHAPTER XL

THE moon was high in the heavens, flooding the night with light. Mademoiselle du Chambon scrambled down the hillside with more agility than she had shown on the way up. Paul followed her, glad that the episode was over, not at all sure what sort of figure he had cut, or what consequences might follow. They reached the beach and ran toward the boat. It was not there. There was no sign of it.

"What the devil!" Paul began loking angrily about him. A figure rose from a log and came toward them. It was Chiktek, one of the Micmac sailors. He began to explain.

The *Oiseau de Mer* had signaled by flares to the longboat to return at once. The officer in charge of the longboat had left Chiktek behind to explain what had happened. He would send the boat back for Paul and the lady as soon as possible. He would report their predicament to Captain de Morpain at once.

"Well!" said Paul.

Mademoiselle du Chambon beside him shivered suddenly and drew her shawl about her.

"Heavens!" Paul said, "you have nothing on but that thin dress."

"I had no time to change," she murmured.

"We must get you home at once. Here, you," he said to the Indian, "go along the shore and see if the boats belonging to the garrison are there."

The man grunted.

"No oars, no men, no manage."

"Then we must go back to the battery at once, and get Captain Thierry to lend us one of his boats and a crew."

"I'll stay here," Mademoiselle du Chambon said. "I'd rather."

Paul hesitated, as unwilling as she was to confront Captain Thierry again. But she was shivering, doing her best to conceal it. It was folly to be out on a winter night in a silken dress. Paul swore beneath his breath. He hit on a compromise.

"The shelter, the hut half way up to the path! Gather driftwood," he said to the Micmac standing stolidly naked beside him. "Build a fire in the hut. Be quick."

He took his cloak from his shoulders, somewhat unwillingly, and draped it about the girl's shoulders.

"Wait for me here," he said, and disappeared.

Moonlight flooding into the shelter showed it to be clean, if bare of any comfort or sign of occupation. There was a log in the doorway, thick enough to be used as a seat. She brushed it off with her hand and sat down, pulling the cloak about her, awkwardly. Chiktek appeared beside her. He began to build a fire between two blackened stones.

"I suppose it will smoke and fill the place with it."

Chiktek shook his head. He pointed upward. She saw that there was a hole in the top of the shelter.

"Well," she said doubtfully, "I suppose it's too cold not to have a fire."

Chiktek smiled patiently. He set to work. The flames crept up between her and the opening of the door. She crouched over them, stretching her hands to the flicker. She was thinking:

"Vergor! Of all the tiresome, exasperating, dearest people in the world. I did what I could. I got the mesage to him. How could you put your life into the hands of such a worm? Don't you ever think of risks, Vergor? Not you! Remember when you fell into the bear trap and I had to get you out and we both had to lie about our being in the woods?"

She laughed, shifting closer to the fire.

"It's lucky for us there's another fool in Louisbourg almost as wrongheaded as you. And right-hearted. At least I think so. I'm taking that risk. I had to. Look out for Thierry. Can't you get free of him? Oh, do get free, and settle down. Please, Vergor, take care of yourself."

She had a habit of talking to her brother as though he were there. It had comforted her often, bringing a sense of companionship into her rather lonely life. Ever since she could remember Vergor and she had been allies. Now they did not often meet, but he was there. Tonight he was there in a special way. Once again she had strained everything to save him from the sort of disaster that was always overtaking him. Probably he was being pressed by some of his creditors or else he was expensively in love; he had grown careless, someone had found out. Vergor just wouldn't see the wood for the underbrush. When he wanted money he would sell illicit furs, his honor or his country, just as cheerfully. Yet no one could consider Vergor a traitor. That would be ridiculous. He did not mean to betray, he just did not think . . . or did he? Did he see the shadow of the gallows, as she had seen it once, when she was a little girl in Paris, walking down the Rue de la Santé with her nurse? There was an execution that morning, and a man hanging from it, twisting in the wind, round and round. She tried to brush it from her memory, afraid that it might twist and show the face and be Vergor.

The sound of footsteps coming rapidly toward her down the path, shook her from her morbid reverie. Monsieur de Morpain blocked the entrance to the shelter. She could not see his face, but she was certain something had gone wrong before he told her.

"I am sorry, Mademoiselle."

"What is it?"

"We cannot get a crew for the boat at present."

"Why?"

He came into the shelter. She made way for him to sit on the log. He passed his hand across his forehead nervously.

"Why?" she asked again.

He scraped with his toe in the dust of the shelter.

"They're all drunk. They've been broaching the hogsheads that are left."

"Where's Captain Thierry?"

"Fighting with the engineer over blowing up the works.

·[172]·

There's no discipline left. It would not be safe for you to go there now."

A picture flashed before him of the men on their bellies swilling the rum that spouted from the broached hogsheads, the engineer with his sword out, stumbling and weaving in front of Captain Thierry. Thierry himself, angry and flushed.

"They were drinking before we got there. I don't suppose you noticed it. But I did."

"I noticed one man," Anne said.

"It's all the men now."

"I see."

"They'll be worse later. I suppose they think that as long as they are abandoning the place they won't be fools enough to leave any wine behind."

"What shall we do?"

"Wait here until the longboat comes back for us. If it doesn't come before daylight, we will go with Captain Thierry's garrison in one of the boats. They will be sober enough then."

"I see."

Paul leaned his shoulder against the doorway, looking toward the beach. He was anxious about the fate of the *Oiseau de Mer*. If the longboat had been recalled so suddenly it might mean any-thing—action against the enemy (with himself stuck here!). It might mean an attack by the New Englanders on the town itself, though that was fanciful, because of the marsh between and the guarded harbor and the difficulty of moving troops by night over strange terrain. It was exasperating not to know what was going on out there. He stared across the moonlit water in the direction of the town. Lights were burning here and there. He thought he could make out the two tall spires rising from the convent and the church.

Mademoiselle du Chambon was speaking to him.

"I want to thank you. I should have been afraid without your help."

Paul grunted.

"It was kind of you. I shall not forget it nor will Vergor. You do not know him, do you, Monsieur de Morpain?"

Paul brought his attention back to her with an effort.

·[173]·

"No, Mademoiselle, I do not know your brother. I left Louisbourg when it was still under Monsieur du Quesnel. I returned . . ."

"I know. I know all about you, Monsieur de Morpain."

Paul was nettled. Bother this girl with her talking. He wanted to see what was going on, and to strain his ears for telltale sounds coming across the water. He knew it was illogical to blame her for the boat's disappearance, but he was inclined to blame her for everything. Most certainly he could blame her for having his warm cloak so that he was beginning to ache already from the rawness of the cold.

"You would like Vergor, I think," she went on. "He is a sailor like you."

Paul said nothing.

"There never was such a—such a spirited boy. Nor a better brother. I know he's wild and likes bad company. . . ."

"Mademoiselle," Paul broke in coldly, "I have no wish to hear intimate family history."

"Oh? I thought perhaps after what you did for me tonight some explanation was due to you, but I am glad you do not want to hear it. It would not be easy to tell. What shall we talk about?"

Paul was silent. He knew that he was being churlish, but he felt a perverse pleasure in his churlishness. Chiktek came to the door of the shelter with an armful of firewood. He dropped a load on the fire. Flames shot up, the wood began to crackle.

"Ah, that's better," said Paul. He stretched his hands out to the blaze. The firelight flickered over Mademoiselle du Chambon's face. He looked at her and his churlishness vanished. She had an appealing face, though it was not good-looking, with that outthrust chin and determined mouth—it was more like a boy's face, perhaps, some sensitive boy with dignity and pride and helplessness. Just now she was looking thoroughly miserable. He realized as the firelight revealed her expression that it could not be a particularly pleasant experience for her either, to wait in a damp shelter, indefinitely, and that he was behaving like a pig. He smiled at her.

Instantly the dark eyes lightened with genuine warmth and gratitude. She turned toward him eagerly and began to talk. She told him first of Vergor, determined to make Paul understand that he was not a traitor. A lot of people dabbled in the illicit fur trade who were not traitors. He was unusual, brilliantly gifted. Few people understood Vergor.

"I'm sure of that," Paul said with his tongue in his cheek.

Then she questioned him about bringing the news of the attack to Louisbourg. He found himself telling her about his life as a prisoner of war. He described the Moodys; she laughed. Her laugh was low and very spontaneous. He found himself trying to evoke it just for the pleasant sound. He talked of Will's estrangement from him and she sighed. He described his flight and Randy's death. She put her hand out to him impulsively.

"I assure you," he said, moved by the recollection and by her sympathy, "it was a scene I cannot forget. Suppose, Mademoiselle . . ."

"Call me Anne," she interrupted. "My friends do. I haven't many, but I have a few like your Randy and like William Vaughan as he used to be. After tonight I shall count you among them, in spite of what you think of me."

He began to protest. She laughed a little shakily.

"I saw your thoughts pass in an ugly procession across your mind. I am glad that you did not act on them."

"I did not really think them . . ." his voice dwindled before the honesty in her eyes, searching his. "Not for long," he added. "I am glad to have been of any help and glad to have found you for a friend."

He put a log upon the fire noisily.

"You should rest," he said. "You should try to sleep. Captain Thierry will not be ready to leave before dawn, if he gets his men and himself together then. Chiktek will rouse us if the longboat comes back. Don't worry, we'll get to Louisbourg somehow."

"I am not sleepy," she said.

Paul smiled in the darkness beside her. They sat in silence for a little while, then Anne's head jerked toward him. She was falling asleep as he knew she would if he did not speak. He edged nearer till it dropped upon his shoulder; then he eased his back against the wall, stretched his legs and tried to relax, staring into the fire.

·[175]·

"Well," he thought to himself, grinning in the darkness, "this is the strangest situation I was ever in."

He began to think of other times and places when he had been alone with a woman who attracted him. He moved his tongue softly against his teeth. A soft smell of perfume and powdered hair and the clean smell of a girl's body drifted to him. He tightened his hold instinctively, putting his free arm about her waist. She stirred, moaned a little and settled down more earnestly to sleep like a child exhausted with play. She was exhausted, no doubt, and so was he.

"Perhaps exhaustion accounts for my good behavior," he told himself, grinning. "Perhaps her being the Governor's daughter has something to do with it too. But principally it's her confounded trust in me. I've always thought a man must be pretty hardened to rape a girl, especially with so many others who don't need to be raped. This is a little trying to my vanity. I never saw anyone so unconscious, apparently, of what might happen to her. Am I so unattractive that she thinks me harmless? Harmless! I could show her!"

Another wave of perfume rose about him.

"Phew! I hope I do not have to pass many such hours," he thought. A sudden vision of San came to him. If it were San beside him what a night they would spend! Oh, hell, why did he have to think of San? This was no place for a married man. He felt the ground beneath his feet. Cautiously he whistled:

"Pssst!"

The Micmac crawled forward.

"Put some spruce boughs here between me and the fire," Paul whispered. Anne stirred a little. He held her quietly while the Indian arranged a primitive bed, then together they lowered her onto the boughs and covered her with Paul's cloak. Paul stepped out of the shelter, and stretched himself, looking at the stars.

"Quite foolish of you," he told himself. "Wouldn't Hortense laugh. Hortense! Ah, well, one can't have everything, or everyone." He squatted beside the Micmac's fire and presently lay down by it.

"Watch!" he ordered.

Toward dawn Captain Thierry and his garrison took to their

boats. They had put in a halfhearted night's work between drinks spiking the cannon without burning the carriages or knocking off the trunnions. They had thrown the loose gunpowder into the well, but they left two hundred and eighty bomb shells, a great number of cartridges and other stores behind.

They did not take the short cut to the beach, past the shelter, because of the equipment they were carrying and the number of drunken men they had to drag along. Captain Thierry staggered sullenly behind them. His head was bandaged. From time to time he looked with dismal satisfaction at the prostrate form of the Engineer carried on a litter. They embarked quickly. The sound of their voices drifted away on the offshore breeze, until it sounded from a distance like the squawking of sea gulls, which had been going on all night. The launching of the boats and the splashing of oars were drowned by the waves of the incoming tide breaking on the rocks below the shelter. Paul and Anne slept on.

Chiktek watched the detachment go. He had been ordered to watch and he obeyed. It did not occur to him to wake Paul or the sleeping squaw. Nobody had ordered him to report anything except the arrival of the longboat and there was no sign of that. The last boat dwindled to a glimpse of black like the last porpoise in a school of porpoises. The sun rose higher; now its rays were reaching out, past the crouching Micmac, over Paul, who stirred and covered his face with his arm, into the shelter where Anne lay beside a dying fire.

Chiktek rose and spread his arms above his head. Solemnly, in silence, he saluted the great spirit rising for another day.

"Make Chiktek strong as you are strong," he prayed, "send the fingers of your warmth into the heart of Chiktek and his tribe."

Then he sat down again, content to wait.

CHAPTER XLI

EARLY in the morning Lieutenant Colonel William Vaughan marched on the town of Louisbourg with four hundred New Englanders. They were weary from the unaccustomed labor of landing guns, ammunition and stores, stiff from wading through icy water and sleeping on the ground in their wet clothes. They were glad to be marching away from further back-breaking labor at the encampment, toward adventure and possible loot. They were nearing the purpose of the expedition for which they had been willing to enlist; for which they had crowded into evil-smelling fishing boats and suffered seasickness, buffeting and storm; for which they had waited in Canceau Harbor from day to weary day listening to Parson Moody's eternal sermons preached in the open air: "Thy people shall be willing in the day of Thy Power";—encounter with the French, victory, the sack of Louisbourg.

Will led his men to a hilltop near the town. He was elated. It was the first time that he had found himself alone and in command. He was young, inexperienced, but so were all the other officers. He was a Lieutenant Colonel because he was Shirley's protégé. He would make his reputation in this war. Afterwards every door would be opened to him. He would make a fortune, he would rise to whatever post he wanted, he would do what he liked.

He halted the company in sight of the town but out of range.

"We'll give the frogs something to think about!" he cried, flourishing his sword. "Three cheers!"

They rolled out threateningly across the marsh. A few heads bobbed up along the ramparts, taking stock of this maneuver.

"Forward march!"

The company stepped out a little raggedly. They skirted the town, marching behind the hills in the rear of the Royal Battery, to the northeastern arm of the harbor where there were magazines and naval stores. Will expected fierce resistance. He drew his men up in formation and made them lie down where they stood. After half an hour's rest they moved forward cautiously, nearer, nearer, until they were near enough to rush the place. They sprang to their feet and stormed forward, each man braced to meet the enemy.

The magazines were deserted. When he was quite sure that there was no ambush, Will started to go through them, taking stock of what was there. He decided to set them afire for the moral effect it would have on the French rather than attempt to salvage the stores and drag them back over the rocky scrub to Pepperell's headquarters. They spent the afternoon piling pitch, tar and other combustibles conveniently left for them, in places where they would be fanned by the wind.

Will lighted the first torch and laid it to the nearest pile. A great cloud of black smoke rolled up. He stood back, satisfied. The men, black-faced and grimy, began to laugh and rub their hands, contented with a good day's work.

"That will bring the Frenchies out!" one of them said.

"If they were fools enough to leave it in the first place, they may be fools enough to try to save it now," the sergeant commented. Will said nothing. They camped where they were, watching the red glow of the burning magazines. He was uneasy, listening for sounds that might escape the sentries, for the stealthy creeping of men's bodies through the dark. Off and on he slept in spite of his anxiety. He was glad when the long night was over and he could see the dawn.

The sergeant saluted.

"Are the men to eat their emergency rations, sir?" he asked.

Will considered this and decided against it. He gave the word to return to camp. The men fell in by companies, some of them

·[179]·

sulkily twisting their belts as a hint to their officer that they were hungry.

"Forward march!"

The men set out, breaking step to crawl and climb and twist through undergrowth and squelch through swampy places. They went quickly, with the thought of food in their minds. A party of thirteen of them was in the rear with Will. They were going more slowly, to act as rear guard in case of a belated attack. They were some distance behind the main body when Will's body servant, a boy of eighteen whose name was William Tufts, caught hold of his officer's arm.

"Look!" he said excitedly, pointing to the Royal Battery, "there's no flag on the flagstaff and no smoke in the chimneys. I'll wager there are no Frenchies there."

The party halted, while Will stared through his glass at the queer-shaped towers. It was true, he could see no sign of life in the place. Incredible! Where could all the Frenchies be hiding? He beckoned to one of his men, a Cape Cod Indian.

"Here, Sagawatek! You may have a swig of this brandy now and the whole flask when you get back. Go and see what's happening there." He undid the flask from his belt and held it out to the Indian. The man put it to his lips and threw his head back. A glitter came to his eyes. Will took the flask away from him and he was gone like a brown flash across the frozen ground. He disappeared from sight, wriggling on his belly to the walls. There was a long pause. Will shifted from foot to foot, reflecting that he had only thirteen men; the rest of his company was far ahead; he would stand no chance if the French made a sortie; he would have to give the order to retreat. He looked over his shoulder. It was devilish country to choose for a getaway. He began to feel his own hunger and to think of those emergency rations. There was an exclamation from his sergeant, then another man spoke, and now all the watching men could see the savage's far-off figure waving them forwards frantically. They advanced in a run toward him. The place was empty, deserted, abandoned by the French. Even the gate was unfastened. They marched in.

"We haven't got a flag, sir," said William Tufts, eagerly beside him, "but this will do!" He tapped his red coat.

Will looked at him doubtfully. He thought of calling upon Sagawatek, but he was in a corner drinking himself silly, and besides, any Indian who could hunt and trap was worth more to them than poor Tufts.

"All right," he said.

The boy went to the flagstaff and began to shinny up, holding his coat in his teeth. He reached the top and started to make it fast. There was a whine, a shriek; a volley of cannon shot from the town batteries passed overhead. The boy slid down again, breathless. Will leaned against one of the spiked guns.

"Eat your emergency rations now, men," he said. "We're staying here and they'll have to send us a reinforcement."

He dug in his knapsack and brought out paper, a silver inkhorn and a pen.

"The third day of May 1745," he wrote, "May it please your Honor to be informed that by the grace of God and the courage of thirteen men, I entered the Royal Battery at about nine o'clock, and am waiting for a reinforcement and a flag."* He added: "rations" underlined, and called to the sergeant.

"Send a messenger with this to General Pepperell, and keep men posted on the lookout."

He started on a tour of inspection, very pleased with himself. It would not take much to drill out the spiked touchholes of the cannon and train them against the town itself. There were twenty-eight 42-pounders, and two 18-pounders. This was better than anything Pepperell had dreamed of, or Shirley with his optimistic draft of instructions that Will had penned. It was a curious document, ludicrous in the light of what the expedition had encountered when it arrived at Louisbourg. He recalled fragments of it, smiling:

"It is thought that Louisbourg may be surprised if the French have no advice of ycur coming. To effect it, you must time your arrival about nine of the clock in the evening, taking care that the fleet be far enough in the offing to prevent their being seen from the town in the daytime."* It went on, Will remembered, to prescribe how the troops were to land, after dark at a place called Flat Point Cove, in four divisions, three of which were to march to the back of certain hills, a mile and a half west of the town,

·[181]·

where two of the three were to halt and "keep a profound silence,"* the third was to continue its march "under cover of said hills till it comes opposite the Grand Battery, which it will attack at a concerted signal; while one of the two divisions behind the hills assaults the west gate and the other moves up to support the attack."* There was a good deal more, taking no account of the rocks, surf, fog, gales, underbrush and swamp, or of the impossibility of landing troops without being seen. Will smiled again. Well, the Grand Battery had fallen at nine of the clock, all right, nine in the morning instead of nine at night, and to thirteen men instead of three divisions. Probably Shirley would court-martial him for not taking it in the prescribed manner. He continued his tour, marveling at the actions of the French. He could only suppose that when the clouds of smoke from the magazines they had set afire the day before, drifted over the battery, the French garrisoned there must have thought they were going to be attacked, and for some reason had abandoned everything in panic. It would be a great feather in his cap with Pepperell. Two hundred men he thought could have held it successfully against five thousand without cannon. The water front was impregnable, the rear defenses —a loopholed wall of masonry with a ditch ten feet deep and twelve feet wide, a covered way and a partly demolished glacis— were flanked by the two towers with swivels still mounted on them. Will was amazed. It would have taken the New Englanders a week or more to drag cannon from the landing place to a point where they could be turned against this battery, at least four miles over the hills that he had traveled with his company, through marsh, briar and rock. He was recalled from these thoughts by a cry from one of the sentries.

"The French are coming! Look there! Look there!"

Will sprang to his side. Four boats were approaching from the town. They were filled with soldiers. This was a sortie to retake the battery and save the stores. It might even be an ambush. It would be better to fight in the open and see the enemy from whatever side he might come. He called his men together. They ran down to the beach, by a little path that passed a shelter of driftwood and stone. The embers from a fire were still burning there. Will kicked them with his foot. Another fire burned a few feet away.

"See?" he said to the sergeant, "someone was here not too long ago. It may be a trap after all."

They arrived together, loading their muskets.

"We must stand them off from landing until reinforcements come. Our men will have heard the row the French are making, they'll have seen the red coat we are flying for a flag. They'll come to help us, never fear. Now then, lads, let's show what fourteen of us can do against the French. Remember Canceau! Hold your fire till you know it will go where it hurts."

The Island Battery opened up on them. They were fired at by the town batteries as well. They stood their ground. The firing was wild, dropping short into the sea, for the most part endangering the French detachment.

"Ready, fire!"

A rain of bullets spattered the first boat. The French came on.

"At them again, boys!"

Another round, this time taking toll in the second boat. Still the French came on. Will set his teeth.

"Keep it up, men!" he cried, "unless you want to be taken prisoner. They'll sell your scalps, remember, if they get you. Now!"

He took aim himself at the French officer he could see in the foremost boat, urging his men on. The shot went wide into the sea. There came a shout behind him. A man toiled down the bank and panted to his side.

"Lieutenant Colonel Bradstreet's compliments, Sir," he said, "he is here with his regiment."

"My compliments to Lieutenant Colonel Bradstreet and will he show himself and his men to the French out there," Will grunted, as the French boats came nearer still. The man ran back, clambering into the battery. Five minutes later a line of men appeared on the ramparts, on the hillside. A great cry went up. The French heard it and stopped rowing, startled. Then they drew off, retreating slowly toward the town. The Island Battery continued to fire, but Will and his men were able to take cover with the reinforcements.

·[183]·

"Congratulations!" Lieutenant Colonel Bradstreet said, as Will appeared, "a master stroke."

"Good for us both," Will said. He was tired now and glad to share responsibility.

"We'll get these guns trained on the town as soon as we can," Bradstreet said cheerfully. "Whatever made the fools abandon them?"

CHAPTER XLII

PAUL finished questioning Chiktek. It was no good getting angry with a savage, he would simply glide into the forest and stay there. They needed Chiktek. He had been fool enough to let Captain Thierry and his men embark without waking them, but he could keep them fed, he could hunt and fish for them.

"Bring us something to eat," Paul said resignedly.

He looked at Anne and saw that she was crying. She had one hand to her eyes, the other groped for a handkerchief which she did not find.

"What is it?" he asked exasperated. "You have nothing to cry for. We'll get back safely sometime. I am beginning to like it here, can't you?"

She tried to smile, looking up at him, blinking away her tears. He swore beneath his breath. If women weren't the devil's contrivances! Here he had been priding himself upon his chivalry, his kind restraint, letting her sleep alone in the shelter, giving her his cloak, and all she did to reward him was to cry, with her hair shedding powder over everything and her face a sight—a pretty sight, though. He grinned. Perhaps she was crying because he had been too chivalrous, because he had disappointed her.

"Here," he said cheerfully, "I admit that the prospect of spending a few hours more in each other's company is a matter of tears, but I refuse to shed them. Food is what we both need."

Anne looked up. She made an effort. She smiled, and sat down on a rock, spreading a scarf on the bank in front of her.

"Table cloth."

"That's better."

The sun grew hotter. It was a bright and sunny day. They sat side by side watching Chiktek preparing breakfast. He brought them sagamité and smoked fish and a bowl of hot chocolate.

"Not my favorite breakfast," Paul said, "but it's hot."

They finished all of it. Then they walked down to the beach and stared across the water toward Louisbourg. There was nothing to be seen, no boat, no sign of life. The sea was moderately rough, and spray dashed up into their faces.

"It won't do to get wet," Paul said. "It's too cold to stand about. We had better get back to the fire, and keep it going."

Anne took a last look toward Louisbourg.

"Do you think," she said, "there's any real danger of the town being taken by the New Englanders?"

"If we had prepared for it . . ." Paul said, and stopped himself. Anne sighed.

They reached the door of the shelter. The fire was getting low. Paul went to find more fuel, cursing Chiktek for not being able to anticipate anything. He must be told; like all savages he seemed to lose initiative in front of the white man. Now he had disappeared, and there was no more wood. Paul broke off some spruce boughs that were not too green and dumped them at the door of the shelter. Then he went back to the beach to look for driftwood. He found some boards and a piece of a tree worn smooth and white by the sea, and carried them up the path.

"Look," said Anne, when he reached her, "at the smoke over there."

Paul turned his head.

"Captain Thierry must have sent a detachment round by land and told them to fire the magazines on their way. That's just as well, it wouldn't do for the enemy to get them or the stores." He frowned. "This abandoning the battery makes me sick," he said, "it's the most senseless blunder anyone could make. I don't understand the Governor. Not that I want to criticize your father, Anne."

She sighed dreamily.

"What will happen when we get back?" she asked, watching the smoke obscure the sky.

"A great many unpleasant things," Paul laughed. "Your father will run me through, and then court-martial me. My uncle will take over where he leaves off. I should be with him now, on the *Oiseau de Mer.*"

"And Madame de Saintonge will finish what remains of you."

Paul reddened.

"Will she not?" Anne insisted.

Paul groped for words in which to speak of Anne's father's mistress to her.

"Madame de Saintonge has too many interests in her life to bother about me."

"Hmmm," Anne said, cocking her head to one side. "These interests that you speak of must have cropped up suddenly. Until yesterday you were the main figure in the tapestry." She decided to let the matter drop. "I could manage Father well enough if this were not a time of emergency. His mind is full of war; any further worry will drive him distracted. One night out of the nest might be accounted for, but an indefinite stay," she shrugged. "I shall have to tell him some cock-and-bull story. He must not find out about Vergor, and it will have to be a good story, otherwise he will kill you and put me in a convent."

"I am not so easy to kill, and convents have doors and windows."

"You sound as though you had experience. Have you eloped with a number of nuns?"

"Not more than twenty-five. By this time Captain Thierry will have told your father that we visited him last night. He will guess where we are and send a boat for us."

"I think Captain Thierry will hold his tongue."

"Why?"

"Because of what was in the dispatch. It would finish him and he knows it. He would not want my father to know why I came to him."

"Plenty of other men saw you."

"They were drunk."

"One of them will tell the Governor."

·[187]·

"So much the better. I hope you are right. Then the boat will come and we can leave. What is the matter?"

Paul's face contracted. He was looking away from her, toward the hillside where the smoke was billowing in black clouds. There was a sudden sound behind them. Anne turned her head. The Micmac was standing there, panting. Paul looked at him from a long way off.

"What is it?" he asked.

"A party of English are coming this way," Chiktek said. "I saw smoke and went to see. They have set the stores on fire."

"Are they coming here?" Anne asked.

Chiktek grunted.

"I don't suppose so," Paul said quickly, "but of course they may." He smiled at her. "The longboat will be back for us before then."

"Are we to fight?" Chiktek's eyes glittered. He was thinking of the price an English scalp would fetch in the open market or from Abbé le Loutre. He could sneak up and get one, perhaps two, and run away. Paul shook his head impatiently.

"You are to watch and this time bring us news of everything that happens. We will stay here. If the longboat comes before you return we shall whistle for you twice."

Chiktek disappeared. Paul looked at Anne.

"We may have to stay here for another night, and without a fire if the enemy comes any nearer, Anne."

She shivered.

"I suppose," she said after a moment's silence, "it will make things worse for father if they take me prisoner. They might try to bargain with him, you know, using me as a hostage. Well, if they do take us, Paul, they mustn't know who I am. That's all. Things are bad enough for father and for Louisbourg without that. We'll pretend I'm your sister."

"Make it cousin," Paul said. "I might be able to make that more convincing. One can be attracted by one's cousin."

She swept the tangled hair from her eyes, clouds of powder falling round her, and shook the folds of her dress with an odd preening movement like a bird.

"Do you think a fire would be seen in this shelter?" she inquired, changing the subject.

"Perhaps not. But I think we shall be safely in Louisbourg before the night. I never had a cousin that I liked before, one that was pretty, and unusual."

Anne worked the toe of a soiled satin slipper in the ashes of the fire.

"This time last year I was in France," she said, seizing on a subject at random. "I liked it for a time, but to live there would stifle me."

"I said you were unusual. Most women pine all their lives to go home as they call it, never having been there. Most women model their existences on the lives of ladies of fashion in Paris, as they conceive them to be."

"That's absurd. Life there and life here are entirely different."

"In what way?"

"Well, you need a great deal of money to live in France, and influence as well. And there are endless intrigues and nobody seems natural. My heart is in the life out here, the space, the freedom, the good life for the people. My father says the peasant here is better off than anywhere in Europe. He can hunt, in France he would be hanged for that, and eat what he has hunted—how many peasants in France see meat on their table more than once in a blue moon? If they do they've stolen it, and transportation or prison catches up with them."

"I've heard that too."

"I met Voltaire when I was in Paris."

"Who is he?"

"Voltaire! The writer."

"I never heard of him."

"He's a great man, with a biting pen. He's perfectly fearless. He has attacked the church, the state, and he has been exiled and persecuted."

"Well, that usually happens when a man attacks the church or the state, let alone both of them."

She made an impatient sound.

"He gave me two of his pamphlets."

"Dangerous stuff for a girl to carry about with her. What would your father or your father confessor say?"

She snorted.

"I can see that danger does not daunt you, cousin Anne."

He found that he was taking pleasure in saying her name. It was short, sturdy, dependable, appropriate.

"Tell me about yourself."

She snorted again.

"I am trying to. I have never tried so hard with so little effect."

"You have been telling me about a writer and about the peasants."

"Yes, I have."

"Well?"

She shrugged.

"I hoped you would understand. The most important thing we can give a friend is our real opinion on the things that matter."

He was a little baffled, but there was something warming in the way she brought out "friend" that went to his heart and started a glow that he tried to disguise from himself.

Chiktek returned, popping up beside them suddenly.

"The English have pitched camp," he said. "I crept close. I heard everything they said. Their officer is young, with authority. Officer Vo-am."

Paul looked startled. Vo-am, Vaughan, Vaughan, Vo-am.

"What was this officer like? Tall, blond and blue-eyed?"

Chiktek nodded, grinning.

"Nice scalp," he said.

Paul waved him away. There were plenty of blond young men in this attack with unpronounceable names. All the same, he turned to Anne.

"It would be strange if that were Will Vaughan," he said, "so near to us."

"Why don't you go and see? I shall be all right."

Paul shook his head. The last thing in the world that he wanted was to see Will, unless he could greet him from the deck of the *Oiseau de Mer* or take him prisoner. It was one thing to tell Anne that he was body servant and prisoner of war, another to have her see the way Will would treat him, the contemptuous superiority. He found himself growing hot at the thought of it.

"I suppose it's a confession of human weakness," he said, "envy, malice and all uncharitableness."

"What?" Anne asked.

A smell of cooking fish came to their nostrils.

"I don't mind confessing that I'm damned hungry again," she said, sitting down.

Paul laughed, still thinking of Will and the *Oiseau de Mer.* From that he went on to the longboat. What in God's name had happened to the longboat? Here he was marooned next to the enemy, with a girl to look after—and she was right, if she were taken prisoner and it was known that she was the Governor's daughter, they would make an issue of it somehow. He choked on a bone.

"If the New Englanders stay where they are now for the night," Anne told him, "we can still have a fire, in the shelter."

Paul mastered his bone.

"Would you like to go up the hill now that the drunken louts are gone, and spend the night in one of the rooms of the battery?"

"No," she said, "I would be more frightened there. I like to see the water and to know that if the longboat comes we shall see it come. I would rather stay here, in the shelter."

Paul was relieved. He had no mind to spend the night pacing about the battery on the lookout for the enemy. At least here one man, Chiktek, could do all the patrolling. He was grateful to Anne for speaking so stoutly, for swearing like a man, and setting him at ease, and particularly for her natural way of taking things. She did not flirt, she did not blush—too often, she did not appear embarrassed by all the intimacies and implications of their situation. She had cried that morning, but she made no attempt to explain her tears. She tried to talk of general things. If she had to be a girl of good family, instead of a woman, or a native girl like San, it was fortunate that she was the sort of girl she was. It was fortunate for her, and for him too, in the long run. She sat serenely in the sunset eating fish with her fingers, as calmly as though nothing out of the way were happening to her, yet surely the prospect

·[191]·

of spending another night alone with a young man who was a complete stranger to her, on a deserted shore with no means of escape and a prowling enemy near, must be an ordeal even to the bravest girl. All the worse ordeal if she were innocent, Paul thought. "It is the unknown that we fear." He smirked, and changed the smirk to a smile as he looked at her. There was something about her that appealed to him to protect her. The appeal was strong. He would laugh at this throwing away of opportunity later, but at the moment, though he might toy with a picture of what would happen, of how she would look if he took her suddenly into his arms, he knew that it was impossible, knew too with what rage he would kill any other man who attempted it.

She turned her frank eyes to his and smiled at him. There was something a little tremulous about the smile.

"She *is* frightened," he thought, and his heart went out to her. "She doesn't find me altogether harmless then, that's something."

He crooked his finger. Chiktek came to his summons.

"Build Mademoiselle's fire up in there," he said, "and arrange a bed for her."

"The sooner you get to sleep," he added to Anne, "the less you will feel the cold."

"But you?" she faltered.

"I have a lot of things to do with Chiktek. We will take turns watching, and we will wake you in case of an alarm. You have nothing to fear. Good night, Mademoiselle."

He had gone back to the formal address unconsciously. A twinkle came into her eyes as she heard it. She said a low "good night" and went into the shelter. Paul turned his back and walked to the shore.

"Pest!" he said, looking up at the stars, listening to the water breaking at his feet, "I wish the longboat would come back. It is ridiculous to be cut off from news in the middle of the attack! Especially when I was the one to bring the news of the attack in the first place."

He began to reflect upon his journey from New England and all that had happened to him since. Then he speculated upon the chances of the siege. Louisbourg was strong, in spite of the Governor's weakness and indecision, in spite of abandoning this battery to the enemy—he glared angrily across the water—that was criminal! But perhaps the New Englanders would not find it or realize that it was undefended. Perhaps the Governor needed those four hundred men. It was a hard position for a governor to have in his command nothing but mutineers and suspects. Still . . . a rustle behind him made him jump. An owl flew over his head, skimmed over the surface of the water in a circle and returned, whirring and gliding, to the shelter of the trees.

Paul returned up the path, and sat down by the fire Chiktek was kindling in a hollow on the hillside where it would not easily be seen.

CHAPTER XLIII

THERE was a flurry of snow that night. Anne, lying on the spruce boughs that Chiktek had piled high for her, woke and looked out. She lay still in the darkness trying to keep warm, but her teeth chattered. She tried to drag a branch of spruce over her legs and feet. Suddenly the entrance to the shelter was blocked by a tall figure.

"Who's there?"

It was Chiktek.

"Has the longboat come for us?"

"No."

He kicked the embers of the fire and piled more wood on it. Anne sank down again, reassured, but not to sleep. A thousand confused thoughts were racing through her mind. She thought of the sick man who should have brought the message in her place, wondering why Vergor had chosen him. It seemed so dangerous to trust your life and other people's lives to a stranger. Vergor was always finding friends in people he had never seen before. Then she laughed a little to herself. Vergor would retort if he could see her now: "What about you? Don't you consider Paul de Morpain a friend?" She thought of that, trying to disentangle her impressions from her feelings, trying to get things straight. The more she thought of Paul the less she kept things straight. She knew for instance that he was not as her father would put it "in her world." He made all worlds but the one he was in seem false to her. She knew that he was neither strikingly handsome, nor rich, nor clever, nor a courtier like Monsieur de Vaudreuil, and others—what was it about him that appealed to her? She did not deny the appeal. She analyzed it. Well, in the first place there was a certain frank enjoyment of himself, of life, of her; an enthusiasm over simple things, the fish he ate, the sun that warmed him, the smooth feeling of a piece of waterlogged wood. She had seen him stroke the pieces that he fed to the fire. Most men did not notice things like that or care. He was vain in an obvious and pleasant way, and diffident in another. He was brave but not, she imagined, the sort of man to be pigheaded about honor when the situation held a deeper significance. Honor! Anne was sick of it. Honor made the French King raze Canceau, honor made the New Englanders retaliate. Honor brought wars and needless suffering to men. They were fools when it came to their honor. Paul de Morpain, like Vergor in another way, would not be taken in, Anne thought, by such a word. She began to place him in a variety of situations, seeing his expression, hearing his voice, as he dealt with them all in unusual ways. Presently she drowsed. Then she began to dream. It was all mixed up with a meeting between Paul and Vergor in an old dark house in Paris. She woke with the sun high above the water. Chiktek was frying fish. Paul was waiting for her in the spring sunshine. She made a hasty inadequate toilet with her handkerchief, recalling a controversy with her nurse outside the salon door, when she was brought in from the garden to see a cardinal.

"I don't care who's in the salon, nurse, I won't be washed with spit!"

She ran her fingers through her hair; powder sifted from it, like snow from a spruce when the first wind strikes it after a snow storm, and she emerged from the shelter awkwardly. Fish, always more fish!

"At least we've been lucky in the weather," Paul said, passing her the water bottle. "It might have worked up to a real snowstorm."

Anne nodded, looking up startled as Chiktek towered suddenly at their sides.

"Oho," said Paul, "what is it now?"

"The English are entering the battery," Chiktek answered, "listen!"

·[195]·

A clicking and scrabbling noise could be heard and the sound of voices. Now that their attention was drawn to it they could not imagine why they had not heard it all along. It seemed an extraordinary din. Paul took Anne's hand. She was very pale.

"Quick," he said, "we must hide in the bushes, near the shore. Chiktek put out the fires."

He put his arm round Anne. She leaned against him and at once all fear left her. They scrambled down the hillside to the beach, and made their way to the next inlet, with Chiktek following.

"Paul, do you think the longboat will ever come back? Hadn't we better try to go round by land?"

"You couldn't make it," Paul said. "It is hard country for a strong man in moccasins to travel. Besides, the New Englanders are between us and the town."

"Then what are we to do? We can't stay here forever!"

Paul was silent. They lay side by side on a flat rock, with their faces peering out from the lowest branches of a spruce. It was very cold, and the spruce shed snow on them.

"Chiktek," Paul said, "start toward Louisbourg by land. Go to the Governor. Make him send a boat for us."

"We should have thought of sending him before," Anne said.

"I did, but I don't trust him. If he runs into one of his people, or anything else catches his attention, he will be diverted for hours, perhaps for days—Micmacs have no sense of time. The only way my uncle gets them to pay any attention to the ship's bells on the *Oiseau de Mer* is by telling them that a spirit is speaking from the bell when it strikes. 'Now it says go, now it says come, now it says eat, now it says sleep.' That way they remember, but not always even then. I thought Chiktek would be useful to us if he stayed, but now we must send him and hope for the best. Let me keep you warm."

He took her in his arms. Once again her senses played her a queer trick; her spirits rose, she became lighthearted and breathlessly gay; she just did not care what happened next, but she hoped something further would happen, though she made no move, no sound. For a long while he held her. She could hear the beating of his heart close to her own. When she stirred the beat seemed to increase or was it her own heart she listened to? Suddenly his head turned, his lips sought and found hers.

"You're so sweet, and so exciting, Anne," he said huskily. "Don't be afraid."

She was not afraid. His kiss held comfort, reassurance, warmth, happiness, and passion. It roused, and yet it soothed in some strange way. She almost laughed. It was not what she had expected from a passionate kiss. A slow warmth crept over her. It was like a drug. She began to feel relaxed and even a little sleepy, in his arms. He had not moved. After the kiss he lay beside her holding her close. Suddenly he sat up with a jerk, startling her. She pulled her arm away—he was grasping it tightly so that it hurt—and sat up too. Something was moving close to them, coming nearer, a twig snapped, the branches of the tree began to rustle. Chiktek's face peered in. He grunted and made signs.

"What is it?" Paul whispered indignantly. "What has happened? Why aren't you well on your way to the town?"

"The longboat is coming back."

"Where?" Paul swept aside the branches and peered out. There was a black streak in the direction that Chiktek pointed.

"Don't let them land at the battery," Paul said. "Make a smoke signal, and bring them farther along the shore, to the inlet here. Hurry, Chiktek, make them understand; they must take us off without the English seeing, without any noise to attract their lookout."

He took Anne's hand in his, but it was different now. They started to creep together down to the rocks, dodging out of sight of the battery.

"I want to tell you," Paul said suddenly, as the boat drew near at last, "that no man ever had a more memorable experience."

She laughed.

"I mean a more enchanting experience."

She was silent, looking out over the water. He could not see the expression in her eyes. He walked round in front of her.

"All right, Governor's daughter."

"Why do you say that?"

"Because when we get back you'll change, you're changing now."

·[197]·

She laughed again, raising frank eyes to his.

"I think it's the other way about."

The boat grounded. She walked to the water's edge and without hesitation into the icy water to scramble on board. The noise behind them, in the battery seemed to grow louder. At any moment the officer who might or might not be Will, would send a detachment of his men in pursuit to take them and the crew of the longboat prisoner. Those last moments while they waited for the stolid Micmacs to push off were tense with strain.

"Take us to the town," Paul ordered, "not to the *Oiseau de Mer*."

Anne stirred.

"I do not want to go home at once, I need a little time to think up a story, to get adjusted. . . ."

"I will take you to my sister's home," Paul told her. "You can stay with her while I tackle the Governor."

She pressed his arm gratefully. The space between them and the shore widened. Presently Louisbourg came so near that they could see the people on the quays. There seemed to be great activity in the town. Bugle calls drifted across the water, guns were firing in the distance, evidently across the marsh. The longboat made for the middle wharf; the Micmacs shipped oars, she glided in, the man in the bow jumped out and made fast. Anne sat still with Paul reluctant to move. He glanced at her, suddenly aware of her appearance, but there was no help for it, he took her by the arm and drew her to her feet. She leaned on him for a moment, as though she were afraid. He stepped on to the wharf and drew her after him. They turned to face the crowd.

There were murmurs, leers, smiles, nudges, here and there laughter choked off abruptly as Paul put his hand to his sword hilt and turned to glare in the direction of the sound. All he saw were mulish faces, stubborn, secretive. When he turned his back on them the laughter broke out again. Anne walked through the crowd with her head held high, in perfect composure, sweeping along in her crumpled dress as though she were in her own salon at a ball. Paul stumbled along beside her, red to the ears with rage and embarrassment. They reached Marie's house after what seemed an eternity to him. He fumbled for the latch. The door swung open. Charles Godet was standing there.

"Oh," he said, seeing Paul, and then "Ah," seeing Anne. He stood aside awkwardly to let them in. Marie was alone in the room. It was an unusual hour for calling, Paul thought. The confusion in Marie's face and the absence of the children told him the story. Godet was eager to tell it too.

"Paul," he began, "we want your consent to our betrothal."

"We'll talk of it later, Charles. You have my consent, but this is an emergency. You must look after Mademoiselle du Chambon while I go to the Governor. Marie, get her some clothes. I will leave her in your care. She has had a distressing experience."

He turned to Anne.

"I will do my best with your father," he said. Their eyes met. Paul lost his composure. He bowed awkwardly and bolted from the room.

He found himself in the street in the fresh morning air, hurrying toward the Governor's house, shaping sentences as he went. He wondered whether Captain Thierry had been to the Governor to report Anne's visit. He thought not, or the Governor would surely have sent a boat for them. Even if Thierry held his tongue, by now busybodies from the quays would have run to tell the Governor of their arrival, of Anne's appearance. The Governor would be justified in thinking the worst. He disliked Paul already; that dislike would color his thoughts, if they needed color to believe what seemed so obvious. "And after all," he sighed, "Lord knows what would have happened if we'd stayed beneath that bush!" But perhaps the Governor knew Anne's quality. There was a chance that if he or any man knew Anne well enough, he would believe in her. Paul braced himself to meet with any reception as he walked over the drawbridge into the courtyard full of hurrying soldiers and turned toward the private apartments. He reached the Governor's door. A sentry challenged him.

"Tell Monsieur du Chambon I have come with important news of the enemy's movements, and I have news for him of Mademoiselle du Chambon too."

The sentry disappeared and returned to admit him at once.

·[199]·

The Governor was seated at his desk. He looked up and there was cold hatred in his eyes. Paul's heart sank.

"Mademoiselle du Chambon is safe," he said, putting the best face on it he could. "She is at my sister's house. The enemy have taken the Royal Battery with a small force. It will not take much to dislodge them if we go about it at once. I carried out your orders to Captain Thierry as he will have reported to you, no doubt, though I did not agree with them, Monseigneur. I consider that we have given the enemy a great advantage in surrendering the battery to them." He talked on, aware of the Governor's eyes fixed on his, as though he would draw the truth out of him, yet did not dare to ask for it, lest it should be the truth he feared.

"I have been under heavy anxiety, Monsieur de Morpain," he said, "for two days and two nights. I would have had troops out scouring the countryside, but this is war, and each man must stand to his station. There is no time for a father's anguish."

"And happily no need for it, Monseigneur. Mademoiselle du Chambon is safe and well."

The Governor passed a hand over his forehead.

"I wish I could believe you! Mother of God if it were true!"

"Your daughter was under my care, Monseigneur," Paul said stiffly. "My sword was ready to protect her from the enemy."

"It is not always the enemy that a woman has most need of protection from," the Governor said, looking fixedly at Paul.

"As to that, Monseigneur, Mademoiselle du Chambon will doubtless render an account of the way in which she was treated when she returns home."

"I will send an escort for her at once, and I hold you responsible, do you hear, I hold you responsible for anything that may have happened. I have yet to hear why she was with you in the first place, and where."

Paul bowed.

"I am happy to hold myself at your disposition, Monseigneur," he said, "and entirely at the service of Mademoiselle. You are not forgetting, I trust, that the English are even now entrenching themselves in the Royal Battery?"

The Governor clapped his hands; the sentry appeared and stood to attention.

"Send Monsieur Bigot, Monsieur Forant and Monsieur de Vaudreuil to me immediately," he barked, "and pass the word to the officer on duty to get two detachments of men ready for a sortie. Prepare boats. Send two trustworthy men with a chair to the house of this gentleman's sister . . ."

"On the corner of the Rue St. Louis and the quay," Paul interposed.

". . . to fetch Mademoiselle du Chambon home. You will stay here," he added to Paul, "until this disgraceful affair has been sifted."

Paul shuffled his feet. The excitement died out of him. He was back in the old atmosphere of court intrigue and class distinctions. The exhilarating air of the sea and the forests had blown society and all its ramifications out of Paul's head, not for the first time. It created the illusion that a man standing upon the free earth of New France was the equal of any other man, free to live, free to love, free to work for himself and his family, free to build up his life as high as he could reach. What else would they be fighting for, when the New Englanders attacked? Not Louisbourg. Louisbourg was just another town, a collection of stone houses, a place to shelter men and women from the storm. It could be built again. Another Louisbourg could be erected, painfully and slowly, somewhere else. The stones were not what they were fighting for, it was the idea of Louisbourg, the idea of a free French town in free New France, for free men. That was what they would be fighting for. Did the Governor know that? Paul glanced at him. No, he had the air of what he was—a nobleman from Paris, impoverished, so that he had to be here, seeking his fortune in New France. He would go back, to strut among his kind when this was over, when he had scrounged enough wealth out of the place. This was the man who had the defense of Louisbourg, of the gateway to New France, in his plump paws. He was Anne's father. Anne was different. She knew what Paul knew. She was real and sweet, achingly sweet. That kiss had been real and revealing. But Anne was not for him. She had used him, prettily, as she would have used anyone else. She was her father's daughter. It was not her fault. She was a horse of a different color, but the stallion had the last word, he sired her.

Paul grew tired of standing. He asked the Governor's permission and without waiting for it to be given sank on a bench near the window, staring out of it. He could see four boatloads already setting off against the Royal Battery. He watched their progress, saw their reception and the puffs of white smoke that hovered over them, saw them turn and head for home, with good men killed and wounded, no doubt, while the Governor sucked at his quill pen, writing a report to the Minister in France. It was just like this weak, vain, indecisive man, Paul thought eyeing him resentfully, to give orders to Captain Thierry to abandon the battery, and then to change his mind and try to take it back.

"The God-damn fool," Paul thought, "he's handed a pretty present to the New Englanders. I'll wager Will makes use of it."

"We've lost the battery," he said aloud, "a bad day's work."

The Governor looked up.

"I am not aware that I asked your opinion, Monsieur de Morpain," he snapped.

PART FIVE
THE FALL OF LOUISBOURG 1745

CHAPTER XLIV

ANNE came, but Paul was not allowed to speak to her. He spent the night in a cell. He was so tired that he managed to sleep, in spite of his anxiety. Toward dawn a soldier brought him some food. A little later his cell was shaken as six cannon opened fire on the town from the Royal Battery. As soon as the English gunners got the range they began to inflict heavy damage to the houses along the quays and to the west bastion. When the first shots dropped into the town, women screamed and ran for shelter, men stared with their mouths open, shaking their fists in the direction of the guns, and some went so far as to shake their fists toward the Governor's apartments in the citadel. It was a colossal blunder that even a child could see, to abandon a battery of heavy guns, before it had been attacked, so that the guns could be used against the people they were installed to defend.

Worse was to come. The marsh which was supposed to keep any enemy at a safe distance from the town was no obstacle to these crusading New Englanders. When the first gun they tried to drag forward toward the town sank to the hub in the mud, then to the carriage, finally to the piece itself, then disappeared completely, the New Englanders did not give up the attempt as any sane people would have done; instead they built sledges of timber sixteen feet long and five feet wide, mounted a cannon upon each sledge, harnessed two hundred men with rope traces and breast straps to each sledge, and dragged them inch by horrible inch through the mire and the marsh. They could do this only at night or in the fog, as they were exposed to the cannon of the town. The French were astonished and bewildered by these feats; horses and oxen would have foundered, men barefooted, in tatters, waded to the knees in a slough of churned and stinking mud, forward, always forward, until they had planted a battery of six guns on Green Hill, a mile from the King's Bastion.

The Governor did not dare to order a sortie against them. He distrusted the mutineers and feared desertion; besides, he could not altogether take the besiegers seriously, looking upon them as an ignorant, unmilitary rabble. Monsieur Bigot urged him to order sorties and make a spirited attack before the enemy could get entrenched or bring more cannon nearer, but the Governor preferred to wait. He was morose and preoccupied.

Many things were troubling him. Anne his daughter had returned, but he could make nothing of her. She was dignified, serene, and laughed at his authority. If she wanted to go away for two days and two nights, in the company of a whippersnapper, a man of humble origin and no standing in the community, she took the line that that was her affair, she could look after herself, and his suspicions were dishonorable. He could do nothing with her. She was bent on bringing disgrace upon him. If he married her to this man, the marriage in itself would be a disgrace. He was enraged and anxious. He consulted Madame de Saintonge.

She listened sympathetically, in her restful apartment, sewing on a piece of tapestry. When Paul de Morpain was mentioned, she put the needle down, and gave frowning attention to the recital. Monsieur du Chambon was soothed. Here was somebody who could appreciate his feelings, who could understand what a mésalliance such a marriage would be.

"Does she want to marry him?" Madame de Saintonge asked, leaning forward.

"She says nothing happened."

"And you believe it?"

He shrugged. "How do I know what to believe? Anne has not lied to me so far, but this is different."

Madame de Saintonge nodded.

"Have you had her examined by the apothecary?" she asked, taking up her tapestry again.

Monsieur du Chambon looked startled.

"No," he stammered, "I . . . er . . ."

"Then do so," she advised. "There may be no need for a marriage. At least you will know what to expect. Perhaps you are doing your daughter and Monsieur de Morpain an injustice. After all, his uncle is somebody, you know, and you need the *Oiseau de Mer*."

He nodded unhappily.

"Where is he now?"

"The young man?"

"Yes."

"In the dungeon below us."

"Oh."

The Governor leaned forward.

"Supposing things should be all right . . . I hardly dare to hope it, but . . . what then?"

"Why then your troubles are over, aren't they?"

"I don't know. Perhaps Anne has conceived some sort of a romantic notion about this fellow. Perhaps she will insist on marrying him."

"Don't be absurd!" Madame de Saintonge said sharply. "Such an idea is preposterous—unless she has to, and that, my friend, the apothecary can tell you better than you or I or Anne. If I were you I should send her home to France when the siege is ended, to a convent there, to teach her manners and sense. And I should detail the Morpain lout to a nice dangerous post in the forefront of the war, where he could be useful, either way, dead or alive." She laughed grimly. "If you keep him in a dungeon, his uncle will get restive, make inquiries, make trouble, noise the scandal abroad. It would be wiser, I think, to release the fellow, as though he were of no importance to you or to anyone else."

"I do not want him free around the town, making a hero of himself," the Governor objected.

"You can't very well kill him where he is; too many people know."

The Governor shrugged.

"A plague on him. What does Anne see in him? What, for that matter," he whirled on her, "did you?"

"I? I? My dear Governor!"

"It seemed to me you took a certain interest in this boy, always walking out with him, and receiving him at odd hours!" He spoke petulantly.

She laughed.

"I must confess, when you are busy I get a little bored. He has a melodious voice, and plays the harpsichord. Occasionally I had him come and play and sing for me. If you had told me that this worried you, of course it would never have happened! But how could I dream that you would descend so low as to be jealous of a stripling fisher boy, a lout, with a tuneful note in his voice! My dear, was that worthy of you, of us?"

The Governor looked confused, and a little pleased. She got up and came over to him.

"I am glad," she whispered, laying her cheek close to his, "that you can be jealous, but amazed that you could be jealous of Paul de Morpain! What humility, and absurdity."

"He's young," the Governor brought out, huskily, catching her hand in his and covering it with kisses.

"Callow," she said.

"And you were—seemed—cooling to me."

"You were neglectful, but I understood. You have so much upon your mind. I only wish that I could rest you."

"You both rest and excite."

He buried his face in the décolleté of her gown, where the hollow between her ivory breasts showed beneath its lace, and stayed there a long time. She stroked his neck, his head, and stared frowning, over his shoulder. Presently she pushed him gently away.

"It will be all right," she said. "Everything will be all right. But you must go."

He stood up regretfully. A distant booming shook the room, chairs rattled, and a pewter dish fell from the wall. He gathered his hat and cloak in silence, smiling at her, meaningly. She smiled back, and escorted him from the room. Then she went to the pewter dish and kicked it three times, took her tapestry and tore it, breaking the threads, pounded a cushion, and finally went to the bell rope, which she tugged viciously. The soldier servant answered, after an interval.

"Bring me a stoup of hot wine," she said, "and make it strong."

·[208]·

CHAPTER XLV

THE Governor sent for Paul.
"It appears," he said, when he stood before him, "that you deserve well of me, Monsieur de Morpain. I was too hasty in my judgment."

Paul bowed.

"I am glad that Mademoiselle du Chambon has convinced you, Monseigneur."

"My daughter has never lied to me, Monsieur de Morpain, and on this occasion I had her testimony checked by the apothecary." He coughed dryly.

Paul looked at him quizzically, then he reddened as the meaning of the words reached him. "Old fool," he thought resentfully, "I could have told you—I did tell you. I knew your daughter was a virgin when I kissed her underneath a bush." The memory of the kiss came back to him, sending the blood a little faster through his veins. Poor Anne! He could imagine how she would hate the humiliation he had brought to her. Part of him was glad to have his certainty confirmed. There was no other man. "Why do you care, you idiot? She's not for you!" "I care," he answered himself with dignity, "because if there had been another man I would have taken the blame, of course." He smiled, his eyes sought the floor.

"You have a father's thanks, Monsieur," the Governor said, but there was no warmth in his voice, no light in his eyes. "I am sending you to the Island Battery in command of reinforcements, to Captain d'Aillebout."

Paul bowed.

"May I not return to the *Oiseau de Mer* instead?" he asked. "My uncle is expecting me. He needs an officer. I know more about the sea than I do about land fighting. I would prefer . . ."

The Governor held up his hand.

"Captain d'Aillebout has a greater need. There is no one to command these reinforcements. You have shown yourself to be a young man of integrity and spirit; I am happy to appoint you to this post."

There was finality in his voice, Paul recognized it.

"I am honored, Monseigneur, and shall endeavor to give you every satisfaction."

Then a thought came to him. He would be leaving Marie and the children at the mercy of his enemies. Now he had added Captain Thierry to the list. He cleared his throat.

"I would ask one favor . . ."

"Yes?" the Governor eyed him warily.

"A little time to arrange my personal affairs. My sister's marriage . . ."

"I thought it had been canceled."

"Her marriage to Monsieur Mercier was canceled, Monseigneur is right. But now she is betrothed to a young naval officer."

"I see."

"I would ask your permission for enough delay to see that the wedding takes place."

"You must leave tonight."

"Very well. A word from you to the priest might hasten things. The priest is a friend of Monsieur Mercier's."

The Governor reflected. After all, why not? If this boy's sister had married into the Mercier family he would be altogether too powerfully protected, and would know too much, through his in-laws. Let her marry a simple naval captain and be out of the picture. The Merciers could not very well object to his sanction of the marriage, or if they did, he could smooth things out. It was better so. He took up his pen and scribbled a note, sanded it and handed it to Paul, who bowed, thanked him and left the room.

Paul was depressed as he crossed the courtyard and saw the damage that the guns from the Royal Battery had already done to the town. Several houses were in ruins, others were scarred and two were smoldering. The wall of the quay was riddled and streets within range were being raked. People ran for refuge toward the stifling casemates. It was no time to be careless. He hoped Anne was taking care. He knew these fantastic New Englanders with their brains still fevered from the "Great Awakening"; they thought that they were Israel doing away with idolaters, egged on by Parson Moody and his kind. They were dangerous because they were mad. Louisbourg was impregnable by all the rules, but the New Englanders from Pepperell to Will paid no attention to rules. They would fight on until they had taken Louisbourg and laid it in ruins. Then the whole dreary pattern of his life would begin again, he would be a prisoner of war, all the good life gone. He raged. People had put love and thought and labor into those crumbled heaps of stone, people had planned their lives, dreamed their dreams, hoped their pitiful small hopes, and now an unseen enemy was taking the last few days, the last few hours perhaps, of happiness away from them. By what right?

He reached the door to Marie's cottage just as a whistling shriek went over him. He ducked inside; the shot fell with a thump against the wall of the next house, sending up a cloud of dust and stone.

"You and the children must take shelter in the casemates."

She nodded.

"It's so airless there. I would rather take a chance out here."

"Charles would not like you to," Paul twinkled at her.

She blushed.

"Where is he now?" he inquired, sitting down.

"He'll be here presently. He's gone to the quay to see about the brig."

"Tomas," Paul called, "run to the priest with this note. Show it to him but do not give it up. Tell him he is to come here immediately."

Tomas started up.

"Is it safe?" Marie asked anxiously. "I have not let him go outside."

"He is a clever boy, big enough to be some use. Run quickly, dodge the shot. When you have told the priest to come here, go to the quay, tell officer Godet he must get leave and come at once, then be back as soon as you can."

Tomas went out.

"Now," said Paul, "get yourself ready for your wedding."

Marie looked startled. The children clapped their hands and crowded about her.

"The wedding! The wedding!"

"Yes," Paul said, "the Governor is sending me to the Island Battery. I cannot protect you from there, I want you married and off my hands, another man's responsibility." He smiled and kissed her cheek. "Charles will make no objection I imagine."

There was another screech, whine and thump close to them.

"I wish you did not live on the quays," Paul said. "This house is dangerous."

He was thinking of Anne as he spoke. The fort would be more dangerous he supposed. It would be difficult to be so far away, not knowing what was happening. Far or near, he could do nothing for Anne.

"Stop thinking about her, you fool!" he told himself angrily.

There was a rapping on the door. Paul turned his head. Marie went to open it.

Anne stood in the doorway, panting and a little disheveled. She had run, dodging cannon balls. Once she had thrown herself down on the quay when a volley came near. She was pale, but her eyes sparkled. She greeted Marie cheerfully and turned to Paul.

"I heard that father had ordered you to the Island Battery. I thought you might be here. I've come to say good-by and to thank you . . ."

Paul interrupted her.

"You're just in time to stay for the wedding," he said.

Anne looked surprised. Marie slipped from the room to get herself ready. The children followed her.

"It was good of you to come here," Paul said awkwardly. "I was wishing that I could see you before I had to go. But should you take so many risks? Your father . . ."

"Don't speak of him!" she cried indignantly. "I regard myself as an orphan from now on. And if he knew that it was all for the sake of his precious Vergor . . . oh, it chokes me!"

Paul began to smile. His heart was beating fast again.

"I came to thank you, to tell you . . ."

"There is no need, Mademoiselle. It is I who am grateful for the memory."

"Don't say that my father has made you go back to Mademoiselle! I know he was insulting, because of all the hateful things he said to me, but don't let that change our friendship, Paul, I have such need of a friend."

He melted.

"I have, too," he said, swallowing hard, "here's my hand on it."

A sound at the door interrupted them. The priest came in, followed by Godet and Tomas, all three flurried and red-faced. Godet hurried to Paul.

"What is it?" he asked. "What has happened?"

"You are getting married. At once. Marie is preparing herself, you are prepared, I take it, you look very well, and here is the priest. We have the Governor's blessing, in this note, you have my consent. Tomas, go and hurry the bride. Father, we are at your disposal."

Godet's jaw dropped. The priest looked a little sullen, but he placed himself with dignity beside the table and opened his book. Marie came out of the bedroom, dressed in white. She had taken a branch of green spruce from the kindling for her bouquet. It looked very well. Godet moved toward her, hands outstretched. The priest cleared his throat.

"Face me," he said, and raised his hand. The marriage service began.

Paul took up his stand behind the pair, a little to the left. Anne stood near him, with the two youngest children on either side. Her eyes were shining, her cheeks were flushed. Paul watched her through the ceremony. Now and then he dragged his eyes away but each time they came back to her face traveling hungrily from her forehead with its widow's peak of soft powdered hair to her eyes, large and dark like the waters of Fundy on a moonless night, to her nose, small and irregular—one side of it was crooked, he had not noticed that before—to her mouth, generous and passionate. He had felt her lips beneath his, soft and warm and full of life.

·[213]·

The ceremony was coming to an end. He pulled himself together with an effort to pay the priest, thank him, open the door and watch him go. Godet took Marie in his arms and turned to Paul.

"I can't thank you enough," he said. "I was afraid we might have to wait."

"Take care of her," Paul said absently.

"I will."

"You see," Paul's eyes were still on Anne, who was congratulating Marie and kissing her, "I have been sent to the Island Battery."

"And I have been dismissed from the brig."

"No!" That startled him out of his dream.

"Certainly. It was bound to come. You did not think Captain Mercier would stomach me there when I was engaged to the girl who publicly jilted his brother!"

"I had not thought of that." Paul frowned. "What will you do?"

"I don't know. I'll find something."

"Go to my uncle," Paul said slowly, "offer to take my place on the *Oiseau de Mer*. He needs an officer, he was expecting me, but the Governor intervened, for reasons of his own." He remembered that Anne was listening and stopped. There was no sense in criticizing her father to her face.

Godet's expression brightened.

"I will," he said.

"And keep in touch with me."

"Are you going to live here through the siege?" Anne was asking Marie.

"Yes. I shall send the children to the convent if it gets much worse. They will be safer there, and nearer the casemates. I can join them if the house is hit."

"We have a better shelter at the fort," Anne said. "In one way it's more dangerous, being fired upon more frequently, but the shelters are deep and comfortable. I am having beds put there for the wounded that the Frères de Charité cannot take care of in their hospital. I need somebody to help me nurse them. Would

·[214]·

you consider coming to the fort and staying there with me until the siege is over?"

Marie looked at her husband. She read the answer he would like her to give in his anxious face.

"Yes," she said and sighed, "I will come and help you."

It was not the start to her married life that she had dreamed. Charles took her into his arms and they disappeared together into the other room. Paul turned to Anne.

"Thank you for coming," he said simply. "I will see you home."

"No," she laughed a little ruefully, "I must sneak back by alleys and streets out of range. Good-by."

"Good-by."

They stared at each other.

"Paul," she said softly, "real things only come once to real people."

She closed the door and was gone. He stood there dumbly for a moment; then he ran to the door, opened it and took three steps after her, but she was already out of sight. A flash and roar, followed by a confused din of shrieks and the crackle of flames sent his heart into his mouth. A bomb had dropped on the tavern in the next street.

"Anne!"

He caught himself together and turned back reluctantly. Charles and Marie were in the bedroom with the door locked, poor lucky young things, snatching at what they could get. Paul took the children to the table and set them to dividing up the gold that was left in the hiding place behind the stone.

"This for Marie, and this for the children and this for me," he said, making three piles of it. All the time he was thinking: "What for me and Anne?"

CHAPTER XLVI

THE Island Battery was a sturdy fortress, guarded by strong walls, by rocks lashed by the surf, and garrisoned by a hundred and eighty men. There were two mortars, seven swivels, and thirty cannon, all in good order. Captain d'Aillebout, the Commander, was a good disciplinarian and unlike the Governor knew his own mind. Paul, prepared for the worst, was surprised to take an instant liking to him. He was assigned to the third battery. From his station he could see Louisbourg besieged by the enemy and watch the clouds of dust and smoke go up to mark each hit. The town was taking heavy punishment, there were five enemy batteries now in good positions, well in range, dragged there in the night by teams of men. Bad as things were, Paul was glad he was not on the English side, harnessed to a gun like an ox. Here the good sea came up in clouds of spray; he might be on a ship. The Island Battery commanded the entrance to the harbor, nothing could pass until her guns were silenced. They could watch the enemy squadron hovering at a safe distance like beautiful birds of prey. On the nineteenth of May they saw a large French vessel, hotly engaged with the squadron. They watched as long as they could see. Captain d'Aillebout thought she might be the *Vigilant* with supplies and dispatches from France. Vital supplies! It would be a disaster if she were taken. Anxiously they strained to keep her in view, but she drifted out of sight, still fighting; the sound of guns went on above the roar of the surf. There was no means of knowing how she fared.

Boats went regularly between the Island Battery and the town, running the gauntlet of fire from the Royal Battery, to gather news, receive orders, and generally keep in touch. It would not be Paul's turn to go with the boat for some time, but he could receive letters and send them. He carried one from Marie.

"I am sending with this some comforts, and a scarf to keep you warm, for the nights are still cold, though it is spring. Take care of yourself, keep out of the enemy's way as I do. I am constantly below ground with the wounded. The children are well. There are very few houses that have not been hit. Every evening I take the air when the English cease firing at their suppertime. I look across toward you and wonder how the day has gone, and when we shall be together. Charles is well suited in the *Oiseau de Mer*. He wishes she could engage the enemy, but she is not ready yet. I am glad of that. I see him several times a day. I can never be enough thankful that God sent you back to me in time to prevent my unhappy sacrifice, and gave you the courage to protect me. Also I met Charles through you. I shall never forget that first evening. Some Indians have arrived and placed themselves at the disposal of the Sieur de la Valière. They tried to burn the English storehouses near Flat Point Cove. I am so tired of this war, and how will it end? The Governor is depressed. The ammunition is running low. It looks as though it might be possible—I say this to you alone—that the New Englanders win. But they will have a ruined town for their pains. As long as they don't get Charles or you, as long as neither of you are like these poor wounded men, suffering, dying—oh Paul, keep safe for us. Mademoiselle du Chambon is good to everyone. She is a real friend. She works here unsparingly. I have come to have affection for her. Oh, and who do you suppose comes here a lot to talk to the men and write letters for them, and make them laugh? Madame de Saintonge! I suppose you are reddening, Paul. I must say she has a way with the wounded men. I like it in her. I never thought she was anything but a light woman, vain with her looks. I have seen her almost compassionate and tireless in working here. Mademoiselle du Chambon and she do not like one another. This is obvious and sometimes funny. I suppose they are too unlike. Mademoiselle du Chambon is direct."

"Direct," Paul thought, putting the letter back into his pocket. "Real things only come once to real people." That was direct enough. He left the guardroom to take what he called his watch. There was a bright moon and northern lights. He could see far to sea and over the harbor. The sentries paced below him, calling their rounds in peace. It was a beautiful scene. Paul snuffed the cool night air. On such a night war and the makers of war seemed far away.

A few nights later, on the twenty-sixth of May, the night was dark, moonless and still. Paul found himself listening uneasily to the surf lashing the rocks below. The tide was coming in, but it seemed to him that there was a noise above the noise of the tide. It was nearing the end of his watch. He called to a sentry and sent him to rouse Captain d'Aillebout. When he came, they paced the battery platform together, but now there was nothing unusual to be seen or to be heard.

Suddenly a sound of cheering tore the night. It came from below the walls. The enemy had landed in the only place that landing was possible.

"Obliging of them to warn us!" Captain d'Aillebout grunted, giving the alarm.

A moment later the island blazed with fire from cannon, swivels, and small arms. Straining through the night, the garrison could dimly see a crowd of boats standing a little distance from the shore. Only three boats could nose in at a time between the breakers. The defenders knew in what direction to fire, even if they could not clearly see. Langrage shot and musket balls rained on the attacking party, which came scrambling on. Some boats were shattered and sank, others behind them sheered off. The men already on shore stumbled forward, carrying scaling ladders, but the French were ready for these. They had placed lanterns so that a bar of light shone between them and the enemy. They spattered this pathway of light unceasingly, until the attack was beaten off. Paul firing his musket and reloading it to fire again, wounded three men in one of the scaling parties and killed a fourth.

The firing went on till the sun rose. As the light became clearer the French shooting improved. Paul, taking careful aim at an officer directing operations, saw him duck and leap aside. He seemed to be rallying the men about him for a final charge. They ran forward, cheering and shouting. Paul raised his musket to take more careful aim. He would get the fellow this time. He fired; a man leaped in between, met the bullet and crumpled to his knees. The officer came on. Now Paul could see his face. He looked closer, lowering his gun unconsciously. Yes, it was Will, Will mad with rage at the turn of events, and the failure of the attack. He ran on as though he would take the place himself with his bare hands. Paul held his fire but the men about him were aiming steadily. Musket balls whistled about the advancing troops. They wavered, broke, and turned. Two men caught Will by the arm and retreated, dragging him with them to the edge of the shore. Another officer ran forward, waving a white silk scarf on the end of his sword. Surrender! The New Englanders were surrendering! There was nothing else that they could do, Paul conceded. Out of the tail of his eye he saw a boat push off. Shots were fired at it, splashing into the sea around it, but it pulled away. Paul searched the shore. Will must be in that boat. He felt relieved.

"Ciel!" he said to himself angrily, when he realized this, "why should I care what happens to Will?"

The sun was shining now, full upon the surrender. A hundred and nineteen men gave themselves up. Many were wounded, three men died while the white flag was being waved above them.

"Victory, complete victory!" Paul exulted, "and heaven knows how many of them were drowned when we hit the boats. The Governor will be glad of this."

The news sped to Louisbourg; shouts of triumph rang through the town; cheering could be heard rolling across the harbor and over the marsh. The sound of it reached the Island Battery in a faint echo. Bells were rung. Paul stood to his station, looking toward the town. He was tired, but the thought of the engagement thrilled him with pride. He went along the ranks of the men under him, congratulating them.

"That was good fighting," he said, "that was showing them how!"

The men grinned and shuffled their feet. They were an ugly-looking lot, the sweepings of France and Switzerland, jailbirds and brigands, but he was proud of them.

"Ah," he said, looking across the sunlit waters where Will's boat had disappeared into Gabarus Bay, "which is the master of us two, now?" He wished he could tell Anne.

·[219]·

CHAPTER XLVII

T HE joy and excitement," Marie wrote to Paul, "with which your victory at the Island Battery was received here, has been clouded. An English officer brought news under a flag of truce, in a letter from the Marquis de Maisonfort, a prisoner on board his own ship. The letter has dismayed us all and Mademoiselle du Chambon says the Governor is confounded. Commodore Peter Warren has arrived with English ships. He is reputed a great sailor, a dangerous enemy, and the *Vigilant* has been taken, Paul, with all the ammunition and supplies we need so desperately here. Nor only that, but these same supplies are now being used by our enemies against us, and to crown all we are being constantly bombarded by new batteries dragged nearer in the night. Our walls are crumbling, our houses falling, we get no sleep and we have no food. You will know beter than I what all this means and whether we can still hold out. Tomas ran to me today with his eyes shining. He had found a litter of kittens and taken them to the convent to be turned into soup. God forgive me, I heard his tale with hunger and envy! What are you eating, Paul?"

The Governor sent a dispatch:

"Ten cannon have been unearthed by the enemy from the flats near the careening wharf where our men had hidden them. They are being mounted at Lighthouse Point and I fear you will hear from them. I have sent another messenger in appeal to Marin to raise the siege of Annapolis and hasten to our relief with his body of regulars and Indians. The West Gate has been shattered. Our men labored with energy under cover of night to repair the damage. They have made a wall of stone and earth twenty feet thick to protect the circular Battery. Three out of its sixteen guns are left to us. We have stopped the throat of the Dauphin's Bastion with a barricade of stone, and built a cavalier on the King's Bastion, where, however, the enemy fire ruined it. We planted three heavy cannon against their most advanced battery (the Batterie de Francœur) to take it in flank.* These produced a marvelous effect, dismounted one of the cannon of the New Englanders and damaged all their embrasures, which did not prevent them from keeping up a constant fire; and they repaired by night the mischief we did them by day.*"

Paul sighed. Lighthouse Point on the eastern side of the harbor's mouth was a short half-mile from the Island Battery. Already one battery of cannons and mortars carried in boats, hauled up the steep cliff and dragged over rocks, had been planted there by the enemy. It was firing with deadly precision, dropping shells among the French gun crews so that several times men had to run into the sea to escape destruction. Several guns were dismantled, Captain d'Aillebout was wounded, Paul found himself in command of a place fast becoming untenable. And now ten more guns, their own guns, were being mounted against them!

He peered out from the shelter of a hogshead filled with stones, taking stock of the situation. Two cannon were responding to the English fire, their crews working under sergeants. Ten of the remaining twenty-eight cannon were out of action, with five of the seven swivels. The two mortars could still be worked but thirteen men had been killed at one of them that morning. Paul had given orders that they were to remain out of action until darkness fell and the enemy fire abated. He knew that his ammunition was running out and he must keep enough to repel an attack.

He watched the work of the two crews, sweating at their guns. He crouched, and made a dash past them to enter the garrison house. It had suffered badly but so far was not made uninhabitable. Captain d'Aillebout was here with seventy other wounded men, and no one to look after them. Paul passed between the long lines of suffering companions who peered up at him in desperate hope, quickly changed to despair. He sweated at the stench of wounds and corruption, trembled at the pitiful sights and sounds, averted his eyes and hurried on till he reached Captain d'Aillebout.

"How are you, sir?" he asked, kneeling beside him.

The yellow face seemed to grow yellower, the tight lips parted.

"Not dead—yet!" the Captain mouthed.

Paul tried to smile reassuringly.

"That's fine, sir, that's fine."

"What about—up there?"

"We're holding our own, sir."

"Don't hear much firing."

"Only two cannon being worked just now, to save the ammunition and the men. It seems to be enough to keep off any attempt to take us by storm."

"They won't try that again," the Captain whispered. "They'll just keep on firing at us till we're wiped out. It's easier. Any news from the Governor?"

"Yes sir, a dispatch came just now."

"Well?"

"He does not give us any orders, just relates conditions in the town."

"Pretty bad, I suppose?"

"Yes sir, almost as bad as here from what I can make out."

The Captain groaned and shifted his weight a little, his face beading with drops of sweat. He fumbled with one hand for the coat that covered him. Paul pulled it straight. He went to a pitcher of stale water in a corner of the room and poured a little into a bowl. He held this to Captain d'Aillebout's lips.

"Have you any orders for me?" he asked, as he took the bowl away.

"Orders? Orders?"

The Captain spoke thickly and his eyes were vague.

"Oh, orders. Yes, do the best you can, best you can."

Paul saluted, and withdrew, passing the long line of wounded men desperately, with his head high and his eyes looking straight ahead. He drew a long breath as he came into the air even though that air was acrid with dust from crumbling stone. He took up his station behind the hogshead again and turned his glass upon

·[222]·

the Lighthouse Point. Yes, the enemy appeared to be dragging something into place. The ten guns.

"We seem bent on giving them our own arms to use against us," he reflected; "first the Royal Battery, then the *Vigilant* and now these. When I think of the preparations that might have been made if Anne's father had listened to me from the first." But he dared not think of that. He must keep his apparent confidence, it was the only thing that he could give these men. "What orders, sir?" they asked, as though any orders of his could help. He sighed. A ball landed on one of the cannons still firing, even as he looked. When the smoke and dust cleared, he saw three men carrying a fourth, followed by a fifth with his hands to his head, staggering toward the garrison house. He turned away.

"Number seven cannon prepare to fire!" he shouted. "Sergeant get a crew there to that other gun. Now then!"

CHAPTER XLVIII

EARLY on the morning of June 18, Paul with four gaunt and
ragged men, crept to the beach and launched a boat to take
them to Louisbourg. The position was desperate, the battery
was in ruins, all but three cannon had been silenced by the enemy's
fire, ammunition was so low that before another dawn these
would be silent too, unless reinforcements could be found. Paul
decided the time had come to go for them himself. All the messengers he sent returned with the same answer:

"The Governor regrets that further supplies cannot be furnished
to the Island Battery, except in case of emergency."

It was the last part of the message that infuriated Paul.

"What does he think an emergency is?" he fumed. "Does he
want to lose this battery as well as the one he gave away?"

He left a sergeant in charge with orders to fire one cannon at
regular intervals.

"We must hope that this will be enough to keep the enemy
from sending a landing party over to attack," he said. "I will come
back as soon as I can, with balls and powder, if any are to be
found in Louisbourg!"

The man grinned, and wished him luck.

Paul grinned back. Grimy scarecrow, in charge of grimier,
more villainous-looking scum! They were magnificent, and he
had come to respect and like each man. He could never forget the
hardships they had endured together, hunger, thirst, fever, wounds,
death, burial. He turned his head away, and looked toward the
town. They were approaching the quays, but he would not have

recognized them. Half the wall was down, gaping, jagged holes showed where the enemy shot had carried stones away. The landing stages were gone. Paul had a difficult time getting the boat moored and scrambling from it with his men. He stared about him, aghast at the destruction forty-six days of siege had brought to the town. The streets were heaped with debris, stones, wooden beams, window frames, chimneys, broken furniture, shoes, clothing, bric-à-brac, the bodies and bones of dead animals from which the flesh had been scraped, cows, pigs, dogs, cats, rats. One of the men said in a tone of satisfaction:

"So they've been eating rat the same as us. Mice, too, by the look of it." He spat.

The houses behind the quay were drunkenly askew, roofless, with crumbling walls and broken windows. Every street opening out to their view presented the same picture. It began to look as though there were not a house left intact in the town. Paul saw the spires towering from convent and from citadel. They at least were still there. He turned up a side street leading to the fort, followed by his tattered escort. They met nobody, passed nobody, saw no signs of life. It was a deserted city in the dawn light.

Presently as they went along a street near the citadel whose houses seemed less damaged, though one of them had crumbled and others showed scars, shutters were opened here and there and heads began to peer out. Doors were unlatched, children and older figures staggered out with buckets and pitchers, going to the well. The children were white-faced wraiths, with protruding bellies and pinched, vacant faces.

"Looks as though these hadn't found even a mouse in a long time," the same man muttered behind Paul's shoulder, "bloody little skin and bones!"

A volley of cannon shot crumped ahead of them. The children scattered into different doorways, peering out until the dust settled, when they ran on their way. Paul and his men made a dash for the gateway to the fort. A sentry challenged them. Paul panted out his errand and was passed inside. The men were detained at the blockhouse.

"All right," he said, "stay here where I can find you when I want you."

He disappeared, making for the Governor's rooms. He found another gaunt sentry at the door and was made to wait. The Governor was in conference with Monsieur Bigot. The sentry swayed as he stood. Paul questioned him.

"Yes, the town is terribly hard put to it for food, for ammunition, for sleep," he whispered. "The enemy keeps up a constant fire. We have not lost so many men—about a hundred—but we are pretty well exhausted, that's the truth."

He dared not say any more. The door opened and fragments of conversation drifted out.

"Where is Marin?" somebody groaned.

Paul heard the Governor reply:

"I have ordered him to join us. I can do no more."

Two officers whom Paul had difficulty in recognizing, Monsieur Forant and young Monsieur de Bonaventure, came out. Monsieur Bigot followed them. He was passing Paul who put out a hand and detained him.

"Monsieur de Morpain! What has happened? Have you—is the Island Battery lost?"

"All but, Monsieur," Paul replied. "Unless we can get more ammunition we shall be taken. We have held out so far only by a miracle. I sent messengers to the Governor, now I have come myself."

"More ammunition!" Bigot said. "We are down to our last barrels of gunpowder now."

Paul paled.

"But I must see the Governor. Perhaps . . ."

"Perhaps he has some up his sleeve? See him of course, my boy."

He turned away and went dejectedly down the passage. Paul called after him:

"Have you any news of my uncle?"

Bigot stopped and turned his head.

"No. The *Oiseau de Mer* sailed a month ago for provisions and reinforcements. We think she eluded the enemy squadron. No one knows."

He left the Governor's apartments. Paul drew himself up, fumbling at his soiled clothes to put them straight, wiping his face with a rag that had been Anne's scarf. His face lightened for a moment as he thought of her. At any moment he might see her, round any sudden corner . . . Anne. He closed his eyes. The sentry said:

"You may go in now, sir."

The Governor looked up from the table where he was sitting, staring straight ahead of him. His face was yellow and lined and his eyes sunk in his head. He looked twenty years older than the man who had appointed Paul to the Island Battery. This was a very different Monsieur du Chambon. He greeted Paul with a weary nod and a forced smile.

"Monseigneur, I have come for ammunition," Paul stammered. "If we do not have it, the Island Battery will be taken."

"Then the Island Battery will be taken," the Governor answered dryly, "there is no ammunition here. We have thirty-seven barrels of gunpowder left."

"That is terrible!"

The Governor nodded.

"Terrible." He plucked at the tassels on his sword. "Unless the enemy is as badly off as we are. I would give much to find that out. Monsieur de Morpain, you are a young man, you do not appear as exhausted as the soldiers here, you seem to have eaten something—never mind what—at a more recent date than most of us. I shall send you out in charge of a scouting party to report the enemy's movements, and particularly, if you can, to capture a prisoner or discover by some other means how much ammunition they have left."

"But Monseigneur, the Island Battery," Paul stammered. "I have left no one there but a sergeant. . . ."

"A sergeant can surrender the battery as well as an officer," the Governor interrupted harshly.

Paul thought of the dirty, weary, valiant men he had left, of the wounded lying in the stifling shambles of the garrison cellar, of the sergeant's grin.

"They will think I have deserted them," he protested. "I cannot do it, Monseigneur."

" 'Cannot' in war is treason," the Governor barked. "I know your feelings for your command," he went on more sympathetically, "but consider, which is the most important for our cause, the town of Louisbourg or the Island Battery?"

Paul was silent.

"I am at your orders," he said at length.

A dull roar shook the room, rattling the doors and window frames. The Governor wiped his forehead.

"You have men with you?" he asked.

"Four."

"They will go with you tonight. In the meantime you may like to go about the town, visit the wounded; your sister I believe is there."

He did not mention Anne. Paul did not dare to ask for her.

"Only take care not to get killed or wounded. That is an order." He smiled.

Paul felt tempted to smile back. This emaciated, sad-looking man was paying for his mistakes. Unfortunately the people of Louisbourg were paying too. Paul hardened his heart. So much might have been done if the Governor had listened to the warning Paul had brought him months before, and had acted on it promptly. If he had ordered Captain Thierry to continue fighting in the Royal Battery, if . . . if . . . if . . .

The Governor had dismissed him. Paul saluted and went out. Beyond the door his heart began to beat a little faster. He was going to see Anne.

CHAPTER XLIX

P AUL crossed the courtyard toward the blockhouse. His men were sprawling against the stone wall, telling a dozen open-mouthed soldiers all that had happened on the Island Battery. They stood up when they saw Paul, not smartly like trained troops, not sullenly like mutineers, but slowly and easily like men sure of themselves and of him.

"We can't go back to the battery today," Paul told them, "the Governor has work for us tonight."

"What about the ammunition?" the nearest man asked bluntly.

"Perhaps tomorrow . . ."

"Tomorrow?" The man spat.

Paul signed to them to follow him away from the listening group.

"The Governor cannot spare us ammunition."

"What?"

"There isn't any."

"Do you believe that?" the youngest hissed fiercely. "Let's break into the arsenal and see for ourselves!"

"There are thirty-seven barrels of powder left," Paul answered him. "Now this is what we are to do."

He outlined the Governor's plan and dismissed them till the evening. They went off grumbling. As he turned toward the casemates where he thought he might find Anne, a woman ran across the courtyard, waving her hands and muttering to herself. The sentry paid her no attention. She darted past him and plunged toward the Governor's apartments in a flutter of streaming cloak and flying skirts. Paul watched her progress idly, wondering who she was and why the sentry did not halt her. "Someone will get a reprimand for this," he thought.

She came nearer. Her hair was unpowdered, her face unpainted, lined and gray; her lips were yellow, parted to let out a stream of hurrying words.

"Imperative! Cannot be borne! An instant longer! Must!" Paul heard as she ran by. He recognized her, amazed, and caught at her arm:

"Madame de Saintonge!"

She wheeled. Her eyes were blazing with indignation. She looked at Paul for a moment without seeing him, then her expression changed.

"Monsieur de Morpain! Paul!"

"Hortense!"

She stiffened and drew herself up as though she would rebuff him, then she forgot resentment in the relief of finding a new listener. She took hold of his arm and began to pour out a complaint:

"The condition of the wounded in the casemate under my care! The Governor will not listen. But he shall! He shall!"

She plucked and fumbled at his sleeve while he stared fascinated at the ravages the siege had made in her. Her face was positively ugly, gaunt and strained, only her fine eyes remained, blazing with energy and passion. Looking at her and watching her speak Paul guessed that she had found a mission at last, to possess her completely as no man could ever do. He was interested, amused, startled, a little sad. Forty-six days seemed to have added twenty visible years to Madame de Saintonge. She broke off her recital to ask him breathlessly:

"What of the Island Battery?"

He told her gravely. She nodded.

"He is telling the truth. No ammunition! Why in heaven's name didn't he foresee the shortage and increase his stores?"

Paul smiled.

"I know what that smile means," she said quickly. "You brought the news in plenty of time and nobody believed you."

"You did, and you converted the Governor."

·[230]·

"Far too late. And even I didn't take it seriously. I did not know, I had not seen the things that I see daily now and cannot help. O Paul, the wounded men, the sick children, the emaciated, famished, hopeless people! What have they done to be treated so?"

"Fortunes of war."

"Bah!" she cried. "You men make me sick! War! War! War! What does anyone get out of it?"

"We must defend ourselves when we're attacked."

"Yes, I suppose so." She sighed, her anger disappearing into lassitude. "I've seen courage and endurance here that will last me the rest of my life. The pity is that it's in vain."

"In vain? You surely don't believe that we're defeated yet?"

She looked at him and seemed about to speak. There was a sudden clamor from the street. The house nearest the citadel collapsed in cascading dust. The sound reminded Madame de Saintonge of her errand. She began to run on, calling back to him:

"I'm glad you're here. Where can I find you?"

"Where can I find Mademoiselle du Chambon and my sister?"

Madame de Saintonge stopped.

"Your sister, of course!" she said. "She's a most courageous person, Paul. Invaluable. In spite of her anxiety . . . she hasn't heard from her husband for a month, poor child, and she's so in love with him. It's tiresome, but I suppose it's touching, too."

"Where is she?" Paul broke in.

"Past the church to the right, the basement below the prison. There's a distribution center there for food. The kitchens for the garrison are next to it, and the wounded that the Frères de Charité can't take at the hospital."

"Thanks," said Paul. "Good luck with your errand to the Governor. I shall see you later on I hope."

He turned away and marched briskly forward toward the prison door and Anne.

CHAPTER L

A FOUL stench of rottenness, of human bodies packed together in the heat, of suppurating wounds, stale food, damp mustiness, rose into Paul's face as he stood at the top of the steps leading into the prison basement. He coughed, peering through the gloom.

Presently his eyes made out a long line of bodies, so close that they touched one another, lying on what appeared to be one bed, with their heads to the wall. Between them and a second line, feet toward them, was a narrow strip of stone floor. There seemed to be a light burning at the other end of the room and a door open with a second stream of light on the floor. It showed three of the wounded men's faces, turning restlessly to escape the light. Paul went to the bottom of the stairs and stepped carefully forward. All about him he could hear and sense the desperate agony of fevered bodies, he could smell caked blood and gangrenous wounds. Once a childish wail set up, a whimper from the corner he was passing. So there were children here, too. He felt sick. It seemed a long time before he reached the lantern at the far end and slipped through the open door.

The room he entered was an old dungeon transformed into a storeroom for potions and bandages, with a table in the center that was used for amputation as its stained wood showed. The bucket beneath it was still full of blood in which a hand and part of an arm were dumped. Paul turned his head away. The heat and the smell were overcoming him. He called softly:

"Is Mademoiselle du Chambon here, or Mademoiselle de Morpain—er, Madame Godet?"

The sound of a distant voice reached him. He closed the door of the storeroom and turned down a corridor. Moaning, muttering, vomiting came to his ears more distinctly as he went toward the voice. He heard it again, raised in soothing authority. Marie!

He hastened toward her. Then she came in sight, bending over a groaning heap, adjusting the straw beneath it, holding a drink toward a white tortured face, while her forehead puckered above an attempted smile and a lantern smoked at her feet.

"Marie!"

"Paul!"

Her whisper was incredulous with joy. He took the bowl from her and took her place. She straightened herself wearily, picking up the lantern.

"What has happened? Why are you here?"

He told her in a few words. She sighed.

"Water! Water!" a voice cried from the darkness outside the lantern's light. She took the bowl from Paul who guided the wounded man's head back upon the straw and clumsily tried to arrange him more comfortably. She went with the bowl and the lantern to several men, kneeling beside them, helping them to drink. Then, regardless of the moaning, the feverish cries and the eternal muttering that wrung Paul's heart, she left the room, beckoning him to follow her. They reached the passage. She continued ahead of him until they were in the storeroom again, with the grim bucket beneath the table.

"Help me to empty that," she said, "then we can talk."

She stooped to lift the bucket, he took it from her, averting his eyes.

"Where do you put such things?" he asked.

"We have a trench outside."

"Do you mean you have to carry this thing right through the place where those men are lying and up the stairs?"

She nodded.

"They're too sick to notice or to care," she said dully. "Even when I stay beside them I can do so little for them. It's almost

·[233]·

time for me to be relieved. Madame de Saintonge takes my place."
She grimaced. "She has twice our strength. Anne and I are pretty
near the end of everything when she's as fresh as if she had just
slept."

"Doesn't she sleep?" Paul asked stupidly. His mind was full of
pictures of Anne, moving about this dismal refuge.

Marie clucked as she did when he was clumsy or one of the
children spilled something.

"I don't know how it has been with you," she said, "but nobody here gets any sleep. The enemy pounds away at the town
all night. In the daytime it slackens a little, we try to sleep then."

"I'm sorry," Paul said humbly, "the sound of the sea breaking
on the rocks of the Island Battery drowns the firing and we have
been able to sleep quite well."

"And eat?" she asked avidly.

"Yes, after a fashion."

She sighed enviously.

"Where is Anne?"

"Let's go outside. There's nothing more I can do for these poor
souls. There's nothing anyone can do. Oh, Paul . . ." she stopped
herself.

They walked together to the opening of the long room and
Paul nerved himself to cross that horrible darkness filled with
suffering. He walked behind her to the stairs and up them into
the better air of the prison itself, and then to another storeroom
with an open window. A door led out of it. He put the bucket
down.

"We sleep in there," Marie pointed to the door, "and receive
in here!" she laughed, looking about her. "And eat, when we eat,
on this."

A rough deal table that had served the jailer stood in the middle
of the room with four wooden stools drawn up to it. Paul sat
down on one of them. Marie dropped beside him and took his
hands in hers.

"Have you news of Charles?" she asked.

He shook his head, stroking her wrists.

"The children?" he asked, remembering the whimper in the
dark with horror.

"All well. They are at the convent. The nuns manage somehow to feed them once a day. Skin and bones," she murmured, "skin and bones. How is it to end, Paul? What will happen to us all?"

He was silent. She snatched her hands away and began to drum them on the table.

"We will have to surrender, we can't go on like this!"

"Hush!" he said, "don't distress yourself, you must rest."

"Rest!" she cried wildly, "rest! With no news of my husband, no future, all of us at the mercy of the English, and you—" she turned to him with panic in her eyes, "you will be in worse danger than anyone if they find you! What about the man you killed? What about the gold?"

"Hush!" he said sternly, clamping a hand upon her mouth. "Somebody may hear you! Are you mad?"

She stopped and looked piteously at him.

"I'm sorry, Paul. I'm tired, I suppose."

"Of course you are," he said, patting her clumsily. "Why don't you lie down and take some rest? Where is Anne? I'd like to speak to her."

Marie rose and staggered to the door of the far room. He followed her. Peering over her shoulder he saw two heaps of straw by the farthest wall. A girl was lying on the nearest, face downwards, her arms outstretched along the grimy floor. She started up as they came in and cried out:

"Is that you?"

Then she saw Paul and sprang to her feet.

"Paul!" she cried, running toward him, "Paul!"

She flung herself upon him, laughing and choking. He opened his arms and she was in them.

"Anne!"

His voice broke. He strained her to him. All was clear between them, simple, natural, right—blindingly, achingly clear. Marie behind them gasped. Paul stared at her unseeingly over Anne's shoulder. She turned her back and began to make noisy preparations to rest. Paul drew Anne with him into the other room.

Everything had receded from him, even Louisbourg. He walked on ice cut out of stars, he walked on air, he did not touch the ground at all. There was a shimmering mist about him, an aching, longing excitement. Then the thought of San came into his mind as winter sea mist blots out the land, as driving snow makes everything bleak. He knew that he should tell Anne about her or go away and stay away, and he knew that both these things were impossible.

"Anne," he said abruptly as they sat down at the table together, "there are reasons why I can't let you care for me."

"But I do care!" she said.

"I have nothing to offer."

"Everything. Yourself."

"Your father would never consider . . ."

"My father, you and I, all of us, may be killed, imprisoned, separated."

"That's another reason. If the New Englanders find me, as an escaped prisoner of war . . ."

She caught him by the shoulders and stared into his eyes.

"Don't you see we have only *now*?"

"I know, but there's something else." Pain came into his eyes, he drew a long breath, he would try to tell her now about San.

"You're safe and we're together, that's all I care about." She saw the expression in his face. "Paul, Paul," she whispered, suddenly afraid, "you do love me, don't you?"

"Oh, my darling!"

"You don't love anyone else? Not her?"

"Who?"

"Madame de Saintonge."

"Oh. No. I love you and no one else."

That much was true and was hers, whatever folly he had committed with San. And this moment was theirs. He cupped her face in his hands and drew her close. She shut her eyes. He kissed her forehead, her eyebrows, her cheeks, the tip of her nose and finally her mouth. If this had to be a farewell kiss it would be a good one.

A voice behind them spoke sharply.

"Monsieur de Morpain!"

They wheeled and stepped apart. Monsieur Bigot was in the doorway.

"The Governor sent me to find you. He wants you at once."

"Mademoiselle!" he bowed to Anne who returned the salutation with an embarrassed curtsy. She looked at Bigot a moment, then at Paul, then she said abruptly:

"Monsieur Bigot, chance has made you the first to congratulate me in my happiness."

Bigot bowed. "Mademoiselle."

"We have always been friends. I want to ask you a favor. Please do not report this to my father until we have time to talk to him."

Bigot bowed again.

"My felicitations to you both."

He turned to the door. Paul hesitated. Anne motioned him to follow Bigot and blew him a kiss. The two men went out together. Anne's eyes fell upon the bucket. She shuddered with distaste, took it up and walked with it to the courtyard. She dumped its contents in the trench, averting her eyes and smiling at the sunny afternoon sky. June! It was dangerous in the courtyard, it was dangerous in the room where she slept, and dangerous in the room where Paul had told her he loved her. The only safe place was where the wounded lay in the fetid atmosphere of the deepest dungeons. It was the only place where she did not want to be. The sights and sounds of suffering were more than she could bear in the sharpened mood of her new ecstasy, but it was time for her to relieve Madame de Saintonge. Presently the surgeon would be coming to make his rounds. She drew a last long breath of summer air, looked toward the gate where Paul had disappeared and went below.

CHAPTER LI

"**M**ONSIEUR BIGOT," Paul said as they hurried warily across the courtyard, "spare me a moment, before I see the Governor. Anne says you have been her friend; she needs one now and so do I. I have no one to advise me and I must have advice!"

Bigot looked at him quizzically.

"The Governor will be impatient."

"This is important," Paul said, "please."

"Very well."

They stepped into a doorway and passed through the guard-room to Monsieur Bigot's quarters.

"Here," he said, "we are less disturbed by the racket. Sit down, Monsieur de Morpain."

Paul obeyed. He fixed his gaze upon Monsieur Bigot's shrewd kind eyes.

"Anne told you we were engaged," he said. "God knows I want to be. When you came upon us I was trying to say good-by."

"A charming way of saying it," Bigot commented, "but a trifle ambiguous. Mademoiselle du Chambon did not gather your meaning and neither did I." He frowned.

Paul leaned forward. He began to pour out the story of what had happened to him with San. Bigot listened without interruption, his expression gradually changing. Then he lolled back in his chair crossing his finger tips.

"Monsieur de Morpain," he said pleasantly, "you have a refreshing sense of responsibility and unusual scruples for this day and age. If you were to get any officer in this citadel—the Governor himself for that matter, not to mention present company—" he smirked, "in a state of confidence induced by drink, you would find that every one has had some traffic with the savages, and that native so-called marriages were more frequent among us than the ladies suppose. Your marriage with this savage is a little more serious, you will say, a little more binding, since it was performed by a Catholic priest and she is a convert. Doubtless the Abbé le Loutre intended you to do well by the girl, to leave her provided for as you seem to have done and to see her treated fairly by her people while you lived with her. The abbé is a man of the world as well as a priest and a man of much experience. He would not expect any more than that."

"Do you think so?" Paul asked eagerly.

"Of course I think so. The abbé married you for several obvious reasons. First in order to secure the savages' respect he must not seem to encourage vice, he cannot sanction promiscuity. Second, the girl was a convert and he was responsible toward her people for taking her away from them; he was bound to see that she got respect and fair play. Third, there was a chance, I suppose, in his mind, that you might want to continue living with her. Some men, chiefly trappers and coureurs de bois, live with their native wives by choice and would not marry Frenchwomen if you paid them to. The exigencies of their lives require savage mates. Your case is different but the abbé was not to know that for certain when he married you."

"But the church upholds marriage . . ."

"Did you have a Mass?"

"No."

"Did you sign a register?"

"No."

"The abbé merely pronounced you man and wife with a blessing?"

"Yes."

"That's it, the typical compromise. Don't you see the girl can go back to her people now, holding up her head? She is probably some chief's first squaw by now. Her wedding to a white man took place in front of witnesses, she had her wedding dance, that's the main thing, and you left her some gold. She has an added value now, my boy. Don't worry about her."

"Then you think it's all right?"

"Absolutely all right."

"And I don't have to tell Anne?"

"You'd be a fool if you did. Women, especially young girls in love, don't see these things as men do."

"What about the Governor?"

"I wouldn't tell him either. He would make use of it to separate you from Anne. He isn't overfond of you, Monsieur de Morpain. You are going to have a hard time to get his consent."

"Perhaps the siege will make it easier," Paul said.

"It may, especially . . ."

He broke off. Paul became conscious of the noise and confusion going on outside. He had forgotten everything in his relief.

"Thank you," he said. "I shall never forget this talk. Whatever comes to either of us, count me as a friend."

Bigot rose and bowed gravely to him with the ghost of a smile. Paul dashed from the room.

He fairly ran to the Governor's office. The sooner he could get the interview over, he could get back to Anne. But when he entered the room and saw the papers spread upon the Governor's table and the grave, weary men, leisurely going over them, his heart sank. He realized it would be a long affair.

The Governor looked up frowning.

"At last!" he said. "I began to think you'd gone back to your battery. Sit down Monsieur de Morpain. You must acquaint yourself very thoroughly with these plans before your raid tonight."

Paul drew the map toward him and dutifully bent his head. His thoughts were with Anne and his lips would smile in spite of every effort to keep them straight.

CHAPTER LII

I T WAS a June night, brilliant with stars, soft and warm, languid with summer smells. Glowworms flickered above the marsh to the monotonous croaking of a thousand frogs, obliterated now and then by the thud and roar of guns firing at the town.

Paul, lying on his stomach outside the walls, felt the ground beneath him shake, air pressed against his eardrums so that his head throbbed and his tongue grew dry. Behind him the sound of crumbling stone showed where the cannon balls were hitting. He could hear men panting and swearing as they labored to repair the damage before the next shot fell.

In the darkness ahead other men were panting and swearing as they tugged shot and powder to the guns. Paul could hear them moving about in parties over the marsh and round the batteries they had placed on the high ground. He could hear them above the noises of the night. There was another sound that puzzled him. He wriggled forward cautiously toward it.

As he felt his way stone by stone, through bushes, over brambles, with the sound of his rustling enormous in his ears, the noise that he was trailing grew louder. It was the sound of wood falling against wood. It puzzled him. He crawled nearer till the voices of men talking in undertones came to him.

"Three hundred and four," someone said contentedly.

"That will do for here," another answered. He spoke more sharply than the first man. An officer, perhaps.

Paul lay still until the sound of their voices and the trampling of their feet died away. Then he crawled forward, inch by inch, his heart pumping unnaturally, his mouth dry. The noise he made seemed to him to fill the night. He could not imagine why he was not set upon. He reached the spot where he had heard the men talking. There was a pile of objects there that he could not distinguish in the dark. He pulled himself forward and stretched out a hand. His fingers closed around a wooden stave and traveled upward till they came to a thicker piece of wood. He moved them back and forth, up and down. It was a ladder, a pile of ladders heaped together. "Three hundred and four scaling ladders," the man had said, "enough for here." Then there were more than these, lying at a stone's throw from the town walls! Paul withdrew. It was agonizing to have to crawl so slowly, so carefully, when he wanted to run, but he must be very silent, very sure, because he had to warn the Governor.

"This will be the second time," he thought confusedly, "that I've brought him a warning."

He reached the wall and whistled twice, straining his ears in the darkness. Presently a man crawled up to him in answer to the signal. Three others crept out of the bushes.

"Have you seen anything?" Paul asked.

"Scaling ladders," two of them answered, "in heaps. They're unguarded. We might set fire to them."

"The enemy would put fires out before they did enough damage. Was there any sign of a sentry whom we could surprise and take prisoner for the Governor to question? Did you discover anything about the enemy's ammunition?"

"Not so far."

"Stay here and keep on trying. Take a prisoner if you can. I'm going to the Governor."

He scrambled up the wall. A sentry rushed forward.

"Saint Louis!" Paul gasped. "Friend."

The sentry took hold of him with a grunt and marched him through the darkness to a redoubt behind them.

"What's the matter?" Paul asked. "I've given you the password."

A lantern swung in his face.

"Listen. There are a thousand scaling ladders piled outside these walls. The enemy may attack this night, this hour. I have to report to the Governor."

There was a wail in the darkness that startled him.

"Pst!" said a voice, "you shouldn't have blurted that out, Monsieur de Morpain. It will be all over town. That was some fool of a townsman listening."

"I'm sorry." Paul strained to see beyond the lantern. "Who is speaking to me?"

"Captain de Bonaventure. I'll go with you to the Governor. This is bad news, but I suppose it is to be expected that they'll try a grand attack." He lowered his voice. "It will be like cutting through butter to take this town."

Paul said nothing. He did not know Captain de Bonaventure well. He had seen him once or twice at the citadel with Monsieur Bigot. He seemed straight enough but there was never any telling when a man might be a spy and lead men on to saying things that sounded treasonous when repeated to the Governor. "My future father-in-law." Paul grinned. Then he thought of the cry in the dark and wondered whether there would be fresh trouble. The townspeople were afraid, and sick and tired of the siege, and hungry. It looked bad. Thirty-seven barrels of gunpowder left. Yes, it looked bad for Louisbourg.

CHAPTER LIII

"SURRENDER! Surrender!"
"Send out a flag of truce!"
"Surrender!"
"We're not strong enough to resist a general assault!"
"Down with the Governor! Mutiny and surrender!"

The Governor walked to his window and looked down on the shouting crowd, surging in the courtyard of the citadel. Men, women and even children were there, packed together so that they swayed in a compact mass out of which their white, strained faces turned upward, their open mouths looking like holes in a large yellow cheese. Other crowds were gathering behind them in the streets of the town. The news of the scaling ladders waiting to be used by the enemy had dismayed them so that they preferred to come out of their casemates and shelters and take their chance of cannon ball, langrage and musket fire, if they could persuade the Governor to give in and save them from the attack. He held their petition in his hand, frowning as he read it again and again, unable to make up his mind. A little group of officers stood watching him. Paul was among them. Monsieur Bigot sat in a corner. He was wounded in the knee, in great pain, but his eyes were fixed upon the Governor with fiery courage in them, an entreaty all could see.

Presently the Governor turned from the window.

"Monsieur de la Perelle, have the drums beat a parley and take a flag of truce."

Bigot let out his breath in a long sigh. Paul's empty stomach contracted. He looked about him for a place where he could vomit. The spasm passed, his vision cleared, he saw the officers leave the room, each man pale as though he had seen a ghost. He turned to leave with them but the Governor called him back.

"It is on your information that I am acting," he said fretfully. Paul did not answer. Bigot spoke from his corner, wearily:

"Monsieur de Morpain is not to blame if the townspeople riot." The Governor snorted.

"He did not bring me the information I required. I do not know what ammunition the enemy has left. It may be they are as near running out of it as we are. I send out scouts to report to me and they do not carry out my orders."

"Monseigneur," Paul began, "I thought it important you should know . . ."

"Bah!" The Governor waved him away. "You have roused the townspeople into panic, so that they cry and clamor and force my hands. The enemy spies will see and hear the noise they are making. They will report that the morale here is broken. So it is. What can a man do with such a pack of sheep, cowardly sheep!"

He began to pace up and down the room twisting his fingers, his face working as though he would cry. Bigot sat staring at the floor, a somber sadness in his face. Now and then he winced and his mouth contracted as the pain of his wound throbbed and burned. Paul looked from one to the other. Suddenly he felt he must have air. He stumbled toward the door and ran down the stairs.

When he reached the courtyard he faced a solid mass of sullen people, white-faced, gaunt-looking men, weeping, haggard women, pinched and silent children, wedged together, facing the Governor's door. The church behind them was filled with more people, praying. The sound of their murmuring responses to the priest's sonorous intoning, drifted in snatches across the courtyard. A sharp crackle and roar came from the cannon mounted on the ramparts, firing at steady intervals. This was drowned by a dull booming roar that shook the walls and made dust rise in clouds about the people, choking them so that they coughed and wiped their streaming eyes, never turning them from the door or the Governor's window.

·[245]·

Paul saw that he could not get through this crowd to go to the town or even to the casemates where he could find Anne. He was able to shoulder his way as far as the nearest rampart. From here he could look across the marsh to the enemy camp. Far in the distance he could see the little group of French soldiers, with Monsieur de la Perelle in their midst, staggering valiantly across the uneven ground, carrying a flag of truce. They disappeared. Firing ceased. The silence was heavy with fears, each man shivered uncontrollably, straining to hear the accustomed sounds that now his tired body seemed to crave.

Hour followed hour. Nobody moved to go home. Soldiers and citizens alike stood in the heat of the day, muttering, shifting their feet, looking toward the Governor's windows. They stood thus and Paul with them until the flag of truce reappeared in the distance, and the word went round:

"They're coming back!"

Women began to cry, men to shout:

"Surrender!"

It seemed a long time before Monsieur de la Perelle appeared, pushing his way through the crowd, answering the outcry of impatient voices with a tranquil:

"Presently! The Governor will speak to us all presently."

The soldiers with him began to clear the way, dropping their musket butts on men's feet, elbowing women aside, shouting threateningly. Even so, Monsieur de la Perelle's clothes were torn and his wig knocked off before he could reach the Governor's door. Paul pushed and scrambled after him.

"They give you until eight o'clock this evening to make your proposals," Perelle was saying as Paul came in, holding out a paper which the Governor took. He cleared his throat nervously and began to read aloud:

*"To Governor Duchambon. Camp June 15th 1745.

We have yours of this date, proposing a suspension of hostilities for such a time as shall be necessary for you to determine upon the conditions of delivering up the garrison of Louisbourg, which arrived at a happy juncture to prevent the effusion of Christian blood, as we were together, and had just determined upon a general attack. We shall comply with your desire till 8

o'clock tomorrow morning; and if, in the meantime, you surrender yourselves prisoners of war, you may depend upon hu-
mane and generous treatment.

We are, your humble servants,

Peter Warren,

William Pepperell."

"Gentlemen," Monsieur du Chambon looked up, avoiding the
eyes of those who stood around him, "we have no choice but to
send our conditions in the morning. Monsieur de Bonaventure I
detail you to bear them to Commodore Warren and General
Pepperell. Monsieur de la Perelle, announce this decision to the
townspeople and tell them to disperse."

"Will you not speak to them, Monseigneur? They have waited
a long time."

"I have nothing to say." The Governor's voice was thick with
self-pity. "I have done what I could. They have forced this upon
me." He glared about him. Then his expression relaxed. "We
should," he smiled the ghost of a smile, "get a good sleep tonight
with no guns firing and no attack to be feared. Good night,
gentlemen."

The group dispersed. They waited on the stairs while the crowd
was being sent away. They waited in silence, each man plunged
in his own thoughts. Presently the way was cleared, they staggered out and went upon their separate ways.

"Well," Paul thought, stumbling after Perelle and Bonaventure
to the quays, "it's all over. The New Englanders have won! They
have taken Louisbourg!" The words made no sense to him, con-
veyed no meaning. He did not believe them though he knew
that they were true. The town looked as it had for the past
twenty-four hours, the same grim dusty fortress that he was used
to now.

"All this for nothing," he repeated, looking at the ruins round
him. A lump came in his throat.

A group of women smiling contentedly together, passed him.
The townspeople had had enough. They did not care what happened so long as the siege came to an end, so long as they could
eat and sleep, even if they were prisoners.

Prisoners! Paul's mind darted forward to the bleak days ahead. What would happen to him now? To Anne? With the thought of Anne, some happiness and warmth flowed back to him, but it was mixed with new and terrible anxiety. He turned a corner. There was Marie's cottage, badly battered, with the chimney and one wall gone, but still standing. He decided to spend the night there, at home.

A man greeted him from the next doorway.

"Well," he called out cheerfully, "it will be over soon. Even if the terms are hard and we're all prisoners, at least we'll eat."

Eat. Paul put his hand to the ache in his stomach. His mind went to the Island Battery and the men waiting there for his return. They wouldn't know of the surrender, but they would guess perhaps, when no sounds of firing tore the night.

"This is the first time I've dared to sleep at home," the man went on, "with my wife in our own bed. We've been lucky. Nobody in this family was even scratched. There are not many of us can say that. Well, good night."

He went inside and closed his door. Paul hesitated. Perhaps Marie would leave the wounded and come home. Perhaps Anne would guess where he was and come too. He wanted Anne. But he was so fatigued and so hard spent he rocked on his feet and staggered drunkenly. He would not go to her till he could rest and bring her comfort and courage in his strength. He went inside and looked about him. Everything was covered with dust and soot, driven down the chimney by the explosion of the guns. He swept a place clear on the table, lay down and went to sleep.

CHAPTER LIV

PAUL'S hunger woke him when the sun was high. At first he did not know where he was. He called out sleepily:

"Is it my watch?"

When he got no answer he sat up, startled. There was no sound outside, no firing, no shouting, no trampling of busy feet. He rolled off the table. The events of the day before came back to him. He brushed off the dust that stained his clothes, straightened them and made for the door.

Men and women were gathered in little groups along the quay and at the corners of the streets, saying nothing, waiting, waiting.

"What has happened?" Paul asked.

Several voices answered.

"The Governor has sent out his proposals."

"An officer took them."

"Over an hour ago."

"Captain de Bonaventure took them."

"Oh." Paul thanked them and turned toward the citadel. The Governor's windows were closed, there was nothing to be seen in the courtyard. The church door was open, and a group of people were on their knees, praying earnestly, while the tinkling of a hand bell showed the priest about to begin another Mass. Paul crossed himself. He turned toward the prison door and started down the steps to the basement where the wounded lay.

Anne was coming up as he was coming down. They met on the stairs and she stopped, startled. He put his arms about her.

"Oh, Paul," she said.

He held her close and turned her face to his, looking into her eyes. His heart was pounding, a queer dizziness assailed him.

"Here," she said, observing the pallor that spread over his face. She drew him after her to the storeroom, went to a hogshead of rum and poured him a stiff drink.

"There's plenty of rum," she made a grimace, "left in the town."

Paul swallowed the drink.

"Anne," he murmured, putting his head against her cheek. "You mean my whole life, you fill it completely. Love, passion, happiness, contentment, everything . . . just you, Anne, just you."

She sighed and stirred to look at him, but he recaptured her and put his head back into the place where he could talk to her and feel that they were close, so close that even their eyes were not looking at each other across the smallest separating space.

"You become dearer and closer to me all the time, even when we're apart."

"I feel that too."

"Anne I mean this, I ask no greater gift from God than that I should keep your love, that nothing should ever mar it or weaken it."

He was silent for a long moment. She trembled a little and waited for him to go on.

"Through all my life's stupid and meaningless gropings, I have been looking for you."

"My perfect love, my perfect friend!"

"Let us find in each other peace and safety. They are not to be found in the world outside. I will be unselfish and always faithful."

"You are as much a part of me as my own heart which I have given to you."

They kissed. It was a long kiss.

"Now nothing matters," Anne told him. "I am not afraid of the enemy, of surrender, of anything! We'll take what comes together."

"The New Englanders have some serious charges against me. We'll have to be prepared for anything."

"Charges?"

"Yes, a man killed, a purse taken, other things. I am an escaped prisoner of war. I was desperate, Anne. I had to get here and warn the town."

Anne raised proud eyes to his.

"If you were a coward you would have gone to a safer place, Quebec or France, and left the place to rot, especially when nobody believed you, when my father was so slow in making any preparations to meet the attack. But you stayed. I don't care what things you had to do before you came here, you were right to do them. I can't believe that anything bad will happen to us now when we've just found each other! Oh, Paul let's get married at once, before the surrender. Don't you see, to be my father's son-in-law would be some protection?"

He laughed.

"Dear Anne. All I want to know is that you love me. The rest can take care of itself."

He felt the rum die out of him. Shyness and despondency took the place of his confidence. He moved a little and cleared his throat. The sound of shouting and running feet came to them from above the stairs. They had forgotten where they were in the excitement of being together. Now the prison walls closed down on them, the groans of the wounded being attended by the doctor with Marie, came to their ears. The airlessness of the cellar oppressed them. They started up the stairs to the door. A roll of drums beat the assembly.

"Monsieur de Bonaventure's back."

"Let's go to my father and hear the terms."

They emerged, blinking in the sunlight and made for the Governor's apartments. Anne ran up the steps and into her father's room, pushing her way forward till she found herself at his elbow as he pored over the communication Monsieur de Bonaventure brought. Paul stood in the background with other officers, desperately anxious to hear what the enemy had sent.

"Read it, Father!" Anne urged.

The Governor looked up at her, seeming not to recognize her. She took his arm in sudden tenderness and distress.

"Read it," she said again. "These gentlemen are waiting, we are all waiting, the people outside are waiting for the terms."

He did not answer her. He drummed with his fingers on the table. Paul saw that he could not control his voice to speak. He turned his eyes away. After a moment's agony, the Governor made an effort and began to read:

"Camp before Louisbourg, 16th June 1745. To Governor Du Chambon. We have before us yours of this date, together with the several articles of capitulation on which you have proposed to surrender the town and fortifications of Louisbourg, with the territories adjacent under your government to His Britannic Majesty's obedience; to be delivered up to his said Majesty's forces now besieging said place under our command, which articles we can by no means accede to. But as we are anxious to treat you in a generous manner, we do again make you an offer of the terms of surrender proposed by us in our summons sent you May 7th last; and do further consent to allow and promise you the following articles, namely:

"1. That if your own vessels shall be found insufficient for the transportation of your persons and proposed effects to France, we will supply such a number of other vessels as may be sufficient for that purpose; also any provisions necessary for the voyage which you cannot furnish yourselves with.

"2. That all the commissioned officers belonging to the garrison, and the inhabitants of the town may remain in their houses with their families and enjoy the free exercise of their religion and no person shall be suffered to misuse or molest any of them until such time as they can be conveniently transported to France.

"3. That the noncommissioned officers and soldiers shall immediately upon surrender of the town and fortresses, be put on board His Britannic Majesty's ships till they all be transported to France.

"4. That all your sick and wounded shall be taken care of in the same manner as our own.

"5. That the Commander-in-chief, now in the garrison shall have the liberty to send off covered wagons to be inspected only by one officer of ours, that no warlike stores may be contained therein.

"6. That if there be any persons in the town or garrison which may desire not to be seen of us, they shall be permitted to go off masked."

Paul and Anne looked at each other. She nodded. He smiled.

"7. The above do we consent to and promise upon your compliance to the following conditions:

"1. That the said surrender, and due performance of every part of the aforesaid promises be made and completed as soon as possible.

"2. That as a security for the punctual performance of the same, the Island Battery, or one of the batteries of the town shall be delivered, together with the warlike stores thereunto belonging, into the possession of His Majesty's troops before 6 o'clock this evening."

"They couldn't get it any other way," Paul thought, his chest heaving. The Island Battery, with its handful of ragged defenders! He found moisture gathering in his eyes, and forced himself to look straight ahead.

"3. That the said Britannic Majesty's ships of war now lying before the port shall be permitted to enter the harbor of Louisbourg without any molestation as soon after 6 of the clock this afternoon as the Commander-in-chief of such ships shall think fit.

"4. That none of the officers, soldiers nor inhabitants of Louisbourg who are subjects of the French King shall take up arms against His Britannic Majesty, nor any of his allies until after the expiration of the full term of twelve months from this time;

"5. That all subjects of His Britannic Majesty who are now prisoners with you shall be immediately delivered up to us.

"In case of your noncompliance with these conditions we decline any further treaty with you on the affair, and shall decide the matter by our arms, and are, etc.

your humble servants,
P. Warren,
W. Pepperell."

"The terms are fair enough," Monsieur Bigot said, when the Governor stopped reading. There was a long silence in the crowded room. One by one the officers saluted and went out. The Governor stopped Monsieur de la Perelle and Monsieur Forant.

"See that this proclamation is copied and posted on the walls of the town," he said, "and give a copy to the town crier to be called tonight."

He turned away. Paul stood awkwardly, looking on at his distress.

"Be comforted, Father," Anne begged, "you did everything that could be done."

"It is ruin," Monsieur du Chambon whispered, "ruin!" He covered his face with his hands. Paul and Anne looked at each other. Suddenly the door opened. Madame de Saintonge came in. She went straight to the Governor and put her hand on his shoulder. He turned and looked up at her. His face changed from despair to eagerness, to hope. Anne beckoned to Paul. They stole out of the room together unobserved.

CHAPTER LV.

A T TWO in the afternoon on June 28 which was beautiful and cloudless, the first of the British men-of-war came slowly into Louisbourg harbor. Most of the population was upon the quays, watching the procession. The men, shading their eyes with their hands, looked critically at the handling of the vessels. Now and then a man would grunt approval, unwillingly. The women beside them looked with childlike pleasure on the bright pennants flying and fluttering from the tall masts, and the colorful pigmies running about the decks. Children hopped and squealed and said: "Look! Look!" as each new ship appeared.

The crowd still seemed pale and sick, but a few days of good feeding and the knowledge that the siege was over had done wonders. The terms of the surrender left them the right to live in their own houses, and to practice their religion, until they could be sent to France. Many of them had never crossed the sea to the far-off motherland. They were excited and curious. Others looking at the ruin of the town were glad enough to leave the rebuilding of it to the enemy and to pull up their roots to start again wherever they might be sent. Here and there a peasant who had lived in France and knew the misery of the poor, the harshness of the laws, the hopeless struggle to make a living at the foot of the social scale, felt his gorge rise at losing all the liberty that he had crossed the seas to find in the sweet freedom of New France. But at least they were not starving and the enemy seemed willing to treat them with more fairness than they had been told to expect. Remembering some of the tales of the officers urging them to fight—that their scalps would be sold to the Indians, that the New Englanders would put them to the sword to pay for Canceau, that they would be thrown into dungeons and left to starve—they wondered resentfully why the siege had been dragged on so long, until their homes were in ruins, their friends killed and wounded, their healths impaired, all to save the Governor's face. He would be deported to France to stand his trial. Some of them nursing grievances against him, smiled.

The long procession of stately vessels continued to arrive, dropping anchor in formation in the wide waters of the harbor till it looked like a fair ground with tilting poles crowded together and men swarming up and down them. The sound of whistles and pipes and shouting came to shore.

"A beautiful sight," the baker said, nodding toward them.

"Not so beautiful as one loaf of bread, crisp and brown."

There was laughter and nudging in the crowd. Paul standing with Anne at the door of Marie's house said:

"No wonder they beat the *Vigilant*. I wonder which of them will bear us to France?"

He was wearing a black velvet mask that Anne had made for him from an old hood.

"I do not know whether it is better to wear a mask and proclaim myself someone with a guilty secret, so that the New Englanders will stare at what they see of me and perhaps someone will recognize me by my walk, my talk, my general shape, or to risk showing my face."

After a long discussion Anne, Marie and he agreed that he must wear the mask and go out as little as possible. Others were doing the same. Monsieur Mercier, for instance, who had spent the siege crouching in his house, refusing to come out or to help anyone, now appeared in a long cagoule, a mask which covered his face and neck completely, with slits for his eyes and which made him look like an inquisitor.

"Only I would know that belly anywhere," Marie said contemptuously. "I wonder what he has to hide?"

"He probably only wants to make himself important."

"That's what people will say of me."

"Who cares what people say?"

A shout went up:

"They're coming! They're coming!"

·[256]·

Tomas, galloping through the crowd to find Marie and Paul, cried excitedly:

"The soldiers are coming through the South Gate!"

The crowd surged forward. The quays emptied. The streets around the South Gate began to fill. A roll of drums announced the enemy's approach to the French troops in the citadel drawn up to receive them. The Regulars, the Militia, the Swiss, stood to attention, their colors floating before them. The Governor waiting in his room with Madame de Saintonge, took up his sword and sighed. He looked about him.

"Well, it has come," he said, and drew himself up with an effort.

"Courage!" she whispered. "You never looked better. It is a bad moment but it is soon over."

He did not answer. Soon over! What was there to say to that? He braced himself to meet his officers, his men and the enemy to whom he must surrender presently, in a few minutes, in the sight of all.

Anne's thoughts went to him as she waited in the streets with Paul. The sound of drums and fife and marching feet on cobblestones came to her as they turned to the South Gate. The crowd parted on each side to let the conquerors through. They stared silently at the men who had poured nine thousand cannon balls and six hundred bombs into their town and had taken it.

"A ragged lot to have fought so well," one man whispered to another.

The New Englanders were not a military-looking army. They were undisciplined, careless, free. They walked without precision, each man grinning to the right and left of him, but they were obviously pleased with themselves and sure of the righteousness of their cause.

"Fanatics!" Paul murmured. He looked at each passing officer sharply. He recognized General Pepperell as the same bovine-faced merchant who had ridden with Randy to the Moodys' house so many eons ago. War had hardened him somewhat, Paul decided, but his eyes were still childish and bewildered, roving from side to side uneasily as he looked at the destruction his troops were responsible for.

Near the end of the marching men, who were only a handful

of Pepperell's army, a young officer strode quickly, head in air. Paul ducked before he remembered his mask.

"That's William Vaughan," he said to Anne.

Will had come through the campaign well. He was pleased and full of his own importance as he went to take part in the surrender. Paul clenched his fists.

"Never mind about him," Anne whispered. "Please, Paul. Why do you care?"

When the last soldier had passed, the crowd broke rank and followed after them. They pressed into the citadel and took up positions round the parade. Silently they watched their Governor hand over his sword and with it the town and everything that had been theirs. The ceremony was brief. The French were dignified, the English courteous. Soon the drums beat again and the defeated troops marched out, carrying arms, with their colors flying. They were accorded the honors of war. They looked neither left nor right as they passed from the citadel into the streets and through the town they were leaving forever. Transports were waiting to take them on board. The wounded men were there already. They had been moved from the hospital and prison cellar earlier. Women ran beside the marching column shouting good-bys, waving, crying. Friends called out encouragement. The officers shouted their orders in voices unnaturally sharp and high. Monsieur de Bonaventure, Monsieur de la Perelle, Monsieur Forant, Paul counted them as they went by, spruce and pitiful, to be shipped home as men without a country, men under arrest to be court-martialed with the Governor when they reached France.

The Governor left the parade ground and went to his quarters. He was allowed a little time in which to pack the cartload of belongings he could take away. Paul watched him climb the steps with some compunction. Anne darted from the crowd and went to her father's side. Paul called out to her. He elbowed his way forward, caught up with them and went inside.

"Monsieur du Chambon," he said breathlessly, on the spur of the moment, "I have the honor to ask for your daughter's hand."

"Father," Anne cried before he could speak, "things are different now. We are all ruined together. You might not have considered Paul the son-in-law you dreamed of before the defeat, but today . . ."

Monsieur du Chambon looked from one to the other.

"So you want to marry a man who goes about masked like a criminal with some dirty secret to hide, and you choose this moment to tell me so," he snapped out bitterly.

"Father . . ."

"A man without money, family, connections. You tell me we are ruined, but in France you have a family with whom you can take refuge. You will have entrée to the highest circles at court. You want to throw all this away."

"We love each other," Anne begged. "Please, Father, give us your consent. Let us be married here, now, while you are Governor."

"I ceased to be Governor ten minutes ago."

"You still have authority. You can have Paul included with your suite on the same transport."

Paul took a step forward.

"Monseigneur, I do not wear a mask for any disgraceful reason, unless you count it a disgrace to kill an Englishman and take his purse. I needed gold to get here in order to warn you of the attack. The Englishman was a recruiting officer who barred my way."

"Any brave man would have killed him," Anne said proudly.

"There are men here with Pepperell's army who would recognize me, so I wear this mask."

The Governor sighed a long, weary sigh.

"Very well," he said. "It is a stupid, sad mistake. You are throwing your life away, but if you want it, you have my consent."

"Father!"

"Monseigneur."

Anne threw herself into his arms and kissed him again and again. Her eyes were shining. She was exultant.

"I suppose," the Governor disengaged himself gently, "I might as well share my responsibility for your protection with a man as powerless as myself. The whole world's crazy, everything is gone, my hopes for you among the rest."

"Don't croak!" Anne laughed at him. "You are giving me to the best husband in the world."

CHAPTER LVI

THE day after the capitulation Louisbourg was filled with troops and camp followers, shouting, singing, laughing, reeling through the streets. More than a thousand hogsheads of rum were found and spirited away before Pepperell and his officers could prevent it. The New Englanders, disgusted at the terms of the surrender which protected the property of the townspeople, were determined to get something for themselves after all their hardships. Many of them had enlisted to the tales of loot and of plunder promised them in Louisbourg. Now there were sentries from their own troops posted at every corner in front of every other house to prevent them from picking up what they considered honest booty. Therefore they were drunk, disorderly, complaining and noisy.

Paul, picking his way through the sights and sounds of their discontent, with Marie on his arm, toward the church, thought that the sooner they could all get out of Louisbourg the better. He had sat up half the night discussing plans with Anne and with her father. It was agreed that they should go to France on the same transport, that Paul should endeavor to find his uncle and ship on the *Oiseau de Mer* until a better position could be found for him. Anne would live with her father until Paul's salary permitted him to offer her a home. The two young people hardly listened to Monsieur du Chambon's dissertations on expense and the requirements of life in France. They were living in a dream, a heady excitement that could see no farther than the dawning of their wedding day.

Now it had come. Paul went through the streets in a daze, brushing past the New Englanders, wriggling his way through shouting groups past this and that familiar landmark, till at length he reached the citadel and turned toward the Governor's chapel that was used as parish church. He had been baptized there, had made his First Communion there, had worshiped there between his father and his mother; now he was to be married there. He quickened his pace. Marie took his arm.

A strange noise was coming from the church as they drew near, a sound of shouting, cursing and breakage. Marie drew back, but Paul went forward angrily. Some of the drunken revelers must have broken into the church and were now defiling it. He opened the door.

An odd sight met his indignant eyes. At the far end of the church, in front of the altar itself, a man was swinging an ax. It crashed into the holy things, breaking the tabernacle sheltering the Host, knocking over the candlesticks, splintering the altar wood and tearing through the silken cloths embroidered and brought from France. All the time the man shouted and cursed:

"Popery!" he screamed. "Down with the heathen idols!" Then he lunged at the image of the Virgin to the right of the altar, splitting the statue in two. Paul gasped. He ran forward to catch at the madman's arm. Marie fell to her knees and crossed herself at the sacrilege. The dim light of the church shone faintly on the man's black clothes and did not show his face.

"Here, you!" Paul cried out in English. "Stop that!"

The man swung round to face him. It was Parson Moody. A red rage came over Paul at the sight of him. He rushed and ducked, with one eye on the ax, to grapple with him. Parson Moody shouted:

"Leave me alone to do the Lord's work."

"Devil's work!" Paul grunted at his ear. "You damned old fanatical fool, leave these sacred things in peace!"

Parson Moody was old and no match for Paul in a rage, ax or no ax. He found himself on his back in the aisle, glaring up at his masked opponent. Paul glared down contemptuously. He turned his back on the old man after kicking his ax to one side. Then he genuflected and went to the altar to repair the damage.

"I swore an oath," Parson Moody shouted behind him, "that with my own hands I would tear down the idolatrous heathen idols if the Lord would give us the victory."

"Be quiet!" Paul straightened the tabernacle and pulled the curtains together in front of it.

"Leave this place!" he said as Parson Moody got to his feet. "Commodore Warren and General Pepperell promised freedom of worship in the terms of the surrender. I shall report you to them, you old dog."

"Who are you?" Parson Moody asked, holding on to a pillar while he gasped for breath.

"Never mind who I am," Paul answered between his teeth. "I know who you are, and that's enough. Get out of here!"

Parson Moody stooped for the ax, retrieved it and plunged it into the statue of St. Anthony. Paul whirled round and ran at him again. Parson Moody brandished the ax wildly.

"Touch me or try to stop me and I'll sink this in your head, you heathen!" he shouted.

Paul stood still.

"A nice Christian pastime," he sneered, "for a man who calls himself a minister. If it weren't for you and people like you with their fool ideas, this war would never have been fought. You stirred them up, you and other hornets like you. You have murder on your soul."

Parson Moody came nearer. Paul was too worked up with what he was saying to notice what the old man was doing. Suddenly Parson Moody sprang at him and tore at the mask. It broke and fell from Paul's face. They confronted each other in the dim light of the church.

"So, a runaway servant! Paul, the renegade."

"I spit in your face," Paul said, beside himself, and with all his force he struck Parson Moody between the eyes. He fell on the floor and hit his head. Paul went to him where he lay and kicked him again and again.

"Paul," a voice behind him called, "Paul, Paul, don't, oh don't!"

And a man's voice demanded: "What has happened?"

Anne had come with her father to the church.

·[262]·

"This old fool was hacking at the altar with an ax. I know him, he's a fanatical preacher."

Paul stooped and put his hands beneath the unconscious man's shoulders and started to drag him out of the church.

"There," he said, when he had rolled him down the steps into the streets. He came back wiping his hands.

"Where's the priest?" the Governor asked, looking about him. "He was to be here to marry you."

"I don't know."

"You had better go in search of him. We'll lock the door to prevent this happening again."

He crossed himself and looked at the broken statues, the torn altar cloths, the tabernacle crookedly swinging open.

"I shall stay here," he said. "Perhaps my authority or my presence . . ."

His voice trailed into silence. He buried his face in his hands and began to pray. Marie and Paul went out of the church. Anne looked at her father, then she slipped softly after Paul. The two girls hesitated by Parson Moody's unconscious figure sprawled upon the steps.

"You hurt him. Perhaps we should . . ."

"Let him be!" Paul stepped over him contemptuously, giving him a nudge with his boot as he passed. "I hate the very air he breathes!"

He adjusted his mask with Anne's help.

"Now that he has recognized me," he whispered to Marie, so that Anne should not hear, "it will be very dangerous until we get away."

"If we can't find the priest, what about a frère de charité?" Anne asked.

"A good idea. One of them will do."

They walked quickly through the courtyard of the citadel, deserted of its familiar sights and sounds and turned toward the hospital. Marie went home. She was anxious about the children with so many drunken soldiers in the streets, and besides she felt de trop.

"We'll send for you," Paul promised, "if we find a priest."

Marie nodded and walked away. Her face was screwed up and

her mouth working. She did not want Paul to see. She was thinking of her own wedding day, so short a time before, to Charles, and of how she loved him and wondered and worried about him every hour of the day. There was no news of the *Oiseau de Mer*. Now Paul was getting married, his future was uncertain . . . poor Anne, if she were half as much in love as Marie was with Charles, but that, of course, couldn't be. She hurried on.

CHAPTER LVII

THE hospital was one of the longest buildings in Louisbourg, two hundred eighty feet, but it had come through the siege without being hit. So had the buildings round it, the bakery and laundry, but the garden where the Frères de Charité grew herbs and vegetables was plowed into desolate heaps. A red light burned in the distance, mounting guard over the tabernacle. Dim, dusty light streamed from the door, making patches of sunlight on the stone flags, the wooden, handmade benches and the altar steps.

"We could be married here," Paul said.

Anne caught his hand and drew him to a bench. They knelt together, praying in silence. Paul finished his incoherent supplications first, raised his head and looked at Anne. She was so young, so independent, so absurdly brave and tender. She had such a large heart in so small and beautiful a body. He was so in love with her.

She rose and gave him her hand.

"That was very sweet, a prelude to marriage."

They stepped into the sunlight. He stopped her for a moment.

"I wish that I had wealth and power and protection to give you."

"I don't want those things."

A distant shouting reminded them of what the peaceful atmosphere in the chapel had made them forget—danger, haste, the enemy in the town, transportation, imprisonment. They walked quickly into the hospital and turned to the little room on the right which served as a reception room. A young brother was seated there, scratching in a ledger as though nothing had happened to make his accounts valueless. He looked up as they came in. He had a pleasant brown face with inquiring eyes and a wide smile. He looked more like a farmer or a coureur de bois than a monk.

"We are looking for someone to help us," Paul said, taking a liking to him. "This is Mademoiselle du Chambon."

The brother rose and blessed her, looking over her head.

"I am Paul de Morpain," he crossed himself, being blessed in turn. "We have Monsieur du Chambon's consent to our immediate marriage. We went to the chapel in the citadel where Father Dominic was to meet us, but he wasn't there."

He decided not to mention the desecration of the altar, as the brother might be more interested in that than the business in hand.

"So we came here. Will you marry us in your chapel now?"

"I will speak to the Reverend Father," the brother said. "Stay here and make yourselves comfortable till I return."

He glided from the room. Paul and Anne gazed at each other, blissfully silent. It seemed no time at all before the monk returned.

"Reverend Father will marry you himself. You must excuse him, please, for a little delay. He is with some Indians who need his help."

"Some delay is necessary," Paul said, "at least until we send for Monsieur du Chambon and my sister. Is there anyone else you want?" he turned to Anne.

"No."

"May the children come if they behave?"

She laughed.

"Of course. It wouldn't be a wedding without Tomas."

"Is there anyone who could take a message for us?"

The brother rose and went to the door.

"Joseph!" he called.

A small Indian boy ran in. He was thin, half-starved, and badly dressed in a coat too large for him, but he had the native grace of his people. He was bronze-colored, with large black eyes and straight black hair cut in a fringe. When he smiled his teeth looked like small sharpened pearls.

"This is Joseph. He will run very fast on any errand that you give him."

Paul began explaining to the boy.

"Tell them that the man in the mask wants them to come at once to the Chapel of the Recollets, do you understand?"

The boy shook his head.

"To the hospital!"

The door opened. A tall, lean, silver-haired man came in. The young monk knelt and crossed himself. Paul did the same. Anne knelt and bent forward to kiss the Reverend Father's ring.

"We are sorry to disturb you," Paul began, rising from his knees.

"And I am sorry to have kept you waiting. Did Brother Constant give you my message?"

"He said that you were helping some Indians. Is this one of them?"

Anne pointed to Joseph, who ducked and slipped from the room.

"Forgive me if I follow him for a moment to make things clear," Paul interrupted, going out after the child.

"Ah, Joseph!" the Reverend Father said, smiling. "No. Joseph is one of our children. We have fifty-seven Micmac and Malisite children here. They are a problem we take in our stride, but this is something different, something less encouraging." He sighed. "A woman, looking for her husband. She insists that he came here to be in the siege. She does not know his name and we are afraid he is dead or has deserted her." He sighed again. "He has probably deserted her. The old story. She is going to have a child."

"Oh," Anne said impulsively, "how sad! Is there nothing I can do to help? Perhaps I can talk to her while we are waiting for my father and the other witnesses to the wedding."

She looked toward the door, hoping it would open and Paul come back to her. The story of this woman's misery upset her and made her want to cling to him.

"I am so happy," she said shyly, "I cannot bear to think of any unhappiness today."

"That is very right and natural, my daughter. I am sure that

·[267]·

you can be of help. She will tell you more than she has told to us, perhaps, a woman to a woman. Come with me."

Anne hesitated, sorry she had volunteered.

"I do not know how to speak to her."

"She speaks good French. She is an educated Malisite, a Catholic."

"Oh."

Anne cast another glance backward. Where was Paul? Reverend Father walked to the door and held it open for her. They went out together. Brother Constant sat down at his desk and began a long column of addition.

CHAPTER LVIII

"HERE is the Governor now!"

Marie turned where Tomas pointed and began to smile. She tried to conceal it but really the more she looked at the two figures gravely approaching the more absurd they seemed. Monsieur du Chambon was picking his way through the debris of the convent garden in the preoccupied way of a man whose thoughts are focused on weighty matters. Joseph trotted beside him, stride for stride, a perfect caricature. Both brows were furrowed with silent thought and both figures looked weighed down with responsibility.

"Monsieur du Chambon," Marie called out, nudging the children into respectful attitudes.

The Governor started and looked up. He had been a thousand miles away, plunged in pictures of the past, conjectures of the future, anxiety for Anne and for himself. He did not like this fellow she was marrying, had never liked him from the first time he had seen him. He tried to tell himself that part of this was prejudice, because he had disregarded the fellow's warning which had turned out to be right. He tried to put this personal dislike aside and judge Paul on his merits.

"Precious few," he grumbled to himself, "no family, no money, no position. I am mad to give my sanction to such a mésalliance."

But he knew Anne. He could not bear to shatter the small chance she had of happiness, and drag her down with him into the disgrace of the court-martial ahead of him, failure, perhaps prison, perhaps death.

"Then where would she be with no one to look after her?"

Paul came out of the hospital with one of the Frères de Charité. They reached the group of children and bent down to talk to them. The Governor stared hard at the two men, comparing them, trying to see Paul with impartial eyes.

"He is well enough as far as strength and figure go, he is young —some would call it callow. He is sure of himself, too sure. He is what I have always thought him, a cockerel."

Paul turned to him and smiled, holding out his hands.

"Where's my daughter?" Monsieur du Chambon asked, stiffly, putting his own hands behind his back. Joseph copied the gesture, throwing out his stomach.

"She is with the Reverend Father, talking to some Indians," Paul answered, carelessly. "Some sad tale or other caught her attention. Just like Anne."

The Governor winced. This easy familiarity upset him. If the thing had to be done it had better be done and over with. He hoped he would not have to see much of his son-in-law.

"I'll get him a job at sea and keep him there," he thought. "I should have enough influence left for that. Then Anne will live with me and all will go on with us as it did, but she will be married, and have a husband's protection when she needs it."

He looked at Paul again.

"Well," he said, "you sent me a message . . ."

Paul was about to explain. The door behind them opened and Anne came out.

"Paul," she said. "Oh Father, there's such a sad thing here. I don't like savages . . ."

Joseph stuck his tongue out at her.

". . . but this is different. She is so young and appealing, and she has been so badly treated. I want you to help her, Father."

"How can I help anyone?" Monsieur du Chambon grumbled. "Where is the priest? Have you made up your mind? You're sure you want to marry this . . . this . . . this Monsieur de Morpain?"

"Of course I'm sure."

"Then let us go to the chapel and get it over. You can tell me about your protégée afterward."

Anne looked at Paul, smiling, her eyes shining.

"I said she could come to the wedding!"

Paul laughed at her.

"That will cheer her up," he said tenderly.

Brother Constant who was teasing Tomas straightened and said to Paul.

"Reverend Father cannot marry you in a mask," he made a gesture toward Paul's face.

"Take it off," Anne said.

"We are all friends here," Marie added.

Paul struggled with the fastening.

"Here, let me help."

Anne went behind him and put her fingers to the string. The door of the hospital opened again. Reverend Father came out, talking to an Indian girl. They moved forward together toward the group.

"There!" Anne said triumphantly.

The mask fell from Paul's face. He turned and kissed her. Suddenly a strange and dreadful cry rang out.

"My husband! My husband!"

The Indian girl was running, laughing and sobbing, toward Paul.

"San!"

She reached him and took him in her arms.

There was a terrible silence. Paul's face was green, he trembled, trying to speak, his lips worked but no sound came out of them. The Governor was the first to recover.

"You scoundrel!" he sputtered, drawing his sword. Anne rushed to him. She was pale, so pale that she looked as though she would faint.

"Father," she said, "take me away, take me away from here!"

Paul looked at her in anguish over San's shoulder. She did not look at him. She took her father's arm and leaning on it heavily, drew him away from the staring group, transfixed in interested horror. Marie, Tomas, the frères de charité, Paul's sisters, were all looking at him as though they saw a ghost.

San was running her hands over him lightly, tenderly, search-

·[271]·

ing for a hurt, holding him stiff and unresisting in her arms. Every now and then she murmured:

"My husband, my husband."

Paul broke away from her.

"Anne!"

He tried to run forward.

"Wait!" Reverend Father's voice was like a whip. "Let her go, my son. You have no business with Mademoiselle du Chambon now."

Paul stopped. His eyes were fixed on Anne's disappearing head. Her father's arm was round her, his cloak about her shoulders as though he would protect her from the elements at least. The day was scorchingly hot, but she was feeling cold. Paul knew that deadly chill from the iciness in his own heart.

His arms dropped to his sides. He stood where he was, watching until Anne disappeared. San, kneeling to him now, took his hand, kissing it, pressing it to her heart.

Marie passed him with the children, eager, curious, afraid. Paul remembered how they hated Indians. Marie did not look at him. Reverend Father touched him on the shoulder. His breath escaped in a little strangling sigh.

"San," he said. "Oh, San."

PART SIX
RESTLESS SAILS 1746

CHAPTER LIX

CAPTAIN WOODES of His Majesty's brig *Hastings* heard eight bells strike and with satisfaction and relief saw the men of the first dog watch take over from the afternoon watch. It was a mild September day. Already the brig, with a following wind, was halfway across the Bay of Fundy. Soon the Gap leading into the Annapolis Basin would be visible. The *Hastings* should pass through it and come to an anchor before the tide changed. Then the long perilous voyage would be over, the precious cargo of supplies and ammunition landed, the reward his. He smiled, putting his glass to his eye. There was no sign from the quarter deck of that elusive opening in the dark forested shore line ahead of them. The mate came to stand his watch, but Captain Woodes lingered. He had no mind to go below while he could have the sun and the bracing air on his face. He watched the sparkle on the clean green water. A porpoise rolled, another and another, a school of them.

Suddenly the midshipman in the maintop hailed the deck.

"Ah," thought Captain Woodes, but the cry that followed was not what he expected.

"Sail ahoy! Coming up on the starboard quarter!"

Captain Woodes swung round and walked briskly toward the helmsman. Standing beside him with his glass sweeping the horizon aft, he could see nothing but the foaming wake, sea gulls swooping, and an occasional whitecap. Presently, however, he thought he caught the white gleam of a sail.

He watched until it was certain.

"She's overhauling us fast," he muttered. "Mr. Hood, set all sail, we must keep ahead of her no matter who she is."

The mate barked orders. Men began to swarm up the rigging. Royals bellied into the breeze, followed by studding sails from the yardarms and watersails beneath them. The brig felt the tug and pull of the extra canvas, heeling under its pressure. Captain Woodes looked anxiously aloft.

"Can you make out what she is?" he cupped his hands and shouted. The mate repressed a shudder. Captain Woodes broke all the rules of decent discipline, ignored the watches and tried to be on deck and in command himself most of the time; but he was a good sailor, no question about that.

The cry came echoing down:

"A barque. French by the looks of her."

"What flag?"

"Can't make out."

And then: "Ahoy! She's flying the black flag with a red design."

"Privateer," the mate said, "a French privateer."

"I'm afraid it may be worse than that," Captain Woodes said pleasantly, snapping his glass into its case and taking out a pistol. He primed it lovingly.

"I think, Mister, we may be in for something."

"Pirate?" the mate asked.

Captain Woodes nodded.

"I think it may be the fellow we've heard so much about."

"The *Oiseau* . . . something, sir?"

"The *Oiseau de Proie*. Bird of Prey. She flies a red hawk's head on a black ground and carries a crew of savages. Have the ship lightened, pile on the canvas we have."

The mate gave the order.

"Aren't we going to fight her, sir?"

"We're going to run. If we can make the Gap before she does we may get away. I doubt if she will follow where the shore batteries might get her range." He sighed. "She has the speed of us all right, confound it."

The mate looked at him disapprovingly.

"It goes against the grain, sir, to run without a fight."

"It does," Captain Woodes admitted, "but you see, Mister," he continued softly as he turned away, "the cargo is important, I might say vital, to the garrison in there." He waved his hand toward the dark shore line. "We've come all this way with it. We have to get it to its destination at whatever cost to ourselves, even if the cost be paid in pride. I fear, however, that we shall have to fight."

He padded away on his elegant booted legs to where the Officer of Marines was placing twenty-four musketeers about the deck. The First Lieutenant greeted him from the main deck.

"Man the guns," Captain Woodes commanded.

The First Lieutenant sent gun crews aft to the long-range stern chasers. They scrambled aft eagerly, with two boys to fetch the powder for them. The Second Lieutenant took command of this detachment.

"Battle stations for all the crew?"

Captain Woodes nodded.

Four men to each of the six guns on a side took their places, with twelve boys to fetch the powder, one beside each gun. The First Lieutenant commanded the six foremost guns, the Second Lieutenant commanded the six aftermost. Two master's mates attended the braces and stood by to work the ship according to orders. The boatswain's mate with two seamen stood by to assist in working the ship and to repair the main rigging. The boatswain was in command on the forecastle with men to work the ship, repair the forerigging and fetch powder for the two three-pounders that were mounted there. Nine musketeers commanded by the Second Marine Officer, eight musketeers in the barge upon the booms with the Third Marine Officer, five men with a midshipman at small arms in the maintop, and five men at small arms in the foretop, completed the regular battle stations. Seven extra men ranged back and forth along the decks with buckets of sand which they sprinkled liberally, without a thought for the reason they were spreading it. They had seen decks sanded before and the bloody sand swept up again. They grinned cheerfully, envious of the men in the Second Lieutenant's crews, bringing the stern chasers to bear on the approaching barque.

"Try to knock off some of her canvas, boys. See if we can't carry away her masts."

The brig was ready for action, and the Gap was far ahead.

·[277]·

CHAPTER LX

THE *Oiseau de Proie* overhauled the *Hastings* before six o'clock. She signaled "Heave to!" a little drunkenly, and when the signal was disregarded, fired her forward port guns. The round dropped short in the sea except one ball which hit the stem and splintered the bowsprit without breaking it. Captain Woodes, intent on making the Gap less than a mile ahead, kept the brig to her course. It was no use. The *Oiseau de Proie*, maneuvering superbly, sharpened up and headed for the *Hastings*, forcing her to choose between being rammed or sheering off from the Gap and losing the narrow entrance to safety.

Captain Woodes brought his starboard guns into action. He could see the First Marine Officer placing musketeers to stand off the boarding party from the *Oiseau de Proie*, now near enough for them to see the naked savages swarming in her rigging and on her decks, manning her guns and handling the barque.

"I don't believe there's a Christian on board her," the first mate murmured below his breath.

A cloud of smoke and flashes of fire obscured his view for a moment. When it cleared, the *Oiseau de Proie* was still bearing down, her grapnels manned and her boarders ready with cutlasses and muskets in their hands. Some of them were sharpshooting at the musketeers on the *Hastings'* deck. Every shot of the volley fired from the *Hastings* had taken its toll, but evidently the savages had no fear of death. They came on grinning.

Captain Woodes gave the order to bear-up but it was too late. The vessels came together with a grinding, tearing shock. Men poured from the *Oiseau de Proie*. Hand-to-hand fighting began on all the decks. The English did their best but they were outnumbered and taken aback by the ferocity and unexpected tactics of enemies who fought without any rules, with anything that came handy, uttering shrill, piercing, disgusting cries as they hacked and tore their way over the *Hastings'* decks, leaving scalped and wounded men behind them.

The tide that Captain Woodes had hoped to catch turned while the vessels were engaged and they began to drift back from the Gap into the Bay of Fundy. It was all up with any hope the *Hastings* had of rescue or escape. Captain Woodes decided to surrender.

The long rays of the setting sun threw bronze and purple reflections over the decks of the two ships, littered and powderblackened; over the savages forming in orderly ranks, officered by other savages; over the small group of unwounded men, breathing heavily, gathered about Captain Woodes; over the wreckage, the blood, the masts towering and straining aloft, the rough freshening seas below.

Silently and efficiently every man who could walk was transported to the *Oiseau de Proie*, manacled and sent below. The wounded who could not walk were left on the *Hastings*. A crew of forty savages prepared to man the brig. One of them stepped up to Captain Woodes, standing disconsolately on the quarter deck, the white flag still in his hands, and made him understand by signs that the Captain of the *Oiseau de Proie* wanted to speak to him. Captain Woodes hesitated, the savage signed more urgently, taking hold of his arm. Captain Woodes brushed him off and stepped forward. The savage followed, frowning. They stepped from the deck of the *Hastings* to the deck of the *Oiseau de Proie*. A huge savage met them, brandishing manacles, but Captain Woodes' escort waved him aside.

The deck was cluttered with savages repairing damage from the action. Captain Woodes estimated that the *Oiseau de Proie* must have a crew of a hundred and fifty to two hundred men, if you could call them men. He wondered what sort of captain he was going to see. He must have directed the operations of the barque he commanded, but during the fighting nothing had been seen of him. Presumably he was a savage too. Captain Woodes faltered in his stride. The full weight of what was happening came home to him. He had not believed up till that moment that everything was over, in spite of the evidence of his senses. He had known, but without feeling it, that his cargo and his future were lost, that he was a prisoner, his men killed and wounded, manacled in chains.

The savage escorting him stopped in front of a door and pointed to it. Captain Woodes hesitated a moment, then he knocked.

"Come in."

The words were spoken pleasantly, in English. He pushed the door open, stepped over the raised sill and moved into a spacious, well-furnished cabin. A young man was seated at a table facing the door. He was not an Indian. He was dressed in a suit of sober blue, with silver buttons, and silver lace. He wore silver buckles to his belt and his shoes and a silver sword lay on the table in front of him.

He looked up, half rose, and motioned Captain Woodes to a chair.

"Sit down, Captain," he said a little haltingly, with a strong French accent. "I am sorry to take you prisoner. You resisted gallantly, but far too long." He waved a hand awkwardly as Captain Woodes remained standing. "Please sit down. I know you will want to hear what is to happen to your brig, your men and yourself."

Captain Woodes nodded. His face relaxed a little. This man seemed to be reasonable and human, although, remembering his crew and their methods of fighting, one could not trust him very far.

"We are, as you will have gathered, pirates."

Captain Woodes said dryly:

"Yes. You fly the Black."

"With the head of a bird of prey to relieve its gloom."

Captain Woodes stirred restlessly.

"We have taken your brig as a prize, for herself and for the cargo. A prize crew is now aboard her and will work her into port."

"What port?"

"There is no reason for you to know till we get there. Your wounded will be put ashore and you with them. You will be able to come to some arrangement with the port authorities, no doubt, regarding the exchange and ransom."

Exchange? Ransom?

"A French port, no doubt? Are you French?"

"Possibly."

"You speak excellent English."

The young captain bowed.

"It is useful in my profession."

Captain Woodes looked at him appraisingly. He was probably in his twenties. He had a sallow face, with brooding, burning eyes, black and melancholy. He did not look the sort of man to command a pirate ship with a crew of two hundred savages. Yet there he was, seated composedly before him, disposing of him and his affairs with courtesy but with finality.

He struck a bell. The door opened. Two impassive savages came in. Captain Woodes listened, fascinated, to a stream of orders in a liquid lilting dialect.

"Will you do me the honor of dining with me in an hour's time? These men will show you to your quarters."

The savages grunted.

"I hope you will find them comfortable."

Captain Woodes bowed and went out. He was very tired. He staggered a little as he followed the savages forward. Food and drink would be reviving. Perhaps if he responded cheerfully and courteously to these overtures from the pirate captain he would get better treatment for himself and for his men. He was interested, with a strange and gruesome interest, in everything that happened on this barque. Any vessel manned entirely by savages was grotesque and unreal, terrifying even to a man with years of experience and some fighting.

He heard the sound of waves, and wind through the rigging, the creaking and the groaning of metal and wood as the barque moved swiftly into the Bay of Fundy, under full canvas. She was expertly handled, but he missed the familiar accompaniments to a normal crew, piped about its work. No bells rang. Everything

·[281]·

was silent. He breathed deeply, looking about him at the cabin. It was neat and even luxurious. He picked up a broken compass and put it down again. He opened a drawer and took out a dusty logbook, opened it idly, turning the pages. It was written in French. He laid it down then took it up again as the title page caught his eye: "*Oiseau de Mer*." "Captain Pierre de Morpain." That was the Sea Bird, not the Bird of Prey. Was it this barque or another?

There was a tap at his door. He slid the logbook into place. "Come in."

A savage glided in with hot water and towels. He placed them neatly on the locker and slipped out.

"Quite remarkable," Captain Woodes said, smiling wryly. "I shall recommend to the Admiralty a widespread use of savages to man our navy."

He took off his coat and waistcoat, plunged his hands into the water and began to bathe his forehead and his eyes. He washed and washed as though he would erase the memories of the last five hours from his brain—pictures, endless pictures of men in agony, men for whom he could do nothing, men whose every gesture was familiar, men a part of his daily life, men for whom he was responsible, butchered because of him. Pictures of the garrison at Fort Anne, waiting for the supplies entrusted to him. Pictures of the future, disgraced, without his brig. He raised his head and stared at himself in the mirror above the locker. It was strange to see the same face that had stared at him in the morning from the mirror of his cabin on the *Hastings*. Yes, that was strange.

The beating of a gong summoned him to dinner. The familiar sound made him think for an instant that he must be on the *Hastings* and all this about him a bad dream. It died away. He stepped from his cabin. It was dark on deck with the cool air of a September night, moonless, starless, refreshing. He walked toward the Captain's cabin, trying not to peer through the darkness astern for the lights of the brig.

"Come in."

The pirate was not alone. Captain Woodes started, repressed his start and stepped forward gallantly bowing.

"I want you to meet my wife, Captain . . . er . . ."

"Woodes."

". . . Woodes."

The woman looked at him and smiled. She wore European clothes but she was an Indian. He let out his breath slowly, taking her hand. She was beautiful. She reminded him of some swift bird poised for flight.

"Naturally," he complimented them, "the Hawk would marry an Eagle."

"My wife," the pirate said dryly, "does not understand English."

"Oh."

"You can speak to her in French."

CHAPTER LXI

SEVENTY-SEVEN barrels of smoked herring. Why do they want to bring fish across the ocean to Annapolis? Herring! Men can go out here and catch lobster, tuna fish, cod, pollack and eat them fresh, but the English send smoked herring to their garrisons and we take it as a prize!"

Paul pushed the ledger in front of him impatiently. It was late. Captain Woodes had retired, leaving the *Hastings*' ship's papers with him, bills of lading, lists of cargo and the logbook.

"Fifty bales of silk. That's better, though I don't know what the soldiers of Fort Anne would do with silk."

San laughed at him. She was sitting on a bearskin at his feet with her arms on his knees. From time to time she rested her cheek against them. From time to time he patted her head absentmindedly and kindly as he might have patted the head of a favorite dog.

"You can have a bale for yourself if you like, and another to make some breeches for Tom. Sixty-two kegs of powder. That's worth having. One hundred and ten round shot. Why the ten?" He went on murmuring to himself, scratching figures with a pen which he handed every now and then to San to be trimmed. Presently he yawned and pushed the books aside.

"That makes the fourteenth prize in less than a year," he said.

"The abbé will be glad."

"Well, he deserves his share, I suppose. He got us most of the crew and some of the information."

San nodded.

"I will go and see to Tom, then we can go to bed. You must be tired."

He yawned again.

"I am."

He watched her get to her feet with one lithe spring and balance herself cleverly against the rolling of the barque. It was beginning to be heavy weather and the *Oiseau de Mer*—the *Oiseau de Proie*—was given to wallowing and worse—to a pitch and toss that felt as though she would break in two until one got accustomed to it.

San disappeared. Paul sat for a moment at his table, then he rose and wandered restlessly to a cabinet behind him, opened a door and got out a bottle and tankard which he filled. He returned to his chair and sat sipping and staring ahead of him. His mind went to the past. Every time that he took a prize he seemed to be conducted back over his career as a pirate, especially the start of it.

There were those three wretched months of June, July, August, 1745, when he lay like a hunted wildcat hiding from his enemies with only San to care for him. There was a reward on his head. The Merciers, the Governor's men, Will Vaughan and Parson Moody, hunted him. San had hidden him from everyone and nursed him back to a wish to live. She had dragged him from the town. He sneaked back. She followed him. He watched Anne sail with her father. He stood on the shore at Pointe Platte and bared his head. His heart was bared already, bared and bleeding.

Later he had watched the *Oiseau de Mer* sail into port, deceived by the French flag kept flying over Louisbourg to lure French ships into harbor, where they were seized and sold. The *Oiseau de Mer* was a fat haul. His uncle and Charles Godet were taken prisoner, the barque was left at anchor with a skeleton crew and her cargo stored on board. There were no empty storerooms. The New Englanders had a number of other prize cargoes on their hands stored in the vessels which brought them.

It was San who had the great idea. She stole forth to talk to the Micmac sailors left on board, then she came back and shook Paul from his sleep to tell him what she had planned. The idea soothed and excited him. He followed her to the harbor. That night they outwitted the English sentries, swam to the *Oiseau de Mer*, stole her from her anchorage and took her out to sea.

Days and weeks of hardship followed, while they worked the barque shorthanded, in danger of losing masts and gear or going ashore. Paul's seamanship was exposed for what it was and the savages laughed at him. San made him take the barque to La Hève. She sent the insubordinate Micmacs ashore. Then she found out where the Abbé le Loutre was camping. Paul wrote to him. The abbé sent a hundred picked Malisites in return for a share in the enterprise.

Paul had the barque careened and re-equipped. When they sailed again as the *Oseau de Proie* they were in a position to hold their own. Paul learned how to handle the barque every day that he captained her. The new crew learned their work from those who had shipped with Pierre de Morpain and like Paul from experience. So far the *Oiseau de Proie* had done very well. She had taken fourteen prizes, all of them reasonably lucrative. The abbé obtained his share and sent them news of English vessels due to arrive, of others sailing and advised which ports were safest for the barque to use.

The winter was full of hardships, with terrible storms and very little profit to be made, so they fished from the barque and lay up where they could. It was in April that the letter came. The first sloop to make the crossing that year brought letters and dispatches for all New France. These were sorted in Quebec. The letters addressed to the scattered inhabitants of Louisbourg were given to Abbé le Loutre to distribute to the fugitives where he could find them. There was a letter for Paul. The abbé sent it to him by a Micmac runner.

Paul took it from his pocket, unfolded it slowly and laid it on the table. He knew every word of it but he liked to read the words, tracing the blobs and dots that Anne had made.

"I have been thinking of what happened to us, Paul. I want you to know that I understand things better now. They hurt me as much, but I think I know how it happened and why you did not tell me and what you must have felt and what you are feeling now. It is right that you should stay with her and with your child, but I believe, and it is all that I have left to me, my love, that you loved me and not her. I believe that you will always love me and I know that I will always love you. Monsieur Bigot who is here has talked to me and made me understand a lot of things. If you see him when he goes back to Canada, for he is to go to Quebec, he will tell you what he said. Pray for me that I can get through the long, lonely years ahead. I thought at first that pride would be enough and anger and my father's contempt for you, but they were useless. Real things only come once to real people. Do you remember when I said that? It is true. It does no good to deny that we ever loved. We loved, we still love, we are apart. It is through your fault, through something you did before we met, that other men have often done without paying for. It is hard for us both. It must be hard for you to know that it is your fault, while for me there is jealousy as well to endure. She is beautiful, Paul, and loyal and honest and the mother of your child. I think so much about your child, and about you. I wonder, often, when I shall hear of you. With all the dangers round you when we left . . . but I have prayed for you and thought of you and suffered and endured for you, at least you must be safe!

"Father is much broken. It is believed that he will be acquitted. He will not return to New France, nor will I. Your sister with whom I have kept in touch has heard that her husband is safe and has been taken prisoner in Louisbourg. He is to be exchanged. The children are well, except for poor little Andrée who died on board the transport from the effects of the siege.

"But how are *you*? Send me, if you can, some word that you are safe and well in health. Speak to me, Paul, and when you speak know that you are speaking to your Anne."

He folded the letter, kissed it and put it away. The door opened a few minutes later. San looked in.

"Tom is asleep now," she said. "You are tired. Come and I will put you to sleep too."

Paul looked at her. She ran to him and strained him to her, alarmed.

"Don't look like that," she whispered. "You are safe. There is nothing to hurt you here."

Paul let her lead him from the room.

·[287]·

CHAPTER LXII

THERE was a crisp September tang in the air. The day was sunny without much wind, a weather breeder, Paul thought, watching the cloudless skies. The water, breaking green and white against the prow, was too transparent. The outline of the rocky coast was too sharp, too visible. He lowered his glass, grunting.

He hoped to make La Hève with the *Oiseau de Proie* and the *Hastings* before a storm blew up, catching him shorthanded, with prisoners on board. The *Oiseau de Proie* needed repairing and reprovisioning. Shots from the *Hastings* had torn holes in the topsides, the afterdeck house and along the decks, charring and splintering uneven pockmarks, traps for the bare feet of the crew. Some of the sails were torn and clumsily mended. The main lower topsail was gone and in its place an oddly shaped substitute offended the eye. With any luck he could anchor at La Hève for several days and set all straight.

They were off Cape Sable now, rounding treacherous shoals to turn north, always an ugly passage. Paul, glancing at the rocky cliffs and the dark line of forest, remembered the storm that had flung him there with Randy. He re-lived for an instant that agonized groping toward the firelight. A voice beside him brought him back to the present with a start, it was the same voice that had greeted him then.

San was beside him, holding Tom in her arms. Paul's face lightened as he looked at his son. It was absurd that a year-old baby should resemble a grown person so exactly as Tom resembled his grandfather. He had the same humorous mouth on which one expected to see a beard, the same level eyes, the same mannerism of raising one eyebrow instead of two in surprise, and he always threw back his head and laughed heartily whenever the sails strained in the wind or the barque pitched heavily or a sea breaking along the side sent a cloud of spray on deck. Paul remembered his father standing on *La Belle Louise* with his great head thrown back, laughing at the storm.

"I wish that he could see you."

The baby swung himself forward with a plunge that nearly sent him overboard. San smiled proudly and placed him in his father's arms. She walked away, leaving the two men together.

Paul held the little bronze body dressed in nothing but a scarlet handkerchief, kicking and springing against him. The child's strength and vitality, his fearless, lusty laughter, coming from so defenseless a minikin, melted the cold raw fog about Paul's heart and gave him something nothing else could give.

He held the child up to the taffrail.

"Look!"

The child held very still against his father's chest, peering downward. He watched the break and wash of the water against the hull. A shout from the rigging startled him. He tried to see where it came from. Then he bent over again, looking at the sea. Paul stared at the green water too, seeing a thousand half-formed pictures. The backs of their heads looked exactly alike, black hair, round head set on the same shoulders, even their ears were alike, a little pointed, but Tom's were already pierced and he wore golden rings.

Captain Woodes coming upon them both like that was startled and amused. He was prepared for most things but this young pirate captain was continually surprising him. He joined the group and stood beside them.

"No need to ask whose baby that is," he said presently, when Paul looked up and greeted him. "I never saw a more astonishing resemblance."

Paul smiled, a little embarrassed. Captain Woodes held out a finger which Tom ignored, staring at him gravely. Now he looked more Malisite than French.

·[289]·

"There's no denying it, they're a handsome race," Captain Woodes said half to himself. "And I suppose a half-breed can have a good life as long as he sticks to the woods."

"Or the sea."

Captain Woodes bowed.

"I had forgotten; this is my first experience of savages as sailors."

Paul was silent.

"This boy will have a good life," he said after a pause. He said it resolutely, almost grimly. "His grandfather was a seaman, his father's a pirate. He'll be able to sweep the seas. You in England don't understand these things. The French have intermarried with the Indians often. Look at the Baron St. Castin, a half-breed, and there are many others, coureurs de bois, adventurers, sailors. He'll be all right. He'll have a better time than I did."

"Forgive me if I sound impertinent. You are young enough to be my son. I never saw a captain so young as you. Yet now and then you speak as though your life were over."

"I've crowded a good deal into it," Paul said.

He called to a passing Micmac. The man stopped and ran back to him. He held out his great naked arms for the baby and carried him away. Paul put the glass to his eye and stared toward Cape Sable. Then he put the glass under his arm and turned away. Captain Woodes stared after him. Above their heads the great square of canvas flapped and gently filled, the barque slid forward, smoothly, talking to herself in the interminable murmuring of ropes and spars and rigging and creaking bulkheads and spray. Captain Woodes sighed. The *Hastings* was behind them, following their course. He could see every move aboard her without his glass. It was hard, but it might have been worse. He had expected savagery and bloodshed, what he got was a combination of Indian boudoir and nursery and a sulky boy brooding over some mystery. He shook his head.

"If I get out of this and can wheedle another command . . ."

CHAPTER LXIII

THE sky was yellow at sunset with black clouds streaked across it.

"Mares'-tails," Paul said to Captain Woodes. "If the moon rises red we'll know what to expect."

It was a comfort to him to be able to talk to a white man experienced in seamanship. His crew of savages worked well and fearlessly, but they were ignorant, indifferent and superstitious. If a gale blew up they attributed it to some bad spirit and like as not they would start dancing and howling on the deck instead of shortening sail. The mate was more help. He was a half-breed who had sailed oi the *Oiseau de Proie* for seven years. He was always telling Paul what Captain de Morpain did, and when Paul told him: "I am Captain de Morpain now," he would grin and shake his head. He drove the other men on with a leather whip and he could have handled the barque alone. Paul sometimes saw him in command of her, grinning beneath a new cocked hat. If he were a mutineer and decided to take the ship there would be nothing for Paul to do but grin back. Fortunately Quanopin was not ambitious. San, who was a good judge of her people, said that he was midway between the authority of the white man and the happiness of the red man to obey. She had no fear of him.

The night grew cold, a late moon rose and there was a red reflection. Paul was anxious. He did not want to be caught short-handed in the gale that he believed was blowing up. He decided that there was nothing he could do but keep on his course for La

Hève. He went below to change his clothes and drink something warm. He would be up all night.

He found San in the cabin and Tom in his hammock. The hammock was made of buckskin embroidered with quill work. It was slung across the middle of the cabin where it could not hit anything even with the most violent rocking of the barque. Tom spent a great deal of his time in it, waking or sleeping. Sometimes when the weather was fine it was slung on deck. Then no one had to watch him. He would lie for hours contentedly watching the sails and the sky, the sea gulls and the clouds.

He was awake now as Paul came in. He was strapped in but he could raise his arms. He lifted them to Paul crying: "Pé, Pé, Pé!"

Paul brushed his forehead with the back of his hand and set the hammock swinging.

"It looks as though it would be rough," he said to San. "I thought I'd have a bowl of soup now before it begins. We'll have to put the fires out and set a watch on the lanterns presently."

"After the soup, some sleep."

Paul shook his head.

"Not with all those English prisoners on board and that Captain Woodes."

"Captain Woodes is not a bad man," San said, "only curious and vain."

"Vain?"

"He walks as though he thought his coming made a difference to others instead of to himself."

Paul yawned.

"I wouldn't trust him in a gale not to try and take the barque. After all, we got her that way. We stole her."

"We took her from your uncle. He would have said 'take the *Oiseau de Mer*, don't let the English have her!' if he could have spoken to us. That is different. Your uncle would never have given up his boat to Captain Woodes."

Paul yawned again and sat on the edge of his bunk to draw on heavy boots. San came close to him. She watched as he laced the leather leggings into place, put out her hand to touch them, then she let herself slide to the floor beside Paul. The barque was rolling badly now, meeting heavier seas. Everything was in creaking motion back and forth complainingly.

A sailor opened the door and came in dripping wet.

"Quanopin says please change course. He thinks the wind will blow us to Cape Sable Island."

"All right," Paul said, "I'll come. Go to the galleys and get me a bowl of soup. Tell the cook to serve out something hot and then to put out his fires."

The savage nodded and retreated. Paul stood up. There was a rap on the door.

"Come in."

Captain Woodes stepped over the sill.

"It's blowing up," he said. "I think it's going to be a bad one. I'd appreciate your letting me go to my men."

Paul considered this.

"They are being well looked after," he answered. "Although I'm shorthanded, I have spared them three of the crew. Only five have died. Nothing further can be done for them. They will have rough going down there but they must be used to it."

"All the same I should like to visit them and I should like to be able to assure them that in case of danger to the ship they would be set free."

Paul did not answer. He made a movement as though to leave the cabin. Captain Woodes barred his way.

"If you had not taken us," he began bitterly, "those men would have been safely ashore. You must have some feeling of responsibility toward them, haven't you?"

Paul stared at him uncomfortably.

"Must I remind you," he blustered, "that you are a prisoner yourself? There is one way for you to visit your men in the hold, and that is to be thrown there permanently. If you want that I shall be glad to give the order, and now get out of my way."

He brushed past. He was troubled. Men in chains in the hold of a sinking ship—it was not a pretty picture. But the *Oiseau de Proie* was not sinking yet, and the men were too numerous to release. They would try to take the ship. They might succeed. Take the *Oiseau de Proie* from him and everything would be gone: the chance to make a future for Tom, a living for them all, the freedom, the good roughness of the sea contending against him so that he had to keep his wits, so that he was forced for long healing hours to live in the present and forget the past. These were the realities. His life still held pleasant meaning while he was in command of his own barque. Here walking his own deck he was the equal of any man. Here he could introduce his Malisite wife and half-breed baby and watch due respect paid to them as his. Naturally there was danger. One had to be alert, that was all. One had to be alert and not taken in by fine-speaking English captains with mutiny in their minds. What was it San had said of Captain Woodes? "He is only vain." San always knew. The methods of her knowing were beyond him. The impulses and intuitions she obeyed were hers alone, shared with her people. He did not understand them though he had mastered her. She was a squaw, always crouching at a man's feet, crooning comfort to him, not an equal like Anne. Anne, San, San, Anne! Oh, God, to get away from that refrain, to lose, to forget! It was like a pendulum, back and forth, back and forth, in his heart and his brain so that one half of him was always hollow, bleeding, wanting Anne!

He saw her again sitting beside him demurely in the morning light at the foot of the Royal Battery, the powder scattering from her hair, seriously discussing Voltaire and the peasant with him! He kissed her under the spruce. He knelt beside her in the chapel, "a prelude to marriage." "It does no good to deny that we ever loved. We loved, we still love, we are apart."

He ran up the companionway, throwing back his head to meet the blustering wind that leaped at him and whipped and tore at his face. The moon was hidden behind black clouds, the water showed black and angry, hissing and roaring, buffeting the barque so that she staggered, trying to escape.

"Like me!" thought Paul as Quanopin came up to him. They found it necessary to shout at each other above the din.

CHAPTER LXIV.

THE storm which struck the *Oiseau de Proie* was worse than a September squall, it was a gale with thunder and lightning. The wind blew over fifty miles an hour, rain came down in sheets, splashing up from the deck, driving close to the barque so that nothing could be seen a foot ahead.

Paul gave orders to furl the foresail and forestaysail and close reef the fore and main topsails.

"We'll have to brace her up sharp and keep her head reaching," he said, "till we get clear of this."

He stayed to watch the sails furled and caught at Quanopin as he passed. The half-breed looked sullen and afraid.

"What's the matter?" Paul shouted.

"Quanopin doesn't like it."

"Quanopin will have to put up with it!"

"We should not be here in a big wind too close to the rocks, too near to Cape Sable Island."

"We've changed course."

Quanopin grunted close to Paul's ear: "Not soon enough."

Paul bellowed back: "Let me know if the wind increases."

He went below. San was soothing Tom, awake and startled by the noise. His hammock swung with the motion of the barque, keeping him from being seasick, but he didn't like the bangs and bumps, the buffeting of the gale. He looked more reassured when Paul appeared.

"Is it very bad?"

He nodded.

"Blowing up. Where's Captain Woodes?"

"He has gone to his cabin. Can you rest?"

Paul sat down with his eyes on the lantern circling above them.

"Take care of that," he said, "though it is a safety light."

He reached up to steady it on its hook.

The wind was increasing. They could feel it growing more insistent, more savage. The barque staggered, plunged forward, shook, balanced upon the crest of mountainous waves, slid into the trough, plowed through the heavy smashing of a wave breaking on the deck.

The door opened. A sailor, dripping water over everything, swayed in the doorway.

"What is it?"

"The wind's blowing harder. Quanopin asks what shall he do?"

"Tell him main staysail, storm trysail only. Jump to it!"

The man disappeared. Paul took a step toward the door, holding on to the table.

"Don't go out," San pleaded. "It's Quanopin's watch. He can manage as well as you. You will be needed later. Please, please rest."

He sank into a chair, half heeding, his eyes still fixed on the door. San staggered to him and put out her hands. She was flung against him and she clung there.

"Look after Tom," he said, pushing her away.

She looked at him, hurt.

"Tom, always Tom," she muttered. "Tom is a papoose. I am San, your wife."

Paul paid no attention to what she was saying. He was making calculations with his eyes closed. Suddenly San was shaking him, pouring out a torrent of passionate words, jealous, pleading words, ludicrous and pitiful. He stared at her. She plucked and twitched at his hands as she was thrown against him by the violent rocking.

"Love me—me—me!" she said. "I hate her! I hate her! I have cursed her and you."

Paul looked over her head to where Tom swung in his hammock, watching them with startled eyes.

"You are frightening the child." He tried to free himself. "You are nervous. It is the storm."

·[296]·

"There is no storm outside as strong as the storm here!" she struck her heart. He frowned. What a time to choose for a scene! Anne would have been some help to him. She would have laughed and have said something silly and brave. She would have smiled at him. He found himself smiling at the thought of it. San screamed and struck him on the mouth.

Tom began crying.

Paul grasped her hands and twisted them behind her.

"What is the matter with you?" he asked sternly. "How dare you strike your husband? You are frightening the child. Behave yourself!"

San glared at him furiously. Suddenly the rage died out of her. She slumped a little in his grasp and turned her eyes away.

"That's better," he said, releasing her.

He groped his way to the hammock and bent over Tom. The child stopped crying and stared up at him. The swinging light of the safety lantern cast shadows and lines across his face, so that he seemed all Indian, not even a child, but a Malisite chief. Paul watched him for a moment, disconcerted. This was not his little son.

Tom smiled, trying to say "Père."

"Pé, Pé, Pé!"

Paul smiled back.

"Papoose!" he said and set the hammock swinging.

CHAPTER LXV

BY MIDNIGHT the gale had increased to hurricane force. The barque was practically hove to with only a patch of sail showing. Paul and Quanopin with their minds full of shoals to leeward and the strength of the rudder, relieved each other's watches, hanging on to ropes and spars to steady themselves. The helmsman was lashed to the tiller. Paul, when he could draw his breath after being knocked off his feet and swept along the deck and thrown heavily against the after deckhouse, wedged himself beside the helmsman. They peered together through the darkness, seeing nothing, feeling nothing, but whipping spray, the surge and slapping of water on the decks, the merciless force of the wind shrieking by.

The barque, still making some headway, was tossed about like a twig in the rapids. The most they could do if the rudder did let go was to try to keep her from being driven among the shoals and reefs to leeward.

The waves seemed to run as high as the masts, the barque was submerged for minutes at a time. Sometimes it seemed as though she would never come up, but she always lifted, dripping and hissing and shaking from the trough.

Paul lost all count of time. He was numb to the bone. It was the worst storm that he had ever experienced on land or sea. He thought of the wounded men in the hold battered about and shaken like rats in a terrier's jaw. He thought of Captain Woodes cowering in his cabin. Paul had bolted the door on him. He thought of his father and storms they had encountered on *La Belle*

Louise. He tried to remember what his father had done, going over the steps in his mind. He tried to imagine what his father would do if he were there, in command of the *Oiseau de Proie*. Nothing. There was nothing more to do. The barque must do it for herself and for them, she must fight and hold together and survive. She was game enough, a beautiful, courageous ship, great-hearted, seaworthy in every straining inch. His uncle had taken good care of her, she was the pride of his life. Paul smiled.

"Seabird, you are more than that now, Bird of Prey. Live up to your new name. An eagle would survive this storm."

As if in answer the *Oiseau de Proie* was shaken by a great tremor. She heeled over to port and remained there, listing, while wave after wave washed over her windward side.

"Throw over the port guns!" Paul cried, shouting through the dark. He screamed again: "The port guns! Lighten her! Cut the gun tackles and let them go overboard."

Blurred forms responded, washed beneath the breaking waves but holding on, creeping forward, dragging, heaving, pushing the guns overboard: "One, two, three, four . . ."

The fifth gun stuck and rolled back upon her crew. It broke loose and smashed bulwarks and stanchions until the crew subdued it and finally got it overboard. Slowly the *Oiseau de Proie* righted herself, shook herself clear of water and staggered on to face the raging seas, smothering her with their weight, pushing, pulling, tearing at her. She rolled and righted herself and rolled again.

Toward dawn she was again listing badly. Several seams were sprung. The prisoners of war, banging on the hatches, shouted that the water was pouring into the hold. Paul ordered buckets passed to them by men loaded with pistols and muskets, ready to stand off a rush. The prisoners were to stay where they were and bail or drown.

Paul had no time to spare for them as the growing light revealed new and terrible dangers. The gale had driven the *Oiseau de Proie* in among a fleet, and the fleet itself onto the shoals off Cape Sable Island. All about them French transports and men-of-war were scattering before the storm. The nearest to them was the *Amazone*, and as Paul watched, he saw a transport, out of control, dash against her and go down with all on board. It was all over between two horrified glances. The *Amazone*, rudderless, plunged helplessly toward them.

Half-blinded by wind and spray, Paul watched her tower over them.

"Hard up! Hard up!" he screamed.

The helmsman flung his weight against the tiller. The *Oiseau de Proie*, lifted on a wave, did not respond. She sank into the trough, rose on the crest of another wave. . . .

"We'll be rammed!" Paul shouted.

The crew on board the *Amazone* yelled. The noise drowned Paul's words. It was too late, anyway. There was nothing they could do. The high prow cracked down upon the *Oiseau de Proie* amidships, crushing and grinding her. The shock was terrific. The *Oiseau de Proie* shuddered, a wave swept over her decks, another followed. She slid sideways. The *Amazone*, her headway checked, eased away, as the next sea lifted her, exposing a gaping hole in the side of the barque. Water began to pour in. The *Amazone* crashed forward a second time. All was confusion, men shouting, screaming, running, choking, slipping beneath the waves that mounted higher, higher. Paul felt himself seized from behind. He turned his head. San was holding him.

"Paul! Paul!"

Her face close to his was in agony of terror, not for herself but for him. She held him tight, strained against her as though she would protect him from the fiends of hell. A wave swept them from their footing. Paul went down. He felt feet trampling over him as men rushed frantically forward. He hit his head against a stanchion. When he could get his breath, sputtering for air, he saw San lifted into a wave above him. She hung for a moment motionless, then she was in the sea.

Paul shouted. He was lying on his back by the gunwale while another wave swept over him and more men rushed through it, more and more. They wore boots, for one came down on his face. It was the English prisoners. Paul found time to wonder dully who had set them free and to be glad. Then he remembered Tom.

Tom was in his cabin and San was in the sea. San was in the sea, San was in the sea! Tom was in his cabin and San was in the sea. The words went through his head like a silly song. He found his lips pursed to whistle it. No whistle came. Instead a roaring, deafening crash and a long red streak that filled his brain went round and round and round, until he became the streak of red, with black circles and dots in it and something heavy on his chest. The curtain of the world came down upon him. He was pitched into the sea.

CHAPTER LXVI

PAUL opened his eyes. He was lying on a deck, rolling and heaving beneath him. Faces stooped over, peering at him curiously. Rough hands were pulling and tugging at his clothes. He moaned and tried to sit up. Water streamed from him, icy water. He was cold.

"That's better!" a voice said gruffly. "Are you hurt?"

Paul tried his arms and his legs. They were stiff and numb, but they moved and no new pain shot through him.

"No," he gasped, "just wet and cold. What happened?"

"Your ship must have foundered in the storm."

"What a storm!" a little man with a red woolen scarf round his throat said grinning.

Voices took it up all about him.

"What a storm!"

"That was a storm!"

Paul shook his head, bewildered.

"Were you on a transport or a man-of-war?"

"What was the name of your ship?"

His ship! Paul tried to struggle to his feet, threshing his arms wildly. His ship! The *Oiseau de Proie!* He remembered everything, heard the crack as the towering stern of the *Amazone* came down on the deck, and saw the wave sweep up, up, up with San in its claws.

"My wife!" he cried. "My wife, my son, my barque!"

The sailors round him laughed and touched their foreheads.

"It's lucky for you we're shorthanded," one of them said,

·[302]·

tapping him on the shoulder, "or we'd have left you where we found you. You had a rendezvous with Neptune that time all right."

"Yes. You floated by in a tangle like the rest of them. We fished fifteen in an hour. But we need a good hundred to make up for the sick and the dead. How many did you bury on the way out?"

Paul swayed to his feet and staggered to the rail. The gale had blown itself out. The storm was subsiding. A gray even light spread over angry waters. Casks, hencoops, buckets, chests, oars, tackle, broken boats, bobbed and floated aimlessly at the will of the tide.

"We were a fleet last night, and look! Only five sail!" a man behind him said.

"What vessel's this?" Paul asked him. "I must see the Captain."

The men laughed again. They were a wild-looking lot, brawny, bearded, tall, with something reckless and despairing in their expressions. It was in the way they stood with one eye out for a kick or a blow and the other roving, ready to steal a dead man's shirt. Paul recognized the breed—pressed men in the service of the navy. He asked again:

"What vessel's this?"

A lanky fellow answered him, drawling the words through his nose while the others laughed again, as though it were a rich and rare joke.

"This is the flagship *Northumberland*, under his grace the Duc d'Anville."

"*Northumberland?* That's an English man-of-war."

"A prize," the same man drawled, "since 1744. Here's a fellow who's been sailing with us since the twentieth of June and doesn't know the name of the flagship nor who commands the fleet!"

Laughter broke out again.

"Oh, well," a short, fat man said kindly, poking Paul, "he fell on his head. Perhaps he's seasick. Perhaps he's one of the God-damned soldiers. That's it. He's a landlubber. Eh?"

Pipes twittered behind them. The men disappeared. In the time it took Paul to turn his head they were scattered, every which way, some in the rigging, some below deck, some vigorously attending to launching the longboat. Paul was alone, looking at the sea, with confused, conflicting thoughts.

His wife, his son and the *Oiseau de Proie*. Lost. Taken by the sea that never gives back what it takes, never. He saw San's passionate brown face look up at him from a dark patch of water. The sun moved over it and the vision changed. He saw Tom. Then he cried out and started, surprised at the sound of his own voice. An officer going by, stopped and shouted at him:

"Here, you! What sort of discipline's this? Look alive, there! Do you want to be flogged? Off the deck! The Admiral's on his way."

"Sir," Paul stammered, "I am not a member of the regular crew. I'm a survivor from a barque that foundered in the storm. I was picked up . . ."

"All the better. We're shorthanded. Go forward and take any place assigned to you." Then as Paul still hesitated, "You are a sailor, I suppose?" He looked doubtfully at Paul's coat. "Or are you a member of the transport?"

"I'm a sailor, sir," Paul answered, his mind made up. It would do no good to say that he was master of his own barque. He would have to give the name of it. The *Oiseau de Proie* was well known. A pirate got short shrift from either side, English or French. They would torture him to find out where he had hidden his "treasure" and put him in chains. Life, intolerable enough on a French man-of-war at any time, would be sheer hell. That would not help San or Tom or anyone.

"What was the name of your barque?"

Paul took a deep breath.

"No, don't tell me," the officer said hastily. "If it isn't lost by any chance you might have to go back. We're shorthanded here. This cursed plague. Just go forward and pitch in. Step lively there, unless you want to be warmed by a rope's end round your legs. Pst, here's the Admiral! Get out of the way, you scum!"

Paul backed hastily toward the nearest companionway and flattened himself against the hatch coaming. A gorgeous figure was climbing out of it. The Duc d'Anville was tall, lean, handsome, all gold braid and gold lace, and white skin gloves. He set his feet upon the deck, looked about him, sniffing the air deliberately, wrinkling his nostrils and closing his eyes, but for all his unhurried grace, Paul caught a glimpse of anxiety deliberately concealed.

The officer standing at attention, glared at Paul. He plunged down the companionway, his head still reeling and his knees weak. Worst of all, there was a settled icy chill of loneliness and of defeat. He could not, he would not, think of Tom, swinging in his hammock in the cabin of the *Oiseau de Proie* below the waves. He choked and staggered against the wall. Two of the crew ran by, heads down, panting heavily. They carried something with them in a sack. A stench rose into Paul's face as they passed, the stench of rotting carrion. The sack slipped a little as they hoisted it to the companionway. A bare foot and part of a leg showed, purple, black, swollen, disgusting, horrible. Paul stared.

("On account of the sickness . . . we are shorthanded . . . how many did you bury on the way out?")

That was plague.

"Hey," a third man shouted to him, "you there, come here!"

CHAPTER LXVII

BY THREE o'clock the lookout counted thirty-one sails from the *Northumberland*. Paul learned the names and peculiarities of some of them from the men of his watch. The *Argonaut* was rolling helplessly, without masts or rudder, the *Trident*, with the Vice-Admiral on board, was in difficulties and flying the "distress," the *Caribou* had thrown her starboard guns overboard, but was still badly listing, the *Terrible*, the *Monarque* and the *Glorioso*, men-of-war carrying seventy-four guns each, were badly battered and had lost rigging, longboats and tackle.

The others were too far away to see what was wrong with them, and presently a thick fog came up, curling silently about the *Northumberland*, cutting her off from everything about her. Guns were fired in the distance, the guns of the *Northumberland* replied. Paul was posted with four other men ringing hand bells and beating drums. He stood staring into the white clammy mist, rolling thickly round him. Rub-a-dub, ting-a-ling, rub-dub-dub, he beat his drum and shook his bell. Faces came to him out of the mist, men dying at the Island Battery, people laughing in the streets of Louisbourg before the siege, Marie with her arms full of spruce boughs, getting married, Parson Moody hacking at the altar, Captain Woodes locked in his cabin, they came in the oddest sequence, Randy, San, Tom springing and kicking against his chest. His throat ached and his hands faltered. Last of all came Anne. She floated before him, smiling tenderly, with understanding and compassion in her eyes and something more—faith in him.

Yes, she seemed to have faith in him. He tried desperately to keep her face before him. It faded, but a message seemed to stay.

"You are free now. There is no bar between us. You are free. Come home to France, to me."

Free! The first small ray of hope and comfort came to him then out of the curling mist, and with it the will to survive.

San was dead. He had not treated her very well. The hatred in his heart that he had felt for her at times had been too strong for him. Poor San. He would think kindly of her now, brave, devoted, passionate San. She was dead and he was free. He would go to France, he would seek out Anne, he would find a living, they would be married. His thoughts stopped with a sudden chill. Anne might be married to someone else. But there was the letter: "I believe that you will always love me, and I know that I shall always love you." Brave words. Oh, Anne, let them be true!

For the moment he was on a French man-of-war headed to Chebucto, with orders that the crew could only guess at, but they involved fighting the English and it would certainly be months, perhaps years before they would see France again. He did not dare to let himself think of the worst hazard of all—the creeping, devouring scourge that was at work in the fleet. Men were dying every day. Every day corpses were being fed to the sea. Every day the plague increased and with it scurvy. In some of the vessels the crews were starving. Survivors picked up like himself, hammering beside him at bells and drums, were glad to have been washed overboard and to escape from their transports and men-of-war. The long voyage had exhausted provisions. The food on the *Northumberland*, rotten and stinking as it was, seemed good to these men. Paul sighed. It was a hard transition, from Captain with money, provisions, wine, a comfortable cabin, a crew to command, a prize taken—idly he wondered what had happened to the brig—to simple hand before the mast with a rope's end licking the breath out of him and nothing to his name but the water-soaked rags he stood up in. He shifted his feet in the sodden, shrunken boots and adjusted his belt. There were twenty gold pieces sewed into the lining. Nobody had stolen them while he was unconscious. They would be something to fall back upon when he reached France.

·[307]·

The *Northumberland*, nosing her way through the fog, pushed forward steadily. She was a much heavier vessel than the *Oiseau de Proie*. She was the largest ship Paul had ever been aboard. Her stern came up in the heavy broad fashion of the French navy, she had a naked figurehead at her prow, part of which could be seen from the deck. Its head was as large as a man's. She had three tiers of guns, the lowest with hinged ports to protect them from the seas in heavy weather. From what he had seen of her so far she compared well with the *Oiseau de Proie* in worthiness, but she was overcrowded in spite of the shortage of hands the officers complained about. The Admiral's quarters were large and well lighted, but the crew's quarters were cramped, dark and dirty. Paul would not have lodged his savages in such airless holes. His corner seemed the worst of all. He was a newcomer; late come, late served. He was not allowed to draw lots with the others for the latest dead man's berth and equipment. He was not altogether sorry, remembering the glimpse he had caught of the corpse before it disappeared. He took over the space of the man who won. It was on the lowest tier, dark, crowded and smelly. He did not care, he had set himself one task—to survive. When they reached Chebucto he might escape and get to France some other way.

He slept heavily that night in the bowels of the ship, among tossing, groaning men, the creaking and shaking of timbers, the clanking of chains and the multitudinous noises of a strange craft at sea. He was roused roughly, with the middle watch. The night had cleared. There was a full moon, shining on the water. The swell had subsided. Paul, glancing aloft, estimated that the wind must be blowing about fifteen miles an hour, a moderate breeze, just enough for the ship to carry royals full and by. That was how he would have set the canvas on the *Oiseau de Proie*.

The *Northumberland* sailed on, apparently alone. No other sails were near her. When morning dawned she had lost the rest of the fleet, except for one far-off transport and a sail, rapidly disappearing. Chebucto could be seen ahead, lonely and savage, set in a ring of forested hills. Paul's spirits rose when he saw how near they were to it.

CHAPTER LXVIII

THE man next Paul nudged him. It was an imperceptible movement. Paul knew what it meant. The crew of the *Northumberland* was drawn up on deck. They stood rigidly at attention, in long ranks. In front of them, the Duc d'Anville was interrogating a prisoner, taken from a small English ketch that morning. The man had agreed to pilot the *Northumberland* into Chebucto Harbor, in exchange for his liberty and a hundred louis d'or. Now he was turning sullen, full of last minute scruples. His fellow prisoners he said had called him traitor. He was refusing to keep to his part of the bargain. The Duc d'Anville, handsome and undecided, seemed perplexed at the turn the affair was taking. He sat behind a table, lashed to the deck, clasping and twisting his ringed hands together. He did not look at the prisoner. His eyes traveled along the lines of waiting men, stolid in the sunshine, then to the dark hills of the harbor, then to the deck.

Suddenly the Captain of the *Northumberland* stepped forward, and this was when the man beside Paul nudged him. Captain du Perrier was known and feared throughout the fleet. The man beside Paul pushed at him again. Paul watched out of the corner of his eye.

"Listen, you!" Captain du Perrier barked in execrable English, mingled with French, "either you keep your word to pilot us into the harbor there, or you go overboard with a pair of cannon ball made fast to your feet. Which is it?"

The man blinked up at him stupidly. The Captain wheeled to the men nearest him.

·[309]·

"Fetch up a pair of cannon ball."

Two men ran to the storeroom. There was no sound till they came back. The Captain, striding up and down, made an impatient gesture. They knelt obediently to fasten the shot in place.

The Englishman, a fisherman from the settlement, said nothing while his legs were being tied.

"Hoist him up!"

He was lifted to the gunwale and held there, looking at the water.

"Overboard with him!"

"Wait!"

It came out in a high-pitched yell.

"I'll pilot you!"

"Lower him. Take him to the bridge, but leave his legs fastened."

"If you should change your mind again, or anything should happen to this ship, you will be the first to drown," he added, thrusting his red face close to the Englishman's. "Crew take your stations. Monsieur le Duc," he bent over and murmured something, perhaps an apology for his show of authority, to Anville, who was still sitting staring ahead of him.

"Oh, ah, yes, Captain," Paul heard him say as he ran past on his way to the main topsail brace, the station assigned to him.

The *Northumberland* got under way. Before night fell she had anchored in the harbor. Whispers went about among the crew. Paul, sitting on an upturned bucket with the rest of the watch off duty, heard that another fleet had been expected here, Monsieur de Conflans with his vessels from the West Indies.

"The Admiral's in a pretty state of despondency over it," a steward reported. "He's in his cabin, holding his head in his hands."

"If you ask me, something's gone pretty far wrong."

"What more could go wrong? Plague, starvation, storm. This voyage's been the worst I ever knew."

"Pipe down, the mate's out there, listening."

"I'd like to pour some boiling oil down that swab's big ears."

"What are we waiting about for? Don't any of us go ashore? How about reprovisioning?"

"Those hills are full of savages, that's what it is."

"What did he want to bring us here for anyhow? What say we desert. . . ."

"None of that. That's serious trouble."

"Beats me what the King sees in his New France. Nothing but a lot of desolate woods and a rocky coast."

"Pretty, though."

"Pretty! Give me Le Havre on a day when the fleet's in!"

"Or La Rochelle!"

"Or the Sailor's Den in Toulon. Ah, good wine, a nice piece of a skirt . . ."

"With you there, Shorty!"

At two in the morning, in the middle of Paul's watch, there was a sudden commotion and a sound of bare feet running over the deck, a shout and a lantern bobbing. Voices broke out and were hushed. Doors slammed. The noise came from the Admiral's cabin. Monsieur le Duc d'Anville had died of apoplexy, Captain du Perrier announced to the crew drawn up on deck to hear the news in the morning.

"Or poison!" it was whispered among the men.

The *Northumberland* swung at anchor, waiting, waiting, no one knew for what.

CHAPTER LXIX

A T SIX O'CLOCK on the same afternoon, the Vice-Admiral's *Trident* limped into port with some of the scattered fleet behind her.

"Monsieur d'Estournel will have to take over," Shorty whispered to Paul. "I've sailed with him. He's a hellion."

Paul was among the crew chosen to man the longboat taking Captain du Perrier to the Vice-Admiral to acquaint him with the news. When they returned they were full of gossip.

"The *Trident's* leaking like a sieve."

"Half the crew dead of the plague."

"And more dying."

"No food."

"I heard them say they'd bury the Duc on an island in the harbor, probably tomorrow."

"When are we going ashore?"

That was what Paul wanted to know, and how soon he could get to France, but for the next twenty-four hours there was no change in the routine on the *Northumberland* except that the food grew worse and five men died.

On the next day, which was the twenty-eighth of September, the Duc d'Anville was hastily and unceremoniously buried on a small island, while the crews of all the ships in the harbor, whispered and stirred and grotesque rumors went around. The officers met in council afterward. Paul found himself once more in the longboat taking Captain du Perrier to the new Admiral. The longboat stayed this time, bobbing alongside the *Trident*, with the crew in it.

"It's the hell of a long council," Shorty growled.

The midshipman in command glared at him.

"Perhaps they're discussing food."

"They'd better be!"

"Another word out of any of you," the midshipman barked, "and you'll all see irons."

Shorty grinned. He knew, and the midshipman knew, that with the *Northumberland* shorthanded nobody would be put in irons.

"Flogging then," the midshipman amended.

That was more likely. Silence reigned in the longboat. Then, when Paul was almost falling asleep, an extraordinary commotion on the *Trident* made him prick up his ears.

There was a great deal of shouting and running about. Two Jesuit fathers paced hurriedly in the direction of the Admiral's cabin. Several men carrying a battering ram went by. Sounds of cracking and heaving and the breaking of a door followed. Presently Captain du Perrier came back, evidently agitated and distressed. He took his place in the longboat and was rowed to the *Northumberland* without saying a word. The men exchanged uneasy glances.

Presently the news leaked out from ship to ship gathering color as it ran. Monsieur d'Estournel had killed himself with his own sword. The debate at the council had provoked him, he was desperate and angry. Apparently he had wanted to return to France.

"Who wouldn't?"

But the council decided against him. His door was fastened by two bolts put on the evening before by his order.

"The boatswain told me so himself!"

"That looks as though he'd been thinking of it for some time."

"It can't have been the council, then."

"Anyhow, there he was, lying in a pool of his own blood."

"Whose blood would it be but his?"

"Refusing to let the sword be taken out. The surgeon overpowered him. Then he wouldn't let the wound be dressed."

"He wanted to die, all right."

"He said: 'Gentlemen, I beg pardon of God and the King for

·[313]·

what I have done and I protest to the King that my only object was to prevent my enemies from saying that I had not executed his orders.*' "

"He named Monsieur de la Jonquière to take his place."

"He didn't have to name him. Monsieur de la Jonquière would have commanded anyway. He comes next in rank."

"Why did he do it, do you suppose?"

"Perhaps he'd started the plague. The *Trident's* full of it."

"No, he didn't want to go on and fight."

"Who does? It's madness with half the fleet and most of the soldiers ill, and all of us half-starved."

"I don't envy Monsieur de la Jonquière."

"I don't envy us."

"How about deserting now?"

"In those hills?"

"Listen, I say Jonquière's a good man."

"Bah!"

"I tell you he has sense. He'll bring us through somehow."

"Imbécile!"

Paul working beside them wondered: "Two suicides in three days! Surely now they'll make for France."

CHAPTER LXX

THE day after the Marquis de la Jonquière took up his quarters on the *Northumberland*, a boat put out from Chebucto, manned by savages. A black figure stood in the stern. As it drew nearer, Paul, staring fascinated, saw the Abbé le Loutre hailing the *Northumberland*.

"I have packets for the Duc d'Anville."

A sailor cupped his hands and bellowed down to him:

"The Admiral's dead! We have buried him!"

The mate shouldered him aside.

"Come aboard!"

The abbé scrambled up the rope ladder flung to him, his robe fluttering behind him. Paul leaned forward eagerly.

"Who commands the expedition now?" the abbé asked, reaching the deck.

"The Marquis de la Jonquière."

"Take me to him please."

The mate hesitated. Paul stepped forward. He was about to speak to the abbé, but le Loutre turned his back.

"I have important dispatches here."

"Very well."

The mate led the way to the Admiral's cabin and rapped on the door.

"Come in!"

The Marquis was pacing up and down the cabin restlessly. He turned as the abbé entered.

·[315]·

"Monsieur le Marquis," le Loutre said, blessing him, "may I present to you these packets destined to the Duc d'Anville?"

The Marquis took them and broke the seals. He read, frowned, and laid them by.

"Monsieur l'abbé," he said, "you could not have come at a better time. We are desperate men. How many cattle can we count on from your Acadians? This paper says that you have corn and other supplies."

"The district is prepared to furnish you with seven or eight hundred cattle and as many other provisions as you need, against good metal money."

"Very well. I will take it all and as much more as may be necessary. I intend to camp the men ashore if it is safe. Perhaps if they get out of the ships they will shake off the plague. What a voyage, Father! Two thousand four hundred men dead since we left France, and more dying every day. The soldiers are reduced to a fraction of their strength."

"Terrible."

"How are the savages hereabouts?"

"Friendly, but a few presents would not come amiss. They can see the fleet from where they hide in the woods."

"Ah. Well, there are all the dead men's clothes. I will give orders that they are to be handed over to the Indians. That ought to please them."

"Munificent."

"Have you messengers you can send for me to the Commander of the troops at Mines?"

"Yes, Marquis."

"Good. We'll order them to take up positions in front of Port Royal, and to wait for us. You yourself, Abbé, could take your Indians and join in the attack."

"Before you come?"

"No. Lie in wait but don't attack until we are there to support you. A bowl of wine?"

The abbé accepted. The Marquis struck a bell. Paul answered it. He saw the abbé start, stare at him, open his mouth and close it again. When he brought the wine he managed to sign to him that they would meet outside.

Presently the abbé took his leave and walked to the companion-way. Paul was waiting there.

"Abbé!"

"Paul de Morpain! What are you doing here?"

"The *Oiseau de Proie* has gone with all on board. Tell my uncle, if you can get the news to him. I had another prize, too, an English brig, the *Hastings*. Did it come into la Hève?"

A sailor brushing by stared curiously. Paul sank on his knees as though he were making his confession. The abbé bent over him with his fingers raised. From time to time he made the sign of the cross, while Paul went on:

"We were driven to Cape Sable Island in the storm, among the French fleet. A man-of-war rammed and sank us. There were English prisoners on board. Your share of the ransom would have been a good one."

"I know. The *Hastings* did reach la Hève. The crew thought you had gone down, with the *Oiseau de Proie*. They have gone back to the woods. I sold the brig, never thinking I should see you again."

"I never thought so either."

"Were all the rest lost?"

"All lost." He paused a moment, then he added: "my wife and child too. Say a Requiem for them, Father."

The abbé touched his shoulder.

"I will."

Paul rose from his knees.

"I was picked up," he said, "and taken for a sailor from one of the men-of-war that sank that night."

"The only thing you could do."

"And now I want to get to France."

"I see. If I can do anything for you I will. Oh . . ." he put his hand into his soutane and pulled out a wallet. "Some letters reached me yesterday from Quebec. There is one for you."

Paul began to tremble. He snatched the paper that the abbé held out to him and broke the seals.

"I hope it is good news," the abbé said. He looked at Paul searchingly, frowned, hesitated a moment, then turned back to him.

"Your wife and child lost at sea?"

Paul looked up.

"Yes."

"You must not bear me any grudge, my son."

Paul stared.

"The Reverend Father of the Recollets Frères de Charité in Louisbourg is a close friend of mine. He told me what happened there a year ago. San was one of my children, my converts, I could not do otherwise than marry you."

Paul smiled.

"I know."

"Peace be to her soul. I wish you happiness."

He turned and swept forward this time without looking back. Paul reread the letter with a blur before his eyes. Then he thrust it into his sleeve. Anne had come near to him again for a breathless second.

CHAPTER LXXI

THE expedition re-embarked on a brisk October morning. Paul was glad to step on board the *Northumberland* again. For six weeks he had camped on the edge of the forest, with the rest of the crew, gorging themselves on fresh meat and corn, brought by the Acadians, and working at the re-equipment of the fleet. The sick were cared for in huts made of old sails. The plague continued. It was spreading. The Micmacs had it now. They were dying in heaps. Three-quarters of the tribe near Cape Sable Island were wiped out. The rest hid from the French, in spite of the tempting gifts of clothes and necklaces. The white men brought ill luck.

The Marquis de la Jonquière had decided to proceed against Port Royal, as he insisted on calling the fort which the English had renamed Annapolis, while he still had soldiers left with which to fight. There were only a thousand in condition. It was no use waiting for more to sicken and die. He gave orders for the *Parfait* and five smaller vessels to be burned and for hospital ships to be given over to the sick. All day long the troops and the sailors re-embarked, cheering and beating drums. It was a gay and colorful sight against the dark fringe of green hills. To Paul it meant a step nearer France and Anne.

He was inured now to the hardships of his life before the mast. He held his own with the crew and had won their respect. He gave no trouble to the officers and did not shirk his share of the fatigue and danger. He was unafraid even when four or five corpses were dropped into the sea each day from the *Northum-*

berland. All around him, on the other men-of-war, the same grim things were happening. Every evening saw a little group of men sliding canvas sacks into the sea. Twice the man sitting next him in the wardroom keeled over in a faint and was hauled away to the surgeon's quarters and later thrown overboard. Paul went on sticking grimly to his work which was doubled as the crew diminished. Rations grew scarce again even before they reached Annapolis and found the *Chester* and the *Shirley* there, waiting to defend the fort against them.

On the night of the twenty-seventh of October, the Marquis held a council on board the *Northumberland*. He decided not to attack the fort nor to engage the two English vessels, but to return to France with what was left of the expedition. It was defeat but the crews cheered wildly when they heard the news and Paul celebrated the evening by leading a rat hunt in the hold. That night the ration of three ounces of biscuit and three of salt meat was supplemented by fresh-roasted rat and stewed tails.

The first mate looked on and smiled. Activities like these would keep the crew from any thought of mutiny. Exercise was good for the men. Sweating prevented the plague. He reported the hunt to the Admiral. That night as the *Northumberland* plowed through the familiar waters of the Bay of Fundy, beneath the full October moon—hunter's moon—Paul was summoned from the foretop to report to the Admiral's cabin.

He found the Marquis de la Jonquière seated at his table with Captain du Perrier and the first mate.

"How long have you been with us?"

"I was picked up in the storm, Monsieur le Marquis. I have been with you nearly two months."

"What vessel did you sail on before you were picked up?"

Paul embarked on a half-lie.

"I commanded a small barque, Monsieur le Marquis."

"A barque? Which barque? The three barques of the expedition are still with us and their captains too."

The Marquis frowned. The Captain stared at Paul.

"It was not one of the barques in the expedition but a fishing barque from New France. I was lost in the fog and found myself among the fleet. When the barque foundered on the shoals off

Cape Sable Island—(Paul decided not to say anything about being rammed)—I was picked up and found myself here. The *Northumberland* was shorthanded, the late Admiral had many affairs on his mind, I was told to take the place of one of the crew who had died of plague."

The three officers exchanged glances.

"I had no other means of livelihood left me. I went about my work with gratitude. I hope it has been satisfactory to Monsieur le Marquis, the Captain and the other officers."

Paul paused. The Marquis leaned forward.

"You commanded this barque, you say. You are very young, Monsieur . . . ?"

"Paul de Morpain."

"Morpain?" Captain du Perrier spoke sharply. "That is the name of the privateer, is it not?"

"My uncle, Pierre de Morpain is a privateer. He and his vessel were taken last year after they had been lured into Louisbourg. The English have kept the French flag flying there in order to trap unwary prizes which had not heard the news of the town's capture. I sailed with my uncle when I was younger, but in the end I commanded my own barque, a modest fishing vessel, the . . . the *Victoire*."

"What was the name of your uncle's ship?"

"The *Oiseau de Mer*."

Captain du Perrier nodded as though this tallied with a score kept in his mind.

"Yes. Well, Monsieur de Morpain, if you had made yourself and your condition known to us we would have treated you with more courtesy."

Paul bowed.

"I have no complaints. When a man is rescued from the sea . . ." he smiled.

"Your work is good. Your influence with the men is good. Even before we knew your story we had decided to try you in a position of responsibility. The third mate is ill. He will be unable to perform his duties. You will take his place."

Paul bowed again.

"The plague promotes us all," the Marquis added, smiling

grimly. "When we reach France I shall have the appointment confirmed and your salary paid to you. It is a good thing that you have had experience in commanding men."

"They were only sa . . ." Paul stopped himself in time. "Sailors," he amended, and as that didn't make sense, added hastily, "sailors accustomed to fishing boats, not to men-of-war."

Fortunately the three officers did not notice his confusion. They had forgotten him and his affairs and were studying the chart on the table in front of the Admiral. Paul stood waiting for a moment, then he cleared his throat and stammered:

"I am very grateful, Monsieur le Marquis, I shall do my best."

"Good, good. Keep clear of the plague."

They waved him away. He bowed and left the cabin. Once outside he rubbed his hands together and began to whistle. Third mate! Before the trip was over he might be more than that. No more rat-hunting, no more floggings for him. He could wear a cocked hat, if he could get one, and a silk scarf at his throat. Best of all, if he did well he could hope for the Marquis de la Jonquière's protection when he reached France.

CHAPTER LXXII

THE *Northumberland*, plowing through December seas ran
into wretched luck. Storm after storm swept her from her
course. She was separated from the rest of the fleet. Food
gave out, water stank, the crew, starved and sullen, staggered
about their work, muttering threats of mutiny. Pestilence increased until there was a real danger that the ship would be left
helpless for want of men to work her.

Paul and the other officers were on their feet all day and all
night, pistols primed, watchful and heartsick.

At last, on the seventh of December, after slipping past an
English squadron, they sighted Port Louis in Brittany. Paul never
forgot that day. It dawned gray and lowering, with a rising mist.
The unlucky fleet's disasters were not ended with the sight of
France. As the *Northumberland* nosed her way past the entrance
to the harbor, a muffled shouting and a commotion sounded
through the mist. Flares went up in front of them. The lookout
hailed:

"The *Borée* in distress!"

The *Northumberland* wore round to go to the *Borée's* assist-
ance, but she had grounded badly in the fog and was sinking
rapidly. Boats put out from shore, the *Northumberland* lowered
her longboat and sent it to the rescue. The *Borée* was a hospital
ship. A hundred and sixty of her helpless sick were drowned before the rescuers could get within reach of her. She turned turtle
and sank. It was all over in a few minutes. The *Northumberland*

stood off and on for awhile and then went on. There was nothing she could do.

She dropped anchor in the harbor and the men, weary and wild-eyed, gathered on deck in silent, furtive groups, eyeing the officers. A longboat put off from the frigate *La Palme* anchored to the right of them.

"Captain Destrahoudal to pay his respects to the Admiral."

Paul received him with one eye on the mutinous crew and his hand on his pistol. The crew pressed forward, leaning over to look at the longboat and shout:

"On shore! On shore! Take us on shore or get out of the way and we'll take ourselves!"

Captain Destrahoudal pretended not to notice this breach of discipline, even when he was rudely pushed aside by the surging men.

Paul shouted:

"You scum! You dogs! Get back! None of you'll see shore. I'll have you put in irons! Get back!"

He edged Captain Destrahoudal through and took him to the Admiral's cabin. The first mate came out, in answer to Paul's whispered warning, to take over the mutinous crew.

"We can't control them much longer," Paul told him. "They will break up the ship."

Captain Destrahoudal told a terrible story. The frigate *La Palme* carried five English prisoners. The crew, crazed with famine, demanded that the ship's butcher should bind one of the men, take him to the hold and cut him up and distribute his flesh to the men in portions of three ounces each. After that was gone, they would take another prisoner, and so on, until the five were gone. The Captain could do nothing with them.

"I walked the deck all night, Admiral, all night. The only thing that I could do was to get them to put off the murder till the morning watch."

"What good did that do?" the Admiral asked, leaning forward, fascinated.

"I didn't know. I prayed all night. The terrible thing, Marquis, was that I was hungry too, so hungry that I could not help speculating . . ."

"Cannibalism! In the fleet!"

"Yes. And it would have seemed quite natural. Distasteful, but necessary."

"Good God!"

"It did not come to that. Instead, something in the nature of a miracle—my chaplain insists it was a miracle—occurred."

"Ah." The Marquis leaned back and his face assumed its normal expression.

"As the morning watch took over, the lookout saw a sail. It was a Portuguese barque, a neutral. She let us get within hailing distance. The Portuguese Captain lowered a boat and came alongside, with five sheep! Five, mark you. I laughed at that. The crew could not wait till they were cooked, they ate them raw, instead of the Englishmen. Providential."

Paul let out his breath.

"My own crew is starving," the Marquis said. "I cannot let them go ashore till they are fed. Not a man would come back."

He laughed.

"Monsieur de Morpain, tell Captain Destrahoudal's story to the men out there, and tell them that they at least have not been eating Englishmen."

Paul went out, but he was spared the horrid recital. The first casks of food had arrived and the men were tearing at them frantically. He watched, his mouth watering.

"Don't eat too much," he warned. "You have been starved. It's dangerous."

Captain Destrahoudal and the Admiral came on deck. They turned their backs on the gluttonous scene in front of them.

"Monsieur de Morpain, I am going ashore in Captain Destrahoudal's longboat. You will attend me."

Paul saluted and took his place. The longboat pulled away from the *Northumberland*. He peered through the mist, toward the harbor. For the first time in his life he would set foot in France. Excitement gripped him. The long trip was over and now he must find Anne.

PART SEVEN
PARIS 1746

CHAPTER LXXIII

O N CHRISTMAS EVE, 1746, a group of riders crossed
the Place de la Concorde. They skirted round the statue
of an equestrian in the center of the square, making
toward the Palais Royale. Paul drew rein for a moment behind
the others. He was weary and cold, sore and very stiff from riding hard day after day over the bad roads between Brittany and
Paris, on an animal that made him remember Frogsmarch with
affection. But he had never seen anything so magnificent as the
long double stone colonnade ahead of him, the crowds walking
and riding, the coaches drawn up at the entrance to the Tuileries,
the gaily colored stalls where vendors were selling favors and
flowers.

It was cold. The tired horse moved restlessly, stable-haunted,
its breath snorting out impatiently in a double stream of misty
gray. Paul's own breath hung round his face in a white cloud. It
was late afternoon. The sun was rapidly setting. He must spur
after the others or lose his way, but this was the first moment
since he landed in France that he really knew where he was—in
Paris, the center of the universe. Behind those gates, at the end of
those gardens, deserted in the winter afternoon, Louis XV, his
Polish Queen, his mistresses and his brilliant court, were preparing to keep Christmas.

Somewhere in this maze of houses, straggling up and down the
two banks of the Seine, the wits, the philosophers, the men of
letters, the soldiers, the galants and the adventurers, were getting
ready for supper. None of them knew that Paul de Morpain had

arrived in Paris. None of them would care. But he would conquer this new world of city and court, and learn to navigate its waters full of treacherous shoals, as he had learned to navigate the Bay of Fundy.

He shook his reins and spurred his restless mount forward, cantering after the disappearing group. They were talking and laughing among themselves, young naval and military officers, home for a spree. Paul had grown to like them on the way to Paris. They had treated him carelessly, kindly. Night after night he had drunken himself under the table with them at taverns along the way. Without their guidance he would have lost himself a dozen times. Now he knew the ropes. He could take care of himself on the way back.

The way back! There was so much to do in the short time that he would be in Paris. The others were dismounting at a hôtellerie in front of them. He clattered up to the mounting block and slid off, awkwardly, holding out the reins to a boy who came forward to take them. Suddenly a memory came to him of Pepperell flinging the reins to him in front of the Moodys' door and at Kittery. He looked sharply at the boy, holding the bridle. He looked thin and tired, anxious and overworked.

"Take care of the horse."

"Yes, Monsieur."

"Here."

Paul fished in his pocket, bringing out a piece of silver.

"It's English silver," he said.

The boy gaped.

"It's for you."

He snatched it, looking over his shoulder as though the devil were at his elbow, ready to take it from him. When Paul saw the landlord, he understood this expression, for the host of the Pheasant was dark and pock-marked and sullen as Satan. He showed Paul into the taproom and went out scowling.

Paul did not intend to get drunk that night. He had other plans. He excused himself from the toasts and tankards waved at him, asking:

"Where can I find a guide to take me about the city?"

There was a burst of laughter. Young Trémont stretched himself and said:

"I can take you to the best bawdy houses."

"How do you know I want to go to a house?"

"Where else would a man want to go after a year at sea?"

More laughter.

"It isn't a church you want, I suppose?"

"Why not, on Christmas Eve?"

"Oh come now, don't pull our legs! What do you want with a guide? The evening's young. Let's drink to Christmas Eve. Then we'll go to La Fantoche. She always has good firm-breasted girls."

Paul was near the door. He made a move to edge out quietly, but a young giant of a lieutenant near it grabbed at him. There was a tussle. It developed into a fight. Paul managed to keep his temper. He shook himself free. Then he thought of the stable-boy and his face cleared.

"I will get him to pilot me," he thought.

A roar of drunken laughter and the chorus of a song reached him as he ran down the steps into the yard:

> "In the morning I make the sagest plans,
> But all day long I engage in follies."

It was their favorite drinking song.

"Voltaire wrote that," Trémont told him one day as they rode to Paris, singing it at the top of their lungs.

So now when he saw Anne, he could talk to her about Voltaire. When he saw Anne!

CHAPTER LXXIV

PAUL fell in love with Paris, with the streets and the bridges, the houses, taverns and shops that he was beginning to know. They crowded into his mind at odd moments, when he was waiting for an audience in the stuffy anteroom of the Ministry for the Colonies, when he was undressing for bed, exhausted, in his cheap room at the hôtellerie, or when he was drinking in a dark and noisy taproom.

At such times the voice of the city called to him urgently and intimately to come out with her and she would show him something magic and miraculous round the next corner, down the next street. Then he would snatch his hat and cloak and go wandering, taking his fill of a beauty that he had never imagined in all his days among the majestic scenery of New France. This was a different beauty, intimate, compelling, that in a moment had become a part of him. He could never again be wholly at ease away from Paris, for he had come home, to an enchanted home. Paris was more than her large spacious parks and avenues, her squares with the chestnut trees that would be blossoming in spring, her fountains playing in gardens and public grounds, her river winding gray and silver round the island of the city, her dark, ill-lit, narrow, winding streets, her villainous-looking corners with houses leaning over so far that they touched and seemed to be whispering evil things together, the prisons, the barracks, the sewers, the smells, the churches, the cathedrals, Notre Dame, the church of Saint Sulpice, the market places. Paris was these, and more than these. The spirit of man dreamed in her stones, whispered, laughed and loved along her quays. Man's vision and his agony had made of her the jewel of the ages, the greatest city of civilization, Paris, "ville de lumière."

Because he had grown aware in every pore of poignancy and longing, of a grotesque tenderness and the need to share a joke, he wanted Anne more than ever. Paris would be the perfect background for their honeymoon. His days were filled with the search for her. It was more difficult than he had thought. When she had written to him she had headed her letters "Paris" never, apparently, expecting an answer to them, although she begged for answers in each letter. Paul was exasperated at this inconsistency. Time and gold pieces were melting away. He began to be afraid.

He went first to the Ministry for the Colonies and inquired for Monsieur du Chambon. He was passed from clerk to clerk and back again. Nobody would give him any information. Yes, they had all heard of Monsieur du Chambon, Governor of Louisbourg; no, they did not know where he might be. Paul had a strong impression that they were hiding something important from him. The expression of their eyes and their wary smiling mouths gave the secret away. They knew what he wanted to know but they would not tell.

He demanded an audience with the Minister. He waited the better part of two long days in the anteroom, to be turned away each evening with a vague apology. The stableboy directed him to cafés and taverns where he might pick up the most gossip and perhaps overhear what he was looking for. He learned that ministers, foreign secretaries and controller-generals were succeeding each other with such rapidity that no one had a chance to get acquainted with their names. The King's mistress, the Marquise de Pompadour, was responsible for all this remue-ménage. Her influence was beginning to make itself felt not only at court but in every branch of foreign affairs. Her friendship with the Pâris brothers made her the most important factor in the new world of finance. Pâris Duverney, sustained by her favor at the court, brought steady pressure to bear on all administrative, military and foriegn affairs. Anyone who refused to co-operate found himself dismissed in disgrace. Even the powerful Controller-

General Orry was kicked out the year before. Cafés and taverns hummed with rumors, tales, and songs about the Pompadour.

Paul listening to them as he drank his wine and ate his roasted kid at the Coq d'Or, began to toy with an idea. If he could have an audience with Madame de Pompadour he could find out what he wanted to know. She had complete information about everything in France. She was probably responsible for whatever had happened to Monsieur du Chambon, or to Anne.

How to get at her in the short time left to him was another matter. Etienne, the stable boy, came to his help. Madame de Pompadour was accustomed to ride each morning at a distance from the city, in the Bois de Boulogne. She and the King frequently spent the night in a hunting lodge and followed the hounds. There was good stag-hunting in the Bois. Perhaps if Monsieur were to hire a horse and post himself near the Royal Hunt, who knows what might happen? If Monsieur were a good horseman ——

"I am not," Paul answered gloomily.

"That is too bad. Both the King and Madame de Pompadour have an eye for equestrian merit."

"My riding would bring me nothing but disgrace."

"Still, Monsieur might post himself nearby and trust to chance to effect an encounter."

Paul had five days left before he must start on the return journey to Brittany to join the *Northumberland*. He thought the plan over and decided to try it. Etienne thought the hunt would be meeting every day in the week between Christmas and New Year's Eve. He would find a horse for Paul and go with him—never mind what the landlord said. He had a brother in those parts who knew the country well. Paul went to bed a little comforted that someone else would back him up in such a startling plan. He dreamed that night of La Pompadour who turned out to be San, riding through the woods with Anne in a bird cage in her hand. He woke to find Etienne shaking him, in the dark.

"It's time to get up. We have miles to go before the meet."

·[334]·

CHAPTER LXXV

"HAL lal lal lal lal li!"

The long notes of the hunting horn rang out through the forest. Paul gathered his reins nervously together. His horse pricked its ears, and shuffled through the fallen leaves. Etienne riding close beside grinned as the music of hounds in full cry reached them from the hillside. Other horns were blowing now. It was the custom for each man to wear his horn and blow it indiscriminately. The joyful confusion of sound encouraged the hunters, horses, hounds and riders alike.

Suddenly there was a crashing close at hand. A huge antlered stag burst through the undergrowth, panting, head thrust forward, sick with fear. His heaving flanks and distended nostrils showed that he was getting tired.

"Don't move!" Etienne said softly, gripping the reins of his startled horse. "Don't turn him!"

Paul pressed his knees beneath the saddle flap, and tried to control his backing, rearing animal, maddened by the sight of the stag, and the noise of the hunt.

The stag crashed on, northwards, through the misty underbrush. The excited quaver of a hound close on the scent sounded to the right of Paul. A solitary hound leaped the bank and dropped beside the horses, nose to the ground. He was followed by another and another, then by the body of the pack. Paul's mount reared and whirled about and plunged forward. Paul, hanging on grimly, tried to turn him out of the way of the pack. He succeeded in making a circle through the woods, to return to the start again, as a company of horsemen came tearing after the hounds.

"Hal lal lal!"

"Away!"

Paul's horse took the bit between his teeth and charged into the group. Paul found himself racing neck and neck with two determined horsemen. Each man was standing in his stirrups, blowing his horn and shouting. Paul, sitting down to it, committed the crime of holding on by the pommel while he allowed his maddened horse to take charge of him.

"At this rate I'll be killed," he thought, "before I can find Anne."

He lost Etienne completely, and had no time to look for him or for anyone. His eyes were fixed on the trees ahead and he swerved and cowered away from the stinging branches and the larger boughs that could crack his skull or sweep him to the ground.

After an uncomfortable eternity, they all emerged on a knoll of cleared ground and there was a halt. The hounds had lost the scent. Devoutly praying that they would never find it, Paul sat still, gasping and crowing for breath while he watched the four huntsmen scientifically casting the pack in a circle to pick up the trail.

Suddenly Paul's eyes lightened with interest. A woman, dressed in a gorgeous lavender hunting suit, sitting sidesaddle on a white horse, was composedly trotting up the hill to join the group of sweating riders. She was not strikingly beautiful, but her face was piquant and there was an air of willful authority about her that was unmistakable. La Pompadour! Paul's admiration for a woman who could be at home on a horse, who could actually go out with men and hunt the stag and yet remain provocative and feminine, was instantaneous and complete, and his hopes rose high as she came near. He was still out of breath, but he began to edge his horse toward her through the ferns. Which of the two men who rode beside her, laughing and talking, was the King? Paul could not determine. Both were richly dressed, both men of a certain age, both sure of themselves. He could not catch what they said. He had just decided that the tall, swarthy looking man with the bushy eyebrows must be the King, when the whole appalling clamor broke out again. His horse plunged forward like a jack-in-the-box released by a spring, and he was once more in torment, guarding his defenseless head from boughs and twigs, rocketing about in the saddle like a chestnut in the fire.

"Away!"

"Hallooo!"

"On, on, on!"

Some hateful hound had found the scent. The whole party galloped forward, down a positive chasm, over a brook, Paul holding on with both hands now, neglecting his reins entirely, crashing up the hillside, and over a plowed field. Here the riders strung out and he could see that there were a great many of them, pink-faced young men in shining boots, and white satin knee breeches covered with mud.

Etienne came up on the starboard side.

"Good sport!" he grinned. He was actually enjoying it. Paul began to suspect that he had suggested the whole expedition just because he wanted to hunt again as he had when he was a stable-boy to the Duc de Choiseul, leading an extra mount for his master. He had told Paul every detail of those golden heroic days of the Duc de Choiseul's pack of hounds.

"How far and how long can they go?" Paul gasped.

"Seven or eight hours sometimes!"

"Great God!"

"She's here and I think she's noticed you."

"I'm noticeable enough. What is the penalty for attending a royal hunt uninvited?"

"Transportation. It depends. If you trampled a hound it's the gallows."

Etienne galloped away, hallooing cheerfully. Paul turned his head. Close beside him, with the wind in her face and mud on her nose, Madame de Pompadour swept forward on her spirited white horse. She sat easily, holding her reins in one hand, her small gold whip in the other. Her hat had a white plume in it which waved in the wind. Her long skirt flowed about her legs in a graceful sweep, from the knee crooked over the pommel to the tiny spurred heel in the stirrup.

She was passing Paul. The men on the other side of her dropped away to manipulate a brook. They were caught up in the hunt. Hoofs thundered by on every side, all the hunt was disappearing, taking the brook with splashing and floundering and shouts. Paul could not believe that he was left alone with La Pompadour.

"On! On!" she said, smiling, waving him ahead. "I am obliged to go round by the bridge."

So there was a bridge, thank God!

"Permit me to accompany you, Madame," he said, restraining his frantic mount from following the rest. He forced it to the pace of hers, and glanced about him nervously. Where was the King? Surely strangers could not speak to La Pompadour so easily?

One of the riders turned at the crest of the hill and shouted anxiously. La Pompadour blew a kiss to him and pointed with her whip ahead. Two others slackened rein and turned to ride back. She rose in her stirrup and shouted angrily:

"On! On!"

They hesitated doubtfully. She waved again more energetically, and blew another kiss to the first man on the hillside. Then she drew rein with Paul beside her and waited until the three of them had been swallowed up in the hunt.

"Ouf!" she said, "I have had enough. If you were a stag, where would you run next?"

"There!" Paul pointed at random, in the opposite direction to the brook.

"Then let us make for it at a decent pace."

She wheeled her horse and began walking it away from the distracting sounds of the chase.

"Hal lal lal lal li!" came on the wind.

Paul spurred after her.

"Oh, Monsieur," she said, "what a heavenly day! Why is it that men cannot enjoy the beauties of nature unless a stag dies or a bird drops killed or wounded?"

"Yet the god of hunting is a goddess, Diana."

"And the patron of hunting is a man, Saint Hubert."

"Oh, a saint!"

"Bah, a goddess!"

They both laughed.

"Now tell me," she said, "what did you want to speak to me about?"

He gaped at her, astonished.

"I told the King you were the son of my advocate at Ville d'Avray," she pointed with her whip across the lake that they could see below them in the distance. "I said I had told you to join the hunt and I think he believed me. He will investigate, perhaps, but not till the hunt is over."

Paul looked at her gratefully.

"Why?" he asked.

"Because I am sick of seeing young men transported and hanged," she frowned in the direction of the fading hunting calls. "Besides, I like my advocate, and you look a nice son for him. Now be quick. What made you take such a dangerous risk? You must have known you would be seen. You're no equestrian."

"I was afraid you would notice that."

"You have bad hands and a worse seat."

"Well, I hate horses. I'm a sailor."

He took a deep breath and began to tell her of his search for Monsieur du Chambon. He did not mention Anne. He had a presentiment that Madame de Pompadour might lose interest in the story if there were a heroine in it too soon.

"I would like to see him if I could," he finished, flicking his horse's ears with the tips of the reins.

CHAPTER LXXVI

MONSIEUR DU CHAMBON was in the Bastille, sent there by lettre de cachet. No wonder the clerks in the Ministry for the Colonies shifted their eyes and evaded Paul's questions. Men who disappeared from general circulation under a lettre de cachet signed by the King of France were as good as dead. Sensible people accounted them dead. If they reappeared to celebrate a resurrection, they were hustled into the far-off provinces to the most obscure country retreat, there to cultivate turnips diligently. But such resurrections could be counted on the fingers of one hand.

Paul was pondering these things as he waited for the turnkey to conduct him to Monsieur du Chambon's cell. He was armed with a pass signed by the King, obtained for him by Madame de Pompadour. A gold piece had done the rest. He was inside the main grille, in a gloomy stone corridor, with a basket on his arm. Food, books, paper, quill pens, wine, a warm jacket, he went over the list of what he had thought a prisoner might need.

The atmosphere of the place stifled and depressed him. Behind these endless blocks of stone, what tragedies of human courage, what cruelties, injustices, and tortures were at that moment being enacted? Paul shuddered. He tried to fix his eyes on the turnkey's striped cotton shirt and long greasy pigtail, instead of on the walls. They walked on.

Monsieur du Chambon's cell was in the part of the prison kept for political prisoners. His room was a bare stone cage with a window high up in the wall, a narrow slit that let in a pallid strip of daylight. There was a wooden bedstead, a mattress with a blanket, a stool and a chair, all hired from the jailer at an exorbitant price. There was also a stone privy in the corner of the room and a small fireplace. A log of wood was burning in the grate, and a pile of logs was stacked in the far corner, but as the window in the wall had no glass, the room was damp and bitterly cold. Monsieur du Chambon, huddled in front of the fire, rose, startled, as the key turned in the lock.

His expression changed when he saw Paul.

"Good God! Monsieur de Morpain!"

They stood staring at each other. The turnkey withdrew, clanking noisily away from them after he had locked Paul in.

"What have they brought you here for, my poor boy?"

"Oh, I'm not a prisoner," Paul said hastily. "Look, I have brought a few things with me. I thought perhaps you might need some comforts."

He put the basket down awkwardly.

"Not a prisoner?"

"Just a visitor, Monsieur du Chambon."

"But I don't understand . . . how did you find me? Is there any news?"

Paul drew up the stool and sat down beside him, stretching out his hands to the feeble blaze.

"This will not be for long, Monsieur," he said cheerfully. "I have seen Madame de Pompadour. The chances are you'll be out of here before another month is up."

"If they would only bring me to trial, not keep me here in the dark!"

"They will. And probably to acquittal for losing Louisbourg. That isn't what you are here for, as you no doubt know."

Monsieur du Chambon was silent.

"Madame de Pompadour told me that the King suspects you of tucking away a fortune made out of illicit fur trading. He is angry because he has lost money on the colonies this year, and for the last ten years. He has poured money into Louisbourg, and instead of getting any return for it, Louisbourg is lost to his enemies. He blames you for the loss, of course, but most of all for the theft of money that he feels should have gone to him."

·[341]·

Monsieur du Chambon said nothing.

"I tried to convince Madame de Pompadour in the short time that I had with her, under many disadvantages . . ." he rubbed his legs thoughtfully, he was very stiff from the saddle . . . "that you had defended Louisbourg to the best of any soldier's ability. I also put in a word about the fur trade, Monsieur du Chambon. I said the leakage could not have been known to you, and I named a red herring. That is to say," he coughed, "I gave the name of the man they are surely looking for."

Monsieur du Chambon looked startled.

"Not Vergor—not my son?"

"No," Paul said, "of course not! Captain Thierry is the man."

Monsieur du Chambon looked at him sharply.

"Captain Thierry was in Quebec when I was imprisoned."

"Yes. By the time they bring him over here to be questioned you will be free, I hope. Captain Thierry really is involved," he said, "and I do not believe he can clear himself. Your daughter has some evidence . . ." he broke off. "Where is Anne?" he asked in another tone of voice. "I have only three more days in Paris before I have to leave to rejoin the *Northumberland*. I am sailing as third mate. The Marquis de la Jonquière has taken me under his protection and I shall rise as rapidly as I can. I want to marry Anne before I sail."

"Marry?"

Monsieur du Chambon seemed stupefied.

"I forgot. My wife and child were lost at sea three months ago. I am a widower."

"Thank God!" Monsieur du Chambon got up and walked the cell. "Anne has never been able to get you out of her head. We had a tragic voyage home, a tragic reception. Poor child, I haven't seen her for six months. She is at a cousin's house, a stone's throw away from here, but I am not allowed to write letters or receive them. You are the first visitor who has entered this cell—the first soul I've spoken to. The turnkey doesn't answer anything I say. I apologize for my agitation. When a man is much alone in a place like this, he broods, he becomes uncivilized. The turnkey tells me, with full and horrible details, that the prisoners in the cells on either side of me have already lost their minds. They have been here twelve and fifteen years!"

"Don't think of them," Paul said quickly. "You will be out of here before the spring. And I will take care of Anne. I promise you that."

Monsieur du Chambon sat down again heavily. His hands and his chin trembled.

"Do you need anything more?" Paul said hastily to distract him from his emotion. "Books? Food? Warm clothes?"

They began to make a list. Monsieur du Chambon wrote a letter to Anne, and his official permission for the wedding to take place. No marriage could be celebrated in France without the written consent of both parents or without their death certificates. No business of any kind could be transacted with the head of the family in prison under a lettre de cachet, which added to the torment of his family. Paul blessed Etienne, the hunting in the Bois de Boulogne, and Madame de Pompadour's generous whim. He gathered the letters up and thrust them into his coat as the dragging steps of the turnkey could be heard.

"Good-by, Monsieur du Chambon," he said, "to our happier meeting in New France."

"Adieu."

CHAPTER LXXVII

E FOUND Anne an hour later on the other side of the
river, in a house in the Rue de Bellechasse.

It was a big house, old, unmoved and formidable, the
sort of place to defend itself indefinitely against an army without cannon. As Paul stood in front of the imposing grille waiting for it to open, his heart beat and pounded, his breath came
unevenly.

Slowly the iron gate was opening. A lackey peered at him.

"Mademoiselle du Chambon?" Paul inquired, his knees shaking.

"This way, Monsieur."

He followed the lackey through a massive doorway, toward a
courtyard with a garden beyond it, surrounded by another high
wall. They turned to the right before they reached the garden,
entering another doorway to a flight of stairs.

Paul mounted them behind the lackey, trying to step evenly
and to seem unconcerned. His breath was coming in sharp gasps
and his heart began to pound again so that he was sure it sounded
loud enough to echo from the walls . . . massive walls, like the
Bastille, of gray stone, and behind them Anne!

They reached the top of the first flight. The lackey paused.

"What name shall I announce, Monsieur?"

"Never mind, Mademoiselle is expecting me."

"But Monsieur . . ."

Paul brushed past him. The door to the salon was open on the
left. He heard voices. He pushed the door wider and went in.

Anne was there. She was not alone. An elegant young man in

naval uniform was with her. They were laughing together. Anne's fingers were upon his collar, his arm was about her waist.

The sound of Paul's footsteps startled them. They wheeled apart, even before the lackey's voice was heard, muttering protestations and explanations.

"That will do, Jerome," Anne said, recovering, "it is not your fault. I do know Monsieur, and you may go."

The color had drained from her face. She looked at Paul. He stood rigid, staring at her. She was dressed in black. She looked very thin. She was the same Anne that he had known. He tried to smile. The young officer, inquisitive and a little annoyed, glanced from one to the other.

"You say that you know him, Anne," he said at length, as neither of them spoke, "but I confess I am curious."

"Oh, of course."

She turned to Paul.

"Monsieur de Morpain, this is my brother Vergor, home on leave from the *Ile Royale*."

"Captain du Chambon."

Vergor bowed. "I have heard of you, Monsieur de Morpain, more than once."

Paul bowed. He was looking at Anne, his expression had changed to one of bewilderment and hope.

"This is the quick-witted fellow who helped us with Thierry, isn't it?"

Anne did not answer. The color had flooded back to her face. She turned her eyes away and stared at the fire burning at one end of the room. Vergor waited a moment, then he grinned.

"Well, this is a most spirited conversation," he drawled.

Paul wrenched his eyes away from Anne's face. He turned to Vergor.

"I have just come from your father."

"What!"

Both Chambons jumped on him.

"He is in the Bastille, under a lettre de cachet."

"We feared so."

"Poor father! How horrible!"

"They took him away six months ago. We haven't known, we haven't dared . . ."

"I know. I think they will bring him to trial before the spring. I was fortunate enough to have an interview with Madame de Pompadour," he grinned reminiscently. "She assured me everything would be done to set your father free."

"What have they got against him? What could he do but surrender Louisbourg?"

"You ought to know it isn't that," Paul said slowly, looking Vergor in the eyes, "it's the money he is supposed to have stolen from the King, through the illicit fur trade."

Vergor paled.

"Somehow the name Chambon has become mixed up with fur trading," Paul went on.

"Vergor!" Anne spoke, low and startled, looking at her brother in dismay.

"I told Madame de Pompadour, which is the same as telling the King, that Captain Thierry was the man they wanted, not Monsieur du Chambon."

Brother and sister exchanged meaning glances.

"I think she believed me."

"Paul, how wonderful."

Anne's voice was husky with emotion.

"May I beg for the honor of a moment alone with you?" Paul looked at her.

"Do you want to be alone with him?"

Anne nodded. "Please, Vergor."

"Very well, I suppose I am not doing the right and proper thing as usual, but I will go and keep watch for Cousin Amadée, for seven minutes. After that I won't answer for anything because I'm going out. I hope I shall see you again, Monsieur."

"I am on the *Northumberland*, and you on the *Ile Royale*. I think it likely we shall meet," Paul said.

Vergor nodded, smiled, waved his long hands and disappeared. Paul took a step forward pleadingly.

"Why have you come here, Monsieur de Morpain?" Anne asked steadily. Her hand closed on the back of a chair and she leaned against it.

·[346]·

"I got your letters."

"They must have told you that no purpose could be served by our meeting again, only bitter misery, Paul."

"On the contrary, they made me hope."

"Hope! Our one hope is to forget. You should not have come here to make it harder."

"Anne . . ."

"Why did you come? Why did you come?"

"Because I love you, because I'm free and I have your father's consent, here in my pocket, because your letters said you loved me still. Do you, Anne, is it true? Do you love me still?"

He pulled the chair away from her and took her in his arms.

"Will you marry me, now that I'm free? Shall we be married as we planned? Do you remember? Love of loves, do you love me?"

There was no answer. She lifted her lips to his. He strained her close. Presently she stirred and pulled away from him.

"What happened?" she whispered, looking in his eyes.

"San died three months ago."

She crossed herself.

"How? Please tell me. I want to know."

"In a storm at sea. We lost the ship."

"Poor—woman." The words seemed to stick a little in her throat. Then she said in a rush, "I will be good to the child."

"He was drowned, too."

"Oh."

Her fingers relaxed. She leaned forward and placed her cheek to his. She whispered in his ear:

"Poor little boy. Poor Paul."

But she was smiling at the fire behind his back.

"So you see," he said after a long pause, "we are free to make a new life for ourselves, here or in New France."

"In New France."

"Paris is beautiful."

"Quebec is better. There is no Bastille in Quebec."

"It shall be as you say, in that and everything."

"I don't believe it, Paul."

·[347]·

"Well, perhaps not everything. But that sounded well, until after the wedding."

They laughed. She drew him to the window. They stood there, looking down on the roofs of the city, over them to the river beyond.

"Poor father . . ."

"He's well and he will be free. Don't worry about him, Sweet."

"I'm not. I'm too happy to worry about anything."

The bells in the convent opposite began to ring.

"We shall spend New Year's Eve together."

They kissed again.

"I'm glad I'm not a nun," Anne said dreamily, listening to the bells.

THE END

Formac Fiction Treasures

A Privateer's Fortune

When Gilbert Clinch discovers a very valuable painting and statue in his deceased grandfather's attic, he begins to uncover some of his ancestor's secrets, including a will that allows Clinch to become a wealthy man, while at the same time disinheriting his cousins. His grandfather's business as a privateer and slave trader helped him amass wealth, power and prestige. Clinch has secrets of his own, including a clandestine love affair. From Nova Scotia, to the art salons in Paris and finally the gentility of English country mansions, Clinch and his lover, Isabel Broderick, become entangled in a haunting legacy.
ISBN 0-88780-572-8

By Charles G.D. Roberts

The Forge in the Forest: An Acadian Romance

Jean de Mer, an "Acadian Ranger," returns, after three years' absence, to his lands on the shores of Minas Basin to find his son Marc in trouble with the Black Abbé — a French partisan leader. Marc is waiting to be tried as a spy. Together father and son make a daring escape but Marc is wounded and Jean must endure a perilous canoe journey with a young English woman to rescue her child from the Black Abbé. This historical romance takes place before the Acadian deportation, when tensions between the English and French were running high. The Acadians, while refusing to take sides, were nevertheless drawn in, accused of disloyalty by both sides.
ISBN 0-88780-604-X

The Heart That Knows

On her wedding day a young girl is suddenly abandoned. Standing on the Bay of Fundy shore she watches her husband's barquentine sail away without a word of explanation. Weeks follows days and she is left to face life as an outcast, scorned by her neighbours and family for being a mother, but not a wife. Over the years her son, like many sailors' children, grows up without a father. Confronted with the truth, the young man sets off to sea, determined not to return to his New Brunswick home until he sought vengeance on the man who treated his mother so heartlessly.
ISBN 0-88780-570-1

By Theodore Goodridge Roberts

Nell Harley: A Backwoods Mystery

In a small New Brunswick settlement, a friendly poker game is suddenly disrupted when one of the players, David Marsh, finds he has a card marked with two red crosses. No one is sure what it portends, but David is afraid that he has been marked and that if he continues to court Nell Harley, he will be in danger. Indeed, a few days later a freak accident with his canoe prevents him from continuing his work as a guide to American sports. While Nell and others are fearful of this mysterious curse, an Englishman, Reginald Rayton, is determined to find a rational answer to this mystery.

ISBN 0-88780-605-8

By Margaret Marshall Saunders

Beautiful Joe

Cruelly mutilated by his master, Beautiful Joe, a mongrel dog, is at death's door when he finds himself in the loving care of Laura Morris. A tale of tender devotion between dog and owner, this novel is the framework for the author's astute and timeless observations on farming methods, including animal care, and rural living. This Canadian classic, written by a woman once acclaimed as "Canada's Most Revered Writer," has been popular with readers, including young adults, for almost a century.

ISBN 0-88780-540-X

Rose of Acadia

One hundred and fifty years have past since the Acadians were sent into exile; now, Vesper Nimmo, a Bostonian, sets out for Nova Scotia's French shore with the intention of carrying out his great-grandfather's wish to make amends to the descendants of Agapit LeNoir. Nimmo finds himself immersed in the struggles of the Acadians to preserve their culture and language while the lure of city life, including money and modern conveniences, draws young people to the Boston states. He meets beautiful, angelic Rose à Charlitte, the innkeeper where he makes his temporary home. When he becomes ill she cares for him, but when he falls in love with her, she cannot marry him — not until she is freed from her past.

ISBN 0-88780-571-X